"HUNTRESS, I'VE GOT A VISUAL ON SOME PEOPLE SNEAKING

out of an outbuilding in the farm closest to the forest. Want me to make a low-eyeball pass?"

People sneaking into the woods could mean many things, including terrorists with reason enough to shoot down a Federation attacker. "Negative," Shores replied to the pilot. "Hold at present distance, scan on max magnification."

Shores studied her map, trying to figure the likely exits from the eastern edge of the forest. Assuming the unknown runners went east, of course, but since that was toward a presumably friendly territory, it was a reasonable assumption. Still, reasonable assumptions could be enough to get people killed.

Suddenly the ground shook. Shores dropped her map, drew her sidearm, rolled to concealment, and stared up at the towering pillar of smoke bulging into the sky beyond the farm. . . .

STARCRUISER SHENANDOAH

THE PAINFUL FIELD

Roland J. Green

A ROC BOOK

ROC
Published by the Penguin Group
Penguin Books USA Inc., 375 Hudson Street,
New York, New York 10014, U.S.A.
Penguin Books Ltd, 27 Wrights Lane,
London W8 5TZ, England
Penguin Books Australia Ltd, Ringwood,
Victoria, Australia
Penguin Books Canada Ltd, 10 Alcorn Avenue,
Toronto, Ontario, Canada M4V 3B2
Penguin Books (N.Z.) Ltd, 182–190 Wairau Road,
Auckland 10, New Zealand

Penguin Books Ltd, Registered Offices:
Harmondsworth, Middlesex, England

First published by Roc, an imprint of New American Library,
a division of Penguin Books USA Inc.

First Printing, July, 1993
10 9 8 7 6 5 4 3 2 1

 REGISTERED TRADEMARK—MARCA REGISTRADA

Printed in the United States of America

Principal Characters

A. Humans

Josephine ATWOOD: War correspondent for Trans-Rift Media on Charlemagne.

Marshal Emilio BANFI: Retired Federation officer, resident on Linak'h.

Admiral of the Fleet Wilhelmina BAUMANN, U.F.N.: Commander-in-Chief, United Federation Navy.

His Excellency Aung BAYJAR: Minister of Foreign Affairs, the United Federation of Starworlds.

Captain Pavel BOGDANOV, U.F.N.: Commanding officer, U.F.S. *Shenandoah*.

Ursula BOLL: Wife of Nikolai Sergeyevich Komarov; Federation Intelligence agent. Mother of two children by Nikolai, Sophia and Peter.

Allard and Sandra BRANDSTETTER: Refugees from the Great Bend region of the Federation Territory, Linak'h.

Leo BUTKUS: Boatswain, R.M.S. *Somtow Nosavan*.

Colonel Malcolm DAVIDSON: Caledonian (British Union) army officer, aide to Marshal Banfi.

Lucco and Teresa DiVRIES: Farmers and intelligence operatives on Victoria.

Sergeant Juan ESTEVA: Security & Intelligence NCO for Candice Shores's Quick Reaction Force and the commanding officer's bodyguard.

Second Lieutenant Rodney FISKE: Platoon leader in the Quick Reaction Force.

Commander Herman FRANKE: Federation Naval Intelligence officer, assigned to Linak'h.

Commander Shintaro FUJITA, U.F.N.: Chief Engineer, U.F.S. *Shenandoah*.

Jeremiah GIST: President, Planetary Republic of Victoria.

Colonel Barbara HOGG: CO of a provisional brigade of Linak'h Command that includes the Quick Reaction Force.

Second Lieutenant Sergei KAPUSTEV: Leader, 4th Platoon, *Shenandoah* LI Company of the Quick Reaction Force.

Nikolai Sergeyevich KOMAROV: Artist and former Federation agent, now teaching art to the refugees in the Federation Territory. Candice Shores's father.

Warrant Officer Second-Class Mitsuo KONISHI: Quick Reaction Force lifter pilot, usually assigned to Candice Shores's command lifter.

Acting Vice Admiral Sho KUWAHARA, U.F.N.: Staff officer at Forces Command, Charlemagne. Commands the Dual-Sovereignty Planet Study Group.

Fumiko KUWAHARA: Wife of Admiral Kuwahara. They have two children, Yaso and Hanae.

Major General Marcus LANGSTON: Senior Army member of the Dual-Sovereignty Planet Study Group.

Commodore Rose LIDDELL, U.F.N.: Flag officer initially commanding the Linak'h squadron; flag in *Shenandoah*.

Charles V. LONGMAN: Chief Engineer, R.M.S. *Somtow Nosavan*.

Vice Admiral Diana LONGMAN: SOPS, Linak'h Command; aunt of Charles Longman.

Lieutenant Commander Brian MAHONEY, U.F.N.: Communications watch officer aboard *Shenandoah*.

Joanna MARDER: Captain, Victorian merchanter R.M.S. *Somtow Nosavan.*

Major Lucretia MORLEY: Federation MP officer, affiliated with Commander Franke and working with him on the same intelligence matters on Linak'h.

First Lieutenant Olga NALYVKINA: Federation Army officer, assigned as Marshal Banfi's personal pilot.

Colonel Liew NIEG: Federation Army Intelligence officer, assigned to Linak'h.

Lieutenant General Alys PARKINSON: Commander-in-Chief, Defense Forces of the Planetary Republic of Victoria.

Karl POCHER: Partner in the DiVries's farm and Team Leader, Victoria Civil Action Group on Linak'h.

Captain Lena ROPUSKI, U.F.N.: Assigned to the Dual Sovereignty Planet Study Group; effectively Admiral Kuwahara's XO.

Acting Lieutenant Colonel Candice Nikolayevna SHORES: Commanding officer, Linak'h Command Quick Reaction Force.

Sergeant First-Class Jan SKLARINSKY: Sniper in the Quick Reaction Force HQ.

General of the Army Maximillian SZAIJKOWSKI: Commander-in-chief, United Federation Army.

First Lieutenant Brigitte TACHIN: Division officer, Weapons Department, *Shenandoah;* assigned to the ground party on Linak'h.

Major General Joachim TANZ: Commanding general, Linak'h Command.

Sergeant Major Esther (Eppie) TIMBERLAKE: Battalion sergeant major, Quick Reaction Force.

Lieutenant Commander Elayne ZHENG: Electronic Warfare Officer in the 879th Squadron (Heavy Attack).

B. Non-Human

Fleet Commander Eimo SU-ANKRAI: Baernoi; former commander of the Seventh Training Squadron off Victoria.

Emt DESDAI: Ptercha'a; representative and agent of Payaral Na'an, also Confraternity activist.

Warbander DRYNZ: Ptercha'a; Confraternity soldier on Linak'h.

Senior Councillor Dollis IBRAN: Merishi; leading member of the Council of Simferos Associates.

Ship Commander First-Class Brokeh SU-IRZIM: Baernoi; Inquirer, assigned to Linak'h.

Ship Commander First-Class Zhapso SU-LAL: Baernoi; Inquirer, assigned to Linak'h.

The LIDESSOUF twins, KALIDESSOUF and SOL-IDESSOUF: Baernoi; elite Assault Force veterans, assigned to the Inquiry mission on Linak'h under Rahbad Sarlin.

Fire Warden First-Class Isha MAIYOTZ; Ptercha'a; a leader in the Administration Fire Guard on Linak'h.

Councillor Payaral NA'AN: Merishi; head of the Trade Mission on Victoria.

Senior Councillor Zydmunir NA'AN: Merishi; a senior executive of Simferos Associates. Father of Payaral Na'an.

Air Warrior First-Class Taidzo NORL: Ptercha'a; Coordination fighter pilot and brother-in-law of Fomin zar Yayn.

Ship Commander First-Class Rahbad SARLIN: Baernoi; veteran field agent of the Special Projects branch of the Office of Inquiry, assigned to Linak'h.

Warbander SEENKIRANDA: Ptercha'a; pair-mate to Emt Desdai; Confraternity activist on Linak'h.

F'Mita IHR SULAR: Baernoi; commander, Fleet-chartered merchant vessel *Perfumed Wind*.

Fleet Commander F'Zoar SU-WEIGHO: Baernoi; retired but still influential Fleet officer. Patron of su-Irzim and Zeg.

Warband First Leader Fomin zar YAYN: Ptercha'a; Legion commander in the Warband of the Coordination of Linak'h.

Jillyah zar YAYN-NORL: Ptercha'a; wife of Fomin zar Yayn, owner of a logging company, mother of one son, Ousso, by her first pair-mate.

Ship Commander Second-Class Behdan ZEG: Baernoi; Special Projects field officer, half-brother to Rahbad Sarlin.

Glossary

AD: Air Defense.

AEW: Airborne Early Warning.

afksi: Small carnivorous fish, native to Merish. Schools of them were traditionally placed in the moats of defended posts for additional security.

Alliance: Freeworld States Alliance, principal human rival to the United Federation of Starworlds.

AO: Area of Operations.

AOP: Air Observation Post.

AS & M: Air Supply and Maintenance.

Baernoi: Sapient humanoid race, highly militarized, whose remote ancestors resembled Terran pigs. Refer to themselves as "the People."

balgos: Dense dark wood of a tree native to Merish; frequently used for making ceremonial or religious objects.

Big Brawl: Colloquial term in the Federation Forces for the ultimate war: the Federation vs. the Alliance, the Merishi, the Ptercha'a, *and* the Baernoi all at once.

blastwater: Baernoi liquid explosive. If allowed to soak into a permeable object, renders the whole object capable of being detonated.

CA: Combat Assault.

CG: Commanding General.

Chadl'hi: One of the older Ptercha'a-settled planets; Seenkiranda's birthworld.

Charlemagne: Capital planet of the Federation and site of Forces Command.

Climb: Merishi term for a subspace transition (see "Jump.")

C-cubed: Command, Control, Communications.

CO: Commanding Officer.

Confraternity: A loosely-knit, theoretically illegal organization among the Ptercha'a, dedicated (also theoretically) to an independent position for the whole race in relation to the Merishi and humans.

Coordination: The independent Ptercha'a government on Linak'h.

CP: Command Post.

dawnfood: Baernoi term for breakfast.

deeochs: Edible bivalve, native to Pterach but extensively cultivated on Linak'h.

EI: Electronic Intercept/Intelligence.

EOD: Explosive Ordnance Disposal.

E & R: Evaluation and Report (on an officer or NCO).

ETA: Estimated Time of Arrival.

EW: Electronic Warfare.

EWO: Electronic Warfare Officer.

flarebase: High-BTU liquid chemical compound used by Federation armed forces. With appropriate additives or containers, can be used for illumination or as fuel-air explosive.

fmyl: High-protein vegetable, a staple Ptercha'a crop.

goldtusk: Derogatory Baernoi term for an idle aristocrat.

Governance: Most common general term for the Merishi interstellar political community.

grode: High-carbohydrate fruit native to Baer; analogous to the Terran breadfruit.

Guidance: Baernoi term for Navigation (of a spaceship or ocean vessel).

haltmeal: Baernoi term for lunch.

holosh: Widely-cultivated Ptercha'a fruit-bearing bush.

House of Light: Ptercha'a fraternal/religious association, of great antiquity and considerable social significance in Ptercha'a life. Divided into quasi-independent Lodges.

Hufen: Capital city of the Governance of the Merishi Territory on Linak'h.

ihksom: Ptercha'a term for a matchmaker.

inward-eating: Baernoi term for a condition equivalent to stomach ulcers.

IOC: Initial operating capability.

JAG: Judge Advocate-General.

JOT: Jack of all trades.

kawde: Baernoi war gas; non-lethal if an antidote is administered within eighteen hours.

Khudr: Baernoi term, literally meaning "First to fight," now extending to mean any leader. The Great Khudr is the founder of the planetary unity of Baer.

koayass: Ornamental shade tree, native to Merish but highly popular among the Ptercha'a.

kuip: Ptercha'a game, similar to *go*. Originally played with fmyl seed pods, it is now played with carved wooden or molded plastic replicas of the pods.

LI: Light Infantry.

LZ: Landing Zone.

Merishi: Humanoid sapient race, evolved from climbing omnivorous reptiles; ruthless and far-flung traders. Refer to themselves as "the Folk," and are called "Scaleskins" by both Baernoi and humans.

nest-free: Merishi term for being of legally adult age.

Och'zem: Ptercha'a capital of the Administration of the Federation Territory.

OECZ: Outward Edge of the Combat Zone.

okugh: Potent Merishi distilled spirit, about 130 proof.

one-plus-three: Standard Federation trooper's ammunition load out of combat—one magazine in the weapon, three in the pouches.

orgint: Organic intelligence, that obtained by a live observer as opposed to electronic or other sensors.

OTC: Officer in Tactical Command

PE & D: Planetary Exploration and Development.

pelsh: Potent Baernoi amnesiac drug; used both for therapeutic and military purposes.

Pek's Fifty: Semi-legendary Ptercha'a Warband, who liberated their native city from a foreign occupation. Said to have among them possessed every known war skill.

Petzas: Nearest major Baernoi planet to Linak'h; Petzas-Din (Petzas, the City) is the capital.

Ptercha'a: Humanoid sapient race with strongly feline characteristics, first encountered by humans when serving as mercenaries for the Merishi. They call themselves "the Hunters," and are called "Catpeople" (human), "Furries" or more formally "Servants in War" (Merishi), and Furfolk (Baernoi).

QRF: Quick Reaction Force.

quickgun: Baernoi term for an automatic weapon.

Rhaym: Merishi arsenal planet.

RHIP: Rank Hath Its Privileges.

R. M. S.: Registered Merchant Ship.

RTB: Return to Base.

SAR: Search and Rescue.

schwerpunkt: The main offensive thrust in a land battle.

Security: When capitalized, the Merishi term for their armed forces.

senior: Ptercha'a term for a person of high rank; capitalized when used in direct address.

SFO: Supporting Fires Observer.

sgai: Spicy fruit-based after-dinner Merishi drink, non-alcoholic.

skrin: Small, voracious predator, native to mountain regions of Baer.

SOPS: Senior Officer Present in Space.

Special Action Band: In Ptercha'a law-enforcement organizations, elite teams comparable to human SWAT or Hostage Rescue units.

thryne: Small, sometimes domesticated ruminant, native to Pterach.

TI: Training Instructor.

TO & E: Table of Organization and Equipment.

True Speech (also "Language"): Ptercha'a term for their native language.

UC: Federation non-lethal gas, inducing violent nausea.

uhrim: A staple of the Baernoi diet: a tuber resembling the sweet potato.

uitsk: Untranslatable Merishi obscenity.

uys: Fortified fermented Baernoi beverage, resembling sherry.

vidjis: Ptercha'a obscenity: one who steals milk from another's young.

Warband: General Ptercha'a term for a military unit of any size.

War Crafters: Ptercha'a term for combat engineers.

Watch: Baernoi unit of time, equivalent to 5.2 hours. The Baernoi standard day is divided into five watches.

z'dok: Merishi obscenity borrowed by the Ptercha'a: one who defecates in another's nest.

zyrik: Coniferous tree native to Linak'h; sap-loaded and, when dry, dangerously flammable.

Prologue

Linak'h:

"Any moment now," the sixteen-Leader beside Seenkiranda said. His neck ruff was up, his ears back, his tail lashing gently. "The communications blocks are in. No messages into the prison, none out."

Seenkiranda would have been amused under other circumstances, to see such excitement in a Hunter who had served in one Warband or another longer than she had lived. She wondered if he had kin unlawfully held in the prison that might soon no longer be one.

She also wondered why this double-four, the observers and farthest from the prison, had only passive sensing devices. The two double-fours actually attacking were far closer, far more vulnerable to detection and retaliation from the prison.

If its guards knew their warcraft. They might not, Seenkiranda reflected. It was certain her doubts would not be welcome now. The leader took his experience seriously and believed everything it had taught him. Seenkiranda could only oppose logic and intuition. The man doubted them; best he not doubt her.

A faint pulse on the hooded display screen—the first rocket was on the way. They didn't need a screen to see it streak across the stubbly fields and the winding road toward the prison walls. The gray smoke-trail seemed to lengthen endlessly. Then the blurred orange flame at its head merged with the wall.

Black smoke and more flame erupted as the warhead detonated deep in the wall. Debris arched out of the smoke cloud, blocking the road, sending up steam as it struck the watery ditch, hurling one guard tower clean off its foundations.

The smoke had not cleared before a second rocket was on the way. After its explosion, smoke hid all but one corner of the prison wall.

But that one corner had a guard tower, and the tower held guards true to their oaths. A third rocket came, this one rising higher, intended to clear the top of the wall.

It also rose clear of the ground-clutter on the guards' sensors. Their micro-radar guided a laser, and the laser guided their heavy-mount battle rifle.

Neither laser beam nor solid rounds destroyed the missile. One or the other sent it off-course, the flame of its motor now irregular and misshapen. It swerved past the corner of the prison and flew along the west wall.

It flew on, past the boundary fence, across the rail line, and past the security barrier of the chemical-processing complex beyond the railroad. Seenkiranda held her breath. The complex was large but well dispersed, with much open ground where the rocket could fall. . . .

The explosion that came made the two warheads at the prison wall seem children's toys. (Seenkiranda thought wildly of the ones she had made with her chemistry set, until one burned off enough fur for her parents to discover what she was doing and confiscate the set.)

A ball of fire rose beyond the security barrier, swelling faster than the eye could follow, engulfing six storage tanks in the time it took to say the words. Those tanks also burned or exploded, and the ball of fire doubled in size in the space of a single breath.

Seenkiranda imagined the screams of workers caught in the flames. She saw and heard burning fragments plunging down like meteorites. She heard but could not see more explosions; some of those fragments must be finding targets.

What was she saying? The chemical complex had not been a target. Its destruction would hurt few enemies of the Confraternity. It might in fact increase their numbers. The Confraternity had been branded mindless killers and destroyers often enough. Now this vile tale would begin to seem the truth.

Seenkiranda had to admit that now logic and intuition would not take the place of experience. She looked at the leader, and without looking back he pointed at the ground. Seenkiranda realized that she had risen half out of hiding to stare at the ruin of the chemical complex. She dropped to a crouch, then lay flat, baring her teeth in frustration.

She had come too far and left too much behind, to see her first experience of war end in this sort of tangle!

The planet Linak'h was a long voyage from either Chadl'hi or Victoria, the two worlds that Seenkiranda had in turn called home. Two hundred light-years from the first, her birth-world, forty-three from the other. Long voyages even for a Hunter who had accepted a Hunter's destiny of voyaging, and well before she came of age.

Nor had her voyaging ended when she left the human ship *Somtow Nosavan* and moved with Emt Desdai to an apartment outside Och'zem in the Administration. The building was old but well-kept; the apartment was comfortable; she and Emt were vowed for a pair-mating. Not less important than these was that the building was guarded and mostly tenanted by the Confraternity and its sympathizers.

There should have been no need to travel farther, to do useful work for her Merishi master Payaral Na'an, the Confraternity that Emt Desdai served, or even the joint profit of herself and Emt. (He expected that his overt mission of chartering ships for Councillor Na'an would generate fees enough to begin his and Seenkiranda's pairing in good style.)

Seenkiranda now knew what a futile phrase "should have been" was. Within twenty Linak'h days of her arrival, it was learned that the Confraternity within the Coordination was seeking to liberate certain human prisoners, whom the Coordination held but whom the Federation wanted.

Within another ten days, it was known that the Confraternity wanted a trustworthy observer from the Administration for their attempt. It had to be a Hunter—no humans could be trusted enough—and (although this was never said aloud) someone the Administration's Confreres could afford to lose.

"They should have asked if *I* can afford to lose you," Emt had said, when he told her of her being chosen.

"What would you have answered?"

"One has to guard one's tongue to save one's reputation at a time like that."

"I see. 'She is precious, honor more so, the Confraternity's victory most of all.' "

"You have been reading the secret histories?"

"Yes, now that I have the rank to access them," Seenkiranda said, wrinkling her nose. "I wish the Confraternity had attracted some of our better writers sooner. When the phrase was turned, the histories were being recorded by the word-deaf."

"They had much on their minds," Emt said absently. "No one knew what the Hive Wars would do to relations among the races who had fought it. Some hoped the Ptercha'a would be given their rightful place. Others thought we would have to fight for it. Still others wished to fight but feared that humans and Merishi alike would unleash the weapons they had used to drive the Hive Folk back to their birth-world.

"The Confraternity left much undone, including having its history well-written. But it was not because we agreed that it was wisest to do nothing."

" 'We'?"

"In a manner of speaking."

"A manner I do not like. We all stand before Judgment for our own deeds, whatever our fathers' fathers did in the name of the Confraternity."

"You have said that before." He was frowning now.

"I know. I will say it again, until I am satisfied that you believe it."

"You are not easily satisfied."

"Of course not." She ran her claws through his neck fur. His ruff was somewhat scanty, the one point of classic good looks (at least for one of his age) that he lacked. "I waited for a pair-mate, until I could have you."

He smiled, and peace returned for the moment. She did not doubt that he had done everything possible to persuade the Confraternity leadership that he should go instead of her. He had service with elite Warbanders to his credit, and much else to make him useful on the mission to the Coordination's secret Confraternity organization.

He also had, or so it seemed, too much knowledge to be exposed to capture and too much work here in the Administration to be risked at all. Seenkiranda wondered how long it would take before those whose brains as well as fur had gone white with age realized that danger would come to all of them before long.

The Coordination had issued an ultimatum that would have had their Warband across the border of the Administration already, if they had not extended it. That extension too would come to an end, in less than a quarter of a Linak'h year.

If it did not, this would hardly be the deed of the Confraternity. The humans might claim the honor, for acting in defense of the Hunters, or the Coordination might do so, for not attacking.

Both would decide for themselves. But Emt Desdai probably already knew that, and if he did not, making him feel ignorant would only end in a quarrel.

It had been the plan, that after the prison wall was breached the rocket team would provide covering fire for the assault team. The assault team would enter through the breach, release as many prisoners as possible, and capture guards enough to trade for the release of the humans if they were not among those freed in the confusion.

It had never been part of the plan to assault directly the high-security block, where the humans were held. (Or *said* to be held; Seenkiranda knew enough about intelligence work to recognize optimism when she heard it.) That would have led to slaughter of Hunters by Hunters, whoever won, and possibly the death of the humans as well if there were Folk guarding them.

Now even entering the breach was uncertain. The explosion at the chemical complex would bring a horde of Hunters from the Guardians, the Warband, and every other service of the Coordination that could find an excuse to send someone. Pushing home the assault could begin the slaughter almost at once.

Either that thought had not occurred to the sixteen-Leader or he had decided the risk was acceptable. He spread his left hand, fingers pointing toward the other Hunters of the observation post, and raised his battle rifle in the other, muzzle toward the prison.

All ten dashed to join their comrades, breaking into fours and then into pairs as they closed the range. The rough ground would have divided them even if tactical sense hadn't, but didn't slow them. Seenkiranda thought herself a good runner, but she had to work hard to keep from being last. Even the Hunter who'd delayed to set the tamperproofing charge in the sensor pack was running level with her.

It was all to no purpose. The third rocket had not yet done wreaking havoc by its ill-aimed flight. From the corner of the wall the guards poured down fire that left half the assault team down before they were in the breach. That took gallantry in the guards; the rocket team had no more rockets but moved to within rifle range of the wall. Weapons drew lines of fire through the air, from tower to ground and back again, until the fire from the tower had ended.

The tower was still smoking when Seenkiranda's double-four came up behind the rocket-launchers. One of them was dead, another binding an ugly leg wound. She studied the ground between her and the wall, and counted five assault-team bodies and only two Hunters moving amid the rubble.

"We have to all move in," her sixteen-Leader said. "We have to control the exercise yard before anything else."

"We can't let our retreat be cut—" the rocket leader began.

The sixteen-Leader cuffed him across the jaw, lightly and with claws in. It was a warning gesture only, but for a moment Seenkiranda thought the rocket leader would take it as a death challenge.

"How do we open the gates, if we do control the yard?" he said, almost plaintively. "Our last rocket is faulty."

"We place the warhead against the door by hand, if need be," the sixteen-Leader said—or rather, snarled. Seenkiranda heard challenge in his voice, to everyone within hearing.

It was not those in hearing who took up the challenge. Literally from the sky, a pair of flyers descended onto the roof of the prison. One mounted a heavy rifle in its nose, and also disgorged six Hunters in Warband tunics. Two of them carried portable bomb-launchers.

When they began shooting, the survivors of the assault

team died swiftly, but none of their comrades knew how. Smoke and dust hid whether the bombs shredded them or the rifle rounds pierced them.

Challenge gave way to indecision on the sixteen-Leader's face. Seenkiranda vowed many offerings at the House of the Light if it granted her the power to remain silent.

The rocket leader bent over his last round, opened a panel, and tapped the darkness inside with two claws. "There," he said. "In five leaps it will explode. The smoke should hide our retreat."

The word seemed to send the sixteen-Leader mad. He would have used nature's weapons to take out the other's throat if Seenkiranda and three others hadn't gripped him. When they finally had him on the ground, he continued to struggle. His head was highest of anyone's when the flyer's rifle shifted its target.

The burst cut through the Hunters at waist level; everything and everyone above that level was hit. Rounds ripped into the rocket; smoke and blue sparks boiled from the opened panel. Seenkiranda prayed again, that the timer was smashed, or none of the wounded would survive the coming explosion.

Her prayer was answered. The rocket died quietly. Another prayer that she hadn't thought to make also found favor with the Light. With everyone who'd been standing fallen and everyone who'd been on the ground staying there, the Warband team stopped shooting.

Without raising her head, Seenkiranda rolled over, hoping this would be taken for the dying gesture of one in agony. She saw that two or three Hunters had climbed out of the second lifter and joined the Warbanders. Distance hid faces, and nothing distinguished the newcomers' clothing, but she recognized the markings on the nose of the flyer. A senior leader in the Coordination's Warband had taken a hand in the fight.

Her first thought was "Betrayal!" Her next was that betrayal made it more important, if less easy, for her to evade pursuit. She rolled onto her back, waited to test the reaction of the watchers, then rolled again when no burst of bombs or bullets came.

She could not stop to look about her, and not only because the movement might arouse suspicion. Sparks from the rocket had ignited dry grass and brush, and

orange flames now flecked the ground. Seenkiranda saw
a tunic flare up, prayed that its wearer was dead or at
least senseless, and kept rolling.

She rolled faster than the flames advanced, still without drawing fire. Smoke tore at her throat and eyes,
and she suspected that it hid her just enough to confuse
watchers.

She also sensed others moving in the smoke around
her, heard coughing, and hoped rather than prayed that
more than she would win clear. It was never honorable
and often embarrassing to others to be the last survivor,
even if one had not deserved to win in the first place.

The rough ground began so close to the prison that
the Coordinator of Confinement had never bothered having the brush and grass cut back. So there was plenty
of growth to burn and raise clouds of smoke that hid
Seenkiranda and five others long enough for them to win
clear.

They all kept their weapons, even the one with a gouge
in the leg and a strip of blood-caked fur running down
one arm. Two of the five tended their wounded comrade,
while another used the sights of his rifle to judge the
range.

"They can't hit us unless the flyer takes off," she said.

"Coordination seniors leave that sort of thing to the
younglings," the wounded Hunter growled.

"Not all," Seenkiranda said. At least that was what
she tried to say. Then she pointed at the burning chemical complex and managed to make herself understood.
"Even if he thought there might be prisoners out here,
they'll need all his people over there."

The rifle-bearer who'd assumed leadership looked at
the wall of flame and made the gesture of an unspoken
prayer. Then he rose to his feet.

"Two of you, help Possandaro. Seenkiranda, can you
take the rear?"

"What of the sensor pack?" a man asked. "It is set
only for tamperproofing, not for timed detonation."

"Easily stated, easily solved," the leader said. He unfolded the braces under his rifle's muzzle, lay down, and
seated the braces in the rocky ground. A moment to
adjust and read the sights, then a long finger squeezed
the firing bar four times. The third burst of the four

touched off the charge in the sensor pack. The explosion took no enemies with it, but reduced the pack to untraceable charred fragments.

The rough, brush-grown ground slowed their flight but also hid them from whatever pursuit was launched. It seemed impossible to Seenkiranda that in a sky so full of fliers there was no one keeping watch on the ground. But all the fliers whined overhead unseeing and vanished toward the fire.

Before they reached the edge of the high forest, the painkillers let Possandaro stand free of his supporters and walk. Painkillers and dressings together left him stiff-limbed, but he thought he could manage as far as the secure hut. It was not always crewed—Hunters of any sympathy, let alone Confraternity, were few in the high forest. But it was watched by the Confraternity, and Possandaro would not be alone long.

"Wager that I'll be home before you are," he said jauntily. "What, no one with faith in the Confraternity's flyer crews? This is a serious breach of disci—"

Seenkiranda gently laid a hand over Possandaro's mouth, with her claws extended. Whenever he came home, it would be as a wounded veteran. It would not be as the bearer of evil news.

One

**Aboard U.F.S. *Shenandoah*,
off Linak'h:**

Commodore Rose Liddell drifted up from sleep to the point where she could answer the intercom.

"Liddell."

"We have a relayed satellite profile on a chemical-plant fire in the Coordination."

Only the fact that the speaker was her flag captain and friend, Pavel Bogdanov, prevented a blistering reply. Nothing could produce a polite one.

"Tell the Coordination's fire departments. They're supposed to be up to their job, except for blazes in the high forest."

"It's less than a klom from the Thunder River Prison."

"I assume the prison healer can treat inmates for smoke inhalation. If—"

She broke off. Wakefulness had not returned, but memory had. The memory produced wakefulness, and when Liddell spoke again she was sitting up and pulling on a dressing gown.

"That's where Intelligence thinks the prisoners from the raid at Marshal Banfi's are being held. Right?"

"Exactly so, Commodore. Also, there are signs that one wall of the prison has been severely damaged."

Liddell tried finger-combing her hair as a way of settling her thoughts, then gave up and reached for a brush. Enlightenment came as she picked it up and turned it on (low-power setting; she didn't trust her half-wakened reflexes with anything higher).

"Not the wall on the side of the plant, right? So it

wasn't the explosion but something else, like a Confraternity attack?"

"Yes. Not just the direction, but the damage pattern is wrong for blast-wave damage."

Liddell applied the brush. "Pavel, wake up the image-interpreters and give them all the computer power they need. Look for any signs of the attackers' approach or evasion. If you find anything—anything *hard,* that is—tell me *immediately,* then transmit it to Linak'h Command."

"If I might make a suggestion, Commodore, it would be better to wait until we can send a full report by shuttle. I've alerted the duty attacker to be on five-minute standby."

"Any particular reason, or just being cautious?"

"Both. We don't know how many Confraternity sympathizers are in the Command network, to say nothing of Ptercha'a eavesdroppers. Also, the Baernoi at least are on the alert. They have already maneuvered one of their satellites for a low-altitude pass over the incident."

The Baernoi satellite network around Linak'h was spread as thinly as all their other resources. Off Victoria it had been different, with the omnipresent Seventh Training Squadron reminding all the Tuskers' enemies to take them seriously. It was some consolation that off Linak'h the Baernoi didn't seem to even take themselves seriously.

But there was that ship, *Perfumed Wind,* the chartered merchant vessel that had also operated off Victoria. There were the shuttles hauling unknown cargoes down from her. And now there was the Baernoi taking an interest in the fate of the Banfi raiders, in a way that couldn't escape Federation notice.

Liddell decided not to be consoled by the Baernoi's apparent lack of strength at Linak'h. That could change any hour, and meanwhile there were any number of Baernoi expert at the art of making wits count more than numbers.

It seemed rather a waste of a good hair-brushing to go back to sleep after this, but Liddell knew how easy it was to run a sleep deficit. She turned off the brush and

the light, lay down, and had just time to be surprised
at how easy it was to fall asleep again before she did
so.

Linak'h:

Warband Second Leader Fomin zar Yayn would not have
been traveling with any escort at all without orders. But
the Coordination's Council of Warband Leaders had
given orders too explicit to ignore.

"Except in an emergency, you travel guarded," their
senior member told zar Yayn. "You know too much and
our loss would be too great, if the humans captured or
killed you."

Zar Yayn could hardly suggest out loud that the purpose of the escort was more to watch him than to watch
for his enemies. Also, if he had any, they were more
likely to be among his own people. His Confraternity
sympathies were not exactly a secret, even if he had
never commanded any of the units almost openly loyal
to the "forbidden" organization.

However, as to arguments that he really could use with
seniors . . .

"I have already told you everything I learned during
my years of duty in the Administration," zar Yayn said.
"Also, the humans had every opportunity to cause an
'accident' in the days after the Braigh'n River incident,
before I was recalled. If they were not bold enough to
do it then, they would not be so foolish as to do it now."

"You surprise me, speaking so well of the humans,"
the senior said. It was as close as either of them could
come to an open reference to the Confraternity.

Zar Yayn did not sigh. The senior was one of millions
of Hunters who thought that the Confraternity was as
hostile to humans as it was to the Folk. After all, had
not both Federation and Alliance accepted the Merishi
view that the organization was illegal? It was impossible
to convince any of these millions otherwise, without revealing far too many secrets that would arm the enemies
of more than humans and Confreres.

"It is not to speak well of an enemy, to recognize his

strength and intelligence," zar Yayn said. "It is also wise to distinguish great threats from lesser ones."

"So—action against you would be a lesser threat?"

"I believe so."

The senior shrugged. "I dispute that."

Zar Yayn nearly asked aloud if they feared being accused by the Confraternity, if anything happened to him. But that would not merely step over the line, it would trample the line and the goodwill of the seniors into feculent mud.

Zar Yayn bowed and accepted the escort. To do the seniors justice they sent eight picked fighters. All of them had the art of always being between zar Yayn and any possible threat without being obtrusive about it. So after a few days he did not mind taking them with him, even to his Lodge of the House of Light.

It was on the way to that House that he saw the rocket flares in the distance. Before he could order a course change, he saw the chemical complex erupt, and the pilots changed course without orders to avoid passing directly over the fireballs.

They still reached the prison and coordinated with the guards in time to make the resistance more effective. Zar Yayn would gladly have lent his men to the pursuit once the firing had ceased, but the leader of the Watch's Special Action Band suggested otherwise.

"You have good warriors, but they don't know the land between here and the high forest, let alone in it. We've practiced there every moon, and chased a real escaper at least once a year for the last ten years."

Zar Yayn then thought of offering his men to help with the rescue work, but that needed the permission of the Fire Guard senior. She was off in the middle of the smoke and flames, moving her heatsuited guards and foam bombs around like pieces in a game of kuip, trying to at least keep the flames contained.

No chance of speaking to her over the radio, either. Zar Yayn had no wish to let everyone on the Fire Guard frequency hear him begging to be allowed to help, like a child at a house-raising. A Warband Second Leader did not have so much dignity that he could give away large amounts of it.

So he took to the air again. As he did, he saw a serpent

of fire wriggle out beyond the complex perimeter, then
begin a swift crawl downhill. One of the containment
walls had broken, feeding burning chemicals into a drain
intended only for clean water.

Zar Yayn saw two Fire Guard fliers take to the air
again, soaring over the serpent's head and racing it
toward the ravine where the drain fed into a stream that
ran under the railroad. It would be a perfect shambles if
the blazing, poisonous mass reached the stream, with the
stream contaminated, the railroad blocked (and it carried
heavy freight traffic, to make matters yet more interesting), and a great deal of blame seeking someone's reputation to devour.

Zar Yayn feared that his departure might make some
think that he feared the blame landing on him. But the
blaze was vanishing behind the hills already; if he turned
about he would look indecisive, even foolish.

Besides, it was the first meeting of the Lodge of which
he was a senior since his return. His presence there was
more of a duty than his presence here, where others
could do anything needed better than he.

"Blessed be the Light, Giver of Peace," he intoned,
then reflected that the Light would need to be very
blessed indeed, to give peace to Linak'h any time soon.

Linak'h:

Behdan Zeg growled the command codes; the computer
recognized his voice even if his own mother might not
have. His mother's elder son, Rahbad Sarlin, looked over
his shoulder. "The machine won't be frightened into displaying any sooner, mother's son."

"Nor will I be frightened into meekness, he whom I
must call kin."

Brokeh su-Irzim looked not too visibly at the ceiling.
The Lidessouf twins were outside and on call, for security
duty. Whether they would consider it a "security" matter, breaking up a fraternal brawl, was another matter.
It was not without some annoyance that su-Irzim had
studied Zeg's record.

In spite of being twenty years younger and ten years

less senior than his half-brother, Zeg had compiled nearly as fine a record as a Special Projects field agent. He also had one talent Behdan Zeg lacked, a command of the True Speech of the Ptercha'a. Humans and Merishi in plenty spoke it, but most of the People dealt with the Furfolk in Trade Merishi.

On Linak'h, in a crisis, that asset could almost outweigh the liability of Zeg's manners, which had not improved since the first time su-Irzim met him, at the house of Fleet Commander F'zoar su-Weigho. Computer translation was swift, precise, and capacious, but sometimes lacked either nuance or security. Both could well be needed on Linak'h.

The display came up. Visual for now, since the heat pulse from the burning chemical plant would scramble blacklight.

"No real-time? No enhancement?" Zeg muttered.

"Forgive that our devices do not meet Your Grace's standards. . . ." Sarlin muttered.

Su-Irzim cut in sharply. "Real-time is too fast, at this altitude. But I admit, we don't have the on-line enhancement they have at the ground receiver."

"What about a fiber line?" Zeg sounded almost amused at having one of his rhetorical flourishes taken seriously. Yet su-Irzim sensed more than amusement. Gratitude? He doubted Zeg had that in him, but who could say?

"Security," Zhapso su-Lal said, or rather intoned.

His solemnity did not rub off on Zeg. "From whom? Can the Smallteeth put anybody on the ground without our detecting it?"

"As you know perfectly well, mother's son," Sarlin said, dropping each word like a stone, "the humans could land an entire brigade on the front lawn without our receiving sufficient warning to organize effective resistance, had we the troops on the planet to make it even if organized."

"Um," Zeg said, scraping a bit of yellowing off his left tusk with his thumbnail and examining it before tossing it to the floor. "I wonder if the Hunters could help us there."

He'd used the True Speech name for the Ptercha'a,

and it now struck su-Irzim that he seldom used anything else. He *never* used the term "Furfolk."

"Help themselves to the cable for a joke, and the repair party for another one, more likely," Sarlin said. "That's if the Smallteeth and Scaleskins aren't running any of them, which they probably are."

At this point Brokeh su-Irzim felt compelled to remind his colleagues that the entire set of satellite images had run past while they were arguing. Ostentatiously he set the machine to run the display again, and this time silence not only descended but endured long enough to be useful.

Not that the images held any surprises. Both the roof of the prison and the ground outside the west wall were dotted with armed Hunters. Of the ones on the ground, some faced inward toward the battered wall, as if they feared a rush by the prisoners. Others were examining the places where the attackers had deployed. One blurred shape on the ground was, to a trained eye, a row of bodies laid out under those vomit-hued groundsheets the Ptercha'a used for the dead. With later enhancement, the Inquirers would be able to count the bodies, though probably not determine their political allegiance, if any.

Before he came to Linak'h, Brokeh su-Irzim would not have called himself a trained observer of satellite images. In so far as he had specialized in the Fleet, he had been Armament, which seldom called for watching the ground unless one was assigned to a ground-support squadron.

Now a combination of curiosity, duty, and the desire to make a new reputation for himself had brought him to Linak'h along with su-Lal and Sarlin. The Inquiry mission was small; the goldtusk Governor kept it not only small but starved. What the three Inquirers wished to be done, they more often than not had to learn to do themselves.

Which had meant Brokeh su-Irzim learning image interpretation and much else, including which Ptercha'a-brewed beers to avoid. (With some he had tasted, it would be a violation of war customs, even treaties, to give them to prisoners.)

"No lifters," Zeg said. And no recording of the radar scan. "Which satellite was it?"

"Sixty-one-C," su-Lal replied. "Modified from a Aunkyn-22 weather model."

"So," Zeg said. It sounded like an accusation. "A weak sensor suite, when it comes to detecting lifter movement at low altitude. Was that your choice of satellite? It was not the only one that could have been moved, I think."

"Explain yourself." Sarlin's voice held both challenge and curiosity.

Zeg called up a display of the People's satellites. He was right. Two others could have been moved as easily as 61-C. One of them was 64-A, an Aunkyn-17 loaded with radar for maritime surveillance, but also useful over level ground like that around the prison.

"Was 61-C the Force Commander's choice?" Sarlin and su-Irzim frowned, but again su-Lal was ready with the answer. He might have few virtues besides his memory, and more than his share of Syrodhi arrogance, but that memory compelled respect.

"It was. We did not think to question it at the time, which was short."

"No doubt the Force Commander and the Governor would agree," Zeg said. "But would they be explaining to you or excusing themselves? Or worse, hiding something?"

"Who gave you the right to come rooting in our patch, this way?" Sarlin snapped. "Make accusations that make sense, or be silent!"

"I promise that I will, when I make accusations. For now, I only wonder if the choice of satellite went wholly by chance. If you think it is worth asking, I trust the rest of the task to you. You are, after all, the ones with the time on Linak'h and the resources to seek others' secrets."

That was true as far as it went. It did not go to where su-Irzim's thoughts swiftly led him. If they did not help Zeg trail this fancy to its lair, he might strike out after it himself.

That might be one way of seeing the last of him. More likely, it would see Special Projects tusk-to-tusk with both the Inquiry mission and the Governor and Force Commander, over what had happened to Zeg and why they had permitted it!

Farther than that, su-Irzim would not let his thoughts go. Even an Inquirer should be only so far ahead of the evidence!

Linak'h:

"A peaceful night, Driver."

"The same to you, Leader."

Fomin zar Yayn stepped back as the flier's fans whispered to life. It drifted off the pad, then climbed steeply. A laser at the perimeter of the Leaders' Land interrogated it; the correct recognition signals flared and the laser died. A moment later the flier itself was lost among the stars as it returned to the skyfield.

All these protective precautions made zar Yayn itch, not only under his clothes, but so it seemed, under his fur. He founded himself reluctant to turn his back on the pad, and was staring intently at a dwarf tree that seemed to be new-planted, when the house door opened.

"Welcome home, Father."

It was his mate's son Ousso. He had used the form of the title that meant the lawful pair-mate of one's mother, which was as respectful as he ever was. Zar Yayn was not ready to ask him to use the honorific intonation, which implied that the legally-created relationship was as valued as a natural one. It seemed very likely that it would be a waste of time to do so, for many years to come.

But then, there was never food without the work of the hunt. Jillyah's first pair-mate, Seb Loyk, had been a fine-bred Hunter, the best Copperlands stock. He lived on in his son's memory in a way that zar Yayn would not try to fight. He also lived on in Jillyah's, as proof that a pair-mate made life sweeter. Without that proof, she might not have accepted zar Yayn's suit—and he needed no further proof than her, that pair-mating could be all it was supposed to be.

Meanwhile, there was Ousso to prove the truth of the old saying.

"Greetings, Son," zar Yayn said. He used the formal form of address to the lawful child of one's pair-mate. He even did it without smiling. At times, Ousso seemed to have more dignity than the Leader. But then, it was said that most sons and more than a few daughters had that kind of prickly dignity at this age.

"Greetings," the boy replied. Then he actually smiled. "Mother has fallen asleep. Was the Lodge meeting good?"

"More so than not." The boy was not yet Initiate, and anyway it would be years after Initiation before he could understand the subtle currents flowing in even the smallest Lodge of the House of Light. Zar Yayn himself did not understand many, and had given up trying to understand any that did not threaten either his Leadership or the Confraternity.

"I thought someone should be awake to greet you," the boy added, the words almost rushing out. "Mother has been worried. The weather predictions say no rain, and the high forest is drier than it has been since she took over the business. She has been worrying over the families of our workers, if we must stop the field operations to avoid starting fires."

"I know there are plans to make them eligible for Emergency Aid, as if they had been flood or earthquake victims," zar Yayn said. "Or has that changed?"

"I do not know."

"Ask your mother."

"I will, Father," Ousso said. "But in the morning." The hint of his displeasure, if zar Yayn woke up Jillyah, was unmistakable.

If there is war, you will be protecting your mother, and your half-sib to be, from more than things I would not do anyway!

"In the morning, I can call the Weather Monitors directly. They may know more than the broadcasters say."

"Perhaps."

Looking at the sky, zar Yayn understood the boy's skepticism. The stars shone with no hint of haze or cloud, the air was dry, and even the north wind held more warmth than usual for this time of year. They were well into spring, too, and after a dry winter the high forests needed a wet spring to keep their undergrowth and debris from turning into a bomb waiting for a fuse.

Not that it would do much good to drag loggers' families into barracks, if folk were going to be fighting a war!

Zar Yayn resolved to go to the basement and exercise until he was tired. For now, he would not have willingly spoken to Jillyah even if she had been awake! His mood was sour, not as it should be after a meeting with the Lodge, but then it was not the Lodge that was most on his thoughts now.

He put an arm around the boy's shoulders. "Now—it *is* bedtime. Or have you forgotten school tomorrow?"

"I have not forgotten."

"Good."

Zar Yayn watched the boy discreetly until he was back in his room, but disobedience was not part of his plans for tonight. When the Leader came up from the basement to wash and comb sweat-soaked fur, the boy was deeply asleep.

Acting Lieutenant Colonel Candice Shores saw Healer Kunkuhn signaling her from the kitchen door. The refugee Confraternity Healer had come to examine the two children of Shores's father Nikolai Komarov and his wife Ursula Boll, and ended up staying for dinner.

Now dinner was over, Sophia and Peter both in bed and (they all hoped) asleep, and the brandy going around. It was better liquor than the home-distilled vodka Shores had drunk at her first meal at her father's house; she'd refused to contemplate tasting that again, and used her new Acting rank to pry loose a bottle or two extra from Supply.

It had hardly been worth it, though. Her father's wife (she still had trouble with the term "stepmother" for a woman about her own age of twenty-nine Standard) had looked sharply at the brandy, then at her husband. Had her father started on a drinking problem? Or was Ursula just being paranoid about bribes by her Nikolai's prodigal daughter?

Probably the latter, Shores decided quickly. And she was definitely the sun complaining of the laser's dazzle; how often had she looked for bribes under Colonel Nieg's goodwill? (She hoped that stage of their renewed relationship was past, along with the eager fumbling of their first physical encounter on Linak'h.)

"Colonel Shores?" Kunkuhn said.

"We call my daughter 'Candice' in this house, my

friend," Komarov said, raising a glass in a sweeping gesture. Fortunately the glass was nearly empty. When he'd remedied that, the bottle was completely so.

After that, though, he sipped brandy in silence. Her father did not become jolly and expansive as so many Bogatyri did when they partied. He still had what Catherine Shores had brusquely dismissed as "a narrow-gauge version of the broad Russian soul."

"Very well, then. Colonel Candice is wanted." Kunkuhn spoke fairly good Anglic. His vocabulary was comprehensive and his constructions usually grammatical or at least only intentionally funny, but his pronunciation needed a trained ear to decipher.

Anybody who had as much to do with the Ptercha'a as Shores did in her post as CO of the Linak'h Command Quick Reaction Force needed that trained ear. That, or what Shores actually had: a knack for languages acquired early by growing up more multilingual than the average, and built on since she came to the Ptercha'a planet.

"Is it a call or a visitor?"

"A call, and from your Warband, with what I think is the 'Urgent Immediate' priority."

Shores's comfortable chair suddenly seemed too comfortable to leave, and the last mouthful of brandy in her glass more precious than cesium. She still levered herself out of the chair and squeezed past Kunkuhn into the kitchen.

The living-room screen was displaying abstract whorls to the third movement of Aksyonov's *Only Symphony* (a title as accurate as most intelligence estimates; the man had composed at least four). The kitchen repeater was linked to the outside, however.

It displayed a flaring notice, simple and direct:

URGENT IMMEDIATE PRIORITY WARNING. ALL FIELD-GRADE OFFICERS AND UNIT COMMANDERS RETURN TO THEIR POSTS AS SOON AS POSSIBLE. THIS IS NOT AN ALERT.

If it's not an alert, why the bloody Hades are they using 'Urgent Immediate'? Somebody doesn't want to cause a panic but is in a big hurry. Too big to think.

However ill-conceived, an order was an order, and in

this case it applied to her twice over. She was both a CO and a field-grade officer, and that meant one thing: time to launch.

Shores turned to face the living room. "People, thanks for the hospitality, but duty calls."

"Really?" Ursula Boll said, neat blond eyebrows rising.

"Really," Shores said.

"Any reason?"

"They didn't say, and I'm not guessing."

"Maybe the Coordination called off the ultimatum and Tanz is holding an orgy to celebrate?" her father said. Definitely brandy didn't relax him, in the face of the tension between his daughter and his wife.

Boll looked as if her husband might not be joking. Shores turned away, trying to keep her shoulders from slumping. Of course she'd had something to do with the Komarov-Boll household being driven bag, baggage, and artwork out of the Merishi Territory, but that would have happened whether she'd come back into her father's life or not! And did Ursula Boll really think that she was going to fade back into the forest after ten years apart from her father? Ten largely unnecessary years?

Boll certainly hoped so. It was written all over her face.

"It has been a pleasure, Colonel," Kunkuhn said.

"Likewise," Shores replied. "Healer, I happen to know that you walked from the camp. I'm flying my own lifter. Can I give you a ride home?"

Breaking up the party didn't improve Boll's temper, judging from her face. But judging from Kunkuhn's body language, he was almost as relieved to be airborne as Shores was. He slumped in his harness as the lights of the rented house faded behind them, and sighed.

"The children are well, at least," he said. "If you care."

"Why shouldn't I? I can recognize a pair-mating when I see one."

"Ah. Then human laws governing half-siblings are somewhat like those of the Hunters?"

"Not as complicated, as I'm sure you know." Kunkuhn could not bring off the Ptercha'a act of being a naive outsider, mystified by humans.

"One hopes so." Then, in quite a different tone, he added, "I am licensed to Heal humans."

"I'm glad you are. I didn't ask, though. As a Federation officer, I'd have been obliged to report illegal Healing. That might not be good for you."

"Ah. Then you feel sympathy for the Confraternity."

Shores tapped the control panel and held her finger to her lips. She doubted the lifter was bugged, but why take chances?

"Of course. Forgive me. You did not ask embarrassing questions. I shall follow your example."

"Thanks."

They topped a ridge and the ground fell away steeply, dropping five hundred meters in four kloms. The refugee camp was less than ten kloms away, and on the same side of the ridge as the Komarov house, but Shores preferred to take the lowland route.

At a safe altitude above the ridge, the lifter might be high enough to register on radars outside the Federation Territory. Why give probable enemies anything unnecessarily?

The automatic pilot took over, swinging the lifter in a ninety-degree turn to the left. Shores strained her eyes, looking for the blur of light in the south that would be Och'zem, capital of the Territory. But the city was a hundred kloms away, and even on a clear night like this probably in the coastal haze belt. Only darkness lay ahead, as the lifter settled onto its eastward course, bobbing gently in the night breezes.

Two

Charlemagne:

Acting Vice Admiral Sho Kuwahara and his wife Fumiko were in lotus position in front of the display tank. Yoga had lost its power to put Kuwahara in a contemplative mood, but then so had everything else. His job as chief of the Dual-Sovereignty Planet Study Group at Forces Command had promised major headaches and long hours. Thanks to events on Linak'h it was more than keeping that promise.

In the tank, Major General Marcus Langston gestured at a display now out of sight to the left. What had been there, and why was he indicating it?

Oh yes. The balance of forces on Linak'h, particularly the Federation and its Ptercha'a . . . call them "associates" . . . in the Administration of the Federation Territory vs. the not-so-friendly Ptercha'a of the Coordination of Linak'h. And Langston was pointing out the figures in reply to Dieter Something Germanic, from the *Freiwelt Kurier*.

"I think you can see that the Coordination has approximately forty-five thousand troops on active duty and nearly four times that many in its reserves. With a Federation brigade deployed, the Territory has a respectable thirty-thousand active, counting both humans and Ptercha'a.

"The Coordination has virtually no navy. The Territory has virtually no reserves. The Alliance, Merishi, and Baernoi among them don't have enough troops or ships at Linak'h to affect the balance."

"So what is the answer to my question?"

The peremptory tone of the voice made this next door to an interruption. The *Freiwelt Kurier* could profitably think of finding a new and politer Military Affairs correspondent, if Dieter held that position.

"The answer is simple. We are reinforcing Linak'h to avoid two undesirable situations. One is small bands of hotheads of any race or allegiance using a military vacuum to make trouble. The other is unnecessary casualties in any evacuation."

"Evacuation?" Dieter sounded confused.

He must have looked that way too, judging from the grin on Langston's dark brown face. Langston looked like a competition shooter who'd just put his team into the winner's circle with three successive gold-ring hits.

"I assume you know what the word means. *If* the Coordination makes an unqualified demand that the Federation leave Linak'h, we will consider giving them what they want. We will of course want to evacuate not only our own people but of any Ptercha'a of the Territory who may not wish to live under the Coordination. That could be a fairly large evacuation, possibly a good fraction of a million beings. So all the expert help on hand won't be too much."

That touched off a babble of voices and shouted questions, most of them sounding like media people calling to each other like a pack of hunt-trained charons. Kuwahara frowned. If he'd been there he might have been adding to the din, and he was definitely going to add to Marcus's worries tomorrow if this confessional hadn't been authorized from a lot higher than the Study Group. . . .

"You will note that I said *consider*," Langston added, raising his voice enough to first cut through the uproar, then beat it down. "There would be so many factors in that decision that we would be here all afternoon if I tried listing them. I would then promptly be arrested for breaches of security."

Some of the laughter at least sounded genuine.

"In so far as we have a policy that I can describe, it is *not* to go to war with the Coordination over the present situation on Linak'h. A war would prevent our getting together to rethink our relationship."

"That sounds like what that ex-sociologist diplomat was saying the other day," Fumiko muttered into her husband's ear.

"Raful Beer? You'd be surprised how many people in the Forces agree with him." Starting with Langston, and *he* was in favor of rethinking human-Ptercha'a relations across the board, on a scale that dwarfed whatever might happen on Linak'h short of all-out war. Which unfortunately couldn't be ruled out.

Several questions passed so unmemorably that Kuwahara didn't remember what they were or who asked them. Then a lady by the name of Kido, from *Meiji Shimbun*, asked a question Kuwahara was surprised hadn't come up before.

"The present situation on Linak'h seems to be at least partly due to our operations against the Merishi Territory. Would you care to comment on that?"

"Certainly. My comment is: very likely."

"Ah . . ."

"The normal limit is one question per conference, but I'll give you a chance to rephrase yours."

"Thank you, General Langston. Did General Tanz exceed his authority, in provoking the battle on the Braigh'n River and conducting operations in the Merishi Territory afterward?"

"It's my turn to thank *you*, Citizen Kido. The answer is no. I admit that the Federation's equivalent of Senior Commander's Initiative isn't as well-defined as the Alliance's. We prefer it that way, for a number of reasons.

"Something like it is inevitable, in any case, given the interstellar communications lag. I'm sure I don't need to give my five-minute lecture on micromanagement, its causes and cures, to a roomful of professional communicators?"

More laughter, and more of it genuine. Kuwahara smiled in admiration of Langston's deft sidestepping of the question. The whole question of whether General Tanz had exceeded his authority, even allowing for his having had Governor-General Rubirosa's consent, was sub judice. Admitting that to a roomful of mediacrats, half of whom had undoubtedly made up their minds one way or the other, would let loose demons and drunkards.

Langston twisted his head. Those high-collared dress tunics always made his neck muscles lock up after an hour or so in one position, and he'd been up there on the Aiming Point for nearly two. *I owe Marcus one for taking this job off my hands. Maybe considerably more than one.*

"Now, the reason I've let the question session go on so long is not to provoke a mad stampede to the bathrooms when we let you go. We had a few delays in getting our written presentation printed, but I've just been informed that the robot with the copies is on the way up now.

"So we have time for one more question. Ah, the lady in the rear? Yes, you—confound this magnifier!"

The camera shifted to show a slim, dark, intense woman in a thigh-length tunic and baggy pants bloused into white boots. "Josephine Atwood, Trans-Rift Media. Why was Marshal Banfi allowed to hold the party that was attacked by terrorists?"

Even before the question, Kuwahara had been at Alert Two. Now he was at Alert One, actively scanning.

Fumiko was looking a question at him. On the assumption that it was *The same Atwood who was on Victoria?* the admiral nodded, without taking his eyes off the display.

"The same Atwood who wrote 'The Cult of the Marshal'?"

"Yes."

"In spite of that, you'll get a straight answer—and please don't look so skeptical before I open my mouth. Think how embarrassed you'll be if I *don't* put my foot in it!"

The camera switched back to Atwood, and Kuwahara was relieved to see her joining in the loudest laughter yet.

Langston squared his shoulders, which Kuwahara noticed brought his two rows of ribbons more clearly into view. One of them represented his Distinguished Service Award from Victoria, for leading the Victoria Brigade against a heterogeneous array of enemies who never seemed to be the same two days running.

Kuwahara hoped that Tanz and Rubirosa could cope with Linak'h's not too different situation as well—and if they couldn't, would shout for help from the Old Vics on hand, like Rose Liddell and Candice Shores.

Langston cleared his throat. "At the time the decision about the party was made, the most serious terrorist inci-

dent had been the abortive kidnapping of Colonel Davidson. That didn't suggest great strength or determination
on the part of the opposition.

"It did suggest that if we canceled the party, it might
encourage the opposition and create that strength or determination. At the same time, it would signal all our
friends that we were frightened of what might be a ridicu-
lously small force.

"Anybody who's a good enough historian to write 'The
Cult of the Marshal' has to know what this mistake can
do. Of course, we made the other mistake, and the raid
took place.

"But before you ask me to hang Marshal Banfi, two
points. I don't have the rank to do it, and I wouldn't if
I could. We drew the opposition into the open, inflicted
far more damage on them than they did on us, and took
a number of prisoners.

"You may say that we opened Pandora's box. Perhaps
we did. But remember that the last thing to fly out of
the box was hope. I think that happened here, too.

"On behalf of Forces Command, I thank you for your
courtesy, your attention, and your patience."

Langston stepped away from the podium and made a
grand gesture, like a Master of Ceremonies ushering on
the drill team from 101 Light. The robot cart loaded with
the printed background files rolled up the aisle, two
Light Infantrymen in dress greens escorting it.

Kuwahara slapped the remote control and the display
died in the middle of the mob scene as the media people
scrambled to get their copies. Then he unfolded from
lotus and leaned back until he was lying on the mat,
staring at the ceiling. He let out a long whistling sigh.

"I thought he handled it very well, Sho," Fumiko said.
"Do you disagree?"

"Not at all," the admiral said. He must have said it
more absently than he thought; Fumiko twisted until she
was sitting astride his lower legs, bracing herself by gripping his ankles with her hands. Kuwahara knew that he
had practically no chance of getting up until he'd given
Fumiko a satisfactory answer, or at least one that showed
he was paying attention to her.

"What was the problem, then?"

"No problem, either. I was just surprised to find Jose-

phine Atwood on Charlemagne. I would have thought
we'd have read about her arrival. Trans-Rift Media is
not exactly a small amateur service."

"She only arrived three days ago," Fumiko said. "That
was when you were in the middle of the two-day session
you still haven't explained. Then when you came home
you were so tired I thought nothing and no one short of
the Empress ought to disturb you."

Kuwahara reached up and patted Fumiko at the highest point he could reach. She held the hand in place and
smiled.

"Shall we blackdown the house?"

"Just the living room. Hanae is getting really good at
screening calls. I wonder if her vocation is communications administrator?"

"Tell me that after she stays interested *and* skilled for
two months running."

"I will."

Kuwahara wanted to tell Fumiko more about Josephine Atwood and how likely it was that she had one
major motive: protecting her old friend and college
roommate Rose Liddell from any blame for the situation
on Linak'h. But that could wait.

Even more, he wanted to tell her about the way the
study group's inquiries were going. The key question had
appeared fairly early: Why had humans been desperate
enough to train as Merishi mercenaries on Linak'h?
Those desperate ones had appeared on both Victoria and
now on Linak'h itself; too many innocent people were
dead because of them. But were the mercenaries the
guiltiest ones?

That was the new key question, and answers to it might
lie down any of a number of paths, including a few
loaded with passive sensors, if not minefields and booby
traps.

For now Kuwahara had decided that the main line of
advance, the *schwerpunkt* of the study group, should be
the emigration files at the Ministry of Trade. Working at
the cross-ministerial level meant that the approval of the
Ministry of War was desirable, if not essential, and the
request for that had gone in several days ago.

Time to follow it up . . .

No. Time to pay attention to Fumiko. She was not

letting him get up, but she was making it more pleasant to remain lying down. And the mat was comfortable, the room was warm, and yoga had kept them both limber—even if it hadn't relaxed Kuwahara as much as his wife would. . . .

Victoria:

Councillor Payaral Na'an finished decoding the letter from Emt Desdai, his agent/observer/spy on Linak'h, and began reading the new text.

At first it seemed to be largely repeating the open version, with perhaps a trifle more gossip and some details about asking prices that would impair Desdai's position in negotiating for ship charters if they were public knowledge. Na'an found himself uncertain about his choice of Desdai. Had the Hunter ignored his second, secret mission on Linak'h, (worse) found it too dangerous, or (just possibly) made his second text a code for the real *third* message?

Unless that third message contained something of real value, Na'an would have something to say about sworn Servants who spent their masters' wealth at playing spy.

Then the tone of the text began to change:

> I have been solicited as to my authority to permit charter of *Somtow Nosavan*. It is apparently no secret, your financial interest in her, although I believe I have been as discreet as Kugh the Simple in the tale of the Swamp Lords.
>
> I have informed the solicitors, who are human and (I suspect) associated with the Federation, that terms must also be acceptable to the government of Victoria and to the officers of the ship. There does not seem to be any great haste in the matter, in spite of the tension on Linak'h, as no price has been mentioned.
>
> If matters reach that point, I promise to take only the most token of fees, that you and the Victorians may both profit and thus build goodwill. I trust I will not be asked to be so charitable in the event of future charters.

Na'an smiled. It was no secret that Emt Desdai and Seenkiranda intended to pair-mate as soon as they had a few days free of other responsibilities. Desdai seemed to take seriously the traditional obligation of bringing to one's pair-mate evidence that one was free, of legal age, and capable of earning a living.

Meanwhile, the Federation has placed a security team aboard *Nosavan,* guards her crew, and has the Folk Security people implicated in the attempted hijacking in custody. I have not heard that they have been charged or even interrogated, and there is discontent among the Federation humans—enough to make me believe this could be true.

Also, there are rumors among the local Folk that pressure on the Federation will force the release of the Security prisoners. This would require a great deal of pressure, as after the loss of their prisoners from the raid on Marshal Banfi's party the Federation authorities are extremely reluctant to let other "criminals" (in truth: intelligence sources) wander off into the hands of the Folk.

That did not surprise Na'an in the least; indeed, he thought "extremely reluctant" must be a well-phrased understatement. He wondered if the Federation had made any progress in investigating its own "Military Police," as they called the Internal Security of their ground forces. On the whole, he hoped they had.

Some among the Folk talk as if it will be easy to exert that amount of pressure on the Federation. I do not see how they can justify their hopes, as giving up territory is one matter for the Federation, giving up terrorists another one entirely. Only the Coordination has the armed strength necessary to force the Federation to do *anything*.

Desdai had not repeated the detailed table of the opposing forces on Linak'h from his last letter. There was no need to. The truth remained the same: The Federation's Linak'h Command would be a match for Folk, Baernoi, and Alliance forces on Linak'h combined.

Na'an began to wonder if the crisis on Linak'h might

in fact fade away without further violence. Had the Coordination's extension of the ultimatum been a device to save its pride, while wiser counsels prevailed on both (or all) sides?

Best finish the letter before he leaped to such conclusions. He did, and by then he felt much less content.

> Seenkiranda has been associating with certain Hunters who are said to be active in the armed-resistance wing of the Confraternity. I have spoken to her on this matter, as severely as I can without danger to our pairing.
>
> I hope you will honor my desire to keep Seenkiranda, or at least not to dismiss our pairing without firm evidence. I also hope you will understand if, with the intention of learning more about Seenkiranda's associates, I myself am seen in Confraternity circles. (I hardly need tell you about the speed with which rumors multiply and spread.)
>
>					Very respectfully,
>					Emt Desdai, Sworn to
>					Simferos Associates

There would be much swearing *at* Simferos Associates if someone in Desdai's position was found openly consorting with the Confraternity. All the understanding and tolerance that Na'an himself could summon up would not keep others from regarding Desdai as a criminal and rebel and Simferos Associates as blind to his crimes, to say the least. (Nor would many be content with saying the least; Simferos Associates was one of the eight largest merchant associations among the Merishi, but that did not make it free of enemies or immune to attack.)

Possibly both Seenkiranda and Desdai were telling the truth. And possibly nestlings were spawned from the morning dew instead of growing within their mothers.

Still, Na'an was not going to repudiate Desdai or withdraw him, still less command him to force Seenkiranda from all association with the Confreres. (Na'an had never served in Security, but knew one of their oldest bits of wisdom: "Never give an order you know will not be obeyed.")

Even if he wished to, there was the matter of the time

needed to send a secure message to Linak'h. This time he would send only a mild admonition about not being seen in dubious company. He would follow it with further messages, each one stronger—until either Desdai and Seenkiranda had finished their work, or it became certain that there was nothing more they could learn worth the risk of their exposure.

Good servants were no more to be risked for bad causes than was the name and reputation of Simferos Associates. But it was not a bad cause, to learn more about the Confraternity. Whatever their ultimate actions toward it, the Folk could not afford to remain in their present state of ignorance about something so important to so many of their best Servants.

Since there were no particularists present to complain about his Human tastes, Payaral Na'an drank a toast to Desdai's and Seenkiranda's success in chilled apricot juice.

Three

Linak'h:

Seventy-two Linak'h days to go. Candice Shores could push the expiration date of the Coordination's ultimatum to the back of her mind, but not out of it. Others in Linak'h Command felt the same way—and no doubt the Coordination's own Warband leaders were even more on edge. (They had the initiative, a principle of war which, since modern sensor nets, often meant only that everyone saw you stepping in it. By the time your opponent reacted, the "fog of war" sometimes provided them with the tactical equivalent of a fig leaf.)

Most of her attention was now on the ground six hundred meters below, matching her eyeball images to what the lifter's sensors showed. Sensor images were always a translation, even if a good one. She backed them up with the Mark I eyeball whenever it could be effective.

The lifter juddered and sideslipped, reminding Shores of where the rest of her attention ought to be. The air was rough here, as the hot updrafts coming off the Syngoon Hills met the cooler breezes in the valley of the Hyssh'n.

"Check your harness," she told her passengers, two platoon leaders from C Company of Fifth Battalion, 222 Brigade. Along with *Shenandoah*'s LI company and a company of Linak'h Reservists, it was one of the three rifle units in the QRF.

Hauled to Linak'h as the first wave of reinforcements, Fourth Battalion had acclimatized well and seemed to be shaping up fine, but Shores would still rather have had a company from the Linak'h BEU. Their officers didn't need this kind of terrain-familiarization hop. In fact, they could take her on one.

"I agree on both points," she remembered Colonel Barbara Hogg saying, refilling her pipe with the potent mixture of aromatics she favored. "But the Linak'h BEU has already been assigned the duty of handling the refugees. That wasn't my idea, by the way."

No, but I wonder how hard you fought it, Shores had thought.

"I can see that would stretch them pretty thin," Shores said. "Well, it shouldn't matter. The Reserve people are pulling their weight. As long as your people do the same, no problem."

"If they don't, stand clear and I'll apply a little nonlethal force," Hogg promised, puffing away.

How sincere that promise was, and how effective the force would be, Shores still didn't know. Hogg was determined to let at least one company of Fifth Battalion show its paces, which could be either loyalty to her unit or hunger for promotion or both. Being from off-planet, she might not know where to apply force to the Linak'h BEU or be able to do so without raising a stink that would have to be mediated by General Tanz, who would not be grateful to any of the officers involved.

The lifter sideslipped again. It seemed they had not only updrafts but crosswinds at this altitude. Shores adjusted the port fans and cut back minutely on the lift field. A few kilos' more effective weight would give the lifter extra stability, without risking a sudden plunge.

Shores's regular pilot, now riding in the copilot's seat, frowned.

"Six hundred meters is enough," Shores said firmly, in answer to the implied question. She wished Warrant Officer Konishi would show a little respect for her six hundred hours' flying time, if not for her rank. Konishi was good, but eighty hours of Shores's time had been piloting Frieda Hentsch, when the Pocket Pistol had her own Command Pilot rating!

The next updraft sent the lifter bobbling and weaving up to seven hundred meters. Shores wished their flight plan gave them more discretion in altitude. But six hundred meters relative was what they'd been given, and what she'd be yelled at for failing to hold.

That altitude was supposed to allow for heavy refugee traffic lower and attackers up higher. She'd seen all of four attackers, two of them heavies nearer six thousand meters than six hundred, and not a single airborne refugee. If anybody was hightailing it toward the coast from around here they must be doing it on the ground, or maybe flying nap-of-the-ground, lifter bellies meters above the treetops. . . .

The emergency warning squalled. Shores started, then recognized the signal for an incoming distress signal. Konishi was already slapping the radio over to the right frequency.

"*Mayday, Mayday!*" blasted her ears. "*Mayday.* This is refugee ship *Five Brothers.* We are under attack, in the Great Bend of the Hyssh'n. Devil's Hill bears zero-one-zero, twelve kloms. *Mayday, Mayday!*"

The armament panel came up green before the call mentioned the Great Bend. Shores cut lift, adjusted the fans for descent, and switched the communications suite to relay. The way the signal was blasting, they ought to be able to hear it aboard *Shenandoah,* but these hills sometimes blocked or distorted signals. At least Linak'h wasn't Victoria, where if you had two kloms' radio range it was a good day!

Linak'h:

Allard Brandstetter hadn't enjoyed being aboard *Five Brothers* even before the attack started. But it was the only alternative to something he knew that he would have enjoyed even less: seeing Sandy and the boys on their way down the river without him.

At times he was almost ready to suspect some of his neighbors. Not of being Cat-lovers, the way Sandy thought, but of being too cheap or too stubborn to think things through. He'd presented the calculations that proved the whole valley could move out if they clubbed together to hire a cargo lifter. But when five of the eleven humans and three of the four Ptercha'a refused to move at all, the cost factor made airlift impossible.

That left *Five Brothers,* the Hyssh'n's Old Reliable since ten years before Brandstetter staked his claim. Co-owned by a Catman and somebody who was rumored to be an ex-Ranger, she trundled up and down the river. Sometimes her regular trips were about all that stood between the settlers and assorted serious problems.

She'd pushed off that morning, her decks crowded with the families who were evacuating and their household goods. Four of the stay-behinds had agreed to keep an eye on the livestock, so *Five Brothers* hadn't had to unload any cargo.

"Just as well," Sandy had muttered. "If those bastards had to unload cargo, they'd tack it on to the fare."

Brandstetter didn't know which owner she was referring to, but it could well be both. Sandy not only didn't like Ptercha'a, she suspected people who got along too well with them. It was an old issue between them, and if he hadn't long since given way on it, the marriage might never have lasted long enough to give them the boys.

Who were fine kids, but if he didn't have them tying him to Sandy for at least another ten years . . .

The first burst of fire ended the old familiar fantasy.

The first burst whipped overhead. The second was lower—solid rounds, some chopping through the railing, some ricocheting off it, a few *thunk*ing into deck cargo. By the time the third burst came in, the marksmen on shore had lowered their point of aim to about knee-level, but everybody on deck was lying down and some lucky ones were behind crates and containers.

Then the first rocket hit. It slammed into the boat's side a meter below the deck. Flame gushed, smoke swirled up, and fragments sprayed outward, pocking the blue-green river with white foam. Brandstetter saw his wife in the open, back to the shore as she pushed the boys behind stacked crates.

As the boys vanished, he grabbed Sandy's ankles and heaved. She slid backward across the deck, snagging one knee of her pants on a deck bolt, ripping cloth and skin. She yelled and struck at him as he pulled her to safety, then let out a very different sort of yell as the second rocket struck.

This one hit the base of the forward pilothouse. It was empty; the helmsman must be in the aft one, if he hadn't ducked belowdecks. Just as well, as the rocket explosion turned the pilothouse into a sleet of wood, plastic, and wire that scoured the decks. Yelps and screams told of people who hadn't found quite enough cover.

"Damn you, Al! What did you do that for? I've got to stay near the boys!"

"For an ex-Regular, you can be pretty damned dumb! Where were you going to stay, that didn't leave your ass hanging out in the breeze or the bullets?"

Before she could answer, the helmsman—a relative of the Ptercha'a owner, Brandstetter recalled—threw the helm hard over. The boat swung more slowly, but the bow definitely was now aimed at the bank to starboard.

Sandy squalled wordlessly. From her expression, if she'd had a gun she would have shot the helmsman on the spot. Then she found her voice.

"Kill the helmsman! The Catturd's turning us over to the terrs!"

There was something wrong with that, but it took Brandstetter a moment to realize what it was. The firing was coming from the port side, while the helmsman was turning them to starboard, away from it.

Then events took matters out of Brandstetter's hands, as a long tongue of flame spewed from the first rocket hole. The deck under Brandstetter shook, and it wasn't his imagination that flames were rumbling under it or that the wood was getting hot.

"Oh, Hades!" It was the cargo they hadn't unloaded— nut and fish oil, both flammable if they were heated enough, plus some solvents that would do the job of heating them very nicely. A hot rocket fragment must have hit the solvents, torched them, and led to the chain-reaction ignition of a fire that was going to eat *Five Brothers* out from under her passengers. . . .

"Sandy! Get the boys forward, as far as you can go without exposing yourself. The bow's going to reach shallow water first."

"Hey, hero, what about you?" She was actually giving him a lopsided smile!

"I'm going back aft."

"No gun?"

"I can relieve the helmsman."

"I can shoot."

"The boys need one of us alive, not both of us dead because we argued too long." He started crawling aft.

The shooters now seemed to be holding their fire, so he made most of the trip without any trouble except that the deck was getting hotter and hotter under his stomach and hands. . . .

He came to the weedy-looking Robinson boy, crouched behind a container. "Don't go any farther," the boy muttered. "The Kitties are all in this together. That was one of their battle rifles that hit us, and look!"

The helmsman was clutching the wheel like a drowning man, and three other Ptercha'a crouched beside it, sporting or hunting weapons in hand and huge eyes scanning the bank. To Brandstetter, they didn't look like conspirators so much as people who hadn't found a worthwhile target for their scant supply of ammunition, but it was just as well that he'd sent Sandy forward. Seeing Ptercha'a standing between her and death wouldn't make things easier afterward, if there was an afterward.

If there was, Brandstetter decided that he'd better think about moving into the Zone. There were jobs for ex-Regulars like Sandy and JOT's like him; not good ones, maybe, but they could raise the boys without the shadow of a Catman falling on them. The only alternative was trying to use Sandy's prejudices against her in court, to take the boys away, and this was a worse-than-usual time to do something that always smelled bad at the best of times.

The pilothouse disintegrated, and the helmsman was the largest of the burning pieces that flew overboard. All three of the other Catmen were in shape to return the fire, not accurately but fast, and Brandstetter thought he heard a secondary explosion on the bank. He wouldn't have heard a scream; the fire belowdecks was roaring too loud.

Then *Five Brothers* ran bow-first onto the bank, hard enough to shift all the deck cargo. Now Brandstetter did hear screams, as crates and containers crushed people they'd been sheltering. More screams rose, to be quickly drowned out as the whole stern opened up in a torrent of flame.

Brandstetter didn't waste breath screaming. He plunged forward, knowing that the terrorists couldn't see to shoot through the wall of smoke behind him. He snatched a son by one arm and his wife by her hair. Somehow Sandy grabbed the other boy and held on.

They all went overboard as the flames started to roll forward. Some of the people who ran ahead of them ran fast enough and plunged over the port side after Brandstetter. Others ran even faster and made it to the starboard bow, where they could practically jump to the land.

Some didn't run fast enough to do either. If they made it overboard at all, it was as living torches. They were dead, so Brandstetter felt vaguely angry with them for still screaming.

Brandstetter half swam, half waded to the shore. He looked around wildly and didn't stop looking until he saw both his boys, grimy, greasy, and coughing out smoke and water, but alive.

It took Sandy's hand on his arm to make him realize that he was still gripping her hair. Then the smoke wall jerked, like a blanket shaken to dislodge a sleeping pet, and a sonic boom slammed down across the river.

Brandstetter looked up, to see a Fed heavy attacker whipping into a climbing turn. He started to wave, then Sandy grabbed his arm again.

"Come on, hero," she said. "If there's anybody alive on board, the Feds can do a better job without our help. Besides, that heavy's chewing up the smokescreen. Want to be around when it goes and the Kitties over there start shooting?"

It didn't seem the time to mention the helmsman who'd saved whoever had lived through this, and Sandy did know more about smokescreens and military air than he did. He helped the boys out of the water and let Sandy take the rear as they scrambled up the bank toward the tree line.

Linak'h:

It took thirteen minutes from receiving the mayday for Candice Shores to reach *Five Brothers*. The boat was off the air for eleven of them. This was plenty of time to realize how green the two platoon leaders were, and how little firepower her lifter really had.

The platoon leaders couldn't be changed in the time available. If this was a firefight waiting up ahead, they would be either less green or less alive very soon. Shores wasn't going to do anything to make their lives harder or shorter—she'd been a new platoon leader once herself—but she was going to pull their files as soon as she got home. Both of them must have been sent to OTC after not much more than the minimum of enlisted service; they had that look.

The firepower couldn't be changed, either, but any tactics she used could be adjusted to what was available. The problem was, the best tactic for a Security Condition Two load with this lifter was the classic maneuver known as "getting the Hades out of the hot area." Ruling that out, what alternatives were left?

Security Two meant personal weapons, body armor, combat helmets (she'd have required those, Two or no Two), a "reasonable" supply of ammunition, and at least one vehicle-mounted weapon. The lifter had an integral pulser in an overhead swivel mount; that was loaded, but the grenade-launcher was empty and the pod racks on either side were bare.

Personal weapons—a pulser carbine and one-plus-three apiece, plus ten magazines and half a dozen grenades apiece in the secure locker. Four sidearms, two flare pistols, and the light hunting weapon in the survival kit that was mandatory for out-Zone flights anyway. More than their allowance, but not enough, thank the Lady, that they'd had to jigger their flight-plan data to hide an extra load.

Shenandoah's task force had loaded up Linak'h with ammunition—the cross-river operation on the Braigh'n had barely dented the dumps—and 222 Brigade was bringing at least its own Basic Load. None of it would save Candice Nikolayevna Shores's tail or reputation if she didn't pre-shrink her tactics.

First move: get help. That meant calling the two heavy attackers and the QRF base. The attackers weren't carrying air-to-ground loads worth mentioning, but they were glad to join the party and could do so at Mach Three. The QRF ready platoon would take longer, unless it rode or at least docked with another heavy, but everything she was saying was getting relayed upstairs; *Shen* ought to be good for some coordination. . . .

A sonic boom made Shores glad that Konishi had the controls while she played Old Lady. A glint in the sky ahead, then a voice:

"Gold One Pest Control. All sorts of household and other pests eradicated at reasonable rates. What's the job today, Candy?"

"Lanie!" Where Elayne Zheng had come from, Shores didn't know, but a familiar voice attached to a competent body never hurt. "Where are you?"

"Circling at eight thousand meters over *Five Brothers*. She's aground, blown up or at least on fire from bow to stern. I see survivors in the water. A couple have made shore. About a klom inland there's a farming village, or maybe just a multi-family farm."

"Can we have a visual?"

"Magnification?"

"Full-view, then zoom in on the survivors."

Zheng was about as good an EWO as there was, and her CO didn't joggle her elbow while she transmitted the telescopic camera's-eye view of the battlefield. Zooming in on the survivors showed that they were all human, apparently civilian refugee. She suspected that most of them would also be in need of medical care.

By the time she'd finished studying the screen, the other two attackers had come on line with ETA's, and she had the first stage of the operation worked out. It was standard doctrine, two attackers at low altitude scanning for hostile presence, one high for overwatch from out of range of antiship weapons.

"Pretty heavy canopy," Zheng said.

"Concentrate on any open ground or possible exit routes from the enemy's part of the right bank," Shores said. "But don't fire except on identified hostile targets."

"What's your ETA?" the senior attacker pilot chimed in.

Shores looked at the panel display. "Five minutes thirty, at our present speed and altitude."

"Okay. If you're late, one of us will try to make contact with the survivors," the pilot said. "I've got my navigator pulling together all our medical supplies for paradropping. If we establish contact, we'll make a low pass and dump the bundle. All right?"

"No problem at all," Shores said. In fact, the pilot was almost embarrassingly far ahead of her. However, with ETA now four minutes, forty-five, she didn't have time to waste feeling guilty about that.

Linak'h:

The announcement of the detection of inbound Merishi ships had come ten minutes ago. A moderately frustrated Juan Esteva and Jan Sklarinsky got out of bed and waited for the inevitable alert.

Five minutes, and no alert. Jan sat back down and started undressing. Esteva grinned.

"Stop looking at me that way," Sklarinsky said, holding one arm over her breasts in a totally unconvincing show of modesty. "I'm going to take a shower first."

Esteva made noises implying unendurable frustration. She patted him on the head.

"Down, boy!"

She peeled off the last garments and trotted into the bathroom. The water had just started running when the alert signal howled.

"Hijo de cabron," Esteva muttered. Then he bounced off the bed and started collecting his weapons, as the intercom cut through the whining alert signal.

"Attention, attention! All personnel assigned to the QRF, report immediately to your alert stations. All personnel assigned to the QRF, report immediately to your alert stations.

"The Alert Condition for the QRF is Red One. Repeat, Alert Condition Red One for the QRF. All other personnel are on Alert Two until further notice. Alert Two, all other personnel.

"This is not a drill. Repeat, this is not a drill."

Esteva started to swear again. It turned into a sound something like "Gmphh!" as Sklarinsky bent over and kissed him. Inspired by the scenery, he kissed her back, then patted her rump. She wiggled it, then grinned.

"Think of it as practice in deferred gratification."

"We haven't been practicing that," Esteva pointed out. "We've been doing it for real." An alert at this point was about as much fun as another bout with Sergeant Dholso.

Esteva was still fully rigged-out in time to help Jan finish dressing. She even let him get the case with her sniper pulser, although she unpacked it herself. (The one time he'd touched the weapon without her permission, she hadn't struck him. The look she gave him, however, was about as pleasant as having a wisdom tooth extracted by an unlicensed Catpeople Healer.)

Outside, it wouldn't have been polite to the LI image to say that everybody was running around. A few people were running, and everybody else was trotting or walking very fast. Some of them even looked as if they knew where they were going. Everybody had a weapon and one-plus-four, and two-thirds of the people Esteva saw on the way to the pad had also pulled on body armor and helmets.

An NCO Esteva didn't know shouted something at Sklarinsky about having a sweater on over her battledress. She didn't break stride, just shot a look back over her shoulder that stopped the NCO dead in his tracks.

"He was probably junior to you, anyway," Esteva said.

Sklarinsky flashed him a white-toothed smile. She had a nice display, and they seemed to grow longer and more pointed when she was heading out on a live-fire mission.

"Well, well, the honeymooners at last," Top Timberlake said, as Esteva and Sklarinsky crossed the pad boundary. "You're in Dryad Two-Six. Move it!"

They sprinted to the indicated lifter and wedged themselves into the last two seats. The rest of the lifter held a squad and SSW team from 4th Platoon. From the cockpit, Lieutenant Kapustev turned and grinned.

"Welcome aboard. We've got a terrorist attack on a refugee boat, up by the Great Bend of the Hyssh'n. The Old Lady's already on the way, and she's called in three heavy attackers for overhead cover."

Esteva ignored sudden bladder pressure by checking his weapons. The SSW loader handed him a bandolier.

He started unsticking magazines and dropping them in his own pouches, which steadied hands and nerves.

"Any more word on those Merishi ships?" Sklarinsky asked. She'd strapped in, and now sat leaning back into her harness, looking rather like a snake basking on a sun-warmed rock. Only the two-handed grip on the sniper pulser between her knees betrayed tension.

"Not even a positive ID," Kapustev said. "But they're coming in fast. To me, that smells like warships."

It smelled the same way to Esteva, too, or rather stank. Had there been a leak, to bring those Merishi ships out when the remainder of 222 Brigade was inbound and only ten hours out?

The whine of the fans starting up cut off further conversation, then the lifter tilted nose-up and shot off the pad at a pace that discouraged anything but holding on tight.

Linak'h:

Candice Shores got good news and bad news at the same time, and promptly passed it on to her companions.

"The bad news is that we have a positive sensor signature on some incoming Merishi ships. Four heavy cruisers, more *Ryn-Gaths*. They haven't made any hostile moves that the Navy's telling us about, but they are coming in fast.

"The good news is that the 4th Platoon of *Shenandoah* Company is on its way, reinforced with sniper, intelligence, and medical teams." She'd bet the sniper would be Jan and the intelligence would be Juan; the medics could be anybody.

"The rest of the QRF is on pad alert. They'll move when we know this is the only action around, and the best place to send them."

One of the lieutenants—FISKE was the name on his tab—looked confused. "Don't we just put them in the places that we can't scan from the air? If I'm out of line . . ."

He was, and if Shores had her wishes, he would be out of any unit she had to work with by tonight. But good fairies were scarce on Linak'h, and light colonels (even acting ones) were supposed to do their own dirty work.

"Take a look at the map. Triple canopy some places, debris layers three meters deep in other places, sometimes both. Ever tried to move in that kind of terrain?"

"Ah . . ."

"I didn't think so. What we're going to do is lay down a network of sensors, to channel evaders into a few possible routes that we can cover. With squads or more, I might add. Sprinkling people here and there like grass seed is a good way to get them killed, even against bargain-priced terrs like this mob."

One minute short of ETA, Shores zoomed in on the battlefield. The boat was a solid mass of masthead-high flames from stem to stern. At least the smoke would be covering the survivors ashore from enemies across the river. It was impossible to imagine anybody surviving aboard.

Konishi followed the bank up to the stern of the boat, then hovered. By this time most of the survivors had reached the shore. Some of them were waving. Shores assigned the two lieutenants to watch the hostile bank, unstrapped, and popped the side hatch. The attackers hadn't been able to reach anybody on the ground by radio, but maybe there was somebody among the refugees who could read Com Standard off a blinker.

She started flicking the lifter's nose light on and off, sending a message:

GET UNDER COVER AND STAY TOGETHER. MEDICAL ASSISTANCE, SECURITY, AND EVALUATION ON WAY.

She had to send it three times before someone—a woman, she thought—signaled back. The woman hand-signaled that the message was understood but that they had no means of reply. Then she pointed at the farm and gave the interrogative.

This time Shores had to send the message only once:

AVOID FARM UNTIL SECURITY FORCES ARRIVE.

That might be hard to do, if the farmers were actually harboring terrs or packing enough firepower to send out a patrol. If they were just sympathizers, they'd probably sit tight. They might even be good guys. It was one of those situations where paranoia was functional.

The smoke whipped about the lifter and the lifter itself bucked until Konishi juggled fans and field. A heavy attacker flashed over the refugees, at minimum altitude and speed but still trailing a slipstream. The belly hatch slid open, and two bundles fell into space. Two parachutes opened before the attacker was over the trees, and both bundles landed before it was out of sight.

One of the bundles got up, stretched its legs, and started climbing out of the 'chute harness. Then the radio came to life.

"Purple Two to Huntress. We've dropped our medpak and our navigator. He's crossed-trained as a paramedic. Can you give us some security?"

Shores looked at the lieutenants. They looked back at her. She decided that if they couldn't meet her eyes by a ten-count, she would have some rude things to say to them, their company CO, and Colonel Hogg.

"No sweat," Fiske said. It was actually popping out in beads all over his forehead, but the first taste of combat had done worse to better men. Shores had been lucky; facing five times your weight in soccer players with rape on their mind was a crash-course in combat-readiness that she'd passed when she was seventeen.

Shores nodded to Konishi. The lifter slid around the flames, which were beginning to die down, and came to a hover near the woods. Most of the refugees hadn't actually hidden inside the tree line, but were keeping low in the scrub and underbrush along the fringes.

Konishi opened the rear hatch and released the ladder. Fiske swallowed, led his comrade aft, and vanished down the ladder. Shores waited until she could see them on the ground, trying to look as if they could protect the medic all by themselves, then tapped Konishi on the shoulder.

The lifter climbed away from the trees, ripped through the smoke, and swung into a wide circle over the smoking wreck of *Five Brothers*.

Linak'h:

They hadn't disabled the distress-frequency monitor or its alarm aboard the Confraternity lifter. It was tempting, but that would never pass a safety inspection, even one performed by sympathetic Hunters. As to what would happen if they came to the attention of the Federation or the Folk . . . Seenkiranda understood why sometimes there was no such thing as worrying too much in a war, at least before the shooting started.

Now the shooting had started—again. Their raid, and now as they finally made their way homeward, thinking themselves safely bound for Och'zem, this mayday for *Five Brothers* and her people.

"If it was just humans aboard, and no Federation Warbanders roaming about . . ." the pilot began nervously.

"That's past hoping for," their new leader (he used the name Drynz) said briskly. "Acknowledge the mayday."

"What about the weapons?" another of the raid survivors asked. "And Possandaro? He needs a Healer, and soon. His father was my science teacher. I will not let him die."

"We hide the weapons," Drynz said patiently. "If you are not plucking your fur out in handfuls as you are now when we land, the Federation will suspect nothing. If they suspect nothing, they will make no searches. Without a search, they will find no weapons. The Federation's Warbanders are no more magicians than ours, maybe less."

"Indeed," Seenkiranda said. "Also, let us give Possandaro a sleep drug. If he cannot be questioned, we can tell the Federation a tale of his being shot in a feud. Many of them will find such a tale easy to believe. Indeed, they may even be willing to aid him."

Drugging humans on their own notions about the Hunters was somewhat like dancing to gain work—it tasted overripe, but did no lasting harm, as Seenkiranda knew from experience.

None of the other five raiders said anything during this exchange. It was Possandaro who ended the debate.

"We go. Or my father learns that we did not, and what

he knows, the kin of the owners of *Five Brothers* will learn."

Seenkiranda thought it might be better not to give him the drug after all. Patiently enduring pain, nimble-tongued in spite of it, he would play even more skillfully on human fancies about the Hunters.

But Drynz was acknowledging the mayday, while the pilot calculated new courses and an ETA that Drynz could give the Federation. They would have more than enough time to talk things over with Possandaro.

She was glad Drynz had assumed leadership. She still had to persuade rather than order. It would take a hand's count more raids at least before she ranked as any sort of leader. There might not be that many more, unless war broke out. The Coordination's Warband would be alert now.

If war did break out, Hunters going up against an alert Coordination might not *survive* five more raids. Better her than Emt, if the Confraternity needed such help, but best of all that it not need it.

Four

Aboard U.F.S. *Shenandoah*,
off Linak'h:

Rose Liddell's conversation with General Tanz was being tight-beamed and scrambled; that would have to do. No EI would affect the Merishi decision to start shooting, if they'd already made it. If they were only going to *look* dangerous, it didn't matter.

The real need for security was from the rest of the Linak'h Squadron (about to be upgraded to a Task Force) and Linak'h Command. She and Tanz not only had to agree, they had to be heard, seen, and smelled agreeing. At the moment this condition was not being met.

"I have to point out the limitations imposed on my people—your people, too—if the 879th isn't available," Tanz said. Liddell wished they had a secure visual link; eyeballing a face during the conversation usually beat computer-analyzing a voice afterward.

"You have three attackers already on station, which is certainly enough cover and support for a reinforced company, let alone a platoon."

"What if we need more troops?"

"Then you can"—*whistle up your light-attacker gang* would not be tactful—"use organic air assets. In fact, I've got a compromise to suggest."

Liddell hoped Tanz would listen. She could disobey even a direct order from the CG, Linak'h Command, if in her judgment it would seriously endanger her squadron. But she would hardly be able to work with him afterward.

The commodore thought that she knew Tanz's goal.

Breaking up a terrorist band that apparently attacked both humans and Ptercha'a would be a diplomatic coup, probably an intelligence haul, and even conceivably a military gain. Or at least it could be passed off as a gain. Forces Command was far enough from Linak'h so that suitably massaged data could make the right impression.

That impression would be one of Tanz as a winner, who should be left alone to win. No more of the over-aggressive independent commander, chasing a third star at the price of causing a crisis.

Liddell would much rather Tanz succeeded, and not only because her own reputation was somewhat at stake. She had not, after all, kicked, screamed, and held her breath in protest against the river-crossing. This was the wrong time to change horses, unless the old mount was definitely either unmanageable or unhealthy, and Tanz hadn't slipped over into either category. Yet.

"You've got three attackers on station. I've got two more I can spare, one on a launcher and the other on orbital-debris patrol.

"I need to leave one attacker on the patrol. But I can load the one on the launcher with a prepackaged load of droppable sensors, mine-dispensers, the usual ground-support suite." She nearly said "garbage."

"How many?"

Speaking strictly from memory, Liddell had to hedge her words. "The equivalent of at least eighteen Mark 40 packages."

"Not the devil of a lot," Tanz said, but he sounded like he was ready to bargain rather than fight. Liddell decided that prayers of thanks still could wait.

"You've got more, don't you?" Taking silence for assent, she went on. "The junk-patrol can ground, load your own packages, and fly out. If we need to scramble the rest of the QRF, it can give them heavy escort.

"I'll also order the heavies and the ground party to help you set up a light-attacker supply point closer to the Great Bend. You pick the spot, you and Sophie, and we'll help you rig it."

Tanz's voice had the tone of a man capitulating, reluctantly, but with enough sense to know he had no choice. Maybe even enough to laugh at himself a little?

"As you wish, *Gnadges Frau Kommodore*. But hurry

things along, please. I beg to doubt if it was a coincidence, the terrorist attacker and the arrival of the Merishi cruisers at the same time.''

"I share those doubts. Good hunting, General.''

"The same to you.''

The connection died. Liddell stretched as far as her command chair would allow, and her eyes met Pavel Bogdanov's. Recruited (*impressed* would be a better word) as chief of staff once *Shenandoah* had gone to Alert One, he was likely to have the job for a little while. His ship was going nowhere, unless the Merishi greatly reduced Liddell's range of tactical options by going after the incoming transports and their escort.

"Tanz may be right," Bogdanov said. "But I have seen coincidence and stupidity produce more evil than conspiracies and cunning. Not that the Merishi are incapable of either, but I doubt that they are more infallible than we are."

Liddell nodded and called up the ship-status display. All the orders she'd given when the Merishi were ID'ed had been obeyed; all the maneuvers called for in those orders were under way.

The transports with the other four battalions of 222 Brigade and their escort of heavy cruisers and scouts were accelerating.

The transports in Linak'h orbit were dropping altitude; shuttles and other noncombatant spacecraft were either grounding or docking. Anything remaining in orbit was adjusting its path to avoid passing over the Merishi territory.

The spare attacker from the junk patrol was already heading for the Zone, just above atmosphere to allow full speed.

Launcher Two (once Charlie Longman's pet; and how *were* things aboard *Somtow Nosavan*?) was ready to cycle and kick its attacker out into space, as soon as the ground-support packages were aboard. That status light was still red; Liddell mentally composed a citation for turning it green in less than five minutes and a reprimand for taking longer.

Three light cruisers were on their way to rendezvous with the incoming reinforcements.

One light cruiser and a scout were on their way to

rendezvous with the incoming Merishi. (Doctrine again: the light cruiser to close in for maximum intelligence, including possibly a visual; the scout to stay back, record, report, and evade if the shooting started.)

If the Merishi were peaceful, so much the better. If they weren't, three light cruisers, two heavies, and the transports' on-board weapons ought to be able to stand off four Merishi heavies until *Shenandoah* could engage. (It might be four light cruisers if the snooper got away, and they would be equivalent to five or six under the mad Irishman.)

Liddell would be quite happy to sit down with her Merishi opposites over sherry and apricot juice. But if she did have to hang some or all of their crests on her belt, she'd use that victory to get a straight answer from Eleventh Zone to at least one question:

Why in the name of everything holy hadn't they sent a capital ship with the transports?

Linak'h:

Candice Shores played lookout and weapons crew aboard her lifter for twenty minutes, while Warrant Officer Konishi did everything to give her a good look at the area where the terrs had to be hiding.

The pilot also did everything to give the terrs a tempting target, short of maintaining a predictable course and altitude. The line between playing bait and committing suicide was always thin, but Konishi seemed to know where it lay.

At the end of the twenty minutes, Shores collected the survival com unit and the rest of her ammo allowance, then pointed at the ground. The pilot frowned.

"All you've got down there is still the two newlies and the locals," Konishi added. "ETA on even the 4th Platoon is fifty-some minutes. Not great security, if you don't mind my opinion, Colonel."

"And all I've got up here is a good view of nothing," Shores replied. "Or at least nothing that's telling me more about who was doing what to whom. That's ground work." She wouldn't insult the man's intelligence by asking if he thought the two lieutenants could do it.

"You have an itch, I suppose you can scratch," Konishi said, wrinkling his nose. "Any particular place you want to ground?"

"The river end of the hide." Shores tapped the display. "If it comes down really hard, get out of here and transmit the latest picture to Lieutenant Kapustev. Give him a quarter of a chance and he'll be able to pull things out of the fire."

One of the things might not be her, but that was doctrine and destiny. Field-grades and even flags weren't exempt from saying "Follow me," and anyway Shores didn't feel *ready* to lead from behind a console even if doctrine let her. Being a light colonel when your contemporaries were sweating promotion to major skewed a lot of things.

Shores went out without the ladder, two meters above the softest patch of ground she could see. She landed and rolled, discovered that the softness was real but under the grass was a web of thorny vines, and stood up with both dignity and clothing a trifle the worse for wear. Konishi climbed out at her signal, and she turned toward the forest to see a Navy attacker navigator and a civilian beckoning to her.

In the bushes with them, Shores listened to Al Brandstetter's story. "No personnel sightings, just weapons signatures?" she asked finally.

"Not a hair, and for the weapons I'm going by what Sandy said," Brandstetter replied. "The Robinson boy also thought it was Ptercha'a stuff, but he didn't make it ashore."

"Anybody make a recording? Sorry, I had to ask."

"I suppose you did," the navigator doubling as medic said. "Now suppose you leave these people alone to get their nerves unjangled?"

Technically, insubordination; realistically, a doctor defending his patients. "All right. One more question, though. Who knows anything about those farms? I wasn't able to raise them, and if the attackers did they haven't told me."

It seemed to lift Brandstetter's spirits, to catch the Federation forces in a mistake. Shores was glad that she

could improve *somebody's* mood; the situation surely
wasn't helping hers.

"From the buildings, it looks like about four house-
holds running a single spread," he said. He peered
through the bushes, muscles taut as if he expected slugs
or grenades to rip him at any moment. "I didn't get
downriver this far very often, and then I didn't stop. But
the buildings look like it's maybe three human and one
Ptercha'a. The Kitties—"

"Better not use that word."

"Try telling Sandy that," Brandstetter snapped. "Do
you want good manners or advice?"

"Advice." At least as long as she didn't have to apologize, and could talk to the Brandstetters later. "You
were saying something about the Ptercha'a?"

"Yeah. They could be either freeholders or a staff cooperative. Eight, ten of them sometimes get together and
build a house, so they've got the right numbers to feel
comfortable even if they're all working for different
people."

It struck Shores that this would probably leave the humans who hired the Ptercha'a with very few secrets. Of
course, the way her luck had been running today, if the
Ptercha'a did turn out to know something, they would
also turn out to be Confraternity. Their price for talking
would be an amount of support she wasn't allowed to
give. (At least not officially; she would have to ask Nieg
about other routes.)

"Where are the other officers?" Shores asked. Apart
from wanting to keep radio silence if possible, she
wanted a tour of the position.

Brandstetter jerked a thumb along the tree line,
toward a large boulder half-buried in fallen poncho
leaves. "They said that gave the best observation, so I
suppose they're up there."

"Fine. Lieutenant Seitz, can you guide me?"

The navigator nodded. As Shores rose on hands and
knees, Brandstetter grabbed her shoulder.

"Ah, Colonel, I'm sorry about the names. But please
don't get into it with Sandy. She's an ex-Regular, and
that makes her about the closest thing to a leader we've
got left."

"I won't pick a fight, okay?"

From Brandstetter's face, it wasn't all he wanted but he knew that it was all he would get.

Shores shifted her carbine around onto her back, flipped her visor down to protect her eyes, and started a low crawl after Seitz.

Aboard attacker Gold One, Linak'h:

Right now Gold One was on high watch (which also meant bait for any really serious hostilities), and the ground-oriented sensors were on automatic. So, technically, were the communications relayed in both directions through Elayne Zheng's console.

However, no EWO worth her flight pay ever avoided playing eavesdropper. There was nothing like being in the know ahead of everybody else to make your crew grateful to you. This wasn't a crew where Zheng would trade that gratitude for liquor or bedroom gymnastics; she'd settle for Shauli's goodwill, if she couldn't earn it any other way.

It looked as if the skyside angle was pretty much under control, about what you'd expect with Rosie Liddell running it. A delaying action against the Merishi all set up, a little more attacker support for the mudfeet on the way, and reinforcements for Colonel Candy likewise. The only thing Zheng would have done different from the way she'd heard it was have an attacker boost about eight suited LI out here at top Mach, instead of a second load of sensors.

A power suit with a good trooper inside was as good as a Mark 40 any day, and had firepower and initiative to boot. Also, sensor packages or troops still forty minutes out couldn't do a thing about the farm, if it needed anything done about it. LI in suits—

The contact alarm went off, both visual and sound modes. Zheng switched off her eavesdropping as the target data came up.

"Aerial contact, bearing one-six-zero, seventy-two thousand meters, altitude twenty-one hundred meters, speed one-eighty km/h. No IFF at all, might be in blackdown mode." The display changed. "Not blackdown, just a civilian lifter suite on low power."

"Check flight plan files," Shauli said.

"Coming up," Zheng said. She'd ordered that from the computer before the alarm stopped. The pilot could still use a little practice in not asking questions that made him sound nervous.

"Could be any one of four, five Catman air-service flights," she said a moment later. "We're going to have to interro—"

This time it was the "Identified Hostile" contact alarm that attacked all the senses. "Missile launch!" Zheng said. It was amazing how easy it was to speak quietly when you were speaking what might be your last words.

Then she saw that the missile was going nowhere near any of the attackers. If it had a target at all, it was the unidentified lifter.

The deck tilted as Shauli adjusted Gold One's attitude. "Weapons free! Laser that bugger! Elayne, give us a POL ten seconds ago."

Zheng had just finished calculating the missile's point of launch when the laser beam stabbed out of Gold One's belly and exploded it. As the explosion faded off her displays, she said, "POL is within a circle eight hundred meters diameter, center one-point-seven kloms from the farmhouse, bearing three-four-oh. Terrain display, please," she told her console.

"That takes in the forest behind the *khosh* and bean fields, that tongue of cleared land off to the northwest," she said a moment later. "Ground tactical frequency, please," she added. "I'm going to warn the people on the ground that the farm's possibly hostile, then warn the QRF about a possible hot LZ."

She got it all out so fast that Shauli didn't have time to interrupt. When she had time to look at him, she decided that maybe he hadn't planned to. She wriggled her toes, wished she could wriggle more, then fixed her eyes back on the display.

At least the lifter had grounded safely; its beacon was clear except for ground clutter. That would give anybody with fancy electronics a good fix on it, but if they used the fancy electronics for another missile shot, they would take out the lifter quite literally over Gold One's dead body.

Oh yes, another little detail:

"Nice shooting, skipper."

"Let's hope that lifter wasn't the terrs calling in the clans on the survivors."

That was a possibility that hadn't occurred to Zheng. "Monitor the lifter?"

"Absolutely. If they move, interrogate; if they don't answer, we'll disable them. And put their position on the air to both Huntress and Purple Flight."

"Aye-aye, skipper."

Linak'h:

Candice Shores checked her watch. Eight minutes, since the missile launch and Gold One's sharpshooting. Four minutes since she'd ordered up an attackerload of LI in suits, from whatever unit had eight people and eight suits available, and praying all the while that previous arrangements weren't yet too solid to be changed.

Thirty-three minutes minimum before the QRF people came in, more if they had to allow for a hot LZ. She could only guess when the armored people would drop.

Could she do anything to cool down that LZ? Three attackers in the air, and Konishi as AOP with a reasonable air-to-ground load, ought to be a substitute for the troops she didn't have.

They were. A partial, even pitiful substitute, that couldn't do much more than put up an easily called bluff unless she was willing to risk civilian casualties. Civilian casualties resulting from her orders.

There were circumstances under which she could be court-martialed for not giving such orders. This wasn't one of them. Nobody had endangered Federation forces, nobody had attacked the refugees again. Her ground strength was four active Regulars (two of them dewy-eyed lieutenants), one ex-Regular, two Militia, and a few farmers who knew how to use weapons if they had any, which they didn't.

Something less than the optimum, for anything except

giving possible bad guys in the farm a more lucrative target than that unidentified (probably but not certainly Ptercha'a) lifter. Being dead was an expensive way of disarming criticism of your good sense. Getting other people killed was an unacceptable one.

Shores put down her binoculars and shifted until she could address the rest of the improvised security team.

"People, we're staying put. We'd have to split up to even recon the farm, and we can't afford that." She flipped her belt comp to sketchpad mode, then discovered that she'd lost her stylus somewhere back during the low-crawl.

"Here." Brandstetter handed her an old-fashioned pen. The grip end at least left a visible trace.

"Wounded in the middle, with Deitz and Fiske. The other survivors in a circle around the wounded, and the rest of security at equal intervals except for the OP toward the farm. I'll take that, along with Lieutenant Botero."

That put each lieutenant with a more seasoned companion, plus giving redundancy in the most exposed position.

"I'm not armed," Sandy Brandstetter put in.

"Fiske, loan her your sidearm," Shores said. "Oh, and Botero, give Thibeaudeaux yours. Code alert for intruders is 'Diamond,' for hostile action 'Ruby.' Any questions?"

There weren't, except Shores's own about how she'd gotten back into the squad-leading business, and she already knew the answer to that one. It was the epitaph of so many good soldiers:

"It seemed like a good idea at the time."

Linak'h:

"It is quite mad, thinking of taking a prisoner under the eyes of the Federation!" the pilot protested. Seenkiranda had a brief fantasy, her fifth or sixth (she had lost count), of gripping his throat until her claws sank in, his eyes bugled out, and his breath (or at least his uttering cowardice and nonsense) ceased.

"Who said a word about taking a prisoner?" Drynz

said. "It will be enough to identify who launched the missile, and perhaps take pictures of anyone who exposes themself."

This time Seenkiranda's brief fantasy was of one of the Folk dropping his shorts. She felt the urge to giggle.

"Does anyone have a camera?" the pilot protested. "If all we can offer is our unsupported word, is it worth . . . ?"

"It will be worth your license if you open your mouth again," Drynz said, in measured tones—rather like a Healer excising a cancer with precise cuts of a small laser. "Possandaro and Bradl, you remain behind and guard the lifter."

The pilot's mouth gaped, showing a fine display of ill-kept teeth. Then he closed it again, remembering Drynz's threat and realizing that he had talked himself into going with the patrol, because Drynz would not trust him with the lifter.

"What about the missile data?" Possandaro asked. He was clearly keeping alert and active by sheer force of will, in the face of the pain of his untreated wound.

"Show him how to record the data and turn on the identification beacon," Drynz ordered the pilot. "If they find nothing compromising in our flight recorder and the . . . the IFF . . . in order, they will suspect less."

Drynz did not say who "they" might be. He probably did not know. They had seven or eight possible enemies around them, and might need the help of as many High Powers merely to win free of this battlefield.

Now Drynz was proposing that instead of hiding and praying, they thrust themselves squarely into the battle, in the name of the Confraternity. (Which had her allegiance, but this much?)

Seenkiranda decided that it did not make any great difference. She would follow Drynz's scouting party, to be able to think well of herself, and plagues carry off the Confraternity!

She would also know ever afterward that the line between those called cowards and those called brave was thinner than any tale had ever led her to believe. Tales were for children; war was for those of lawful age, who could learn its harsh lessons.

Five

Linak'h:

Zhapso su-Lal was as close as he ever came to cursing an inanimate object. He was glaring at the communications console in a way that must have been raising its internal temperature several percent. Brokeh su-Irzim asked the Lord of Works to grant that Zhapso fry neither the console nor his own nerves.

The gray blankness on the screen turned into a gray spiral, then began to show colors. Su-Irzim held his breath until the picture clarified, then muttered an obscenity.

It was *Perfumed Wind*'s First Guidance, Ehmad met-Lakaito, looking out at them. Not the ship's commander, F'Mita ihr Sular.

"Easy," Behdan Zeg said, behind su-Irzim. "The commander may be speaking with the Federation Fleet. I would be surprised if they are wholly ignoring *Perfumed Wind*'s movements."

That had not occurred to su-Irzim, but now that it had been said, as unlikely as the speaker was, he thought it possibly true. *Perfumed Wind* had maneuvered so that it offered high-altitude but constant real-time surveillance of the "incident" (which might earn the name "battle" at any moment) in the Great Bend of the Hyssh'n.

"Good guess, Commander," met-Lakaito said, not bothering to look at any of his audience. "We had the feeling it were best to warn the Smallteeth. From what we've seen, they're not likely to have ships to spare to watch us, so if they protest, it may be an order to move."

This would confront *Perfumed Wind* with the choice of humiliation or danger, if the humans were not merely threatening to see what ihr Sular was made of. Su-Irzim

and Rahbad Sarlin at least had complete trust in both
her courage and her judgment, and doubted that she
would risk her ship.

What would be at risk in any confrontation was the
Inquiry mission's ability to work with the Governor.
F'Mita was branded and bonded one of them. Anything
she did that the Governor thought "shamed the People"
(or even him, as he often confused the two) would be
entered against the Inquirers.

In due course the Governor could be countermanded
from Petzas, even removed. Before that came about,
however, much damage might be done—or as bad, the
little that the Inquirers could do (with scant Fleet or Host
strength to use what they learned) would be left undone.

At least the Governor was not so pure a Consolidationist that the party would fight his removal. For such
small favors, su-Irzim thanked the Judgment Lord.

He had just finished his prayer when ihr Sular came
on screen. She looked rather as if she had eaten a meal
of unsalted marsh grass and unshelled nuts.

"Commodore Liddell has given me permission to remain on station over the incident site, on certain conditions," she said. "One is that we do not actively scan the
area or listen to the military frequencies. The second is
that we remain at our present altitude. The third is that
if hostilities begin with the Merishi, we move immediately to join the Federation transports."

Seeing Rahbad Sarlin gaping like one of the faulty wits
was a rare sight, but su-Irzim suspected he looked no
finer. "Is the last a jest?"

"No. She said—I actually spoke with Ship Commander
Bogdanov, but the words had Liddell's flavor to them—
that the People might be hostile but were not foolish.
She did not wish my ship to be without protection, in
the kind of situation where innocent bystanders can often
be hurt."

The Inquirers had stopped gaping. They were still so
intent on the screen that they did not notice Behdan Zeg
withdrawing.

"If it comes to that, I will observe the Federation
transports at close range and record any additional data
I obtain. Everything I've already recorded about the
squadron is already in a file that I will dump into the

computer of the shuttle if we have to maneuver. The shuttle will take everybody except myself and met-Lakaito down."

"But . . . F'Mita . . ."

Su-Irzim reflected that being speechless twice in a hundredth-watch must be a new experience for Rahbad Sarlin. He thought seeing the old commander that way embarrassed F'Mita as well. Her face was flushed and she had lips half-pulled over her tusks when she broke in.

"We can slave the engines to the Command consoles faster than any Scaleskin ship can approach the planet," she said. "Once that's done, *Wind*'s a one-crew ship, at least for orbital maneuvering."

Su-Irzim thought of damage control. He thought of several other things, including old sayings about arguing with those who have chosen their course. He said nothing. If Sarlin wanted to regain control of his mouth and use it to make a fool of himself . . .

Sarlin said nothing that su-Irzim remembered afterward. In fact, the first event he remembered was the battlefield coming up on the screen, the second Behdan Zeg's return.

"Is that transmitting?" he asked, then looked at the display. "Ah, excellent. I can tell you."

"Tell us what, mother's son?" Sarlin said. His voice was taut, his body the same. It seemed that being unable to argue with ihr Sular had left him wishing to argue with *someone*.

"My friend in the Governor's household has confirmed that he will work with us. Also, he has confirmed that he enjoys the confidence of several Hunters among the servants."

"The Governor gives confidential posts to Furfolk?" su-Lal exclaimed. He looked as one suddenly finding himself weightless.

"I know nothing about the confidence," Zeg replied. "But how else can one we all agree is a goldtusk keep a proper household here without hiring Hunters? If you have an answer, tell me. If not, let us watch the battle. It is more intriguing than your conversation, by far."

Su-Lal had enough practice in keeping his temper with Zeg by now; his nostrils flared but that was all. Su-Irzim had no answer either, but he had one question that he would have to ask before long.

Who had given Zeg permission to recruit spies in the Governor's house? None of his colleagues on Linak'h had, because none had thought he would do such a thing. It was an immoderate, even dangerous act.

As long as it was more dangerous to the Governor than to anyone else, however . . .

Then the computer-enhancement marked four light attackers entering the area of the Great Bend incident. Su-Irzim turned his attention to the display. It *would* be more interesting than arguing with Zeg, watching the Federation's Linak'h Command handle multiple threats.

Linak'h:

Candice Shores had five minutes' notice of the incoming light attackers. She wondered what kind of offensive loads they were carrying and if they were going to need the secure LZ she had no way of giving them. From their ETA, if they'd been scrambled from back in the Zone, they must have been burning sky and fuel.

Her first good visual on them gave her the answer. Two were carrying basic offensive loads, gun and dumb-rocket pods, with conformal external fuel tanks. The other two were carrying both the conformal tanks and buddy outfits, that could be used either air-to-air or as the basis for an advanced fueling/charging depot.

That still needed security, though. Shores hoped the attacker jockeys wouldn't shoot *or* burn themselves dry before the QRF arrived to keep the bad guys out of their hair while they reloaded and refueled. Knowing light-attacker pilots (not the ones she'd known in the Biblical sense) led her to skepticism.

"Barb Flight to Huntress. Where do you want us?"

"Out of range of the missile site"— she transmitted the estimate of its position—"and saving fuel."

"Ah, Huntress. Barb One, and I've got a visual on some people sneaking out of an outbuilding in the farm closest to the forest. Want me to make a low eyeball pass?"

People sneaking into the woods could mean many things, including terrorists with reason enough to shoot down a Federation attacker if it gave them time to get away. She called up the area map again. Once into the trees, the people would have at least eight kloms of double or triple canopy before the nearest open country. Plenty of room to lose pursuit.

"Negative, Barbs. One of you hold at present distance, scan on max magnification. We'll enhance the recording. The other, take overwatch. Fuel-haulers, I want you behind a good solid ridge *now*."

The four light attackers had just started maneuvering when the heavy down from *Shen* with a load of sensor packages arrived. Shores was immediately busy adjusting the map display and transmitting her ideas of where to lay down the Mark 40's or whatever was doing duty as Mark 40's.

The problem with this battle, she decided, was that it kept jumping from squad-sized up to company or even short battalion, then back down again, and at entirely random intervals. *Just think of it as an exceptionally realistic exercise and don't sweat*, she told herself.

The second half of the command was easier to obey than the first. The Federation territory was having a warm, dry spring, but that meant a high of thirty during heat waves. Today it hadn't cracked twenty-five, at least not up here on the western slopes.

"Okay," she said. "Drop your sensors from below the horizon, so that they overlap along what my map calls 'the Inkwell River.' Check your references."

"Coordinates?"

Shores studied the map, trying to figure the right length of sensor line to cover the likely exits from the eastern edge of the patch of forest. Assuming they went east, of course, but since that was toward the (presumably) friendly Merishi territory, it was a reasonable assumption.

And reasonable assumptions could be wrong enough to get people killed, not just in war but—

The ground shook. Shores dropped her comp, drew her sidearm, rolled to concealment, and stared at the towering pillar of smoke bulging into the sky beyond the farm.

Linak'h:

Seenkiranda and Drynz quickly found themselves in the
lead, as the Confraternity patrol curved toward the farm.
Drynz clearly knew woodland as well as he knew weapons, and Seekiranda found that some of her childhood
games really had taught her useful skills.

More recent and valuable, however, was her outdoor-
security course. When she had been studying for her
Guards' Certificate, she did not know whether she would
be working indoors or out, and if out, whether in a city
or far out in the country. She only knew that she would
be competing for both with veterans of the legions (perhaps not the elite, but even four years with a One or
Two-Legion would be more than she had), and every
skill she could learn would be just barely enough.

At times during her service at Simferos Associates she
had wondered if she had spent time and money to no
purpose. Now she had ceased to wonder, and instead felt
pride in her caution. (Time to feel pride in her fieldcraft
when it was better polished.)

The patrol stalked forward, Drynz in the lead, Seenkiranda behind him, the other two in the rear. From time
to time Seenkiranda glanced behind her, to make sure
that the rear was not falling behind or dropping its guard.
They all knew enough to move with their weapons in
hand, held so that they would not catch on foliage yet
be easy to bring into action, and also to study the ground
ahead for leaves that might rustle or twigs that might
snap.

They moved parallel to a well-beaten trail, closer to it
than Seekiranda enjoyed but not so close that they would
be helpless if sighted. The same tangle of vines and fallen
branches that kept them close to the trail would also hide
them if they had to flee. Hide them—and also hold them
in place, like a bog gripping a thryne—but it was odds
against the enemy having the strength to lay siege to
their hiding place. It would be "strike and flee" for both
sides today.

How long it took them to reach the edge of the forest,
Seenkiranda never learned. She knew that she could

smell her own sweat, see her fur matting, and see insect bites begin to swell, before the trees began to thin ahead.

An urgent gesture from Drynz sent them all flat to the ground. Seenkiranda raised her viewer and looked where Drynz was pointing.

Two figures ran from a clump of vines fifty paces ahead. One was Folk, and it struggled to grip and hold another, apparently human.

All four Hunters covered the fifty paces in bounds. As they reached the struggling pair, the human broke loose and plunged toward the edge of the trees. He was dark-skinned and bald-headed, his clothes clean but shabby, his legs long and strong, and his weapon a battle rifle with a bomb-launcher under the barrel.

Seenkiranda had a moment's thought of what that weapon might have done, in the hands of a braver human. Then she raised her own rifle, as Drynz raised his voice.

"Halt!"

Either the human did not recognize even that simple command in True Speech, or fear deafened him. Before anyone could think to use Trader's Tongue, the Folk warrior drew a single-hand from under his cloak and fired a burst at the human.

The human wore body armor, but no head protection. The burst from the single-hand walked up his back to explode his skull. He sprawled facedown in the leaves, blood spreading around him.

Either the Folk warrior thought he had done nothing wrong, or he thought that Hunters would not dare lift a claw against him. Whichever mistake he made, it slowed his turning too much. Both Drynz and Seenkiranda shot him through the head, no great feat at a range where they could nearly have spat on him.

One of the Hunters behind now put his single-hand to work, kicking up leaves, missing the dead Folk by a generous distance, but nearly hitting Drynz. That broke Drynz's silence at last.

He had just warned the eager shot where the single-hand would go, the next time it fired so wildly, when the farm seemed to fly into the sky. The tirade died on Drynz's lips as his muzzle churned up forest soil again. Seenkiranda rolled toward him, and side by side they watched smoke pour up and spread out, from the core of flame on the near side of the farm.

Drynz lifted his head and cursed softly. "Two bodies, two races angry, and not even a picture."

"We can do better than that," Seenkiranda said. She pointed at the Folk body. "Four of us should be able to carry him fast enough."

"Better to remove the human," Drynz said. "If the Federation Warbanders find him, they will be on our trail. If they find the Folk, on the other hand, they will be even more suspicious of the Folk than they are already."

"That they may. Certainly the Folk will hear of it, though. *They* will launch a hunt wherever their Security death-bands can work unhampered. Do you wish that?"

Drynz muttered something about wishing for women who knew either war or silence, and for a flier-sled to take both bodies. But he moved forward as he muttered, crouching over the dead human to strip him of weapons and search him for documents. Seenkiranda motioned the others forward, and pointed at the dead Folk.

They looked ready to roll belly-up and void themselves with fear, but it seemed to be fear of her more than of the enemy. They bent to their work, and the three Hunters with their burden were well inside the trees when Drynz overtook them.

"Baernoi-made, Folk-modified, human-wielded," he said, slapping the battle rifle. "What in the name of Pek's Fifty is going on here?"

Seenkiranda shrugged. All the war-wisdom of Pek's Fifty combined could hardly find the answer to that. Then she handed her weapon to Drynz and hurried forward, to relieve one of the body-carriers. The explosion at the farm should prevent pursuit from that direction, but it would surely have the Federation Warbanders looking in all directions, claws ready.

Linak'h:

Squad-sized units had one advantage, Candice Shores realized. The communications net was incredibly simple.

All you had to do was roll over and shout toward the rear, "Hit the dirt!"

Everybody who hadn't been knocked down by the explosion obeyed, leaving Shores to study the scene. That was another advantage of squads, she decided. You could be well forward, not only inspiring but seeing with your own eyes, and still communicate with the rest of the unit.

Right now there was nothing to communicate except the description of the Hades of a big smoke cloud, with bits of debris falling out of it. Radio discipline overhead seemed to have also taken unauthorized leave; every frequency she tried had someone already on it, talking loudly and not always to much purpose.

Shores waited until the flyers had unjangled their nerves and she could be sure that her own voice was steady.

"Huntress to Gold One. Put a camera on the explosion site and transmit real-time to Dryad Flight. And tell everybody else to get off the air and execute previous orders."

She heard Zheng's acknowledgment and saw Gold One maneuvering for a good angle; she also spared fingers to cross, that Elayne would not be shot down a second time. The lady would not be grateful.

It seemed that the AD and shipkillers had gone up with the blast or gone into the woods with the fugitives. It also seemed that Shauli really was the senior officer in the air. Shores's hunch would pay off, if Zheng could keep her pilot's mind focused on his new command role.

Meanwhile, she had to update the display on the farm, so Kapustev could see what he was getting into. He didn't have much margin with only a platoon, but he ought to be in range of a relay through Gold One in another minute or two. . . .

"Colonel?"

It was Sandra Brandstetter, tugging at Shores's ankle.

"What is it?" Shores didn't try to hide her irritation.

"Just before the big bang—I thought I heard shooting off that way." She pointed to the northwest. "A Kit—a Ptercha'a battle rifle, it sounded like."

To Shores, it sounded like Sandra was seeing hostile Ptercha'a under every bush. "I'll have one of the lights do a visual over flight, as soon as they've finished deploying," she said. "I'll also have our reinforcements put an outpost on that side of the farm."

That seemed to satisfy Brandstetter, even if the outpost was something that Shores would have established anyway. Fear of the Ptercha'a seemed to be making her forget basic CA tactics, not to mention how this kind of forest could distort sound. Somebody might have done some shooting, but who was anybody's guess right now.

Shores thought briefly of pulling her squad back, to where their ample air support had a clear 360-degree field of fire around them. A look at the map killed that idea.

Any place like that was too far for the wounded or for good observation of the farm—still the critical point, even under its shroud of smoke. Better spend the time bringing Kapustev and the chain of command into the picture.

"Huntress to Gold One. Have you established contact with Dryad?"

"That's affirmative, Huntress. Five by five."

"Good. Ready to take a map overlay?"

"Ready when you are, Huntress."

Linak'h:

The relayed map came up on the tac display in Kapustev's lifter. The platoon leader motioned Esteva, Sklarinsky, and the squad leader to gather around, then waited until the other lifters reported receiving the map.

"We start off simple, and let it get complicated if the bad guys want it that way," the lieutenant said briskly. A light above the display indicated that his briefing was being scrambled, squirted, and tight-beamed to the other three lifters of Dryad Flight.

It wasn't as secure as rendezvous and plug-in, but Esteva didn't think they had time for that. Colonel Candy had her ass on the line. It might take a lot of terrorists to hang it out to dry, but there might *be* a lot of terrs at the farm. That explosion might have been fertilizer; Esteva would take bets it was the local guerrillas' ammo supply, which meant sympathizers at the farm.

"Comments, anyone?"

Esteva realized that Kapustev was looking pointedly at him, and tried to recall the deployment. Oh, yes. Standard with one squad left, one right, one back with the weapons team and CP. Two lifters low, one high, one grounded. Deploy and hold position pending orders, which meant word from the colonel.

"What's the mix of lethals and nonlethals?"

"All lifters with one system loaded with nonlethals. One trooper in each squad with a nonlethal load in his launcher, everybody else one nonlethal magazine apiece. Standard Security rules of engagement."

Which meant let the other guy, good, bad, or merely mistaken, shoot first. You could get dead that way, and dead with a clear conscience was still dead. Orders were orders, however, and good relations with the civilians an asset a smart trooper wouldn't ignore.

"What about the time to switch over if the bad guys let fly?" the squad leader said. His eyes met Esteva's,

Kapustev smiled. "A risk, but a small one. We have a fantastic ratio of air support to ground strength. Air support can buy time, if they know where to strike. If the bad ones start shooting, they tell the flyboys where they are."

Kapustev lit an aromatic with three smooth motions. "Remember that the greatest danger went up with the terrorists' ammunition. What else the people at the farm can do besides play innocent, I do not know. Also, I do not know what we can do unless we are authorized to arrest and interrogate on our own authority. We must have that authority from the Territory's Administration."

An anonymous voice from the shadowy rear of the lifter, piled with ammunition crates and bagged shelters, muttered, "When are we going to get it?" Esteva studied the camouflage-smeared faces but none of them gave away anything. Kapustev had the sense to ignore a question he couldn't answer.

"We can establish Protective Security Conditions on the farm," the lieutenant concluded. "Listen instead of talking, and accept no hospitality without my permission."

"I forgot my testing kit," somebody complained.

"With what I've seen you get down, you're immune," a female voice replied. Laughter rippled until Kapustev held up a hand.

"This will not be easy. You have to be polite and alert at the same time, and for a long time. Even when we are reinforced, I doubt that we will being going back to base soon."

A sober silence followed, and greeted Kapustev's "Any questions?" The lieutenant turned to the pilot. "ETA?"

"Fourteen-twenty."

"Assume assault formation at ten-thirty."

"Can do, Lieutenant."

Esteva and Sklarinsky started checking each other's gear. Over Jan's shoulder, Esteva could see the altimeter slowly climbing, as Dryad flight held its altitude above the highlands south of the Big Bend.

Linak'h:

"Ah, Huntress, this is Gold One. We're getting a request from the lifter that grounded after the missile strike. It's Ptercha'a all right, but a private med charter. They say they've got a civilian casualty aboard and no damage. Can they lift out?"

Candice Shores's display was too small to show a really good AO map, but imagination filled in for electronics.

"They are authorized to lift out, provided that they steer two-seven-zero true for fifty kloms before they turn south. If they're short of juice, they can file a claim with us for any unanticipated recharging stops."

"I'll pass that along."

The lifter was a little too close to the shooting for a course straight south. For that matter, there was nothing between its landing site and the farm—and what about that Ptercha'a weapon Sandy Brandstetter said she'd heard?

What about it, indeed? You couldn't detain people claiming a medical emergency on mere suspicion, and suspicion was all Shores had to go on. Anything else was an outright accusation that the Ptercha'a in the lifter were lying. You didn't need cultural-pattern or basic diplomacy courses to know that would be a bad move.

The lifter rose unmolested into the sky, two kloms away and five minutes later. Shores watched until it was out of sight, then shifted so that she could see the platoon come in.

They came in with LI panache, low, fast, flaring at the last minute, and grounding in a formation that might have been measured with tape. Rear doors opened, turrets swiveled, and troopers poured out. Now it was LI doctrine to run, and they did. Shores saw one trooper running from the CP lifter to the squad covering the farm; that would probably be Sklarinsky, deployed against the most likely location of sniper targets.

Better check that they have a sniper covering the woods, too, just in case Citizen Brandstetter isn't hearing things.

So as not to joggle Kapustev's arm, Shores waited until the lifters were unloaded, men and supplies, and off. As she started to call the platoon, Gold One came back on the air.

"Ah, Huntress. Gold One with a RTB request. It seems they have two heavies coming out, one with your second load of sensors, the other with docked lifters *and* your armored squad. We've got the lightest air-to-ground load, so it's been suggested that we provide the escort."

There was no question of the two valuable heavies coming out unescorted, not with mysterious Merishi ships coming in and terrorists swanning about the countryside. Shores wouldn't have suggested it even if she'd had the authority; thirty-three of her people would have their tails in a crack if the flight was attacked.

With their safe arrival, on the other hand, and the doubled-sensor line, any lingering terrorists could soon be filled with alarm and despondency, and possibly with something more solid and lethal.

"Gold One, you are authorized a RTB as soon as the medevac lifter reaches her turning point. I want somebody monitoring them until they reach the fifty-klom mark."

"Roger, Huntress."

The Ptercha'a must have been flying fast, or Shauli shading his timing. It was barely five minutes before a sonic boom marked Gold One's climb-out. By then Shores had suggested a sniper on the forest side of the platoon position, but Kapustev said he had only one and offered one of the overwatch lifters instead.

"In another ten minutes, if they don't come out of the farmhouse, we'll split the left squads. One to secure the tree line, one for security for the medics."

"Put the medics in one of the overwatch lifters and fly them down. We can provide the security once they've reached us."

"You want to keep the lifter, Colonel?"

It was a point for Kapustev, that he asked instead of waiting for orders he assumed the Old Lady had the sense to give. It was a tempting offer, too. There'd be shelter for the wounded in the lifter, and a quick retreat if needed.

It would also be doing what she'd just vetoed Kapustev's doing, dividing thinly-spread forces even further until they were stretched to the breaking point. The "Principles of War" weren't as binding as the laws of physics, but "Concentration of Force" was one that came close.

"Negative. Load a tent and a supply pack in the lifter along with the medics, and you can have the lifter back once it's unloaded."

"Yes, ma'am."

The treetops swayed as the sonic boom from Gold One tore down through the sky to bounce off the ground.

Linak'h:

Gold One climbed out at high Mach and went ballistic as soon as the atmosphere allowed. Elayne Zheng sat at her console and watched with detached interest as one radar after another got a lock on the soaring attacker. They had a reliable IFF, a filed flight plan, and were within the Territory's boundaries at all points and in all directions, so nobody should regard them as a mystery, let alone a threat.

Zheng still felt like the only clothed person on a nude beach, conspicuous if not threatened. Twenty radar operators of four different races all staring at her signature on their displays always made her feel that way.

She didn't have much time to fret. Barely a minute after Gold One broke into vacuum, *Shen* punched a signal through the lingering remnants of ionization. Zheng didn't hear the original message, but she did hear Shauli's request for a repeat, and the repeat itself.

When the exchange was done, the Gold One crew were staring at each other.

"Yes, they're Ptercha'a," Shauli said. "Merishi-built, but Ptercha'a-crewed." He added, with the tone of someone who has just heard his legitimacy questioned, "They say they are being delivered to the Coordination."

"It makes sense, from their point of view," the copilot said. "I mean, if they handed them over here, we might learn too soon and protest. Sending the crews off-planet and having them take over the ships on some Merishi world elsewhere—the training time alone . . ."

His voice trailed off, as he decided that no one had been listening to him. Zheng had been; she had also been listening to an inner voice that was saying one thing and that repeatedly and loudly:

Federation strategy has been based on the Coordination's having no significant off-planet space force. Four heavy cruisers with trained crews is significant.

Then the displays showed that Gold One was now topping out her trajectory, ready for the dive to the Zone and pickup of her convoy. Zheng checked her harness, a ritual that didn't calm her as much as it usually did, and focused all her attention on the screen. She knew it was ridiculous to expect the Coordination's ships to be in radar range for another eight hours at least, but she would be alert when they were!

Linak'h:

Silence followed Gold One's departure, broken only by the distant crackling of flames on the explosion site. It was hard for Candice Shores to tell what was burning. The smoke was still too thick, even though it now rose up in a vast greasy column that left the rest of the farm visible.

A somewhat battered farm, she saw with a little magnification. The roof sagged, one chimney was topless, and if there was an intact window in the place it had to be on a side she couldn't see. If the buildings were still habitable, it would be a miracle.

If the farmers had been doing no worse than turning a blind eye to terrorist activity, they'd probably had enough punishment. If they'd been doing more, punishment was out of Shores's hands—although she could make recommendations to Linak'h Command's Legal Officer, to pass on to the Territory's Administration.

She was drafting those recommendations (and not erring on the side of charity) when the lifter arrived with the medical team. Two of them started erecting the shelter; the other four waded into the casualties. Triage took ten minutes, and the verdict wasn't as bad as Shores had feared.

"First aid was good, so we're not going to lose anybody to shock before we can get them to the hospital," the medical team leader told her. "Most of them also had a dip in the river before they got ashore. That's cold-water first aid in fine style. We've got vital-signs monitors on them all, and when we've got good readings we can up the painkillers."

The implication that the rest was up to the combat troopers was too obvious to require comment. "We'll have them out of here as soon as the reinforcements—" Shores began.

"Dryad Leader to Huntress. We have a problem."

"Huntress here. Go ahead."

Kapustev sounded like a man trying to be analytical when he wanted to yell for help. "The advance to the tree line sighted a body and blood pool about two hundred meters in. Using bounding overwatch, we advanced two people to the body.

"The body was human, shot in the torso and head. Male, late middle-aged, undernourished, clean clothes showing signs of wear, torso armor. Could be any planetary origin.

"The blood pool suggests a second victim. From the color and odor, probably Merishi. The two people also detected a trail leading away from the body, bearing roughly two-four-zero as far as they could see it.

"Ah . . . from the size and configuration of the footprints, the trail was probably made by Ptercha'a. They have taken photographs and are returning to the platoon perimeter without otherwise disturbing the body or the ground around it."

"Well done," Shores said. That was something that never hurt, particularly when it was true. Even when it wasn't it was better than standing there open-mouthed when a good man needed guidance.

"Don't follow the trail," she said. "I want your sniper over on the forest side, best possible position and security. Pull your farmside squads back fifty meters and spread them out. Don't erect any shelters without my permission."

That took care of the platoon. Now for the rest of the farm's perimeter. She called up Purple Flight and the four light attackers.

"I want an eyeball and all-sensor watch on the ground between the farm and the forest. If anything larger than a muskipede moves in either direction, record it. If it shoots, shoot back."

"Range?" That was one of the light attackers, without the spaceship-grade armor of the heavies.

"You're the best judge of your own accuracy, but we don't want to hit the farm if we can help it. It may contain civilians. For damned sure it holds evidence."

Nobody mentioned the Ptercha'a medevac lifter, and Shores wondered if this was tact or her being the only one who'd made the connection. The Ptercha'a trail away from the body led almost directly toward the lifter's landing site. Shores would have bet her next promotion on the dead Merishi being aboard the lifter.

But even that degree of certainty wasn't evidence. At least not evidence enough to let anyone use lethal force against the lifter, if it refused to ground and be examined. And by the time it reached the first recharging point, anything as embarrassing as a dead Merishi would probably be long gone into the forest, not to emerge until winter or possibly the Universal Resurrection. . . .

Shores swore silently to herself, as the air support deployed noisily. She really would like to know who, for today at least, was getting away with murder. She also had to admit that Sandra Brandstetter might be right, in her suspicion of at least *some* of the Catmen.

Six

Linak'h:

It seemed to Candice Shores that the rest of the day was "just one big talktalk," as she put it afterward.

Talking with the troopers who'd found the body. Talking with the farmers, both human and Ptercha'a, without learning very much. Talking with Kapustev, Purple Flight, the medic chief, and the leader of the armored squad dropped to reinforce the sensor line, to make sure that everybody knew what they were supposed to do under various conditions. (Some of these conditions seemed improbable even at the time, more so afterward. Shores realized later that she'd come perilously close to micromanaging the very competent leaders under her command.)

Talking with the Detective-Inspector from the Special Branch of the Territory's police (a computer translation, to save time) and the lieutenant from the JAG's office. Talking with her successor in command at the farm, the XO of Company C, Fifth Battalion—by the favor of some Higher Power, LI-qualified even if not on LI duty, so he could run two LI platoons and their attachments and Shores did not have to turn her own XO loose on a remote post possibly in contact with the enemy.

Finally talking with Colonel Hogg—although by then it was late and they called it a "debriefing." The same attacker that flew out the new Farm Force CO flew Shores back to the Zone, and over a late dinner, in the middle of a cloud of aromatic smoke, Shores told Barbara Hogg of the day's events.

"That 'well done' you gave Kapustev applies to you too," Hogg said, knocking out her pipe into the trash tube. "There are harder things than thinking at several different tactical levels at once, but not many of them, at least the first time you do it."

"Thank you, Colonel."

"Thank me by being honest about Lieutenant Fiske." Hogg held out a large hand, first thumbs-up, then thumbs-down. "Which?"

Shores briefly wished she smoked. "Thumbs up, for now. Today could have just been first-combat nerves making him look . . . inadequate."

"He's not one of the Federation's great bargains at the best of times, but I'll go along with that. I'm glad he'll pass for now. I don't have too many platoon leaders in reserve, any more than you do.

"Besides, if we shuffle him off to Base Augmentation or whatever other hole opens up when the rest of the Brigade comes down, they'll know what we're up to. They'll pack him right back, probably with a nasty note attached, or else we'll have to go to Tanz. Which is something I would *much* rather not do, incidentally." The pipe stem pointed at Shores for a moment, like the muzzle of a sidearm.

"When is the rest of 222 coming down?" Shores asked. She'd seen lots of activity in the Zone when she came in, but no signs of even a substantial fraction of the eight thousand troops coming in aboard the 222 Brigade convoy.

"Probably tomorrow, except maybe for one battalion. I've heard Tanz has a scheme to put it directly down somewhere out to the north, now that you've turned up terrs."

An unacclimatized battalion straight off ship would not be the best proposition for the job, but few major generals would welcome that opinion from temporary light colonels. Or permanent full colonels either, judging from Hogg's sour expression.

"When do we know if that's coming down, and which battalion?"

"Tomorrow."

"And tomorrow, creeps in its petty pace from day to day, to the last drop of patience of those who need to know tonight."

"Need or want, Candy?"

"Want badly, but I could argue the case for need."

"So could I, but I doubt it would do much good. Try a sauna instead."

Shores tried the sauna when she returned to her quarters, but it wasn't quite as relaxing without a follow-up backrub from Colonel Nieg. His mission to visit *Perfumed Wind* and assess her crew and capabilities had been on hold all day after the ship sighting, then been reinstated just in time for him and Shores to miss each other.

Frustration gnawed at Shores, and very little of it had anything to do with sex or even Nieg. It was the frustration of being just far enough up the chain of command to know how many more links there were above her, and how much all of those people knew that they weren't telling her!

Linak'h:

Fomin zar Yayn had forgotten how underground flier-shelters were equally good at keeping out enemy weapons and holding in noise. The din of machinery and vehicles struck at his ears like a padded club as he slipped through the gas-lock into the shelter. What it must be like with fliers testing their engines or even launching with engines on, he did not care to imagine.

The spring-legged young Hunter crossing the shelter floor was busy taking off his helmet. He nearly bumped into zar Yayn, backed away nearly in a fighting crouch, then recognized the rank of the one he'd bumped.

"Forgive me, Senior. I just landed after—ho, what have we here?"

"Your sister's pair-mate, in case you have forgotten due to lack of air at high altitudes," zar Yayn said. They gripped shoulders as kin, rank forgotten as it was easy to do with Taidzo Norl. With Taidzo, it was also easy to see why he was his sister's favorite brother.

They walked side by side back to the gas-lock. "No high altitudes this time," Norl said, as the door opened. He lowered his voice. "I was playing test animal for our warning systems, down where I could look *up* at the tree-tops if I dared take my eyes off the readings."

The door closed, and the elevator whined as it sank to the third level down. "I'll accept any hospitality that kinship or generosity make you give, Senior, but tell me first what brings you here? Is all well?" That meant his sister, whose affection he returned.

"I am not the bearer of bad news, if that is what you fear," zar Yayn said, laughing. "Call it idleness, itching feet, and family duty." It was also the wish to see if the Air Legions showed any signs of preparing for war, but that was understood too well to need saying. Indeed, Norl had already given him one clue, mentioning the testing of the warning network.

"Then let me invite you to the leader's hall once I have changed," Norl said. He unsnapped his harness, rolled it neatly into a bundle, and popped the bundle into the helmet so that he had a hand free.

As they turned the corner toward the corridor marked AIR LEGION ACCOMMODATIONS, a very junior and very nervous Warbander ran up to them. He was so out of breath that it took him three tries before zar Yayn recognized that he was being summoned to the communications center. . . .

". . . which is all that is secure enough, in this place, for what you are to hear," the messenger ended.

Norl tactfully vanished down the corridor, to report on his flight and groom himself. Zar Yayn assumed an air of dignity to banish uneasiness bordering on fear and allowed the messenger to lead him to the communications center.

He had a whole room to himself, which did not surprise him when he recognized the senior on the screen. It was Great Warband Leader Muhrinnmat-Vao, one of the three chief seniors in the Coordination's Warband. He looked half-asleep, but then he always did, and those who took the pose for the reality had earned themselves many fates, short of the death sentence.

"Greetings, Fomin," the leader said. "Your good mate said that you might be found here. She is well and sends her love. Says you were here out of family duty, although I haven't heard there's much to be said for Jillyah's kin."

Taking Muhrinnmat-Vao's words at their apparent value meant blood feud, and it was said that he had actually fought a few duels with tribal Hunters in his

youth. Those who had served with him for up to thirty
years had long since learned to ignore his habits of
speech.

"Oh, they're not as dark as they're painted," zar Yayn
said. "Taidzo's the best of the lot, I admit. But I doubt
you called me to send my mate's love and word of her
good health."

"Cynical, aren't you, zar Yayn? But right, in this case.
You're taking a Legion. Six-Seven, and maybe five cohorts of Tribal Warbands as well. The villages are turning
out in force, this time."

Zar Yayn made all the appropriate gestures and said
all the appropriate words, without his brain being involved at any point of the process. It was devoted to
considering what this news meant.

Calling up the Warbands of the villages whose people
kept to the old ways of the remote lands of Homeworld
meant the next thing to a complete mobilization. At-
taching them to a regular Legion was considered a sign
that war was imminent. Or at least that the Coordination
wished to give the impression that it thought so.

Zar Yayn had that impression already. He also thought
it was an open question, whether a Legion was a reward,
a bribe, or a punishment. He had served well in the
Administration, better indeed than his senior; it could be
a reward. It could also be a bribe, to one known to be
a Confraternity sympathizer, to secure the goodwill of
his Confreres.

The Tribesfolk might make it a punishment; they were
notoriously hard to bring to any sort of discipline, as
fierce and skilled as they might be. But now that he
recalled it, Legion Six-Seven was largely recruited from
the same area as the villages. On mobilization, if not
before, it would have plenty of Warbanders who knew
the Tribesfolk, their dialects, their virtues and vices, and
the art of getting Hunters' work out of them.

Which suggested to zar Yayn a fourth possibility. The
Legion was a trap, which none of his friends would recognize. If he did well, the Coordination's war effort would reap
the harvest, without any benefit to the Confraternity.

If he failed, however, he could be cast aside like or-
dure, his Confraternity sympathies exposed like an un-

shelled deeochs, his career ended and the Confraternity shamed before all.

"I am grateful," zar Yayn said, for what he suspected was the fifth time. "It is an honor. It is also the greatest challenge I have ever been set."

"Cursed if it's not," the senior said, wrinkling his nose and scratching behind an ear. "But you'll do it, I know. You have a one-grade promotion now, a second if you earn it in the new post."

Muhrinnmat-Vao seemed ready to cut the connection; zar Yayn made the gesture to halt. The old senior's pale muzzle twisted all the way up to his eyes.

"Yes?"

"When do I report?"

"As fast as you find it convenient. You have a good second, and all the cohorts who have leaders have good ones too. So a day or two won't stunt the herds."

"I am grateful."

"So you've said, and I don't doubt it. Just be sure I don't doubt you when this worm-riddled business is over and done, that's all."

The screen blanked.

"I've heard the stories, but seeing him . . ." came a voice from behind zar Yayn. He whirled, nearly in combat stance, to see Taidzo Norl raise placating hands. He had somehow managed to groom himself in amazingly little time, and even change his tunic, but the flight report . . .

"Oh, that," the flier said, dismissing it as if it were a red crawler found in his soup. "I dropped off the inflight recording, voice, controls, and sensors. If there's anything else they need to know, they'll find me."

"It's a good thing the screen's off," zar Yayn said, finding it hard not to laugh at this display of a flier's manners. "You'd spend the . . . crisis . . . counting bathroom supplies in the Southern Territories."

"That might not turn out so badly," Norl said. "If there is a war, the Southern Territories will be in the forefront."

"*If* there is a war," zar Yayn chided. "And why will they be in the forefront, if you can say anything besides 'Look at a map' without being a rattle-tongue?"

Norl looked about as chastened as he had it in him

to be. "I will say, 'Look at a map,' he said finally. "We can launch low-altitude flights carrying missiles to strike at the Administration's coast, and that's no secret to them either."

"I suppose not. Just be sure that you don't talk about my appointment until it's announced, or matters such as your forward-position supply packages being assembled."

Zar Yayn had the pleasure of seeing his mate's brother gape. "Who told you that?"

"In the cities, one finds places to hear things," zar Yayn said ponderously, then laughed. "But none of them are as good to drink in, as a flier's hall. Lead on."

"With pleasure, Senior," Norl said. "I've been all day and half the night breathing bone-dry cockpit air. My throat feels like it's been rasped!"

Linak'h:

Colonel Malcolm Davidson found Marshal Emilio Banfi sitting in the atrium, beside the drained swimming pool. Most of the rest of the damage from the terrorist attack had been repaired or at least covered up, but the pool would need a complete rebuilding that they had decided could wait until after the war.

Above was the twilight that passed for a late-spring night here on Linak'h—Yellow Father below the horizon, Red Child just above it—but the ruddy glow filtered through the haze. It gave enough light to silhouette some of the hills around Banfi's home, but left most in shadow.

It also left the Marshal's face in shadow, and his expressions were hard to read even when it was fully lit. So Davidson merely approached, saluted, and stood at ease until Banfi coughed, sounding like a poorly maintained and underpowered robot starting to move.

"You're going to Och'zem," Banfi said finally.

"Sir?"

"You're going to Och'zem," Banfi repeated. "They want someone for Liaison with the Fire Guard. The high forest's getting so damned dry, they went to work out a coordinated plan in advance."

"I don't argue with that, sir. But why me?"

"They want somebody who's human, Federation, military, and knows the high forest. Are you disqualified on any of those points?"

"No, sir." Davidson balanced risks. Banfi was not in his best mood, but he would be in a worse one if Davidson showed signs of overlooking vital data.

"I'm qualified. But I already have an assignment, as your senior aide and chief of staff. What happens if you're . . . needed?"

That word was a hastily chosen compromise. As a Marshal of the Federation, Banfi was on active duty until his death. But he was much too senior not to interfere with the running of Linak'h Command if he came down out of the hills. So far he had not done so.

Banfi also held a Ptercha'a commission, the rank equivalent to lieutenant general. Given by the generosity of long-dead Hunters and carefully preserved by Federation legal technicalities, that commission made Banfi the third-ranking Ptercha'a officer in the Territory, if he chose to come on active duty or was ordered to do so by the Administration.

So far he'd received no orders and shown no inclination. But this could change—might *have* to change—quickly, and when it did Davidson had the feeling he would not be in the right place, off in Och'zem keeping an eye on the Fire Guard's deployment plans and studying maintenance schedules for fire bombers.

"If I'm needed, and you're not busy with a fire, you can come back. I'm sure that Linak'h Command and 222 Brigade between them can find someone with local knowledge. But right now, you're *my* best man for the job because the post carries with it a seat on the Linak'h Theater Command Group."

Banfi had lost none of his deviousness, it seemed. The only question was whether Davidson's being so obviously a spy would reduce his value, by making people less willing to talk.

The Marshal seemed to read the younger man's mind—not really surprising, after their five years together. "They'll have to take you into their confidence on a great many things," Banfi said. "Consider how much firefighting will depend on Federation people. If they forget that in the Zone, the Administration will remind them of it. You may even learn a few new epithets in True Speech when they do.

"Meanwhile, my sending you down will reinforce the notion that I'm too guilt-ridden over the terrorist attack to be fit for anything. That will keep our enemies off their guard, not to mention possibly one or two friends."

Davidson risked a single word.

"Tanz?"

Banfi's head swiveled like a lifter turret, the white eyebrows seemed to jut out farther and become sharper, and the dark eyes were unreadable. Then the scarred mouth twisted in a wry smile.

"Certainly the most important, unless Charlemagne really is sending some hot number out to supercede Liddell."

"I hadn't heard that, Marshal."

"All I've heard is the rumor. Your first job may be to confirm or deny it. Your second job is to sooth Tanz."

"Sir . . ."

"Indirectly, of course." Banfi reached for his walking stick, and was standing before Davidson could offer him a helping hand.

"Tanz is no fool. He's stubborn, hotheaded, and did a lot of damage to our relations with the Ptercha'a by not getting rid of Goerke years ago. But he can count fingers when you hold them up in front of him.

"He's not the man to do a good job with a Marshal looking over his shoulder, either. Few are, so no shame to him. If he fails, I want it to be from real faults, not just Marshal-phobia."

Davidson grinned. "Should I pass that one on to Josephine Atwood, for a companion piece to 'The Cult of the Marshal'?"

Banfi made a noise like a faulty exhaust system. "That . . . female person . . . can damned well do her own research!"

Aboard Baernoi merchanter *Perfumed Wind*, off Linak'h:

The sudden appearance of the Coordination's new cruisers and the terrorists incident in the Great Bend delayed for several hours Colonel Nieg's departure for *Perfumed Wind*. For a while he thought the visit might be canceled entirely.

Then suddenly the crisis passed, or at least shrank to a size that didn't justify canceling a visit that Linak'h Command had spent several days negotiating. The delay turned out to be just long enough for Behdan Zeg to show up, claiming to be Nieg's escort to the orbiting merchant ship.

Nieg had always assumed he would be escorted, and doubted that Zeg was planning any violence, even though they were going up aboard a Baernoi shuttle. Still, Nieg hastily stowed his portable computer in a secure locker, gave the locker code to his bodyguard, and checked his own sidearm and its ammo supply before following Zeg aboard the shuttle.

The flight was fast and direct, taking advantage of *Perfumed Wind*'s favorable position and the high performance of the Baernoi shuttle. Nieg saw that externally it was a non-standard type, possibly a converted interplanetary ship. Internally it had less passenger space than the outside suggested. Heavy-cargo capability, Nieg suspected, probably including carrying lifters, but not CA'ing them.

Zeg was careful not to turn his back on Nieg all during the flight up, and seldom took his eyes off the Intelligence officer. This was a breach of manners that in another Baernoi might have made Nieg change his mind about planned violence.

However, Behdan Zeg's reputation stretched beyond the Khudrigate's Special Projects branch and even beyond the Khudrigate. He had a chip on his shoulder (as much shoulder as any of the People had) and a lack of charm (not to say personal hygiene) that made his not having died in a duel somewhat curious.

At least this rudeness let Nieg examine the Baernoi with equal attention. He was eight cems taller than Nieg and close to forty kilos heavier. Virtually all Baernoi looked stocky, even squat to most humans, but Nieg knew that in proportion to his height Zeg was as long-legged as Candice Shores. (He doubted that Zeg was as good-looking, even to the eyes of a woman of the People.)

How would a bout between him and Zeg come out?

The Baernoi were not like the Ptercha'a, able to move three meters to a human's one, use both claws and teeth, leap higher and jump farther than any human, and generally do a remarkably good imitation of an unbeatable foe.

Baernoi were a mixture of strengths and weaknesses. Their reaction times were no faster than a human's, on the average, and their short limbs limited their footwork and reach. On the other hand when they did strike a blow it landed with bone-crushing force, and their heavy bones and massive torsos, with the internal organs deep in almost a solid wall of ribs, let them take an enormous amount of punishment.

The outcome of Nieg vs. Zeg (which would look good on a poster, but did not tempt the colonel to propose an exhibition bout) would probably depend on who was slowed down first. A human unable to avoid a Baernoi's power strokes was quickly finished. A Baernoi unable to protect his vulnerable spots from a flurry of lighter human blows did not last much longer.

It would be long, messy, bloody, unedifying for the participants, and uninstructive except to martial-arts professionals. One thing Nieg had learned, along with enough skills that he needed both hands to count his black belts: You stay out of that sort of fight.

"Please go before me out of the lock," Zeg said. Nieg looked up to see that they'd docked while he was plotting the bout; the DOCKED signal was clear and green.

It was only the fourth time Zeg had spoken. Like the other three times, both the construction and the accent were marginal. Either Zeg was sounding like a caricature of a Baernoi villain in a cheap 'cast drama in order to be rude, or he had actually not bothered to learn fluent Anglic.

Nieg assumed a mocking version of the Baernoi pose of submission—head raised to bare the throat, and gums pulled over the teeth. Zeg made an irritable noise and pointed toward the door. It slid open as Nieg approached, and closed as soon as Zeg was in the docking module.

Nieg was moderately amused to see Zeg obviously lose his way after a few turns. The *Inquirer* hadn't been aboard the ship so often that he knew his way. They both needed help, which came in the form of one of the crew (female, from Engineering, if Nieg's memory of Baernoi merchanter insignia was correct) who guided them to Commander F'Mita ihr Sular's cabin.

Like most Baernoi shipboard accommodations, it seemed cramped by human standards (unless one was like Nieg, used to emigrant and troopship quarters). The commander herself didn't help. She exceeded the Baernoi female average by as much as Candice Shores exceeded the human one, although she was more of Commodore Liddell's generation. The gray hair and the wrinkles showed both age and a complete lack of vanity about it. No goldtusk here, but then Nieg had hardly expected one.

Refreshments seemed to sprout from the table, the steward came so quickly. Nieg spread a meat-and-vegetable paste on a slice of baked *grode* (freeze-dried, but the Baernoi had freeze-drying down to a fine art) and contemplated warily the clear liquid in his glass. It had to be at least a hundred proof, and he needed a clear head even if he wasn't subject to skin flushes.

Baernoi etiquette about how fast you got down to business varied widely, almost on an individual basis. With F'Mita ihr Sular, it was quick. She made it plain (in fluent Commercial Merishi, with a regional accent Nieg couldn't place), that she was a busy woman, with a ship to run in what might at any moment become a battle zone, and she hoped she would not be thought rude if she asked Nieg to state his business and if possible accomplish it. . . .

Nieg's business had been simply to look over the ship and record his impressions of it. But he decided that it would do no harm to try for more, even if this involved telling what was not quite a lie, but which would need to be hastily turned into truth after he landed.

"Actually, apart from sharing your wish that there be peace, I had another matter to discuss. Have you been keeping records of any ground observations you make? I realize that your orbit keeps you clear of the most critical areas, which is as it should be. But if your scans have picked up something that might be of interest to all peace-lovers on Linak'h . . ."

"What if it did?" Zeg said. In these close quarters, his

lack of personal hygiene was a trifle more noticeable than in the shuttle's larger cabin.

Ihr Sular flicked a glance like a whiplash across Zeg. He showed no signs of noticing her disapproval, let alone being concerned about it.

"It would help if it was available to the rest of us," Nieg replied. Ignoring Zeg completely might lead to a confrontation. "Of course, we would not expect you to cooperate without clearing it with the Governor."

"The Fleet!" Zeg snapped, and then did wince at the look he got from the commander. Nieg held back a smile. It was Zeg himself who had been indiscreet, confirming the human suspicion that the Governor was a superannuated goldtusk not to be trusted in delicate matters.

"We would need Fleet authorization," ihr Sular said, more politely. "But we do keep our recordings in fairly good order. I can pledge not to discard anything currently in our files until the Fleet replies. Will that be enough?"

"More than enough, for now. I would not have expected even as much."

"F'Mita runs a good ship," Zeg said. This drew another look, which said that the use of her first name was unauthorized and the transparent flattery unappreciated.

"This has been obvious since Victoria," Nieg said. This little dagger-thrust chilled the atmosphere, so that Nieg was out the door within a few minutes.

The passageways seemed deserted, except for a trio of crewmen—Cargo Handling insignia, Nieg thought—holding a gripe session. He heard one say "Why we can't stay up here where we can move?" before Zeg's glare silenced them. Zeg didn't keep the colonel from noticing that all three Baernoi crew wore clean coveralls and dirtside footgear, and held hats under their arms.

At the hatch to the docking module, he also noticed a pile of kitbags that hadn't been there before. Considerably more than three, although Zeg hustled him past before he had a chance to match names on bags with names on coveralls.

It looked as if *Perfumed Wind* might be evacuating her crew dirtside, or had already done it. Not illegal, even a reasonable safety precaution, but was that all?

Nieg decided to run that question past Commander

Franke. *After* he'd set up a schedule for visiting the other foreign merchanters in orbit, or appointing people to act as his representatives. If he wanted his cover story for Commander ihr Sular to hold up, he would have to annoy all the other skippers as well!

It would be nice to turn the whole job over to Commander Franke himself, but that was out of the question. Commodore Liddell in particular and Linak'h Command in general needed the commander too badly. Also, Nieg did not care to risk Major Morley's wrath—and not only because he needed her cooperation in intelligence work!

As the shuttle undocked, with the three *Perfumed Wind* crewmen sitting in a row by themselves, Nieg looked at the screen and saw it remain blank. Well, there the Navy could help him, with an estimate of *Perfumed Wind*'s size and crew, and whether the number of kitbags he'd seen represented her whole crew, and if it didn't how many more there might be. . . .

Little questions, but Intelligence estimates were more complex in the assembly than any puzzle. You didn't know how many pieces you had, they kept changing shape as you laid them down, and the final picture was anybody's guess.

Linak'h:

A sonic boom rattled dishes in the kitchen and assaulted Nikolai Komarov's ears. A moment later another noise followed the boom.

"Nikolai! Didn't you shut those windows yet? If the children wake up, it—"

"I know. It will be my fault. You have said that already."

He heard a tense silence in the kitchen, as if Ursula were considering her reaction to this rude, even defiant answer. Another boom ended the silence.

The damned Navy must be bringing that brigade down faster than they planned. What are they afraid of?

He rose and started toward the windows, then remembered that the remote control was by his worktable. He turned back, saw that the pile of pictures had wandered toward the edge of the table, and started to push them back.

A third boom and another shout from Ursula made him start. The pictures fell to the floor.

"Sookin sin!" he growled, and mashed the remote-control plate. He would not have minded shoving it through the wall. The situation on Linak'h was making him nervous, and he needed an outlet for those nerves that was better than teaching art to the refugee children or shouting at Ursula. Especially something better than shouting at Ursula, who had started shouting back, which told him that he was close to the danger mark.

The windows squealed and juddered in their tracks as they closed, but they did close, and the fourth sonic boom wasn't as painfully loud. Just as long as the one after that didn't shatter the windows outright . . .

He picked up the pictures and started sorting them, for the tenth time. The one on top, he'd already rejected. It showed Candy in her soccer uniform, with her foot on the ball. The look on her face made it seem that the foot was on the neck of a mortal enemy.

Picture followed picture, until he came to the ones he'd asked from her, the ones taken after he left Quetzalcoatl and before she marched to the stars. He had looked at these only about five times apiece, but it had seemed until now that he would be as frustrated with the new pictures as he had been with the old ones.

Or could he end the frustration by abandoning the idea of using Candy as the model for his "Young Queen?" Perhaps. Certainly he could reduce the danger of another kind of frustration. Ursula would be happier if Candy was not coming around, there would be fewer quarrels, and less risk of his spending his nights on the couch. (No guest room in this house, unless he wanted to shut down his studio until the war was over, and he would *prefer* celibacy to that fate!)

No. He and Candy were not going to be put apart again. He had let one wife do that already, even though the wife was Candy's mother. Ursula *would not do it*.

Sophia and Peter might. They were his as much as Candy was; he would listen to anything they had to say about Candy. (Some things he would like less than others, but he would not give back to Candy the home she had lost by taking it away from his children by Ursula.)

Another boom, distant but longer. Then a picture that Komarov swore he had never seen before was staring at him. Two pictures, actually. From the celebration at San Miguel Superior School, when Candy and Fredo had led the soccer team to the state championship.

One showed the two of them holding the trophy up between them. Candy looked almost right, but *almost* wasn't enough now.

Not when he had the second picture. Fredo had stepped out of the scene—maybe he knew who had really done the lion's share of the leading. Candy was standing, trophy in the crook of her arm, head erect, looking some fat woman in the eye as the woman draped a wreath of flowers around Candy's long lovely neck.

Yes. That was it. That was the place for her helmet, the position of her head, everything. Now if only she could strike that pose and make it come through when she was wearing power armor. (Kipling was very specific; the Young Queen was armored.)

And if she had the time. *That* was something Nikolai Komarov would pray for, and Ursula might not object—unless she knew what he was praying for.

Seven

Charlemagne:

The call caught Admiral Kuwahara rubbing in the beard cream. His wife took it.

"Sho, there's an 'Urgent Immediate' message for you."

"Coded?"

"It says a lifter will be coming to our house to take you to Forces Command. That seems so unlikely that I thought it was a code for something else."

Kuwahara grimaced at his reflection in the mirror. The grimace and the half-creamed face did not improve the image. He hastily rejected the idea of growing a beard, splashed warm water on his face, and leaned toward the blower vent.

He managed to be outside when the lifter came, by having Fumiko pack his case and running down the front stairs, pulling on his overcoat and scarf, to snatch it from her. They barely had time to brush cheeks, before the lifter's blatting alarm joined the whine of fans and the rustle of fan-swirled snow against the front windows.

"The Empress?"

"If it's anybody else, I will be back before lunch, with their head."

"Why stop with the head?"

"Remember, the rest can be used for transplants."

"If this order wasn't the result of some disease!"

"If they don't have a disease now, they will have one when I'm done with them."

Kuwahara waved good-bye to his daughter Hanae, who had been sleeping late, then sprinted out to the lifter. There was ice on the walk—*the heater must not have adjusted to the drop in temperature; Fumiko can*

110

check that after breakfast—and Kuwahara barely made it to the lifter without losing his balance, dignity, and load.

The pilot helped him in, climbed in after, and took off without waiting for Kuwahara to strap in. Kuwahara saved his dignity by not complaining, which would have been futile in any case. The pilot was a squarely-built South Asian woman, who could have given robots or Merishi Adepts of the Serene lessons in being silent.

A tail wind cut five minutes off the usual time to Forces Command and cleared the skies of some less well-equipped machines. Kuwahara was relieved when they settled down on Baumann's pad; he had lost his initial enthusiasm for massacring whoever had pushed the panic button.

The Empress met him at the door, for the first time with her uniform less than recruiting-poster perfect. (Kuwahara decided that she was one of those fortunate officers who have a built-in neatness-field generator; he had been suspected of that himself, but knew that Chilly Willi was the real thing.)

"Sorry to rush you out here, but there's been a terrorist incident on Linak'h. Have you had breakfast?"

"Not a bite."

"Sorry. I told the chief to send something, but he can do penance by serving you lunch as well."

Kuwahara could contain his enthusiasm for that long a meeting over anything short of full-scale war on Linak'h, but kept his face straight. It was as well. Baumann led him into her office, checked the anti-snooper displays, then closed the door.

"That isn't all. The War Ministry isn't authorizing our approach to the Ministry of Trade for the emigration data."

The picture clarified. The incident on Linak'h was doubtless public knowledge by now. By appearing to press the panic button over it, the Empress had an excellent excuse for bringing him in for a fast, secure conference. It might make people wonder if the Forces weren't hiding something about the incident, but that they could live with.

This piece of bureaucratic harassment, on the other hand . . .

"What are we expected to do about the emigration data?"

"I'd like you to read the Minister's note before I answer that."

Kuwahara read through the three paragraphs four times, looking so intently for certain words that he almost started hallucinating them, ones like "forbidden," "required," and so on. He finally handed the note back to the commander-in-chief.

"Either he's trying to avoid responsibility, or he's less familiar with Anglic than I thought. This is a matter where if I recall correctly, the precedents are on our side. Unless there is a direct order keeping us out of Emigration's files, I intend for the study group to go right ahead."

"Not right now, Sho. I need a digest of your findings so far, including the case for checking emigration data. Make it a case for checking both official emigration data and unofficial impressions."

"Do we want to admit that in public?"

"General Szaijkowski is hardly the public."

Kuwahara's mind took another intuitive leap. "Unauthorized" was not the same as "forbidden," but the lack of authorization meant that they would have to win the Army's cooperation on their own. Support and Training too, to be on the safe side, although this was technically out of their jurisdiction.

"We'll start on the presentation today. But don't ask for a miracle of delivery time. If Szaijkowski is half as finicky as his reputation has it . . ."

"He is." Baumann let the robot in with the first course of breakfast, coffee, and hot rolls, then was silent long enough to pour them both cups and drink half of hers.

"He is, and will be," she said finally. "Whatever is bothering him is unlikely to affect that. In fact, if it is Linak'h . . ."

She gulped the rest of her coffee. "Last night at the C-in-C Conference, the question of a senior naval flag for Linak'h came up. Szaijkowski suggested Batsirvan."

Kuwahara winced. "Did he also suggest somebody to replace Commodore Liddell? She and Batsirvan would hardly be compatible. She's professional enough to meet him halfway, but I have yet to hear the same of him."

"If you do, expect the Last Trumpet to sound shortly afterward," Baumann said. Sausages, eggs, more and sweeter rolls, and a bowl of fruit arrived before she could continue.

"Is he going?" Kuwahara was mentally reviewing the posts that might be in his or Baumann's gift for Liddell, after the kind of E & R she would likely get from Batsirvan. As Eleventh Fleet's Deputy Chief of Staff for Personnel, Liddell had helped keep several of Botsirvan's pets out of posts where they would have been disastrous. Somehow the man had failed to regard this as a favor.

Kuwahara filled his plate and refilled his cup. Flowing adrenaline hadn't yet increased his appetite, but it would leave him weak before dinner if he didn't pile on the breakfast.

"Who are we sending?"

"Schatzi's only spare three-star, Di Longman."

"I thought she'd picked up her fourth already." Then memory stirred him to a smile.

"Something funny about Diana Longman?"

"Probably not to the people involved, but you be the judge." He gave the Empress a carefully edited version of Charles Longman's personality, abilities, and eventual departure from the Navy to become a Victorian merchanter officer and affiliate of an Alliance defector. He gave an even more edited summary of how Longman's relations with the five admirals in his family (including his father, mother, and Aunt Di) had shaped—or distorted—his personality.

"He did damned good work aboard *Somtow Nosavan*," Baumann said reflectively. "Do you think we should put him in for some kind of award? A Civil Assistance Award, at least. Or is his bounce partner Marder a security risk?"

"No to the second, definitely yes to the first. Apparently *Somtow Nosavan*'s crew have become heroes on Victoria. Since I suppose we agree with that notion, we ought to show it."

"The Board of Awards grinds exceeding slow, when it grinds at all."

"I know. There are still awards recommended for Victoria that haven't been approved yet."

"Is that a hint?"

"Would you like a list, along with the presentation for Szajkowski?"

"Yes, as a matter of fact. If we've got another campaign coming up, the more old business we clear out, the better."

Baumann filled her plate again. She seemed more relaxed, and Kuwahara decided to leave her that way as long as possible. That meant not mentioning Admiral Longman again—not that it was really Forces Command's job to tell an admiral how to deal with her own nephew—and maybe even leaving unasked one delicate question.

Why had the Army Commander-in-Chief suggested a highly unsuitable naval flag for Linak'h? He might not know anything about Phoumi Batsirvan except that he was available and senior to both Liddell and Tanz. (It was not a small concession for the Army, granting without argument that the interim theater commander off Linak'h should wear blue and gold.)

Or did he know something about Batsirvan, and suggest him for that reason—possibly hoping that Baumann didn't know or have anyone who could tell her? Maximillian Szajkowski hadn't earned his stars by sabotaging the other Forces or mismanaging his subordinates. Kuwahara did not care to think that he had developed either of those vices in his old age.

One worry at a time. If he wanted to learn more about the general, the best starting point would be a dazzling presentation, complete, coherent, and prompt. The general's reaction would save both Kuwahara and Baumann a good deal of idle speculation.

Baumann held out her cup for more coffee, and Kuwahara refilled it, while probing the sausages with the fork in his other hand.

Petzas:

F'zoar su-Weigho saw that little had changed in the Night of Deep Club since his last meeting with Eimo su-Ankrai. It was haltmeal, almost early enough for dawnfood if one rose as late as a goldtusk, so the star of Petzas lit the rooftops, gilded the flying white clouds, and sparked fire from the sea beyond.

Otherwise the live attendants were as discreet, the robots as numerous, and the food, strongwater, and uys as excellent as ever. Eimo su-Ankrai looked, if anything, younger than he had been. A command in space could do that to one whose life had been the Fleet.

Su-Ankrai's good spirits even survived reading the material concerning Behdan Zeg's request for ground-fighter arms and supplies. Su-Weigho doubted that his longtime associate, sometime friend, sometime rival, never yet open enemy, had come to approve of Behdan Zeg. He thought, however, that Zeg might have lost the power to surprise su-Ankrai. That was certainly true of himself.

"Two questions," su-Ankrai said, putting down the sheets and stabbing a slice of spearfin in light sauce. "Or rather, one question and one . . . hypothesis."

"One is: communications security. This is a long message for a courier ship."

"As it happens, that is less to be feared than I thought. The message was sent the day the ships that are said to be the Coordination's new fleet reached Linak'h. The humans had much on their minds, likewise the Furfolk and Scaleskins."

"Good. If we only fill Zeg's request, without sending more than an acknowledgment and approval, the humans will suspect less. Without suspicion, they can hardly act before the cargo is aboard *Perfumed Wind*, or perhaps even grounded on Linak'h."

"You propose that we allow Zeg to arm a personal host of Furfolk?" Su-Weigho could not keep his voice entirely subdued.

Su-Ankrai's dignity would not allow him to look about for possible listeners. Instead he tapped the sheets with his midfinger.

"Why Furfolk?"

"What else?" Su-Weigho read off the items, and from his still-excellent memory gave the weight of each one. "You see? A pitiful load, for one of the People. But the right weight for a Hunter. The primary weapons, sizes, and supplies of ammunition all say Ptercha'a to me."

"I do not doubt that. But they could also say local-security ground-fighters of the People. Remember the fighters who protected the Great Khudr's baggage train? Their load was no heavier than this, in a time when the front-fighter's load was much heavier than it is today."

"I do not question your knowledge of history. Will the human Inquirers share it?"

"If they see the weapons only in Ptercha'a hands, they may not. But if we send more . . ."

Su-Weigho nodded. "I see. Hide the weapons for Zeg's pet Furfolk in an arsenal for the People of Linak'h. And where is this generosity to come from?"

Su-Ankrai smiled. "I think I command resources sufficient for the work, both supplies and the ships to carry them."

"Better you than the Consolidationists."

"No doubt, although I think they are better friends to Zeg than he is to them, and they may well learn this in some harsh way before long. That was one need to be met before Zeg is allowed to arm Ptercha'a."

"What is the other? Surely not the Governor's approval?"

"We might find it wise to obtain that," su-Ankrai said. "I know he is an old enemy and a goldtusk of the worst sort. But you also know there is such a thing as courtesy."

"He would not know courtesy if it came up and extracted one of his tusks," su-Weigho muttered. "Let us not give him the power to forbid shipping the supplies. He may have a voice in their distribution after they have landed. Enough?"

"More than the son of a marsh-dweller deserves, but I suppose likely to be enough. What *is* the other?"

"The cooperation of Zeg's fellow Inquirers. Have you seen any word in this message, to hint that he has it?"

Su-Weigho decided that his wits were growing faulty with age. Granted that it was harder to see what was missing than to miss what was there, he should have done better. He felt like pulling lips to su-Ankrai, an unfamiliar and disagreeable sensation.

"A whole host of Ptercha'a would not be worth disrupting the Inquiry work," su-Ankrai continued. "I do not think we need to pretend that I value su-Lal, you value su-Irzim, and both of us wish Sarlin every success.

If Zeg has the consent of his associates, their work and his can advance together."

Su-Weigho felt that this might be so, although he did not care to drink to success today. He had not eaten enough lunch to safely take any more uys, for one thing, and if his wits were faltering while he was sober, what follies might he commit if he was not?

Victoria:

Alys Parkinson awoke to the distant whine of a sandstorm and the chilliness of an empty bed. Through the study door she saw the glow of lights and a terminal, and heard Jere's voice muttering. She couldn't tell if it was curses or commands to the terminal. Probably both.

He sounded deep in work, even at 0700. She considered climbing out of bed in the same clothes she'd worn when she fell asleep. That would certainly get his attention, and also give her a complete outfit of gooseflesh and possibly a cold.

Besides, she had reached the Third Age: "Show it off selectively." Jere had certainly selected her, but as what? She hoped they wouldn't wind up disagreeing over that. Neither of them really had the time to play games or recover from a painful affair, entirely apart from their needing to work together.

There were plenty of people who wanted to replace Jeremiah Gist as President of the Planetary Republic of Victoria. Most of them wanted the job for the wrong reasons. There were also a few people who wanted to replace Lieutenant General Alys Parkinson as Commander-in-Chief, Defense Forces. They might have the right reasons but not the right qualifications, or be secretly on the Federation payroll.

Pulling on slippers and a bathrobe, Parkinson punched in an order for two breakfasts of whatever would come fastest, and walked into the study. Jere grunted acknowledgment of her presence, but didn't look up for nearly five minutes. She noted an empty glass on the desk, but no bottle, and it was hard to tell what the glass might have held.

Finally Jere gave another grunt, stood up, and came around the desk to hug her. "Breakfast, anyone?"

"Already ordered."

His face twisted in mock-chagrin. "I was hoping to persuade you back to bed."

"Tell me what got you out of bed this early, and it's a deal."

"I thought if we wanted to move fast on that Civil Action mission to Linak'h, we should have a tentative roster drawn up."

"Do we?"

The idea of helping ease the situation on Linak'h made sense; it would build goodwill in at least some of the places where it was needed. But it presented problems too. Much of the cadre for any mission large enough to do any good would have to come from her own exiguous Defense Forces. The alternative was a mob of civilians, individually competent but not under any sort of discipline, and with too much equipment that might not survive even the trip to Linak'h, let alone a heavy workload when they reached it.

"Could I see the roster?"

"Can do," Jere said. "Print," he commanded, in a voice that must have activated printers three floors below. Jere always treated voice-operated machinery like unruly recruits, but only hurt his listeners' eardrums.

Blrrrpppp! and the sheets popped out. "I came up with a list that would make your job easier."

"Which job?"

"Keeping cadre for on-planet jobs and expansion." He handed over the sheets.

Parkinson started to skim, muttered something rude as she came to a name she recognized, then started reading name by name. By the time she had put the sheets down she knew that her face was flushed by the way Jere was staring at her. He didn't look apologetic, which was very much against his nature anyway, but the present look threatened a fight.

"Jere, this was not a good idea."

"What do you mean by 'this'?"

"Are so many of our bad actors on this list by coincidence?"

She could see an actual struggle against the impulse to lie. She was glad to see Jere's good sense won.

"Hardly. We send maybe two hundred or so of the people who might make trouble again off to Linak'h, and it will keep them busy. It might even keep some of them there, either alive or dead."

"Isn't Victoria a little too new to need a foreign legion?"

"Considering how we slogged through to independence, I'd say we could have used one years ago."

"Maybe, but years ago there wasn't so much anti-Federation sentiment."

"I think cutting off the head of the anti-Federation leadership will make that less of a problem. I admit that we will be working in the Federation's interests, if we send the mission. But we won't be responding to a Federation request. We'll be asserting our right to implement an independent foreign policy, supporting our interests by actually despatching people out-system."

Jere had that much right. It was one of the classic ways for a newly mature independent planet to establish its credentials. Unfortunately, playing this card without regard to logistics had destroyed the independence or even the civilization of a few planets over the last five hundred years.

Parkinson didn't run down a list. She knew that would run into a stone wall of Jere's belief that Victoria was different. However, he had also spent thirty years in the Southern Cross army before the political career that had brought him to Victoria as the Federation Territory's Governor-General. Military factors, he would hear and even possibly understand.

"My problem is with the number, not the idea in principle," she said. "Figure two ships, and half their capacity for vehicles and equipment, unless we want to send them out starkers."

"They wouldn't be as useful or as decorative in that condition as you are, I admit. So what are you getting at?"

"Two ships, half-capacity, means a maximum of four hundred people. If half of them are bad actors, we'll have to practically strip out our most reliable cadre to make up the other half. Not just military, our covert-action people too, if we can't trust Special Branch. And if we can't trust Special Branch, do we want to weaken our covert-action strength by sending *anybody*?"

"We don't want to sit with our thumbs up our arses, either. We've discussed this mission in the Cabinet twice, Alys. Sooner rather than later, somebody is going to prove their mouth is bigger than their brain. Do you want to bet it will be somebody on our side?"

"I wasn't suggesting canceling the mission."

"No? Then what do we do about the bad actors? I don't suppose we could send a list of them to the Federation and ask them to keep an eye on them for us."

"Not unless we wanted barricades in the street. The anti-Feds would be after our scalps, and not necessarily through a vote of no-confidence."

Jere suggested that the anti-Feds had irregular ancestry, dubious morals, and a horrible fate waiting for them. Parkinson waited for him to run down.

"I suppose you're right about the anti-Feds. Besides, half the job of this mission is to generate Federation goodwill. If they have to play cop on people we don't want to handle ourselves, with everything else they already have on their plates . . ."

He shook himself, knocking against the desk hard enough to send a stack of files sliding off. "Bloody hell," he muttered, and bent to pick them up.

"What about going over the roster again and picking, oh, the worst fifty?" Parkinson said. "Then we don't need as many full-time watchdogs. Out of four hundred, three hundred can actually do work on Linak'h."

Gist dumped the unsorted files on his desk and kissed her. "Or maybe we can pick fifty we think aren't hard-core, and hope they'll reform." He hugged her.

"Back to bed, or shall I just clean off the top of the desk and . . . ?"

"Jere!" She punched him lightly in the stomach, knowing that her voice had sounded almost girlish. But his interest was flattering, when you'd reached the Third Age and wondered if some morning you might wake up in the Fourth (keep it on except in the dark).

"If we go to bed, breakfast might get cold." She gripped a roaming hand. "And you will be easier to warm up than breakfast."

"That I can promise you," Jere said, with a grin. "And the desk wouldn't be safe. One of us would have to turn our back to the door, no matter who was—"

The door chimed, and the voice that answered Parkinson was human, so they had to pull their faces and bathrobes straight before registering the code and opening the door.

Merish:

Zydmunir Na'an felt the bearer-chair strike the floor. Ancestors he could name would have punished the bearers for that. But that at least was an anachronism, if bearer-chairs themselves were not (at least for one who wished to maintain the proper ceremonial surrounding a Senior Councillor in a House as large as Simferos Associates).

The curtain slid back—automatically, without hand or paw touching it—and Na'an stepped out onto the polished stone floor. One of the walking Servants handed him the data-carrier. Its lights told a tale of a safe trip and no tampering.

"May the Serene bless you," the chief bearer said, and made the formal obeisance on behalf of his seven comrades.

"And likewise you," Na'an replied. He did not think very many of his bearers worshiped the Serene, although the belief was not unknown among the Servants in War. (Mostly those of higher rank than body-attendant even to a Senior Councillor however; few body servants had any ambition to settle and prosper on a planet of the Folk when their term was done.)

Na'an prostrated himself before the door to the Chamber of the Serene's Vigilance, reciting from memory the twenty-two Principles of the Serene. On this door, each of the Principles was carved into a panel of a different kind of wood.

When Na'an rose, conscious that the cold stone had set his limbs to aching, he noticed that one of the panels had been replaced since his last visit. Polished sweetbark, from Jmaggi, if his memory of what soil chemicals did

to wood tints had not deserted him along with suppleness
of limb.

The doors automatically opened from within. Some
Chambers of the Serene kept the old ritual of live door-
openers and even of not allowing Servants to touch the
doors, let alone enter the chambers. The guide of this
chamber was of a more moderate disposition, and also luck-
ier than some in extracting donations from wealthy patrons
for extensively mechanizing the chamber's operations!

Na'an strode through, prostrated himself again (this
time on the mats, which seemed thicker than usual; had
someone known he was coming, or was it just that other
patrons of the chamber were also aging?), then assumed
the posture of meditation. To his surprise, he was actually able to meditate for most of the time he was supposed to remain in the posture.

But then, he supposed his years made this easier.
Three-quarters of the way through a Folk's normal life-
span, he had gained wealth, outwitted competition, be-
gotten children, buried one wife and made peace with a
second, and avoided making enemies who wanted more
than to diminish his wealth or perhaps a chance to speak
ill of him before his very ashes.

(He might let the second kind of enemy have their say.
It would not be easy for children, let alone grandchil-
dren, and friends, but it would ease the hearts and minds
of those enemies allowed to speak. Their burdens light-
ened, they might be less willing to go to law over his
inheritance. That would save Simferos Associates, as well
as his kin, rather a good deal of wealth.)

The time he could normally be expected to sit meditat-
ing was done. Na'an rose, walked to the center of the
chamber, and stood on the skystone. He raised both
hands and made a series of complex gestures over his
head.

In the seventh corner of the eight-cornered chamber,
a small door slid open, each half disappearing into the
wall. Na'an had to hurry to be through the gap before
the door halves slid together. Looking back, he had to
study the wall carefully to see where the door was—although half of that might be dim light and dimmer vision.

On a bench in front of several ancient robing cabinets,
Na'an's informant sat. From his pose, he must have been

lying down, perhaps even asleep, when Na'an entered. Zydmunir Na'an briefly wished that he might be able to trade half his fortune for the ability to sleep under such circumstances—and on such a bench. It probably had not been here since before the discovery of the stardrive, but it looked old enough.

"So?" he said.

"It is certain," Kep-Fah said. (At least Kep-Fah was the name he gave, and it was not impossible for him to be of Lesser Delta descent.) "Space Security is deeply committed to do whatever can be done to feed the fire on Linak'h."

"That is hardly worth the price of a meal, let alone what I have already paid you and those you hire."

"I did not say that it was." Kep-Fah spread his hands, but one claw tapped the stained and pitted brown stone of the bench. He was not as much at ease with one of Na'an's rank, even in a setting where there could be no real danger to him.

"There is more. I have encountered rumors that your son Payaral is dealing with the Confraternity."

Zydmunir Na'an knew that neither surprise nor outrage would help matters. Indeed, he was far from being surprised. He also realized, with a small shock, that he was not as outraged as he should have been, or even as he had expected to be.

However, Kep-Fah had used the word "rumors". . . .

"Are these rumors arising from some facts, or are they being put about by Space Security to shame my son and his House?"

"I do not know enough to say either way. I must find more informants on Linak'h, as well as at least one or two more in Space Security on Victoria."

Na'an thought briefly of wealth poured into the pockets of hired eyes and ears on two distant planets. He thought less briefly of the need to protect his son.

"Very well. You may do this. But find reliable people on both worlds. Space Security's presence on Victoria is a closely-held secret. They will not be gentle with anyone they find threatening to expose that secret.

"Likewise on Linak'h, the Confraternity will be watching my son's agents. The Confreres have grown more ruthless even on other worlds that do not face war. They will certainly not be slow to wet their claws on Linak'h."

"I rejoice that you know so much of this kind of business, Master Na'an. It is not just a matter of wealth, finding those who will not betray us under torture or truth drugs. But it is necessary.

"If Space Security learns that we are spying on their Victoria mission to save your son, your House might tremble. Certainly your son's work, reputation, and even life might be in danger."

It was a measure of his increasing age that Zydmunir Na'an merely nodded. But after Kep-Fah had left, he found that for some time his legs would not allow him to stand, let alone walk. He was able to return to the chamber and from the chamber to his bearer-chair in time to avoid staying suspiciously long.

He doubted, however, that his bearers would suspect anything. The chief and the runner had looked him in the face in a way bordering on insolence, except that he knew the look of Servants concerned about his health. Also, his breath came short, and his crest and the webs between his fingers twitched slightly as the bearers lifted the chair and began their homeward march.

Eight

Linak'h:

"Conclusive evidence is still lacking, but we are evaluating every scrap of data," Commander Franke concluded. "Exhibit Four, please."

The display in the center of the briefing room darkened, then came up with a schematic diagram of a Merishi warship that looked like nothing Candice Shores had ever seen. She knew this didn't prove much. LI officers did enough shipboard duty to know more about ships than regular mob-job leaders, but that didn't make them serious ship-recognition experts.

"If the conclusion is that the Merishi ship *Shenandoah* destroyed in the asteroids was a Queen Bee, we have to suspect an unpleasant corollary."

"How long do we wait for you to tell us what it is?" Brigadier General Kharg said. The commander of 222 Brigade spoke seldom, still more seldom pleasantly.

"We suspect those four Coordination cruisers may be stripped-out conversions based aboard either the destroyed Queen Bee or another one."

It was interesting to see how the fifteen officers in the room divided between those who understood what Franke meant and those who didn't. Shores congratulated herself briefly on being one of the knowledgeable ones, and listened to Franke enlightening the rest.

"This means that they will have lost their Jump and long-term life-support capabilities, and the personnel to support either. The space made available could be taken up with extra sensors, damage-control, weapons, ammunition storage, in-atmosphere maneuvering equipment—at this point your guess is as good as mine, and I won't pretend that we're not guessing."

From Mad Bill Moneghan's sour look, that admission was letting down the Navy side, but Franke remained unruffled. (His uniform was still below standard; his poise had become resistant to fusers, Death Commandos, flag-rank critics, or Lu Morley.)

"For at least a short engagement, a *Ryn-Gath* cruiser converted along these lines could have either space-to-space or space-to-ground capabilities nearly equivalent to *Shenandoah*."

"Not both?" This from the CO of 222 Brigade's First Battalion—well regarded, wiry, and said to be a gifted amateur actor.

"Not unless either the Merishi or the Ptercha'a have repealed the law of physics about two objects occupying the same space at the same time. Or unless they've been willing to make the ships fit for one *very* short engagement of each kind.

"Remember, the *Ryn-Gaths* are an old design. They're still in production because they can take a lot of punishment, any planetary dockyard can build or at least repair one, and Merishi straight out of merchanters or even straight out of training can crew them. That means the Merishi can keep a lot of them in service cheaply, and if you have enough of anything, it doesn't always matter if it's not state of the art."

This seemed to soothe Moneghan, who was representing the Navy at this conference because he was in charge of ground support, not because he was the smartest or most diplomatic four-striper available. Shores would have given a good deal for Liddell to be able to come down herself, but that would have to wait at least until Admiral Longman and her staff were in and on duty.

Shores hoped that would be soon. Sixty-one more Linak'h days on the ultimatum seemed an eternity unless you treated it that way. Then you would wake up with your unit half in one place, half in another, armed Ptercha'a shooting their way through the space in between, and everything to be done at once before anything else could be started.

Longman had a harsh reputation, but Shores had survived a year as aide to Frieda Hentsch, who had a worse one. If Longman came fast, took charge properly, and gave the right orders, she could—*after* they won—conduct human sacrifices by the light of the Red Child. Shores was even prepared to nominate a few candidates for the starring role in the ceremony. . . .

"Thank you, Commander," Kharg said. He looked at his watch. "The next and last speaker is supposed to be Colonel Davidson, but the printed annex on Fire Guarding that he promised hasn't arrived yet. Colonel, do you want to wait, or speak now and let the paper catch up with you?"

Davidson's face showed that he recognized and disliked an effort to put him on the spot. It couldn't be any secret that he was almost nakedly regarded as Banfi's spy. It might be a secret (to him, at least) that not everyone in the Field Force disapproved of Banfi's spying on them.

It was not, however, something that Shores intended to tell him. Her relationship with Nieg already had a few people bristling; they suspected her of having preferential access to intelligence. Add suspicion of cultivating the Marshal through his spy, and her relations with at least half of her colleagues in the Linak'h Field Force would become impossible.

The display generated a map of the Federation Territory, then the map expanded to include all the portions of all four territories covered by the "high forest." To highlight just how much area that was, Davidson ordered them displayed in green.

"Now that I've impressed you with the size of the problem . . ." he began.

Linak'h:

"Aren't you clean yet?" Emt Desdai asked. He thought he heard a firm negative from Seenkiranda over the sound of running water.

He thought of going in and turning off the shower. But that might lead where he had no wish to go at this time. He was not only weary, but too sober in mood for romping.

"Just remember what I told you about the water!" he called.

A moment later Seenkiranda thrust her head out the bath chamber door. "You told me about the water, but where is the dryer's airflow?"

Desdai had to get up to answer that, and even thrust his way into the chamber, but Seenkiranda contented herself with scratching him lightly under the throat and behind the ears. She was not as she had been during the first days of her return from her first battle, when she had come close to reminding him of the gap in their ages.

The dryer, as Desdai expected, had simply locked down from the excess humidity. By the time Seenkiranda had dried half of herself on all the towels and grooming cloths in their chambers, the warm air was flowing to dry the other half.

Clothed in a robe, she was beginning to trim her claws and chase the last dirt out from under them when she noticed her mate's expression. The knife and scraper didn't fall to the floor, but she dropped them on the side table in more haste than usual.

"Bad news?"

"Do you want me to lie to you or refuse to tell? Or would you rather give up going into the field?"

"It did not seem to me that the Confraternity took such great pleasure in my being in the field that I would have another chance," she said, assuming a pose of injured dignity. Then she deliberately ruined the pose by shifting until she could lift her tail and tuck the tip under her chin.

Desdai laughed and ran his claws gently along the tail, from base to tip. She parodied arousal, but again only worked her claws through his chin fur.

"Drynz isn't the only one who thinks you have the makings of a warrior," Desdai said. "They aren't ready to make you a field leader, but if Drynz or I go out, you can go as our second."

"I thought you were too valuable to send into the field," Seenkiranda said. This time the dignity was no pose. "Is the bad news that the white-muzzle Confreres have changed their thoughts on that?"

She would think it bad news, Desdai realized. But then, Seenkiranda's one taste of battle had not been anything like his years with a Legion. By the time you had seen four such years, you were closer to many in your cohort and most in your band than you were to anyone except pair-mates or younglings. You could easily think that being killed or crippled was worth it, if it happened in such good company.

"The bad news is of what you did in the field. The Folk you killed has been identified. He is Bahrass Je'en, formerly of Space Security, believed in the service of the Hakzos Consortium. How high in their service is not known, but he was a Squadron Leader in Space Security. One of the great consortia would not give him charge of disciplining drunken Hunters."

"How long ago did he leave space?"

"If he left it, five years ago."

Seenkiranda nodded and probed one ear with a finger wrapped in a towel. Her ears had always seemed to Desdai to be extraordinarily well shaped, but then he could say (and had said) the same of most of the rest of her. He knew that his critical judgment was not at its best where she was concerned.

"Five years. Four and a half of the humans'. All the time needed for him to be in from the beginning. To have sunk his claws into Victorian throats. Is it known if he did anything on that world?"

"No, nor is there any way to learn without admitting guilty knowledge of his death to the Federation. Not that they would consider him a great loss, but surely they have in their ranks spies from the Folk. What the Federation learns, so will the Folk. Je'en is mute ashes now. Let us not try to make them speak."

"I was not thinking of the Federation. What about the Victorians? What might they know?"

"What the Federation learned may not have been given to the Victorians. They would have the same fear of spies as we do. Also, who would ask the Victorians?"

Then Desdai realized where her persistence was leading her—and him, and perhaps his master.

"This asks much of Payaral Na'an."

"I think he is willing to give much, if asked," Seenkiranda suggested. "Also, if the Victorians' debt to him is increased by his chartering of more ships, knowledge may be the only way they can repay him."

She began dressing. Desdai propped himself on one arm on the midroom mat and contemplated her grace.

Clad from feet to belly, she stopped suddenly, tunic in one hand and a boot in the other.

"Bahress Je'en. I *thought* that name sounded familiar. Did he do anything between leaving Security and joining Hakzos?"

"He lectured at guard schools, but the Confraternity records gave no names."

"One of them was mine. I remember the name now, because he stayed nearly a quarter of the year. I did not recognize him, though."

"Surgery can do that, and of course his face was a horror after his death. But I wonder if he put you in danger before his death."

"Oh, come, dear heart! He never saw me at the school except as one of a class of twenty. In the forest he had a good look at me for perhaps five heartbeats before he died."

"He might have had a vision-transmitter on him."

"He did not. We searched him, and he had no time to throw it away." She looked at him with a familiar sharpness, then pulled her tunic over her head.

"Emt, dearer than my own soul, you can urge me into the field or you can urge me to stay out of it. You cannot do one in one breath and another the next. Could you put your own thoughts in order, before we ponder this matter again?"

Her eyes told him plainly that she was being much gentler than she wished to be. However, one did not quarrel with such a large gift.

"I will hold my tongue, on one condition. I wish to put your name forward, as one who has deserved well of the Confraternity and may therefore use its escape routes. I also wish to introduce you to what would be your first stop on the route you would need to use, if worse came to worst."

"After lunch, please." She looked in the mirror, discovered that pulling on her tunic had unsettled her ruff and crest, and reached for a comb.

"It would not even be today. I must send the message, await the reply, and decode it to see if it is favorable. Then I must arrange a cover mission into town. Work connected with the charters will serve, I think, although we may have trouble there.

"The news seems to be spreading, that Linak'h is too dangerous to make any profit worth the risk. Word of those four Coordination ships will make matters worse."

"Working in vain is still work."

"How am I to take that?" He grinned, to show that no serious offense was taken.

She grinned so widely that he could count every one of her teeth. "Forgive me for making demands beyond the powers of such an aged one to meet. . . ."

They both resisted the temptation to put those powers to the test, and went to the exercise chamber downstairs instead. A good sweat, and muscles taut as a Legion's parade line, did not drive away either of their worries. It did give Emt Desdai a good appetite for lunch, and it was almost an article of faith with him not to worry while eating.

This time, though, his guardian spirits failed him. He looked at Seenkiranda so often that only her patience avoided a quarrel, but he was not really seeing her. He was looking beyond, to a shadowy battlefield where humans, Hunters of several factions, and even the Baernoi all seemed to be standing to arms at once.

By the time lunch was done, he understood clearly why in old tales the power of prophecy was so often considered a curse.

Linak'h:

Candice Shores's unfamiliarity with forest fires was balanced by Colonel Davidson's determination to do the work of the missing annex. It also helped that the situation they faced was comparatively simple to describe, even if probably complex to solve.

No, make that certainly *complex, barring miracles such as no thunderstorms before a heavy snowfall.* Since the earliest recorded date of a major snowfall in the fire-danger area was still a hundred and two Linak'h days ahead, Shores decided that would be a bigger miracle than mere soldiers were likely to be blessed with.

The problem with the high forest of the inhabited area of this continent was that the past dry winter and present hot, dry spring had followed three years of below-average rainfall. This meant that the dense litter on the forest floor, three meters thick in places, had finally reached the point of drying out. The trees above it were often flammable, and sometimes burned, but the mass of litter twice as high as a man usually kept the fire in the tree-tops, eighty or a hundred meters up.

"Now, though, the debris could be dry enough to *feed* the fire, generate more heat, and generally keep it moving and growing. If we got an inaccessible location and a high wind thrown in on top of all the dry fuel . . . Picture the Black Dragon or the Kuikamani Fires, but an order of magnitude larger."

Those who had heard of either seemed impressed enough to satisfy Shores that she was hearing of a real threat. Fortunately, real remedies were available. They fell into two categories. One was fire-prevention techniques in all training exercises and anything else done in the high forest.

"This may include staying completely out of some areas, unless there's a military emergency," Davidson added. "The relevant Fire Guard regulations are available, even if the print shop has completely wiped the annex."

"Are we going to let a bunch of Cat—ah, Ptercha'a—*firefighters* dictate tactics?" That was the XO of Third Battalion, who seemed to be a spiritual twin of the late Colonel Goerke in his attitude toward Ptercha'a.

"Yes," Davidson said. "If you don't like it, persuade General Tanz to take it up with the Administration."

Kharg's glare took in both men. It would be too much to hope for the general to back Davidson totally against one of his own brigade, but an impartial hostility to public confrontations might be enough. Shores made a mental note to ask Kharg for even fewer favors than General Tanz.

The Administration's Fire Guards and the Linak'h Command Civil Action units had reasonably complete firefighting gear: robocats, water bombers, tree-toppers (civilian logging models, mostly), and so on. The mobilizing human Reserves would help; the mobilization of the Administration's forces could help still more.

But a major fire would need every available pair of

hands, and Davidson wanted Linak'h Field Force to line up those hands in advance. Fifty fighters and a security & logistics detachment would be a reasonable quota from each battalion.

"Pick reliable people, preferably ones who grew up in the country," Davidson added. "I won't say that any of you plan on sloughing off your bad actors to the fire detail, but remember that that kind gets killed in a crown fire."

The bulk of the transportation, training, guides, and leadership above squad level would be provided by forest-wise local Reservists and the Fire Guards. The rest would come from the Linak'h Battalion and the QRF.

That made Shores do quick mental arithmetic. The QRF now had one detachment in the new Great Bend camp and one back in the Zone. If she could get her TO & E frozen, so that she wasn't breaking in a new company periodically, she could cope with a three-detachment plan—one forward, one back, one fire security.

It would leave no margin for error, or for other units using the QRF instead of their own people—which, come to think of it, was no bad idea. A lot would depend on Barb Hogg; if she was willing to leave her C Company under Shores, that would be the freeze right there.

The annex arrived about then, and everybody was too busy adding it to their binders and portable data-carriers for any bargaining. By the time Shores looked up, Kharg had adjourned the meeting, Hogg had vanished, and the one who caught up with her on the way out was Colonel Davidson.

"No problem with your people being tapped for fire security?" he asked.

"I don't see how we can avoid it, until the other four battalions learn their way around," Shores said. She only thought afterward to check for eavesdroppers, but nobody from 222 Brigade was in sight.

"Good. Keep in mind the morale factor, too. Your LI people have done the serious fighting so far."

"The Great Bend farm wasn't what I would call a fight, let alone serious," Shores replied. "Besides, the bad guys got away."

"Nonetheless, you and yours did live up to the LI reputation. Having somebody like that out there between him and any stray terrs could keep some city lad from panicking on the fire line."

"Why, Colonel, you sound as if you believe the LI legends!"

Davidson's grimace showed even under his beard. "Right now, Colonel Shores, I'll believe in any damned thing that I think will work!"

Nine

Linak'h:

Rahbad Sarlin implemented the decoding program and
sat back to await results. A newly unpacked robot rolled
in with a jug of beer and several mugs.

Brokeh su-Irzim reminded himself to establish a schedule of checking the robots for eavesdropping implants.
As security became more crucial to the Inquirers' mission, the support staff had to be excluded from larger
areas of the house for longer times. Two robots ordered
and a third donated by F'Mita ihr Sular helped, but
would hinder if curiosity or disloyalty turned them into
mechanical spies.

Behdan Zeg was pouring himself a beer when the decoded message came up on the computer's display. Sarlin
looked at it, then his eyes widened and he gave every
appearance of being about to commit murder or suicide.

"Mother's son!" he roared. It came out sounding obscene. Then he added several epithets which were explic-
itly so.

Zeg set down his beer and assumed fighting stance.
Su-Irzim took some small hope from the beer's being set
down, rather than flung in Sarlin's face. However, he did
not like the color of Zeg's face or the way his hands
shook. His thumbs seemed ready to take on a life of
their own and gouge out his half-brother's throat.

Sarlin did not look much more peaceful than Zeg,
which hinted of grave provocation. Su-Irzim, however,
refused to act on hints.

"What troubles you both?" he asked, more sharply
than one really ought to with those of equal rank.

"Read this!" Sarlin snapped. Su-Irzim moved to where
he could see the display and obeyed.

He himself felt no urge to kill, but he could understand where the others' urges came from.

"The question is, did the message arrive on Linak'h in this form?" he said. "Or is the mention of 'Furfolk modifications' something added on the whim of our beloved goldtusk of a Governor?"

"Does that matter?" Sarlin snapped. "Zeg had no right to secretly order the weapons at all!"

"What justifies calling it 'secret'? Had I wished it secret from you, I would have used another code."

For a moment su-Irzim had hopes he would be mediating a skirmish, not a war. Then Sarlin glared.

"There are things you will keep secret from us, then. But not, I suppose, your Consolidationist friends?"

Su-Irzim was now prepared to thrust himself bodily between the two half-siblings to prevent bloodshed and the dissolution of the mission into chaos. For another moment he thought it would be necessary, and commended his reputation to the care of the Lords.

Then, to the surprise of the others, Zeg spread his hands. It was not in the least a submissive gesture, but he was ready to admit to bad manners, if not wrongdoing.

"I do not suppose you revealed anything to the Governor, when all is said and done," he said, not looking at Sarlin. "Possibly no one did, and his offer of modifying the weapons for Ptercha'a use is only a lucky guess."

"That still leaves open the question of why he made it," Sarlin said. "Also why your friends—whoever they are—are sending enough weapons for a Furfolk Legion."

"Someone on . . . Petzas, most likely . . . thinks that it will be better to have them here before the war breaks out. When that happens, navigation off Linak'h could become perilous simply through the accumulation of dead ships and debris!"

"Likely enough," Sarlin said. "But we still have problems, even if they arrive safely. Storing them securely, so that if we do not want them in Furfolk hands they need not end up there. Issuing them to the Furfolk if we wish, and if the Governor approves . . ."

"Why seek his approval?" Zeg inquired.

"Oh, I see. Maintaining a private host is merely a form of healthy exercise to purge your system of mineral imbalances and fluid excesses. Somehow, mother's son, I always thought you had led too temperate a life for that.''

Zeg looked ready to erupt again, but when he did, it was with laughter. "I did not inform the Governor, wishing to have the work done and the weapons in hand before he could protest. But you will notice that the message is not worded as a protest. He seems to think that arming the Ptercha'a is not such a bad idea, and is curious if we mean to do it.''

Sarlin sat down, shaking his head. "The idea of that goldtusk possessing either curiosity or intelligence stuns me.''

"Then go lie down until the effect wears off,'' su-Irzim said briskly. He had said little, but his throat was dry enough to need a beer, which he poured himself, with another for Sarlin. All three beers disappeared quickly, although no one raised a mug in salute.

"If the Governor has guessed,'' su-Irzim concluded, "then the Lady of Fortune has smiled on him. If, however, he had been informed, we need to find out by whom.''

Zeg nodded. "The twins and I have all the necessary skills, and—''

Sarlin interrupted. "If you plan on training the Ptercha'a as well as arming them, you will need the twins as instructors. Making them interrogators will not make them more fit for the task. It might turn the Ptercha'a against them.''

"I was not thinking only of Ptercha'a rattlejaws.''

Su-Irzim had his turn. "It is not done, to set the twins on our own people. There would be bad blood enough to give rise to murder within days.

"Zeg, I offer you a bargain. Put those people of yours—the ones you claim to have in the Governor's palace—on the trail of the rattlejaw. Promise no punishment if he comes forward when identified.''

"Is that all you want from my people?'' Zeg muttered.

"It is all for now. But for the future, they must be at our disposal. Zeg, you cannot have both a private host and a private cell of spies in the Governor's palace. One or the other, or even both, must obey us as well.''

"And if I refuse?'' It seemed to su-Irzim but a glimmer of the old, fierce Zeg.

"Then I at least shall wonder whom you serve, the Khudrigate, the Consolidationists, or your own ambition. If it is not the first, then leaving you to run free will cause more chaos than dividing the mission by suppressing you."

Zeg took that more calmly than su-Irzim had expected. The two People who showed agitation—or at least felt it—were Sarlin and su-Irzim. Sarlin, it seemed, had never imagined anyone so addressing his half-brother and living to tell about it. The experience left him befuddled, as his face told plainly.

Su-Irzim did not know what showed on *his* face. What he felt within was a chilling knowledge that in all but name he had just assumed leadership of the mission. If Zeg's spies and Ptercha'a ground-fighters obeyed any orders but Zeg's, they would obey Brókeh su-Irzim's.

He was farther than ever from Fleet Rank, he suspected. He also knew that, for now at least, he did not greatly care.

"If you have not chosen the Ptercha'a for training, Behdan, could you see about doing it quickly? If the weapons are twelve days out, that does not leave much time for training fighters you want ready for the war."

They all three looked at the calendar, as if a single cord bound all three heads. Fifty-two Linak'h days remained before the ultimatum would expire and the planet tremble on the edge of war.

Linak'h:

Candice Shores managed to get her QRF TO & E frozen almost soon enough, and almost at a high enough level. It involved a certain amount of juggling bodies and vehicles. She also had to do more than a little praying that the XO could hold the fort at Camp Great Bend. Finally, she had to persuade Lieutenant Fiske (assigned for fire security) that when it really came down, he should defer to the QRF's own Fire Liaison, a Reserve master sergeant with eight seasons on the North Territory Human Hotshot Crew.

After that, she had, out of every twenty-two-and-a-half hour Linak'h day, as much as a whole hour to call her own, not needed for eating, sleeping, or personal hygiene. The first day she had that hour, she let out a lot of pent-up aggressiveness in bed with Nieg. This did not seem to bother him in the least.

The second day they got together with Shores just in from a field exercise. She nearly fell asleep during the shower and did fall asleep during the back rub.

The third day, Shores called up Nieg after a message from her father. "He's going to be in town on a purchasing mission," she said. "Art supplies at a place called Renko's. Ever heard of it?"

Nieg's screen split while he consulted a directory. "In Big Tree Mall, right. Thinking of going?"

"Of course. I can't get away long enough to fly out to the camp."

"I'll go with you, on two conditions. One is that I do not have to ask your father for your hand. The other is that you produce some additional security."

"Terrs?"

"Yes. There are rumors that Renko's is a Confraternity safe house. Also, the mall gets its name from a stretch of titanhome running right up to the edge. A platoon of snipers could hide within pulser range of the whole mall."

"I'll see if Juan and Jan can be sprung loose. Jan's as good at spotting snipers as she is at being one."

"Pick you up about 1400?"

"I thought we could just walk over. . . ."

"Ah, remember Admiral Longman's modification to the standard Security Two."

"I'd rather not."

"Best be careful, unless you have a very good excuse. Are you pregnant?"

"Is that one of the excuses? I didn't read the edict that carefully."

"What an example to set for your people! Seriously, Longman's supposed to be looking for someone to hang, so people will stop thinking she's just trying to make an impact. I'd rather it wasn't any of us."

Which added up to their borrowing a military lifter with pilot, for an errand that could have be done on public transportation, by taxi, or even on foot. Could

Longman simply be trying to discourage sightseeing, by requiring military vehicles for all Federation personnel movements outside the Zone?

Possibly, but if so, that edict had backfired. Too many people's errands were chasing too few vehicles. If a screening process wasn't instituted pretty soon, essential training and logistic operations might find themselves short of lift.

What was really needed was Marshal Banfi's taking active command. Or else a new Linak'h Theater Commander, senior to both Longman and Tanz and not looking over his/her shoulder for the Marshal to leap and bite. (Forget removing Banfi. Forget, also, that "Theater" technically required a war; there would undoubtedly be one before a new chief could arrive, if only between the Army and Navy.)

Shores looked at the clock. They would be eating in town, she suspected. Grab a snack now, take a long shower, and see if she had a civilian outfit that didn't look baggy. (The routine she'd been on since reaching Linak'h stripped off fat but didn't add muscle mass to keep her contours stable.)

No, wait. Baggy was better. Under Security Two, military personnel also were supposed to go armed. Doctrine and precedent about concealed weapons were fuzzy, but so was this situation. Nieg would certainly have a small arsenal invisible except to a sensor scan, and with weapons as with money, "neither a borrower nor a lender be" if you can provide your own.

Shores opened her closet and her weapons case and started mixing and matching.

Aboard U.F.S. *Shenandoah*, off Linak'h:

"Did you recommend Mr. Longman for a Civil Assistance Award?"

If Vice Admiral Diana Longman had grown a second head or started dancing on the table, Commodore Liddell could not have been more surprised.

No, the dancing might have been all right. Di Longman

didn't get the name "Golden Vanity" for any sort of modesty.

"I did not."

"Good."

"With your permission, Admiral—why is that good?"

There were several other questions Liddell wanted to ask. Such as: Why no squadron maneuvers since Longman had arrived? Why a staff of thirty, apparently hand-picked like the Hentschmen but not, on the average, nearly as impressive? Why a string of "edicts," some sensible, others ranging from the petty through the officious to those that Federation officers were embarrassed to enforce in front of other races?

That seven years of dirtside staff duty might have left Di Longman a little out of her depth with a space command seemed the simplest explanation. It also called for the simplest remedy: Wait until she either sank or swam.

Except that people could be killed and ships destroyed during that long a wait, a lot of them if Longman sank. Some of them would be Liddell's. One of the people might be her, one of the ships *Shenandoah*.

"I don't have to answer that question, Commodore."

Which question? Oh—why was her not commending Charlie the Misfit good?

Longman's face threw a challenge at Liddell. Liddell returned stare for stare, and realized for the first time that Charlie's face hadn't been weak. It had been human, confessing its faults. Di Longman's face was the same, slightly modified for a female, and largely drained of humanity.

"No, Admiral. You don't. But you can't relieve me of my command for asking it." *Or for resenting your refusing an answer, but let's not treat her as a mental defective by spelling that out for her.*

"I was afraid you were going to imitate Captain Prange. Once of *Valhalla*, always of *Valhalla*, and so on. Pushing for a commendation for a discipline case who resigned his commission because he had the hots for an Alliance defector—that looked too close to Prange's style for comfort."

Liddell wondered, *whose* comfort.

"I suppose we can leave it at that," Longman said.

She turned toward the door and called, "Bar's open, people!"

It was generally considered etiquette for even a visiting flag officer to ask a captain's permission before letting other guests in. It was also considered proper for the staff not to descend on the hospitality supplies like a herd of grubbers on ripe crops.

Liddell snagged a drink and a plate from one of the robots just before it ran empty, and her eyes met Chief Jensen's over the rim of the glass. The steward looked ready to sink into the carpet.

Well, Longman did come out in a hurry, and she did bring another capital ship, which you, Rosie, were praying for. Possibly the haste had affected *Roma*'s ability to re-supply, as well as Longman's choice of staff.

And possibly Schatz and Baumann had coordinated sending Longman between them. Send out Di Longman, let her do her worst, and get the Army screaming, praying, and begging on its collective knees for Marshal Banfi to ride forth and slay both the human and the nonhuman dragons.

It was a dirty trick, very unlike the John Schatz she knew, not so unlike the Chilly Willi of legend—but legend was often just that. It was, however, some sort of explanation of why Longman was here. The idea of her being the product of random chance was too painful to contemplate, if one valued a reasonably orderly universe!

Linak'h:

Candice Shores's trip to Renko's made her think even less of Security Two precautions. If she'd walked she would have had open ground all the way to the edge of town, then solid human suburbs and the bustling city center most of the rest of the way. Nobody could reach her in the open, and nobody was likely to try anything in the presence of five hundred witnesses of probably three different races.

But from the Och'zem Municipal Landing Stage, the route to the mall lay through a largely industrial belt, with recycling plants jostling old townhouses and new warehouses crowding into old parks. Beyond that lay a stretch of solidly Ptercha'a housing, more than half of it the kind of workers' dormitories where they had armed guards at the door.

(A backhanded tribute to the Hunters, those guards— Hunters seldom became apathetic and lay down to die. More often they turned aggressive, even deadly. A Ptercha'a who had completely forgotten that he/she was warrior's kin was brain-dead.)

Then the neighborhood began to sparkle again, and just beyond four neat streets of mixed single-family and apartment housing lay the mall. It had both human and Ptercha'a businesses, Shores noted, but no Merishi. Not that there were any Merishi living close by; where it wasn't Ptercha'a the area was human, with several self-contained little villages on the other side of the Big Trees and connected to town by a road that vanished in the shadows less than a hundred meters north.

But there wasn't a single Merishi business in the mall. Not even a spice shop—and Merishi monopolized the herb-and-spice business on some *human* planets.

Renko clearly catered to both races; he himself was human, and in fact ex-LI (one term with 106 Brigade, before he transferred to the Engineers for a Settled post to raise a family). His assistant was a Ptercha'a who spoke Anglic with an accent that even Shores had trouble understanding, but who tolerated her efforts at True Speech. The robots were maintained and operated by a human female who couldn't be more than twenty Standard.

Shores's father was already in the store when she and her escort arrived. Five people, none of them small, crowded the store's narrow aisles, and Nikolai Komarov made matters worse by rushing up and down the aisles like a demented insect. As he ran, he snatched items off the shelves and flung them at whichever of the soldiers happened to be standing within range. The random chase ended only when Shores missed grabbing a jar of blue toner, nearly dropped the rest of her load in the resulting puddle, and finally decided that she'd had enough.

She set down half her load, handed the rest to Nieg, and marched up to Komarov.

"Father, didn't you have a shopping list? Or did you have one and forget it?"

"Oh, I have it right here," Komarov said, tapping the breast pocket of his jacket. "Or do I?"

"Let me," Shores said.

"Oh, if I am going to be searched by a beautiful woman, why waste it on my daughter?" Komarav made a sweeping gesture, which knocked several items off the counter. Renko cringed. His assistant was nowhere in sight, and the maintenance tech was loudly proclaiming that Robot Red Ted needed her touch right this minute in the back room.

They finally compromised by having Jan Sklarinsky search Komarov while Shores studied a picture her father handed her out of the third pocket he had been sure held the shopping list. By the time Sklarinsky came out with the list, Shores had studied the picture and handed it to Nieg.

"I can recognize today's soldier in that day's girl," Nieg said finally. "Or is there more to it?"

"With my father, probably, but I don't know what."

"I tell you what," Komarov said. His Anglic was always more accented when he was excited. "I want you to pose for a picture. You are the centerpiece, the Young Queen, standing like you were, with a helmet where the trophy is."

He went on, while Nieg and Esteva together collected the purchases. Sklarinsky mounted security watch and ordered up a roboporter, although Renko said that the rest of the party from the refugee-camp school had promised to come by.

"Will they, though?" Nieg whispered. "Even if they do, when? Do you want him and his purchases piled up in your store all afternoon?"

Shores overheard, wanted to both glare and giggle, but kept her attention on her father. He had a knack for talking about a painting in a way that made others see it as if he were sketching it in the air before them, one that had made him a good teacher over many years and quite a few planets. It was the first time he had turned the full force of this gift on his daughter, and the shock of realizing that made her turn away and blink her eyes dry.

Wouldn't he have done that before, if he loved me? If I was as important to him . . . as he says?

She felt a slim, muscular arm slip through hers.

"Accept his apology before you complain, Candy."

"Is that what it is?"

"From where he stands, it's the most complete apology he knows how to make."

"Or the only one Ursula will *let* him make."

"Is associating with Intelligence making you cynical, Candy? If so, perhaps I should take my leave."

Shores missed a breath and again wanted to turn away and blink, but Nieg's slim arm now held hers so firmly she would lose dignity trying to break his grip. She closed her eyes until her breath came properly, then bent down and whispered:

"You are going to pay for that. . . ."

"Ah, heads up, people," Jan Sklarinsky said. "I've got a roboporter on the way. ETA about ten minutes. But there's also a bunch of people gathering in the middle of the mall. Some of them have weapons, and there's a couple carrying a sign."

"What does it say?"

" 'Renko Unfair to—"

The explosion in the back room blew the rest of Jan Sklarinsky's words to oblivion.

Linak'h:

Emt Desdai and Seenkiranda had sighted the Federation military party at Renko's from across the mall. They had also spotted two or three suspicious humans loitering about the shop windows or lounging on the benches.

They didn't see the two or three become twenty or thirty, because they were making their way through an alley to Renko's back door. Desdai told his mate that he might as well teach her how the land lay while they kept out of sight and Renko served his customers.

A low rear window left open allowed Desdai to eavesdrop, with the help of an earplug amplifier. Seenkiranda wondered why he was carrying such a thing, when he had not yet told her what he thought about her taking the field. She doubted she would receive an answer.

"The taller woman in street garb is Colonel Shores," Desdai whispered. "The Warbanders wearing uniform

are Colonel Nieg of Intelligence, and Esteva and Skralin-
sky—no, Sklarinsky—of Shores's cohort. It is rumored
that Nieg and Shores are pair-mated, or sworn to it.''

"Is that lawful in human Warbands?'' Among the
Hunters, Warband pair-mating was as complex as inheritance and therefore done with caution. Battle-vows grew
like ripe berries on a holosh just before the first snows,
but pair-matings intended to last for life much less often.
(And of those that grew, sadly many ended a battle or
few later, a thought Seenkiranda did not find any too
pleasing.)

"Who is the last man? Renko?''

"Oh, no. Renko is hardly taller than a Hunter. The
tall one—oh, I see him clearly now. Colonel Shores's
father. An artist, and a good one, I am told by those
who know.''

Then Seenkiranda saw her mate listen more carefully,
turn aside from the window, and reach out to her. The
explosion a moment later knocked her down, and flung
him clear across the alley in a cloud of smoke and debris.

Seenkiranda strangled a scream at birth and leaped to
her mate's aid. He was already sitting up when she arrived, dabbing at a cut over one eye and beating out a
smoldering patch on his fur with the other hand.

Then the screams began inside. The back of the store
was a ruin, blackened robots looming in the murk like
angry spirits, but the screams came from a living throat.
They tore at Seenkiranda's ears and soul, and even her
half-deafened mate shook himself.

With her arm around his shoulders, he lurched to his
feet, fought for balance, then trotted toward the door.

"Thank All that the door's open,'' he muttered. "I
forgot my cutter.'' If that was what Seenkiranda thought
it was, she was just as glad. Having one without a license
meant a work-farm sentence at least, and attention called
to you that anyone working for the Confraternity could
well do without.

Instead she took a deep breath, nearly started coughing on
the spot, but held the air long enough to plunge into the
smoke after her mate. She caught him as he knelt in the
wreckage, clawing an overturned robot away from a
fallen human.

The human was female, young, and if not dead then

gravely hurt. Her hair was gone, one side of her face blackened with more than soot, and blood was trickling from her mouth. Other injuries, inward or to her limbs, Seenkiranda could only guess at.

But the floor was black everywhere and ablaze in three places, one of them the hall to the front room. Before the woman's comrades could fight through that blaze to reach her, one of the others would have finished the explosion's work.

Seenkiranda flogged her wits for memory of what injuries made it unsafe to move a human. More easily, she remembered that the rule with them was the same as with Hunters: If they are doomed where they lie, move them as gently as possible to a spot where they may live to die of their hurts!

The human female was full-grown for all her youth; the two Hunters had much trouble being gentle and some trouble lifting her at all. The smoke eating at throats and eyes did not help. They finally stepped into clear air, and laid the woman as gently as possible on the cleanest patch of alley paving that they could find.

They examined the woman and, not much to Seenkiranda's surprise, Desdai produced a small battle-hurt kit. It held little besides dressings, cleansing sprays, and painkillers for Hunters, humans, and Folk, but that was more than the woman had on her. Perhaps it would even be enough to preserve her until her comrades came.

Seenkiranda was so busy helping Desdai that she lost all sense of time, and was slow to notice two of the uniformed humans looming in the hall. One of them carried a fire-sprayer, wielding it against the flames on floor and wall. As the flames died with hisses and clouds of filthy vapor, fouler even than the smoke, the second advanced to guard his comrade's back.

No, *her* comrade's. It was the sixteen-Leader Sklarinsky, and she carried a battle rifle. As she saw the two Hunters, its muzzle swung toward them.

Linak'h:

Flame boomed up from the hall before the echoes of the explosion had died. It rose as high as a tall man's head, much higher than Juan Esteva, who was crouching to rush through the flames to the tech's assistance.

Shores didn't blame him; the screams were dreadful. But the fire-damping system in the back room was either defective or had gone up with the bomb. Any rescue attempt now would just mean one more person burning alive.

The fire-damping foam was sluicing down from the main room's fixtures in fine style. Shores snatched up fallen canisters and cartons, clearing the edge of the burning patch of floor. From behind the counter came the hiss of a hand extinguisher, as a spotfire there died. (Odd how she'd come to use forestry terminology in only a few days. Odder still how bungling terrorists seemed to be chasing her around.)

No. From the point of view of that girl's parents, the terrs didn't bungle. They did their job.

Then a rock cracked against the front window. Two more followed. Renko stabbed at a control by the cashier's station, then cursed as whatever he'd expected failed to happen.

Nieg pointed, and he and Sklarinsky grabbed the handles of the interior shutters and pulled them closed by force. Then the sniper crouched in the doorway and unslung her rifle. Not her sniper weapon, thank the Lady, just a regular pulser with a magazine of nonlethals already in place and three more in her pouch.

"What sons-of-bitches are playing with us?" Shores's father shouted.

"It may not be—" Shores began, then saw Sklarinsky signaling. The hand signals said:

Mob approaching.

Her reply was:

Open fire. First burst low or high. If that doesn't stop them—

Sklarinsky could fill in the rest from her own training. Her pulser droned a short burst—five rounds, maybe, frangible rounds loaded with something tranquilizing or smelly, Shores didn't know which—and the mall was suddenly a lot quieter.

By then Esteva had given up trying to get through the flames, and he grabbed a fire extinguisher to put them out. Shores positioned Nieg to act as lookout and security for Sklarinsky, took a deep breath, and stepped out the door into the Mall.

A ground truck rolled out of the trees, stopped abruptly as the driver realized something wasn't normal, and went hastily into reverse. That distracted enough people in the mob to let Shores take a place and stance for negotiating—in front of a solid wall (the outer shutters were still jammed open), hands visible and empty (never mind all the concealed weapons), expression and body language curious rather than confrontational.

It also helped that most of the leaders and some of the rest seemed to recognize her. There were advantages to getting your face on the lunchtime mediacasts, at least if you faced opponents who ate lunch. . . .

Shores wondered if she was getting a whiff of the nonlethals, frowned, then took a deep breath. The lungful of smoke made her cough, but not enough to spoil the impression she was trying to make, of someone in command of herself and the situation.

"All right. I'm Candice Shores. What the Hades is going on here?"

A confused babble of voices finally gave way to a couple, shouting accusations.

"Renko cheats humans!"

"No, he lets his partner cheat them and takes the profit."

"He does worse. He lets his partner . . ." and the voice (it sounded androgynous, but Shores was ready to choke its owner on the spot regardless of sex) began the old litany of humans pandering to Ptercha'a sexual appetites.

Shores's hand flashed a signal. Sklarinsky's second burst, three rounds, left stains a meter to the right of the first set.

"Get the message?" Shores yelled.

The mob did. They opened the distance a good ten meters, and a few of the people carrying bags of stones or metal bars put them down before they moved. Two of the leaders had either more courage or less sense. They stayed put. A third actually walked toward Shores.

"I think—" he (it looked male) began, in a voice that wasn't one of the two earlier speakers'.

Then Jan Sklarinsky screamed "Down!" and fired a

burst off toward the left, into the trees. Before leaves and twigs started pattering, Shores was down. The leader stood gawping until she had rolled to within arm's length of him and snatched his feet out from under him.

Then sirens sounded, both on the ground and in the air. They might have sounded from the sewers, for all Shores knew. Certainly Administration police suddenly seemed to come from everywhere. Esteva shouted something that made Sklarinsky disappear, and Shores was left alone to welcome the police.

They'd got as far as exchanging ID's when Nieg came out, and Shores could not have been happier to see Marshal Banfi. Sklarinksy reappeared briefly; what she said brought a medical team on the run.

When the medics reappeared they had Renko's tech on a litter, with every kind of first-aid gear Shores recognized and some she didn't already hooked on, in, or up. The blanket was drawn up to the girl's burn-sprayed face, but not, praise the Creator, over it.

Nieg finally pulled himself away from briefing high-ranking police officers as a load of humans arrived, enough to take the rioters into custody. He handed her his portable and rearranged the soot on his forehead with an unsteady hand.

"As far as we can tell, somebody was set to play very rough indeed. The mob was whipped up or bought, I don't know which, to storm Renko's. Then the bomb was supposed to catch them."

Shores nodded. Either way, a mess. Just wrecking the shop alone would have made enough people angry for somebody to retaliate. Lynching Renko's partner could have meant blood-feud if he had tribal relatives, a circus of a trial if they were law-abiding.

And what would have happened if the shop had gone up, killing twenty or thirty humans who could be charged off as victims of Kitty-claw retaliation . . . ?

Shores decided that there were some thoughts humans were not meant to think.

"Did Jan spot their observer?" Shores asked.

"I expect so," Nieg replied. "But he'd already failed at part of his job. He thought we'd gone into the back, and was so eager to get us that he blew the bomb prematurely. All he hurt was the tech, and a couple of Pter-

cha'a out back pulled her out of the fire and gave her
first aid before they ran off. Juan and Jan have sworn to
that."

"Bless them." Shores badly wanted a shower and
something to replenish her adrenaline supply. It seemed
she couldn't go shopping without something happening
to deplete it!

Then her father stepped out of the shop, and froze in
mid-stride as he saw her. "Perfect, Candy! Hold that
position while I borrow Renko's camera!"

Shores had modeled just enough for her father to know
that if you so much as let a drop of sweat fall before he
wanted it, he might sulk or rage. He was *not* going to
make a public spectacle of himself here and now, even
if the only way to prevent that was her doing the same.

Renko at least could hurry his good customer along.
Nikolai Komarov practically flew out the door, then
aimed the camera, set intervals and number of expo-
sures, and danced all around his daughter while the camera recorded twenty different versions of her pose.

By the time he was done, only concern for Nieg's dignity kept Shores from collapsing on his shoulder. She
turned her head—and the knowledge that her father was
right chilled her.

The reflection in the window was only a ghost of the
soccer shot, with Nieg's portable in place of the trophy.
But everything else . . . yes, it all came together, how
her father had put stance and expression, the right foot
thrown slightly backward, the head even higher than
usual on the long neck.

Yes. The words rolled:

> Her hand was still on her sword-hilt, the spur was still
> on her heel,
> She had not cast her harness of gray, war-dinted steel.
> High on her red-splashed charger, beautiful, bold, and
> brown,
> Bright-eyed out of the battle, the Young Queen rode
> to be crowned.

Except that the Young Queen had come to do honor
to the Old Queen, and be honored in her turn. Where
was the Old Queen here on Linak'h? For that matter,
where was the honor?

Ten

Linak'h:

"Forward!"

The command came from a village chief, in the Thoori dialect, but Fomin zar Yayn understood it as clearly as the chief's Hunters. Many days, stretching from Father-rise to Father-set, with the levied cohorts had sharpened his ear for the tribal Hunters' dialects and his eye for their faults and virtues.

Besides, there was no way to go to carry out the exercise except forward, even though forward meant across a rushing stream at the bottom of a ravine thirty-some tails deep. Behind lay a supposed enemy, and an actual line of sixteen-Leaders from zar Yayn's Legion Six-Seven, as well as several more chiefs.

The vanguard of the levies bounded toward the stream, hooks swinging in their hands and ropes coiled about their waists. As they ran, they uncoiled the ropes and began swinging the hooks.

Tails short of the bank they stopped, swung their hooks until they blurred, then flung them toward branches on the far side. Five of the six hooks caught; four of the five held. Four vanguarders swung themselves across hand-over-hand, with the two unlucky ones and two others following after.

Those eight all carried battle rifles with generous loads of rounds; they vanished into the undergrowth as they took up defensive positions. The next eight who crossed carried only single-hands as personal weapons, but each pair carried a heavy rifle, its mount and sights, and a case of rounds for it.

They too vanished, as eight more came up, these carrying observation equipment. They did not vanish forward; instead they climbed trees as soon as they had crossed. Zar Yayn happened to know that higher trees farther west blocked the view from even the highest perch along the riverbank. It would be a test of the levies' modern war skills, how quickly they realized this and changed their plans.

Another sixteen crossed on the ropes, this one including two War Healers from the Legion. (Each of them spoke at least two tribal dialects, and one of them had tribal patterns in her fur. Zar Yayn wondered how far they really were from the tribal way of life.)

The next sixteen was escorting what at first glance seemed a mob of workmen abandoning a building site, and stealing the tools and materials into the bargain. In fact they were two sixteens of War Crafters, carrying the components for a foot bridge.

The escort was tribal, the Crafters Legion, and zar Yayn had his doubts about some of the looks the two sides were exchanging. No doubt each side had its proportion of rattlejaws, who said that the tribesmen were savages or the Crafters cowards. Zàr Yayn intended to put the band and sixteen-Leaders to work finding out who these were, and applying a little judicious punishment.

Whatever had been said, nothing was done to displease the Legion leader. The long members went across, slung from one set of ropes. The connectors went across on tribal backs, except for a few that rode with nimble-handed Crafters.

The village chief chose this moment to approach Zar Yayn. "Leader, those who have climbed the trees say they can see little. I have asked those of the vanguard to push forward until they have clear sight or find the enemy." He winked as he said the last word.

"But one in a flier rides higher than any treetop. I asked of my people, but none had the art of the far-speaker. Do you have farspeaker adepts you can send with my people, to call fliers for both seeing and slaying enemies beyond the reach of the weapons we carry?"

It seemed to zar Yayn that whoever had taught the chief the True Speech had taught him an almost archaic vocabulary and a range of deferential tones that would have been degrading for a non-tribal Hunter. Not for the first time, it struck him that True-Speech Hunters seemed to look at the tribesfolk rather as humans or Folk did at the Hunters as a whole.

He did not doubt that the Confraternity had the right of it, in seeking a better position for the Hunters. But this matter of the tribesfolk was definitely one that the Confraternity should address when it achieved power. To solve the problem would bring them honor and prolong their influence. To leave it unsolved would hand the honor and influence to whoever did solve it.

But the chief was waiting for an answer, which these musings had not given zar Yayn.

"You know that the farspeaker adepts must sometimes be guarded when they are practicing their arts?"

"Yes."

"Be sure that they are guarded by Thoori who are not as children, believing that the farspeakers will twist their unborn young or blind their eyes. Then they will do their work well."

"There are no such fools among the Thoori, Legion Leader. Do you think we have learned nothing in our travels from the shores of the lake?"

Zar Yayn's apologies were more elaborate than they might have been otherwise, if he had not realized that he had just done what he criticized in others. It was accursedly difficult to strike the right balance with the tribesfolk when they veered between great good sense and utter nonsense, like one of the Folk drunk in a storm!

With the chief satisfied, zar Yayn returned his attention to the bridge-building. Long members and connectors together had transformed themselves into a pair of girders. More connectors linked the girders, and floor plates went down atop the whole structure. In the time it took to eat a leisurely dinner, the bridge was ready to carry a sixteen of Hunters carrying any sort of warload.

Multiply the girders and flooring, and one quickly came to a bridge able to carry light ground vehicles. The exercise would not go that far today; there was no road on the far side of the stream and only a poor one on this side. Besides, the vehicle bridge needed no skills that the warriors had not shown today, only more work.

Zar Yayn allowed the warriors to assemble into their

sixteens and bands for counting and inspection, then ordered his chief of guards to pass the word:

"Break ranks and gather around me."

Two hundred Hunters jostled and pushed and sometimes deftly used their claws to gain position. Zar Yayn waited until all had found places without starting a riot, then climbed onto the driver's seat of a light ground-hauler.

"You have done well today. Do as well when the enemy is shooting at you, and the Hunters will have their ancient power. We do not need to fly or ride. We can walk to our chosen battlefield, and reach it before those who trust to machines."

The cheers came about as loudly from Legion as from tribal Hunters. If they had any secret quarrels, these did not dampen their enthusiasm for upholding the honor of their common race. Indeed, they seemed more enthusiastic about ground-stealth tactics than Zar Yayn was.

But then, his greater knowledge balanced his greater distance from the firing line. He knew how many of those now cheering might well die, and that he was not likely to be among them.

The whine of fans subdued the cheering. Zar Yayn's command flier was sliding in over the trees, the boarding ladder dangling from the belly hatch. The pilot waved from the primary command seat and performed one of those complex manipulations of thrust, lift, and steering that zar Yayn knew would be forever beyond him.

He was fast, strong, and skilled. But when he contemplated the skills of his flier pilot or the more advanced arts of his wife's brother, he understood something of what the tribesfolk felt when contemplating field-communications technicians. His head knew that pilots wielded no magic; his belly told him otherwise.

The ladder was half a tail above his head. Zar Yayn flexed his legs, leaped to the back of the ground-hauler's seat, then leaped again to catch the ladder. This started the cheering again, but the whine of the fans as the pilot climbed out quickly drowned it.

Enough showing off for the tribesfolk, he decided. He had promised them a feast as a reward for working hard at their training and not making brawls and scandals in the towns. So far they had earned it on both counts.

But when the feast was over, it was time to go back to spending more time with the Legion. Otherwise the Legion leaders assigned to the tribal cohorts would think he distrusted them, and the Legion would wonder if he was one of those city Hunters foolishly fond of the tribesfolk. That *would* mean brawls, in both camp and town, and his forces divided in the face of the enemy by the time the war actually started!

Linak'h:

"Candy, could you let me do one more sketch, you holding a sword?"

Candice Shores looked around her father's studio. It held an impressive amount of art supplies, half-completed projects in three or four different media, and odd bits of household equipment drafted into service. Nothing anywhere looked like a sword.

Then she looked at her watch. "I have to load and lift in half an hour, father. Will that be enough?"

"If that piece I carved for the Perseus hasn't been eaten by woodworms or stolen by kittens . . . Ah, there it is." Komarov pointed to a shadowy corner of the studio. "Candy, don't break pose yet. Sophia, can you get it?"

The older of Shores's two step-siblings hurried to obey her father. Peter, somewhat of a tagalong, followed. They returned holding as if in triumph the Greek-style wooden sword Shores recognized from the picture that had put her on the trail of her father.

She quickly learned that Federation standard sword drill and the model didn't go together. The balance was wrong, also the hilt and a few other things. Her father seemed to sense her growing frustration, and finally smiled.

"Try holding it up, hilt-first, as if you were offering it to the Old Queen," he said. "There were more things that you could do with a sword, in the days when people actually used them as weapons."

Shores frowned, and was tempted to correct her father. But the informal agreement still bound her: the veterans of the raid at Banfi's held their tongues about

Rose Liddell's actually skewering a terrorist with her dress sword.

It wasn't just fear of civilians or mediacrats getting hold of the story and blowing it up into something ludicrous, either. The Federation Forces could give any small town lessons in lethal gossip; nobody who respected the commodore wanted that tale to follow her all the rest of her career.

Shores shifted her grip on the sword, her father nodded, and she shifted until he declared that she was properly in pose. He did a quick sketch, applicator set to black-line mode and a board of whiteplast on his lap, then stood up.

"I wonder if you could bring your own dress sword the next time you come."

"If there is a next time," Shores said. "The Coordination is definitely getting their active units tuned up. We're doing the same with ours, and the Administration is at least checking their stockpiles."

"Is any of this secret?" Komarov looked bemused. "Should you be . . . ?"

"Nikolai," came a too-familiar voice from the studio door. "It's only what the media have been 'casting for the last week. Where have you been all that time?"

"Not planted in front of a screen, clearly," Komarov said. Shores could not see her stepmother, but her father could, and apparently saw something he did not like.

"Candy, could you take the children outdoors for a few minutes, if you have the time?" he asked.

With the atmosphere in the house, Shores would have made time (short of risking a court-martial) to rescue the children, even briefly. It seemed to her that they followed as gladly as she led.

In a minute they were all outside. The sky was a flawless dome, except for patches of clouds here and there. The clouds were white, and sun, sky, and cloud-hue added up to one thing: no rain today. None this week, either, if the meteorologists could tell a satellite picture from a plate of beans.

No rain this week. No rain for many weeks past. No rain for many weeks to come? Possibly, and the fire-hazard index in the high forest already at least in HIGH and sneaking toward CRITICAL.

At least the sky was quieter now. From above the faintly waving tips of the poncholeafs and titanhomes, nothing came except the distant whine of a lifter. No, a formation of them, but a good five kloms away.

Lifter-whines had largely replaced sonic booms, now that 222 Brigade and all its supplies and equipment were down. Even Camp Great Bend was down to routine movements, and the light attackers were working low and slow, patrolling suspected areas and cooperating with the ground-pounders. In the Zone shuttles still came and went, splitting the sky in their passing, but the Zone was a hundred kloms to the south.

Shores lay on her back in a patch of woolgrass, and inhaled its musky fragrance. It was horribly tempting to just fall asleep here, bathed in the warmth of both suns, ignoring staff conferences in the Zone and children here. . . .

"Ah, Candy . . ." in Russian.

It was Peter's voice, hesitant and piping. Sophia's replied, quickly and decisively.

"Mother told us to call her Colonel Shores."

"She said me call her Candy."

"I did?" Shores muttered. Then she sat up abruptly. "I did," she repeated, nodding. She refused to give Sophia any cause to call her brother a liar, let alone tell on him to her mother.

"Of course, I didn't know what your mother wanted when I talked to Peter," she added, trying to place a veil of truth over the lie. "Maybe it would be better if I talked to her first?"

"She doesn't like talking to you," Sophia said. It was impossible to tell if she approved or not.

"I want her talk you," Peter said. "You nice."

"Maybe she doesn't think so," Shores said. "You see, your mother wants you and your father and she all to be happy together. She's afraid I might do something to make your father unhappy."

"Then she's wrong," Sophia said firmly. "Peter's right. You're nice. Nice people don't do things like that."

Oh, to be able to take a child's view of the world again, Shores thought. Then she amended the thought: *a child sheltered from a lot of things, including the Hades her mother must have gone through on the way to her present happy domesticity.*

Was that the threat she represented to Ursula Boll, Shores wondered? Breaking down the wall that the woman had built for herself and the children against the nightmares of the past (and now the future)? Demolishing the pretense that she, Nikolai, and the children were a happy brood apart from all the troubles of this or any other world?

Maybe, or maybe she was just speculating far ahead of her data. Meanwhile, there were two children who apparently thought better of her than their mother did and wanted something from her. *Answer them first, Candy, then go back to guessing games.*

"I like to think that I'm a nice person," Shores said. "Was there something in particular you wanted me to do?"

They nodded in unison. "Fly us," Peter said.

"Take you flying?" Shores asked.

Again they both nodded. Shores lay back down and stared at the sky without seeing anything until a light attacker scrawled a vapor trail high overhead.

Joy-riding in service vehicles was out. Everybody up the chain of command as far as Longman disapproved of it. Most had issued some sort of order on it, if not one with bared teeth like Longman's edicts.

For that matter, Shores disapproved of joy-riding, although it hadn't been much of a problem in the QRF. They had a high vehicle-per-trooper ratio, and an even higher mission-per-vehicle load. Which meant she hadn't issued any orders on joy-riding—but couldn't scare up a QRF lifter to take the kids flying without setting the bad example that would make such orders necessary.

Forget borrowing one from another unit; none of them owed her or her force enough. But a civilian lifter . . . There were some available. Expensive (refugees now preferred the air route into the Zone) but what else did she have to spend money on? Not a lot.

What about security? Well, there were those convoys of supplies they were running to the refugee camp. The convoys and the heavy escorts might not be necessary, but they gave the 222 Brigade pilots a taste of local flying conditions. They also proved that Linak'h Command was taking no chances.

Plug a rented lifter into the convoy, and she could follow it out here with Fed firepower packed all around her. On the way, she could get some idea of how one of the convoys looked from a civilian point of view. Once out here, she could take the kids for a hop while the convoy unloaded and the escorts flew a terrain-familiarization mission. Then home, "and so to bed," which would be a very quiet place that night; it was going to be a long day.

She only hoped she could fit it in before the shooting started.

Shores sat up. "I won't promise when I'll do it, because I can't know now. All the military lifters are being used to move soldiers and equipment around so they'll be in the right place. Also soldiers have to eat, drink, take baths, even go to school."

"Ugh," Sophia said. "I don't think I want to be a soldier."

"It's not a job for everybody," Shores said. "But all this means that my lifters are busy. I will have to rent one in Och'zem and come out here. I also have to ask your parents if it will be all right, even before I rent the lifter."

"I'm sure Papa won't mind," Sophia said.

Temptation, get thee behind me. It was becoming moderately obvious which parent the children preferred. It was abundantly clear how easily she could bribe her father by pleasing the kids and not consulting with Ursula. It was certain what would come of that: all Hades let out for lunch.

Sorry, Ursula Boll. I won't live down to your opinion of me.

"If your parents are through talking, we can go ask them now," Shores said. She looked at her watch. "Then I'll have to say good-bye for today."

The parents' talk had ended in a chilly silence that said a great deal to Shores. The children either didn't notice or were used to it. She hoped it was the former.

The good-byes were polite but perfunctory. That wasn't to her father's taste; Shores had learned that much. As she climbed into the lifter, she wished she could also discover what was ailing her stepmother.

One thing: It was beginning to smell like more than just jealousy of a husband's previous family. Nieg the lifelong bachelor was about as useful on that as he was

on brigade tactics; was there anyone else more knowledgeable, and as discreet?

She nodded to Warrant Officer Konishi, who was fin-
ishing the visual scan of the pad.

"Let's head for home."

Aboard Baernoi merchanter *Perfumed Wind*, off Linak'h:

Brokeh su-Irzim nearly had to run to keep up with Behdan Zeg. The Special Projects commander was shorter
in height but longer of limb, in better condition, and in
a rage as well.

Su-Irzim did not care to contemplate the consequences
of his falling behind in the race. Zeg looked ready to do
more than confront Commander ihr Sular; he looked
ready to assault her.

Su-Irzim also did not know which Lord to pray to, for
the wits and strength needed to avoid such a catastrophe.
The situation lacked dignity—so greatly, perhaps, that the
Lords had washed their hands and tusks alike of it.

The two Inquirers arrived at ihr Sular's cabin door almost together. The door was unguarded but closed; Zeg's
lunge at the opener proved that it was command-locked
from within as well.

"Who goes there?" came the voice from the speaker
above the door. At the same time the telltale light of the
visual scanner came on.

Su-Irzim adopted a placating pose and stood still. Zeg
had to be given a chance to open the discussion, if only
to save his pride. Otherwise Su-Irzim's influence today,
and his ability to work with Zeg in the future, might be
as cargo cast into deep space, lost to everything save
memory.

"Behdan Zeg, with a complaint about our cargo."

"So be it. You have come to the right place. Enter
and be welcome." The words were formally polite. The tone
suggested that she was quite ready to set drug-maddened
Hunters on them the moment they entered the cabin.

The Inquirers would have marched in together, if the
door had been wide enough. Instead they nearly jammed

on the way. Su-Irzim broke free first, stepped forward
in the knowledge of a blazing glare directed at his back,
and turned to usher Zeg forward like a servant presenting
his master.

"Commander Zeg asks justice, or at least knowledge,"
su-Irzim added. "I join in his petition." Then he assumed
the stance of a bodyguard watching his master in a dangerous situation, eyes roaming from F'Mita ihr Sular
around her cabin to the door and back to her by way of
Zeg's stiff back.

The diplomacy succeeded to this extent: Zeg did not
at once insult ihr Sular. He described how the Inquirers
had come up to inspect the newly transferred shipment,
in preparation for loading it aboard shuttles for the final
leg of its journey. All appeared to be in order, except
that one container showed signs of opening. One crate
within had definitely been opened, and others showed
signs of tampering or at least irregular movement.

"Which container?" ihr Sular said.

Zeg's mouth opened several times. Su-Irzim kept his
tightly closed, partly to hold in laughter. Zeg's memory
was as good as his, but being treated as he was used to
treating others sometimes froze Zeg's tongue. Su-Irzim,
however, knew that his answering ihr Sular would annoy
Zeg, to say the least.

"Blue-Green Fifty-one," Zeg said.

Ihr Sular surprised them both by laughing softly. "Oh,
Lords. Forgive me, both of you. It never occurred to me
that you would suspect the worst. But it is no shame to
you that you did.

"Only . . . the matter could have been settled with a
call from the hold. The next time—"

"Please tell us what the matter is, before you judge it
easily settled," Zeg finished. By his usual standards this
was almost groveling.

"Easy. We transshipped the load from *Stormrider* with
their crew and equipment. Most of my own people are
still on Linak'h, by the way."

"So we judged," su-Irzim said. "We did not quite trust
the security of the ship communications, and there was
no one on-duty in the hold."

"There are ample security devices to keep anyone unauthorized from the cargo, I assure you," ihr Sular said.

"If you had not been identified, we would now be flushing Kawde gas out of your lungs—or perhaps refusing to do so until you confessed."

The idea of that particular death made even Zeg's ears twitch. "Do you wish to say that you felt a need to broach the cargo?" he said. "Is your crew in need of weapons?"

"Now that you mention it, I might well ask for sidearms and field-medical packs all around, at least. But you may have been in too much haste to note that nothing was removed. We merely scanned the containers, saw that the scan showed items not on the manifests, and did a little discreet physical examining.

"I appreciate that this was unauthorized, and that it gave you . . . caused you some surprise," she went on. "But I could not communicate with the ground without risk of a security breach. I do not trust the Governor, if I may speak plainly. Also, the Federation's electronic monitoring of all non-Federation ships has increased greatly since Fleet Commander Longman arrived."

Zeg and su-Irzim looked at each other, this time colleagues jointly entrusted with a secret: the Governor's trying to join the game. Then Zeg's look said:
Shall we tell her?
Su-Irzim's expression replied:
Not right now.
Su-Irzim nodded. "You feared for your ship's safety, if Special Projects was smuggling something dangerous onto Linak'h?"

"You were at Victoria, Ship Commander," she challenged him. "Would it not have been less bloody for all, and no less profitable to the People, without the sunbombs?"

Zeg looked at the walls, so obviously afraid of being overheard that again su-Irzim held in laughter. Very briefly, because sunbombs had not been nor ever would be a matter for jesting. In the hands of people as witless as the Victorian rebels or Linak'h terrorists, they were a thing to make any Lawbound weep, pray, or perhaps do both.

"I think we have groped our way to peace and even some wisdom," su-Irzim said. "Shall we celebrate with some beer?"

"Most of the beer aboard went down with my crew," ihr Sular said. "I have a bottle of uys, but I would rather broach it after we discuss how to get those curious con-

tainers off my ship and into the hands of whoever they
are intended for."

The simple scheme of shuttle flights, it appeared,
would not be quite the right approach now. Ihr Sular
called up display of the new Federation deployments and
su-Irzim had to admit that it was persuasive.

Fleet Commander Longman had brought not only her
flagship *Roma* but two heavy cruisers, *Drashpil* and
Kyros, more powerful than the four Coordination ones,
a base ship loaded with containerized supplies and engineering equipment (being busily transferred to less vulnerable ships or the ground), and the equivalent of a
squadron of scouts, courier ships, and vessels that had
begun as light cruisers but might now be who knew what!

She had also arranged these ships cunningly. No un-
protected shuttle or transport moved without an escort
of at least one cruiser or the equivalent plus heavy attackers. No non-Federation ship could be free of sensor
surveillance for more than a tenth-watch, if that long.
(Unless she altered her orbit, and that itself would draw
Federation attention.)

For now, she seemed to be sacrificing ability to detect
ground action and support ground forces to keeping the
situation in space under her hand. Su-Irzim did not quarrel
with these priorities; they would have been his in her place.

As he had more recent experience of Fleet duty, su-
Irzim pointed out to Zeg some of the fine details that
showed Longman's mastery of tactics. Zeg finally came
as close to laughter as he ever did.

"Grant that Fleet Commander Longman passes jewels
and fine uys, and let us return to the original problem.
Those ground-fighter supplies do no one any good here
aboard *Perfumed Wind.*"

"I have a suggestion," su-Irzim said. "It may require
recalling some of your crew, Commander. . . ."

"If their travels are secret and they can draw arms and
equipment from this shipment, I will recall them. Your
plan needs extra hands, I presume?"

"And feet, and tusks, and if they can work with their
tails . . ."

"Enough. I will listen. I do not promise more."

Su-Irzim put from his mind the thought that he was in
his second year of Child's School, and the teacher

doubted his reasons for being late three days in a row. It helped that his plan took only a few sentences.

Dock *Perfumed Wind* with the People's base ship, as if she needed repairs. Even perhaps put that story about. Then the recall of the crew would be only logical. So would a long stay docked with the base ship, during which the cargo could be transferred with none the wiser.

Shuttle flights to and from the base ship had already become more frequent. Now the Federation would not complain if they were increased further. The People would plead security, and hint that it was not the Federation they feared (which was not so far from the truth, for now).

If the Federation did not wish the hostility of the People adding to the confusion off Linak'h, they would allow the shuttles to fly freely. Then the weapons could land in what would seem a normal routine, while *Perfumed Wind* lay off, under no suspicion and free to move.

"I approve," ihr Sular said. "But will the Governor?"

"We can give him reasons for approving," Zeg said. He did not quite bare tusks, but his body was stiff with ill-concealed anger.

"This will mean delay, at a time when days count," he added. "But I suppose the Federation will delay us more if they learn of the weapons."

That was true in all points. It would be a wonder if more than a thousand or so Ptercha'a were fit for any sort of battle by the time the ultimatum expired. It would be that many only if Zeg and his gang had been careful to choose former ground-fighters, or at least active members of village Warbands.

But more could be done with the weapons on the ground than with them in space. Nothing at all could be done if the Federation detected them and saw in them cause to closely watch all the People's actions even in their own Territory.

"I approve," ihr Sular said. She tapped her desk and a drawer slid open. "I believe we can now broach the uys, and settle the schedule over a drink."

Eleven

Linak'h:

"Ready on the left!"

"Ready on the right!"

The range officer followed these ancient commands from the range NCO's with an equally ancient one of his own.

"Commence firing!"

Candice Shores watched as the first firer from QRF HQ, Juan Esteva, leaped into the first position. Ten rounds each from the standing/shoulder, sitting, and prone positions, then ten rounds marching-fire and ten more position-optional. The perfect score was 500; the record for the range was 488, set a few years back by a platoon sergeant from the Linak'h Battalion.

Juan's pulser droned off the ten shoulder rounds; he vanished across the range to the sitting-fire point. The next trooper marched up to the point, waited until Juan's score flashed over the target and the light turned green, then snapped her piece up to firing position and went to work.

The range officer didn't seem bothered by having a light colonel looking over his shoulder as she waited her turn. But then, with Linak'h's being turned into a Theater, its population of Federation Forces people had gone from five thousand to nearly twenty thousand, if you counted activated Reservists. Lieutenant colonels were no longer something you could count on the fingers of two hands.

Esther Timberlake seemed to have more of the range officer's attention, but that went with being a sergeant major. Eppie didn't confuse herself with the Deity, but she didn't stop anybody else (particularly young officers) from doing so.

And Jan Sklarinsky was even a step beyond Timberlake, in having the range officer's attention. Any sniper would do that; female snipers could do it a little more easily. A female sniper who'd added to her kill count since hitting Linak'h did it just by being alive and breathing.

The HQ people flowed down and out of sight, the pulsers droned, and the scores came up. So far Esteva was shooting the highest score, but Havighurst was hanging in only a few points behind the sergeant, even if neither was a threat to the record.

Then a shout in True Speech and several more in Commercial Merishi drowned out the pulsers. Timberlake moved to where the range officer could see her and hand-signaled for permission to step out of sequence. The officer nodded, without taking his eyes off the range.

With the officer alerted, Shores and Timberlake were free to turn and face the new situation. Two platoon-sized units, one human and one Ptercha'a, were facing each other on the path to the firing line. The Ptercha'a were still shouting in Commercial Merishi, except for a few who were using True Speech (and not politely, Shores could tell).

The humans looked even less disciplined, except that they all wore Linak'h Command shoulder flashes on their motley upper garments and carried standard pulsers. Most of them were standing stolidly under the verbal abuse from the Ptercha'a, but a few weatherbeaten faces were turning into grim masks.

Shores stalked, Timberlake marched. Both received the new arrivals' undivided attention at they approached.

"What is this—besides a violation of range-safety rules?" Timberlake asked. "One group in line at a time, you know."

The answers came from a dozen throats in three languages, and needed more than translation. They needed, finally, a good sergeant major's bellow to bring silence and then sense.

Some people didn't know the rules (chalk up one point against the CO of whatever Reserve outfit the humans came from). Others knew, but each side thought their group was first.

By now Esteva had finished his firing. He came over from the far end of the range, took one look at the situation, and ran up to Shores.

"Anything I can do here, Colonel?"

"Damned right," Shores said. "Chase up the range CO and NCO, ten minutes ago. If you can't find them, you're authorized from me to call up the range HQ and pull a list of today's schedule. One of these groups has to be first."

Juan reached for the HQ com pack, but Timberlake shook her head. "Try for a secure phone first." Shores nodded.

"Can do." He looked over the two groups, then managed to point without anybody but Shores seeing him. "Those two Ptercha'a at the end of their line. The man and woman?"

Shores nodded.

"I think they're the two Jan and I saw out behind Renko's, giving the tech first-aid."

Which had saved her life, even if she was going to be in the hospital until well after the ultimatum expired. Shores mentally noted the two Ptercha'a as ones to appeal to in a crisis.

"No harm if they are. Now launch!"

Esteva disappeared. Shores turned to the new arrivals. "Now, who are you?"

"Second Platoon, K Company, Linak'h Security Battalion," the leader of the humans said. Shores counted only nineteen bodies, a very short platoon indeed, but then she'd never heard of the battalion's K Company either. A couple of faces were vaguely familiar, though, and one was more than vaguely so—Sandy Brandstetter's.

"All right," Shores said, then switched to True Speech. She still couldn't manage more than a few polite phrases in it, but she could understand somewhat more.

She also saw familiar faces among the Ptercha'a. The man and woman Esteva had pointed out were standing in the rear of the Ptercha'a line—twenty-three Hunters, as Shores counted them. They didn't look at all concerned about possibly being recognized, but that might be just her unfamiliarity with Ptercha'a body language.

Nonetheless, a couple of things she knew added up to a sum she didn't like. Renko's, according to Nieg, was a known Confraternity center, possibly even a safe house and arms dealer. Shores's father shopping there for refugees wasn't a problem; half of the Ptercha'a refugees seemed to be open Confraternity sympathizers.

But Ptercha'a who'd been there the day of the bomb . . . that could be a problem, no matter which side they were on. The terrs certainly had some Hunters working for them, but from their reported behavior, the two Ptercha'a were probably Confraternity supporters coming from some business that the bomb interrupted.

"We are the fifth sixteen plus other fours, from the Tenth Band, Third Cohort, Legion Eight-Two," the Ptercha'a leader said. "We are allowed the use of this range by long custom."

The leader was gray-muzzled, his fur bleached by many years outdoors. Most of the rest were city Ptercha'a, and some of them looked as if they were holding a weapon for the first time.

"An honorable Warband," Shores said. She switched back to Anglic. "All right. Everybody ground arms and relax. There's not room for both of you on the range at the same time, so I'm kicking the issue over to the people in charge."

"Why not alternate us?" one of the Ptercha'a said. That drew what was unmistakably a glare from the male of the mystery pair. It drew worse from the humans.

"No way we're going to let the pussies on the same range with us!" was the way it began, and it got quickly worse from there.

Or at least it would have, if Shores and Timberlake hadn't stepped down between the two groups. Nobody was quite ready to start throwing stones or punches with them in the path. The two women inspired uncomfortable thoughts of what might happen to the guilty parties.

They moved the two parties far enough off the path for a safe distance between them, not so far that either was in the thornbrush or rocks. A few people with canteens had just started passing them around when Esteva returned.

"Colonel, can we step aside?"

Shores followed Esteva back up onto the range, where

the range officer was trying to hide his being out of his depth by doublechecking the scores of the completed shoots. "All right, Juan?" she said. "What is it?"

"The CO is off-post. I got the XO, who said that the Ptercha'a are supposed to be first. But"—and here he whispered—"he also said he doesn't think their outfit really exists."

"Confraternity militia trying to sneak in training and a look at the range?"

"Could be. I've also heard something about the XO. He was tight with Goerke."

"This is going to be a fun day, I can see that right now." Goerke the Ptercha'a-hater, now dead to the great benefit of Linak'h Command. But his coterie of appointees lived on after him, and most of the ones Shores had met so far seemed to share their late mentor's prejudices.

It began to look as if today was one for confrontation. The only question was, who would confront whom?

Aboard U.F.S. *Shenandoah*, off Linak'h:

"We will want two escort forces," Admiral Longman said, tapping a display control. "I think we should make a rule that we only have one of them out at any time, but we should have two organized."

The display showed something more dramatic than just a list of names. It showed three—no, four—cruisers and several lighter ships in formation with what looked like eight merchanters. A realistic starscape flowed behind them.

Longman's penchant for doing conferences and briefings with elaborate visual simulations used up computer capacity, but *Roma* had even more than *Shen*—as much as many whole semi-industrial planets. Otherwise it did no harm that Liddell had discovered so far.

Would that all of the Golden Vanity's vices were so petty.

"Suggestions for names?"

They tossed captains and ships back and forth for ten minutes, ending with TO's of two escort forces, each with one heavy cruiser, three light cruisers, and two scouts. Liddell flatly refused to let Moneghan out of her sight, and for less positive reasons was unhappy about giving Bronstein and scout *Powell* an escort role.

"Is there anything against him, other than what Commander Franke said?" Longman inquired.

"Gordon Uhlig supports Frank's story."

"Uhlig is a *Shen* officer," Longman said. "He also knows about Franke's connection with the Kishi Institute and his affiliation with Major Morley."

Liddell didn't question the facts, only the interpretation. Herman Franke's various connections were public knowledge. Implying that they might have influenced Uhlig to give false testimony—to violate one of the basic points of his commissioning oath. . . .

But Longman had already implied that too much loyalty to *Shen* people was suspect. The admiral wouldn't do more than harass about it, spare commodores being rare off Linak'h, but that could sour the whole atmosphere in Linak'h Command even if the Army didn't take sides.

"All right," Longman concluded. "We'll strip out extra crew from the unloaded transports and organize the convoy in the next thirty hours. You have the cadre for the naval ground party already in place?"

If Longman had been properly briefed, she would have known that the ground party had been down and at work in time to support the original raid along the Braigh'n River that had led to the present crisis. Brigitte Tachin, for example, had been aboard *Shen* for only eight days since the battlecruiser hit Linak'h orbit. (Weapons Department had been heard to complain of this. Brian Mahoney might be even less happy.)

Longman's staff couldn't be spending all their time scarfing up entertainment supplies and reading light fiction. The detailed and polished plan for the redeployment showed that. Maybe they were just playing to their admiral's virtues, like her tactical sense, and not trying to correct her vices, such as lack of tact (which might in any case require Divine intervention, not staff assistance).

"The ground party is up to the strength the Army asked for," Liddell said.

The ploy of forcing Longman to confront Tanz failed.

"Fine, we don't need to assign the people straight off. I'm sure there's plenty of work to be done in the Zone."

There was also plenty of work to be done back on Riftwell and the other Eleventh Fleet bases. Schatz might have plans for some of the two or three hundred transport crew people Longman was planning on appropriating.

Not that this wasn't a standard procedure in crises, even ones less serious than Linak'h. Send out a transport with a full crew, reassign most of them as a unit to whatever jobs needed doing at the crisis point, escort the skeleton-crewed transport to the Jump point, and let it repeat the process until the crisis was over or all the Navy people needed had been moved without taking up billets needed for ground-pounders.

Longman even had the rank to do this, and discretionary orders from Schatz *and* the Empress. But neither had given her the sense to realize that Schatz might like to be consulted before she embarked on a wholesale stripping of his transport crews for the benefit of Linak'h Command.

"We can courier a message to Riftwell while we're putting the escort groups together," Liddell suggested. "The one with the convoy will need at least a day of working up."

"If they do, then somebody hasn't been training them properly," Longman said. "Or can't you read a discretionary order?"

Liddell took a deep breath before replying. "I don't remember seeing that the transports were regarded as expendable. Sending them back with skeleton crews is the same thing as temporarily expending them."

"There is no such thing as 'temporarily expending,'" Longman said, with the precision and finality of a Baernoi war-axe lopping a head.

"Aye-aye, Admiral," Liddell said. "Are you planning on sending *Somtow Nosavan* with the convoy, by the way?"

"She's going back to Victoria, Lord knows what for," Longman said. "Some of their dustball politics, I suppose."

"Dustball politics" was not the phrase Liddell would have applied to the Victorian plan to send a Civil Action Group to Linak'h. (Or at least that was the rumor; she could probably confirm or deny it through Herman

Franke, but he had enough on his plate already.) She would have called it clever statesmanship by Jeremiah Gist, and both moral and physical courage on the part of the Victorians who actually came out.

Liddell resolved that if it cost her her commission, she would not let Longman jerk any Victorian volunteers around the way she did Federation forces. If necessary, she would see that they wound up under Administration command. After hearing a few of the horror tales about the Golden Vanity, any sensible human would rather be commanded by Ptercha'a than by her.

"It could be," Liddell said. "But she can ride with the convoy as far as the Jump point. Even Jump first, if the convoy's being trailed."

"Why escort her at all?"

"I think we have a choice between not sending her home or escorting her. If she sails unescorted and doesn't arrive, we'll never know what happened to her. But the Victorians will blame us, I won't blame them, and it won't improve our relations with the Merishi."

Longman's "I don't follow you" expression seemed to be genuine, so Liddell went on. "We don't know if the Merishi behind the hijacking represent anybody but one faction in Space Security. But that faction still has ships. It may have a second Queen Bee in the Linak'h system.

"It certainly has a score to settle with the crew of *Nosavan*. They turned a planned massacre of Peregrine emigrants into a major intelligence coup for the Federation. Under those circumstances, *I'd* want somebody's head on a platter."

"Was the intelligence all that critical?" Longman asked. Liddell heard genuine curiosity in her voice, raised her opinion of the admiral, and revised still further downward that of the admiral's staff. "We had to release the Merishi, I know. Did the refugees make up for that?"

"Add it to what we learned or guessed on Victoria, yes."

Longman grimaced. "You don't need to remind me that I'm not an old Victoria hand, Commodore."

"Sorry. But they must have sorted the data from the mercenaries' interrogation by now. And there were all our action reports."

"I've got the reports right here," Longman said. "I

even read them. But I drew a blank on the mercenaries'
interrogations. So did Schatz.''

This time it was Liddell's turn to have a "run that past
me again" expression. "They said it could not be ac-
cessed in the time available before my departure.''

"They?"

"The Deputy Chief of Staff for Intelligence and his
people.''

That particular deputy was one of Phoumi Batsirvan's
people, appointed without protest from Liddell because
he knew his job. Did that job include things Liddell
hadn't guessed? Or would it have, if Batsirvan had succeeded in coming out here in Longman's place?

Liddell had heard rumors about intelligence from Victoria falling into black holes. It now began to seem more
than a rumor.

Best check with Herman Franke before she planned
any countermoves. He might know what was missing,
and how. His Kishi Institute connections could also out-
flank any Forces obstacles. Question: Would he be willing to risk Lu Morley's career by using them? (Anyone
more immune to FADS than Commander Franke, Liddell could not imagine. A risk of getting your affiliate
court-martialed posed a harder ethical question for even
the least ambitious.)

Answer: Ask Herman Franke and find out.

Meanwhile, in the matter of buying off Longman, she
was a mass of prejudices. Play on some of the more
potent ones, such as her nephew.

"There's another reason for having *Nosavan* escorted,
too. If Marder goes back, or Charlie loses his nerve . . .''

"My nephew's no coward. He hasn't enough sense to
be afraid.''

That was the biggest piece of garbage about Charlie
that Liddell had yet heard from Aunt Di, but she would
let it pass like the rest. "Nonetheless, I think *Nosavan*
ought to be guarded while she's in the Linak'h system.
We can also put a security party aboard, with enough
watchstanders to run the ship if necessary.''

"Can *Shen* provide it?"

Liddell had been thinking that some of the transport
crews scheduled for kidnapping as ground party could
ship out aboard *Nosavan*. There was undoubtedly work

on Victoria for them. But Longman was going to be territorial about the transport crews, and the best Liddell
could do was stay out of the inevitable fight with John
Schatz. (He didn't need her help, anyway. Only months
from retirement, he had nothing to lose by squashing the
Golden Vanity into a small yellow stain on his reception-
room rug, if it came to that.)

"All right. I'll come up with eight people, four watchstanders and four security. That's *Shen*'s limit, with the
people we've already sent dirtside."

"I'm sure I can find a few people eager to make a trip
to beautiful, scenic Victoria and sample its bracing cli-
mate. What about throwing in one of my intelligence
people too? I understand your Commander Franke is
persona non grata on Victoria."

He's also indispensable here, but let's be polite. "That's
one way of putting it. Let's just say that it will help if
any Intelligence people we send to Victoria aren't on
anybody's little lists."

"Fine." Longman leaned back in her chair; the rigid
formality went out of her body so completely that Liddell
expected to see her glossy-booted feet on the desk. "*Shenandoah* Crew List for Commodore Liddell, please," she told
the computer.

It struck Liddell that she had yet to hear Admiral
Longman address any organic intelligence so politely.

Linak'h:

To Candice Shores, the people who seemed to be the
most alert were Sandy Brandstetter and the two Ptercha'a from Renko's. But Sandy didn't like "Kitties" and
the Ptercha'a were not improbably Confraternity. Alertness didn't preclude dangerous bias; in fact, it might result from it.

*Oh, for a nice quiet garrison posting, on an all-human
planet ninety light-years from Linak'h.*

Shores returned to her previous place and faced the
two platoons. "There seems to be some doubt about the
authorization of both platoons for slots in today's schedule," she said.

Some of both races looked indignant at being called liars. Others grinned in triumph, willing to see Kitties, or whatever the Ptercha'a called humans when they wanted to be insulting, embarrassed.

Nobody showed any signs of reaching for a weapon, although Shores would put a large bet on Jan Sklarinsky's hiding someplace where she could drop any hothead before they did damage. (And a larger bet on her not having consulted the range officer either; tact with officers she did not know was an art Jan had yet to master.)

Well, Shores hadn't consulted the range officer either, but that was only just; what he didn't know about in advance, he couldn't be punished for allowing. At least not without more stench and scandal than Linak'h Command could very well afford.

"However, it also wouldn't be fair to stand on regulations, and make all of you waste your trip today. I know that some of you must have left work behind, and I don't know when you'll have another chance. In another few weeks, you may be shooting for real."

She pulled out a ten-stellar vendor card. "Here's a card. I'll flip it. Logo the Ptercha'a go first, value the Reserves get first shot."

The hot breeze caught the card as Shores flipped it, and both platoons had to crowd backward to give it room to fall. Esteva knelt by it, to keep the curious back until Shores arrived.

"Logo!" she called. "Fifth sixteen, front and center. Do you know the range-safety regulations?" She realized she should have asked that first; getting somebody's head punched off their shoulders was carrying the non-humiliation of Ptercha'a a little far.

She also realized that, like Macbeth, she was in too far to go back, but hopefully in a better cause. (Nieg as Lady Macbeth? No, he would never tolerate someone close to him as reluctant as Shakespeare's brave but bumbling Scotsman; if she ever had a chance at a throne she would be expected to either usurp it at once or stay loyal.)

The gray-muzzle recited the Ptercha'a Warband regulations while the suspected Confraternity woman translated them deftly into Anglic. Weapons being approximately the same for both races, one set of regulations would save about as many lives as the other.

Shores then recited the Federation Army range-safety regulations (the twelve-point short version), while the woman translated back into True Speech. Meanwhile, her companion and Eppie Timberlake had their heads together, recording the Ptercha'a scoring system and transmitting it to the computers of the targets.

Five minutes was all Shores dared allow. Some of the humans were already muttering things it would not help if the Ptercha'a understood.

The Ptercha'a lined up, their lead man unslung his weapon, and the range officer looked at the sky, then called:

"Ready on the left!"

Jan Sklarinsky's voice came back:

"Ready on the right!"

The range officer looked at Shores. She cupped her hands and shouted:

"Commence firing!"

The lead Ptercha'a vanished, as silently and swiftly as a dust mote whipped away by the wind. Moments later they heard his battle rifle ripping into the target.

Shores led her command group away from the platoons, leaving the range officer in charge of work he could handle. "Eppie, divide our people and make sure that we've got two, four if possible, at every point where these two gangs"—she flicked a glance at the platoons— "might bump."

"Will do. We've got a few who don't much like Ptercha'a, too."

"Try to keep them down to one on each team. Unless they're really hot for blood." Timberlake shook her head. "Good. Anybody who ruffles Ptercha'a fur today is going to be hung out to dry.

"Juan, Quick-sneak back to the command lifter, and use my authority to ring up the Eight-Two Legion. Ask them for the TO&E of their Third Cohort. Max communications security."

Esteva grinned. He didn't think much about Ptercha'a, one way or another, although Jan's active like of them was tipping him in their favor. He absolutely loathed Goerke's memory, and the chance to sink the toe of his boot into the arse of one of Goerke's survivors was too appealing to miss.

"Don't look so damned happy, Esteva," Timberlake muttered. "It just could be that our furry friends here really are lying."

Esteva went off down the hill toward the lifter pad with a more sober expression on his face.

Twelve

Charlemagne:

Admiral Kuwahara looked over the letter to his son and said, "Edit"—quietly, so as not to disturb Fumiko in the bed on the far side of the room. If he woke her up she would be irritable twice over, once for his waking her up and a second time for his not moving to the study and using the terminal there.

Write it off to his wits and her temper both being affected by the hours he was working and the general flow of dubious news from Linak'h. *Don't* use either as an excuse for shortchanging Yaso—who was a long way not only from Charlemagne but from a safe port, if the Linak'h crisis did flare up into a Second Merishi War.

Kuwahara scanned the letter and finally deleted only one sentence. "I hope the orphans aren't learning snobbery too early." The request for genuine Charlemagne products for the donation *Sagami Maru* was making to the orphanage on Cuchulain sounded ominous and would be expensive, but it probably wasn't the childrens' idea.

Then he added:

> Your mother and I will be going shopping in the next few days anyway, probably most of it hands-on. (Your sister is going back to school, and says she has nothing to wear except bathing suits and ski outfits.) We can certainly arrange for most of what is on your list and have it shipped out as expeditiously as possible.

> Do not, however, expect expensive miracles of promptness so that you can impress the rest of *Sagami Maru*'s wardroom. You appear sometimes to believe

that your refusing an allowance (quite honorable then
and now) has left your parents with more money than
we can honestly spend. Please reconsider that opinion.

Also, be prepared for a long wait or even the loss
of the shipment, if this political carbuncle on Linak'h
becomes inflamed enough to infect interstellar shipping in general. A reliable team of surgeons (including
Commodore Liddell) is on hand, so we should be able
to prevent a dangerous situation, but Murphy governs
politics and war as well as engineering.

> With affectionate regards,
> Father

The letter would be electronic all the way to *Sagami
Maru,* a matter of some four hundred light-years at last
report, so there was no need to run the printer. Kuwahara added the necessary priorities and codes and was
about to order "Transmit" when the PRIORITY signal interrupted him.

He split the screen, then kicked the letter clear off it
when he saw that it was Captain Ropuski calling. She
had taken over the second watch at the study group three
weeks ago, although watches had become a nearly mean-
ingless concept; most of the senior officers were putting
in seventy- and eighty-hour weeks.

"Admiral, we have trouble with one of our people.
Chief Krazinkow was attacked tonight, on the way home.
I've got Lieutenant Pfalz, of the District Violent Crimes
Division, on another secure line."

"Connect," Kuwahara said. Julie Krazinkow seemed
an unlikely victim for any sort of violence, but of course
Pfalz would tell him immediately that there was no such
thing as a "victim type."

The screen split, and a wiry lieutenant of the Federal
District Police appeared on the lower half. "Good evening, Admiral. I'm sorry to meet you under circumstances like this. Fortunately your people aren't too badly
hurt."

"People?"

"Warrant Yeoman Krazinkow had a male companion,

a Chief Weapons Technician Deere. Isn't he assigned to the same . . . project . . . as Ms. Krazinkow?"

"No," Kuwahara said shortly. "Could you feed me the full report, let me read it, and then we can discuss it?"

"Coming up, Admiral," Pfalz said. The printer whined softly, but loud enough to wake up Fumiko. She stuck her head out from under the blankets, followed the head with a bare arm, and made a rude gesture in the general direction of both the screen and her husband. Then she disappeared again under the blankets.

Kuwahara skimmed the report. Krazinkow and Deere had been on the way to one or the other of their apartments after a late supper at the Adlershof, a thoroughly respectable hotel in a more than respectable district. However, the quickest route to the apartment complex where they both lived was through a largely wooded area, under normal security watch but still with more than the usual number of hiding places for bad actors.

Deere had been shot twice with a medium-caliber wadgun, giving him a heavy dose of Riot Compound 12, popularly known as Flatout. Krazinkow was more seriously hurt, the result of a beating that had cracked several ribs, sprained her arm, and severely bruised her left cheek and jaw. Neither victim had been robbed of anything, even their clothes; neither had been sexually assaulted or injected with any drugs other than the RC 12.

"Is there any chance that they were illegally carrying classified material or access codes? Sorry, I have to ask," Pfalz added hastily.

The apology didn't keep grim looks off the officers' faces. It was always an awkward question, like parents being asked if their child was using illegal drugs.

"Anybody can be careless," Ropuski said. "We're not running a unit of saints or angels. But our key files have several layers of security beyond the ordinary codes. I don't think anybody could penetrate them with what they'd take off Krazinkow, and they would leave a record of the attempt."

"That tight, are you?" Pfalz said, then stiffened at the glares from both naval officers.

"We are," Kuwahara said. "If you have a need-to-know, we'll tell you why." He knuckled his eyes, which did nothing about his incipient headache but made Ropuski smile sympathetically. "Sorry, Lieutenant. I didn't mean to snap at you. I imagine you have even less enthusiasm for this kind of work at this time of night than I do."

"That's about it, Admiral," Pfalz said. "But don't sweat over the need-to-know. I'll bounce that up to the Inspector of Violent Crimes, and he'll get back to you if necessary."

"Fine. Captain, check if there have been any attempts to penetrate our security."

"That was the first thing I did," Ropuski said, in a tone of mild reproach. "The second thing I did was lock down all access until I'd called you. *I* can't get into the files now."

"Let's leave it that way for the rest of your watch, unless something comes up that needs to be handled urgently," Kuwahara said. "Sorry, Lieutenant. I gather you weren't finished?"

"I'm afraid not. Ah . . . was either victim possibly involved in commercial-sex activities?"

Kuwahara was too surprised to be insulted. Ropuski was too insulted to find words. She looked about to find some, probably in her birth Polish, when Pfalz held up desperately placating hands.

"Please. I don't know the kind of background checks your people went through, but I know that even 'Command Secret' checks have overlooked this sort of thing. You would not believe what can fall through the cracks, or be hidden in them."

"What makes you think that twenty-five years in the Navy haven't let me past a few garbage heaps?" Ropuski said.

"I'd like to take that as a no, but to be official . . ."

"Or officious," Kuwahara muttered, but fortunately only Ropuski heard it.

"The answer for Krazinkow is *no*," the captain said. "I'm not authorized to check on Deere, but anybody who makes his rank in Weapons gets all sorts of psych tests. The profile doesn't match."

Pfalz looked his opinion of psych profiles, but had the sense not to put it into words. "This isn't just idle curiosity," he went on. "The MO and area matches a male/

female team who work for the local pimps, trying to keep the commercial sexers in line."

Kuwahara refrained from expressing surprise at the existence of pimps in the Federal District. Among any group of two million people, one could find someone capable of any crime from shoplifting to genocide. Pimping was a fairly demanding crime, requiring as it did either unlicensed practitioners or easily intimidated ones. Lacking either, the career of an aspiring pimp was short, and sometimes his life as well.

"Is there the possibility of mistaken identity?" Kuwahara asked.

"There's always that possibility, but it's a pretty low-order one here," Pfalz said. "If this is the same team, they're about the best in the business. You can practically tell them what kind of fracture you want in which bone, and they'll not only deliver but send you copies of the scans as evidence. For a price, of course," he added.

"Charming people," Ropuski said.

"All right," Kuwahara said. "Lena, get an LI detachment over to—"

"St. Luke's Medical Center, the Emergency Room," Pfalz supplied. "They'd better have credentials up the arse, though."

"They will," Ropuski said.

"Fine," Kuwahara said. "Put them in the Security One ward of Kronje House, my authority, and no visitors until we and the police can both talk to them. Lieutenant, do you want me to come down to your station, or can you send somebody out here? I have a pretty full day tomorrow."

There was no reason why Kuwahara and Ropuski couldn't give their statements over the circuit, except for one: security. Anyone capable of hiring top-grade street soldiers was also capable of hiring the same quality of electronic snoopers. Unless this incident had no connection with the study group's work, something Kuwahara would believe the day after he saw Rose Liddell pick up *Shenandoah* with her bare hands.

"If we can park a ground-wheeler in your garage, we can sneak in, then sneak out with our material. We may want to have a lifter flying security, though."

"Can you provide it? Calling Security at this time of

night causes talk. Oh, sorry, I forgot the LI. We may as well be hanged for a tree as for a sapling. Lena, we want high cover over my house until dawn or when the police leave."

Kuwahara fixed Lieutenant Pfalz with eyes that he was sure were already pink and would undoubtedly be red before sunrise turned the sky the same color—no, it was supposed to snow tomorrow. Before dawn turned the sky the same color as his face? Better.

"Very well, Lieutenant. Are you coming yourself, or sending somebody else?"

"That'll be flipping a token, but whoever it is, expect them in about forty minutes."

Kuwahara looked at his watch. It was remotely possible that he would get as much as six hours of sleep tonight. After an eleven-hour day, this was not the optimum prediction.

However, he would not be sleeping under sedation with major drug doses working their way out of his system or painful fractures and bruises. The people who were sleeping that way deserved a little help from their superiors.

The screen faded. Since he wasn't going to get back to bed, Kuwahara called up the letter to Yaso, and this time he got to "Transmit."

"Better take a shower, if you're going to be up late," Fumiko said. "There's plenty to drink, but I suppose the detective will be on-duty. The snacks are down to crackers and cheese and a few rice balls and pickled vegetables, unless you want me to get up and—"

"Beloved and honorable spouse, if I thought I could get away with offering the man a glass of water, I would. Our cooperating with the police does not require you losing sleep."

But it would require shifting a few things in the garage, such as the gardening robots and three returnable packing containers. The Kuwaharas seldom needed ground transportation except for the vacations they hadn't taken since summer, and the garage had slowly transformed itself into ready storage.

The shower could wait. Kuwahara opened his closet door and grabbed the first outfit and pair of shoes that would fit under his parka and boots. Shifting the garage's contents might mean outdoor work, and it was twenty below tonight.

Charlemagne:

Kuwahara's first shock was the wind. It had come up since he reached home; he did not want to think about the chill factor. He was considering returning for the heated coldsuit when he got his second shock.

There were footprints running around to the side of the garage. Footprints that had to be no more than an hour old, allowing for the snow flurries and the blowing and drifting in between.

Which meant that no one in his family had made them. Hanae was out; Fumiko had gone to bed early; the cleaning team had been gone since mid-afternoon.

Kuwahara crossed the driveway and studied the footprints. Not only was the time wrong, so was the footgear. Nobody wore boots with that pattern.

Well, maybe he didn't know the pattern of all of Hanae's skiing gear. But that meant her sneaking back home by way of the garage, then sneaking out again. She certainly wasn't home, alone or accompanied.

Kuwahara stepped across the footsteps and walked parallel to them as far as they ran, which was to the side door of the garage. The light over the door was a pale glowing worm in the night; Kuwahara remembered his plan to fit a stronger one. He had plenty of security on the second floor for classified materials and family treasures. No need to worry about somebody breaking and entering to steal a quarter-ton gardening robot easily traced by alarm and transmitter.

Weak as it was, the light showed suspicious marks on the door, and more around the lock box. Kuwahara backed off, remembering that compact motion-sensors were not cheap enough for amateur criminals but well within the reach of professionals.

Professionals had been here tonight, if they had opened the door and booby-trapped it without setting off the central alarm. Professionals who might be able to monitor intercom communications, if they were still close enough or had planted anything in the system besides the bomb Kuwahara suspected.

Kuwahara forced a halt to that line of thinking before he started worrying about triggering the bomb by using the intercom. Instead he hurried back to the front door.

"Fumiko. Signal a 'Security Red' to Forces Command, our address, my authentication code. Then get dressed—warm, and come downstairs. Hurry. We've had a prowler in the last hour, and I think he may have put a bomb in the garage."

"Any connection with the attack on what's her name?"

"Krazinkow. I can believe connection more than coincidence. Move!"

Fumiko moved. She wore a coldsuit when she came out and brought a heated cape for Kuwahara. With that over his parka he felt almost cozy. They walked arm-in-arm, stumbling over an occasional snow-covered bush, to the stand of pepperbean in the southwest corner of the lot. There nothing but an IR scan could spot them and nothing but a good-sized rocket reach them, if they lay down.

Kuwahara drew the line at that. Even if response to the alert was slow, the police should be arriving in . . . call it thirty minutes now . . . and discourage anything too insane.

Or was it the too-insane they needed to fear? The people too mad over some aspect of the Linak'h situation to care about their own lives, if they could end Kuwahara's?

A consoling thought for a man driven from his own home into a frigid night, crouching behind bushes, hoping he could shield his wife at least with his own body from any menaces that might be lurking in the night.

The stars that blazed in the Raft, the Helmet, and the Delta were dazzling and wholly unsympathetic.

Help came almost before Kuwahara had managed to turn his self-pity into anger and analysis of the situation. The planned high cover was first, a lifter with Forces Command insignia that flew low overhead, spotted Kuwahara, and landed to drop off three men.

"Something new turned up, Admiral?" the LI corporal in charge said.

"You might say that," Kuwahara explained, over an open circuit to the lifter. He hoped the scramblers were working; otherwise the whole neighborhood would be awake by the time all the police agencies who heard showed up.

Either the scrambling failed or the lifter pilot thought calling in the clans was a bright idea. Lifters and groundcars from the Federal District, Bennington, Forces Security and MP's, and Federal Security Bureau streamed in for the next twenty minutes. Kuwahara's lawn began to look like an air-gypsy encampment or a battalion LZ, and he cringed as he heard bushes crunching under lifters landed with more haste than observation.

He had just about given up hope that somebody had remembered to send an EOD team when a lifter swept in at high speed, circled, and on the third circle dumped a fuse damper slung under one skirt. The damper plummeted down, aimed God only knew where, but hitting squarely on the roof of the garage.

The impact sent slabs of flooring and pieces of railing from the roof deck flying ten meters, knocked out several windows, and buckled at least one wall of the garage. Then the fuse damper itself erupted with a *phoomp* that rocked the whole garage, lighting up the interior with a sinister blue glare.

As the echoes died, Kuwahara heard an ominous sizzling. One of the robots' power packs was discharging. It could (and with the way luck had been running tonight, probably would) set the whole garage on fire. The advantages of an attached garage began to seem less evident.

Kuwahara stalked over to the nearest police vehicle and stuck his head inside. "Get me that clown who bombed the garage on the radio. *Now!* I don't care if it's scrambled or not. The more people who know he's an idiot, the better, as far as I'm concerned."

The lifter crew, a youngish woman wearing Bennington Municipal Protectors badges, stared. "I don't care if the pilot is your husband. I have a few things to say to him." Then he looked toward the garage, where the blue glow was holding steady, likewise the sizzling.

"Better yet, get the Fire Department. Now. Ten minutes ago would be better, but now."

This time they achieved communication. About the time the third fire department acknowledged, Kuwahara's attention shifted to a long red-painted lifter with

Forces Command Engineering insignia, looking for a place to land. The Forces Command EOD team had arrived at last.

Captain Lopez-Wang wasted no time on the first EOD team, the Blitz County one. Instead he positioned his security, surveillance, and communications people in two minutes. A cable-controlled robot carried a fuse damper up to the suspect door. The fuse-damping field was so powerful that the electronics of several police vehicles parked too close died, which at least cleared some frequencies even if the air promptly turned several colors from the language of irritated police officers.

Lopez-Wang was the sort of EOD man who would stay calm even if he heard the ticking of an old-fashioned clockwork fuse under his fingers. In fact, he would probably try to race the timer, so he could salvage the fuse for the Forces Ordnance Museum.

What he actually did was scramble onto the roof, using a stirrup of two sets of hands, then strap on a vest of tools and instruments, tie a belt rope to what was left of the railing, and disappear through the hole in the roof. The sizzling promptly died in a series of hisses; one of the tools must have been a compact foam-projector. Then all was silence and darkness for what seemed like an hour, but Kuwahara's watch told him was only five minutes.

At the end of that time Lopez-Wang emerged, something small and black in one hand. Ignoring a babble of questions, he marched straight up to Kuwahara, and without saluting thrust the black thing at the admiral.

Kuwahara knew that his reputation depended on taking it without flinching, even though he would rather have petted a deathback. It weighed about a kilo, seemed to be made entirely of plastic, and looked as if it had been baked in a microwave cooker.

"All right. What is it?"

"What you suspected. Booby trap rigged to the side door. Also has a motion-sensor and a couple of other backup systems. I foamed it for anything mechanical, and they didn't seem to have an anti-tamper charge."

"That many sensors, in that kind of a package? I didn't think that was possible."

Lopez-Wang put on his best technical-junior-confounding-non-technical-superior expression. "Rephrase that. I don't think it's possible either, with a decent explosive charge." He tossed the black package to a sergeant dripping electronic gear. "Scan this and give me an estimate on the charge."

The captain turned back to Kuwahara. "If you kept the explosives down to a few grams, or just used flash powder, you could cram all kinds of mini-systems into that black can. Thing is, you'd have a warning rather than a killer. Know anybody who wants to warn you?"

"A lot of people, including my wife, but I don't have a list handy."

The admiral knew immediately that he must have sounded like a man too tired or too angry to take real danger seriously. The captain frowned.

"It's not a joke, sir. Whoever did this has pretty impressive capabilities. The next time it could be more than a warning."

"I'll tighten up security, or arrange for it to be tightened up," Kuwahara said. He was conscious of Fumiko at his elbow, out of her depth but grimly determined to freeze to death listening to jargon rather than let anyone except him know it. "But first, I have some evidence to give to a detective from District Violent Crimes."

Kuwahara raised his voice. "Is Lieutenant Pfalz anywhere around?"

Something that sounded like a reply came back, immediately drowned out by at least three other voices claiming superior jurisdiction.

Kuwahara's patience finally vanished. "Attention to orders! I want Lopez-Wang's people, the security squad from Forces Command, and a fire squad—pick one. Also Lieutenant Pfalz and anybody with him.

"As for the rest of you, I can't order you to leave. But if you stay around here much longer, it won't be just the neighborhood you wake up. Somebody's going to put in a complaint to Forces Command. People with even more stars than I have may be waked up to handle the complaint. I really don't want to think what the Empress would say if she hears about this circus."

Admiral Baumann's proved a name to conjure with. The risk of jurisdictional conflicts rapidly gave way to the risk of midair collisions, as a dozen lifters tried to find their way out of the same suburban lawn at the same

time. In five minutes more, Kuwahara was left with the
people he'd asked for as well as Fumiko, now trying hard
not to laugh, and a Navy courier who seemed to have
fallen from the sky like the mis-aimed fuse-damper, although without doing so much damage.

"Who are you?" Kuwahara snapped.

"Message from Admiral Baumann," the courier said. She
wore undress blues under a desperately light coldsuit.

"Come on in and warm up while you deliver it," Kuwahara said.

"I was requested to draw as little attention to myself
as possible," the courier replied.

"You'll draw more if you stand around shivering," Kuwahara said.

The messenger saluted and handed over a message
pack. "If you will acknowledge receipt . . ."

Kuwahara let the courier's portable register his retinal
and finger prints. The courier vanished toward the house.

Fumiko entertained the inside crew, the Violent Crimes
people under Lieutenant Pfalz, while Kuwahara borrowed the nearest terminal to deal with the message. A
particularly ripe Arabic obscenity ripped the air as he
finished decoding.

"Sho?"

"Merely some unexpected business tomorrow, at
lunchtime."

"Oh." He heard the rustling of her robe as she turned.
"Good people, I appreciate that the hour is late and clear
heads are needed. You are also on duty. But under the
circumstances, would anyone care for a snack, and a
drink with it?"

It would take more than the best whiskey to explain
why the Empress had made a lunch engagement for the
two of them with the Foreign Minister. However, the
whiskey might give him better sleep and a milder mi-
graine, which was not the worst starting point.

Thirteen

Charlemagne:

Federation Foreign Minister Aung Bayjar was said to speak seven languages, five of them human, and to be able to lie with a straight face in all of them.

When Kuwahara's alarm went off, the admiral awoke wondering if he would be able to understand a word in any of the minister's languages. A long shower and a large breakfast with plenty of coffee helped bring enough brain cells on-line to restore coherence and even allow hope.

It also helped that Baumann's courier had stayed overnight, sleeping on the rug and rising fresh and ready to pilot Kuwahara to Forces Command. He was mildly jealous of the freshness, but didn't turn down door-to-door service.

It was as well he kept normal hours during the morning, although he needed the help of more coffee to do it. Captain Ropuski had stayed out her watch, briefed Captain Fraziano, then borrowed a bed in the Study Group's off-duty apartment for a nap. Ropuski's briefing must have covered all the worst-case scenarios; Fraziano was as nervous as a second lieutenant facing his first combat.

Fraziano, it appeared, was one of those unfortunately not rare officers who believe that combat should stay in one place and that all other places should be peaceful. He was not going to be much use in the event of a serious terrorist effort against the study group. Kuwahara tried to soothe him down as much as possible, while using part of his brain to compile a list of possible replacements.

Without expanding the study group's roster, there weren't too many possibilities, and all of them would involve taking somebody from useful work they were already doing to replace a man made useless by an attack of nerves. This would not help the group's morale; it was already not helping Kuwahara's.

He decided against asking for more people, particularly four-stripe or one-star people, until after the meeting. The Empress did not break promises, but she would be preoccupied before the meeting and possibly worse afterward.

They met for the lift to the Foreign Ministry just before 1230. Baumann gave every sign of having been up later and having slept worse than Kuwahara, if you knew her. To the casual observer the uniform was as spotless, the elegant figure as erect, the fine features as carefully expressive as ever.

"Thanks for the courier, Admiral," Kuwahara said, as they settled into the rear seats and strapped in. "Having a ride in helped."

"Not enough, I should say," she replied, looking him over. "Anyway, don't thank me. That was Nika's own idea, staying at your place."

"I'll have to do something nice for her."

"Is there anything I can do for you?"

Kuwahara was tempted to suggest that she talk to Fumiko, concerning her and Hanae finding separate quarters. Unfortunately, Fumiko would be even deafer to Baumann than to her husband. Her family sometimes claimed samurai ancestry, but she herself said, "Even farmers with nothing to eat but millet didn't desert their families at the first rumor of bandits."

Last night was more than a rumor, but if the "bandits" really had some organization behind them, they might be able and willing to strike at Kuwahara's family anywhere on Charlemagne. As for him or anyone else persuading Fumiko to return to Akhito and "hide in the family vault" as she had phrased it in the past—he would rather take on the Coordination's new cruiser squadron in a scoutship than face that argument.

"Tell me why His Excellency is planning this meeting," Kuwahara said. "It seems rather sudden."

"It is. I had the courier on the way twenty minutes after Bayjar called me. I then called him back, but he had gone to bed. I did the same."

She was not, Kuwahara noted, saying that she'd slept. So much for his hopes of knowing better what the Empress's mood was or might be, and what chances he had of scraping up more people for the group. She was never an easy person to cajole or persuade; when her voice hardened like that it was hopeless, even if she was smiling.

The smile stayed on the Empress's face all the way to the Foreign Ministry. Kuwahara did his best to match it with his own.

Charlemagne:

Above ground, the Foreign Ministry was one of Wendy Neimeier's masterpieces (or at least it was called one in the guidebooks). Inside it had been from the start an example of conspicuous craftsmanship, with public rooms decorated by the best artisans of the hundred and fifty-two member planets of the Federation in the year it was dedicated. The real work of overseeing the Federation's foreign policy was done in less sumptuous surroundings.

Some of it was done in the suite of offices and conference rooms in the penthouse. Approaching it from the air, at a distance of two kloms, Kuwahara thought that the penthouse looked rather like the gun turret of a medium lifter.

The rest of the work was underground, manipulating electronic pulses in the gigantic computers, the best in the capital next to the War Ministry's. Interstellar distances meant that foreign policy didn't need vast quantities of decision-makers, to respond rapidly to crises. What it did need was a few very good ones, with access to the best possible advice (not all of it human), and with both decision-makers and advisers having access to as much data as possible (definitely something to be turned over to computers).

If the permanent staff of the Ministry exceeded five hundred people, Kuwahara would be surprised. He would not be surprised to learn that half of them worked underground on the computers.

The pad had the usual LI guard, wearing white cold-suits and with weapons and gear also whitened for camouflage. This aggressive pose made Kuwahara frown.

"I hope nobody's declaring a security alert for the whole district because of last night."

"I hope so too, but the War Council can if it feels like it. Here, though, I wouldn't worry. The chief of security for the ministry is an old Ranger. He likes guards to look field-ready instead of ceremonial."

The guards certainly saluted with precision worthy of 101 Light, and Kuwahara did his best to reply at the same standard. A four-trooper escort fell in, two on each side of the admirals, and marched with them to the elevator. Kuwahara resisted the temptation to fall into step with his escorts.

Aung Bayjar was waiting for them in a guarded reception room off the lobby in front of the elevator. The display over the doorway said that this was the Columbian Room, paneled in Giant Logan with a design of Olufsson's Kelp but done in "a universalized Amerind mode"—whatever that was.

The guards withdrew; the door closed; a robot rolled forward. The Foreign Minister waited until the robot had finished scanning the two admirals, his face almost clinical. Then he stepped forward and gripped both right hands at once.

"Be welcome to as close to a house as I can call my own here. Lunch will be in thirty minutes or less, but drinks can come at the snap of a finger."

They all ended up with fruit punch. Bayjar was an abstainer, Kuwahara didn't want to risk drinks after a short night, and Baumann looked ready to kill for a brandy but even more reluctant to be the only one swigging ethanol.

"I trust Deere and Krazinkow . . . are well?" Bayjar inquired, over a silver goblet of iced punch. "Or at least as well as can be expected?"

Baumann's smile seemed a little forced. "Deere will be released as soon as we and the police are finished questioning him. Krazinkow will need bone-boosters, but should recover without any trouble. We may temporarily reassign her to a low-G post like Alcuin, simply for therapeutic reasons."

"One sees," the minister said. "And for security reasons?"

"If we decide that's a factor, of course," Baumann said.

"I would think that is automatically a factor," Bayjar replied.

Kuwahara took his cue from a jerk of Baumann's head. "Not necessarily," he said. "Two incidents doesn't automatically create a security crisis. Or at least not the kind that need concern anybody beyond Forces Command."

"You regard yourself as expendable, Admiral Kuwahara?" Bayjar asked. "I was not under the impression that vice admirals ever fell into that category, or that Admiral Baumann placed so little value on you."

"Admirals and CPO's are equally expendable in a good cause," Kuwahara said, more sharply than he had intended. "Not putting the whole Federal District in a panic is a good cause, at least for now."

"As long as there is nothing to panic about, yes," Bayjar said. "You doubt that this is the case?"

Kuwahara felt a brief urge to drop something bad-tasting in Bayjar's drink, then realized that the bad taste was already in his own mouth. Baumann presumably had her reasons for dealing with the man, but he was going to request an explanation of them before he sank much deeper.

"Yes, we do," Kuwahara said. "We may be dealing with amateurs. We may be dealing with professionals trying to imitate amateurs. We may be dealing with two different groups, one professional, one amateur."

"There is a possibility you have not mentioned," Bayjar said, with a dangerous softness in his voice. "Some highly professional group is trying to simulate a terrorist movement, presumably related to Linak'h."

Baumann's face showed that she had been surprised and didn't like it. "What makes you think that?"

"Because if terrorism is suspected, everybody concerned with it will be looking outward. Few will be looking at our own ranks."

Baumann had not as much practice at yoga as Kuwahara; her nostrils flared and her face flushed. Bayjar held up a hand. "I do not question the honor of the Forces. They are only one of many possible bodies who could gain advantage from using a terrorist threat as as a decoy. My ministry is certainly one of them. The present Government would certainly not be above inventing a security threat to prolong its tenure of office. There are others."

"There is also such a thing as being so cynical people will suspect it's an act," Baumann said. A smile flickered at the corners of her mouth. "But I take it that you approve of our not pushing the panic button?"

"For the moment, I approve more than not." Bayjar emptied his goblet; a robot came at once to offer a fresh drink and retrieve the empty. "In my position, facing this kind of situation, one must balance risks. The diplomatic community and the media will make a howling scandal if someone prominent is killed.

"On the other hand, they will also make one if we declare a crisis and no one is shot by the terrorists we hunt, at much expense and inconvenience to the Federal District and everybody in it. They may not even wait a decent interval for the terrorists to not appear, lest they miss being the first to courier the news back to their home worlds.

"I hope, however, that you both will take decent care of your own safety. I choose not to regard you as expendable, and trust that you will not be offended."

From Baumann's expression, she was anything but. In fact, Kuwahara suspected that one of the more important topics of today's meeting had been settled with hardly more than a raised eyebrow.

He was reasonably certain, however, that other points might not go so smoothly.

Charlemagne:

If lunch was a point, it at least went smoothly. The Foreign Ministry's cooks lived up to their reputations, with puff pastry appetizers, the ubiquitous Firelands bluefish with a pureed vegetable sauce, just enough wine to improve the disposition of the two admirals, and a dessert of fresh fruit with another sauce that hinted of chocolate and a dozen other flavors.

Baumann clearly had missed breakfast. She chewed her way through lunch with hardly a break except to praise the sauces, leaving most of the conversation to Kuwahara. The admiral had the feeling that she would have done this whether she was hungry or not. Was he being thrown into the feeding pit, or given a chance to acquire a powerful friend?

Fortunately Aung Bayjar stayed away from military topics. They exchanged family histories and anecdotes, and Kuwahara found himself telling the old story of how nearly he'd become an adopted husband in his wife's family.

" 'As long as you have even a single coin, never become an adopted husband,' " the minister quoted. "Or was the bargain more promising?"

"Since the Bad Manners Wars, being an adopted husband is much rarer than it used to be," Kuwahara said. "In fact, in my own family's circle the custom has practically died out. But I was a fifth son, which is not common, and being in the Navy brought me into contact with people I might not have met if I had stayed in the transportation industry."

He managed to get through the rest of the story unaffected by the wine, and without mentioning his wife's brother. At the time of Kuwahara's marriage, Shiro Otani had looked so hopeless that someone much below the standard of Fumiko's new husband might have been considered for adoption.

If Fumiko's father Takeo had ever considered the adoption seriously, rather than simply using it to frighten his late-blooming elder son into good sense. If the latter, it had been a triumph. Shiro had been conscientious and discreet, if a trifle too creative at times, for nearly twenty years. A delicate situation had ended with everyone winning. Kuwahara wished he could hope for as much on Linak'h.

The robots cleared the table and vanished, except for one that Kuwahara recognized as a debugger and scrambler carefully disguised as a robobar. He wondered which bottle contained the recorder.

The conversation over lunch had satisfied any traditional notions of hospitality Bayjar might hold. He moved swiftly to the point—the Ministry of War's refusal to authorize an approach to the Ministry of Trade and its Bureau of Emigration.

"It sounds as if your position is one governed by custom and good manners rather than law and regulation," Bayjar said.

Baumann took her cue from his tone. "About right. We're in the gray area between what's absolutely forbidden and what is absolutely required. However, we want to tread cautiously. Without authorization, Emigration might show us the door. They might even complain to their Ministry, and Trade's a zealot even if she's not on the War Council."

"You fear retaliation by an intermediary sitting on the council?" Bayjar said. The ironic tone was almost undetectable. "At the expense of our soldiers' lives?"

"Not that far, no," Kuwahara said. "But Trade and Transportation tend to work together. If they both leaned on the Council, the Navy might be limited to shuffling ships and men, and I might be reassigned.

"Admiral Baumann and I think that there's more to this crisis than can be handled by force-shuffling. I'm in charge of the search for whatever that is.

"Somebody else could do it, of course. I am not that indispensable. But it would take time that we may not have."

"You think vital evidence might disappear in the delay?"

Baumann gave a carnivorous smile. "Let's just say we'd rather not take chances."

"Neither would I," Bayjar said. "Any situation that may set the course for our future relations with both Merishi and Ptercha'a certainly requires a coordinated military-diplomatic effort. I am afraid, though, that my knowledge of Admiral Kuwahara's work is limited."

It ought to be nonexistent, Baumann's face said to Kuwahara, *but let's give the little tomb-robber the benefit of the doubt.*

"I can increase it, if you have the time."

" 'Better to spend time now than lives later,' " Bayjar said, then smiled. "John Kishi might have been a field commander greater than Briggs or Hannibal, if his political career had allowed it."

Kuwahara decided that reminding Bayjar about a few

other quotations on the subject of time could wait. He gave an edited version of the study group's origins, intentions, and suspicions, and kept it under ten minutes.

"I see," Bayjar said, and held out a hand. A glass of cold spicemilk popped out of the robot and slid to within reach. The minister sipped, again contemplating his guests over the rim of his glass.

"There may be no conflict between the Minister of War's reluctance and your need to access Emigration files," Bayjar said. "My own people regularly require such access. Given a list of what you need to know, they could easily add that search to their others. We could even have a cutout running through the Ministry of Planetary Exploration and Development, if necessary.

"Of course, I would need more than the list of what you needed to know. A promise of discretion, which really goes without saying. Deniability, in the event that the War Council finds itself involved. I have a position to maintain in the War Council too, and for the same reason that you have yours. Without it, my work will be impossible." His voice suddenly lost its affability. "Unless you hope to bring about my resignation?"

There were people at Forces Command, and even out in the War Zones, capable of that kind of plotting, Kuwahara knew. Some disliked Bayjar personally; in a career of nearly sixty years he had made the usual quota of enemies. Others simply felt that periodically shaking up the Foreign Ministry strengthened the position of the Forces.

No doubt it could. Whether this helped the Federation, Kuwahara wondered. Since he wasn't sure, he had long since decided that his oath required him to stay clear of that particular form of party-circuit politics.

"No," Baumann said. "It won't help anything to have the Foreign Ministry become a demonstration of chaos theory. Your job is safe, as far as we are concerned."

"I am grateful," Bayjar said. "I am also thinking it best to appoint a higher-ranking political representative to Linak'h. Or . . . are there any plans involving Marshal Banfi, that you know about?"

"What sort of plans?"

"Bringing him into the Linak'h chain of command."

The two admirals did not quite gape at each other.

This was a ploy neither of them had expected. Or was it a serious suggestion?

Kuwahara swore to look up any possible connections between Banfi and Bayjar. Meanwhile the minister had to be answered, and Kuwahara's one consolation was that the question had to have been meant for Baumann.

"That would depend on many things, including Banfi's own health," Baumann said. "I haven't heard of any such plans. But I'd bet the factors are being evaluated."

"Under General Szaijkowski? Your faith in him exceeds mine."

Kuwahara forced himself not to push his chair back for freedom of movement. The tension between the other two at the table was as visible as a laser beam.

Baumann was the first to slip down in her chair, a matter of a few cems but a concession of defeat for all that. Kuwahara wanted to look away.

"Szaijkowski is rather fond of letting the people already plugged in handle a crisis, unless they're incompetent," she said. "He will also find it hard to believe that anybody approved by Hentsch and Schatz isn't up to standard."

"He might even be right," the minister said. "But can we afford to risk his being wrong, when it leaves Banfi unused?"

"Put it that way, I suppose not," Baumann said. "So I should go and raise the question with Mighty Max?"

"Is that his nickname?" Bayjar said. "How was it acquired?"

"Under circumstances about which the less said the better, and on which the witnesses tend to be unreliable anyway," Baumann said briskly.

Bayjar laughed softly. "Do not fear that I expect a miracle. It is merely that Banfi's experience with the Ptercha'a gives him diplomatic qualifications nearly equal to anyone I could send out, and he is already there.

"The less time I have to spend shuffling people to fill gaps on Linak'h, the more time I can spend helping you trace the roots of the crisis. That, I think, is our common goal."

He tapped an intercom switch. "Tea, coffee, or more juice before you go?"

Charlemagne:

They were both silent during the flight back to Forces Command, and Baumann's grim face discouraged casual remarks on the way from the pad to her office.

Once barricaded against the world, Baumann sagged into her chair, which adjusted so enthusiastically to her slump that she wound up nearly flat on her back. From that position, she waved a languid hand.

"The bar is open, or would you like coffee?"

"Coffee would be fine."

"Press Coffee Six, then. Two cups."

The beverage-maker had to start a fresh batch of coffee, which gave Baumann time to resume her normal posture. By then it was Kuwahara's turn to be slipping down in a chair.

"What's the price for the thought I see on your face, Sho?"

"If we can handle this one, we can both put in for Lopez-Wang's job."

"Lopez-Wang? Oh, the EOD man. You've met him?"

"He came out to check that fake booby trap in my garage."

"Oh-ho. He's about the best they have. I didn't ask them to send him, either. The first thing I knew about your situation was five minutes after the Tomb Robber got off the circuit, and the Security team was already on the way."

"I wish they'd been a little faster," Kuwahara said. "That air-dropped fuse-damper—they didn't have the nerve to hand-place it—did more damage than the bomb could have done. The bomb couldn't have hurt anybody who wasn't actually holding it in his hand at the time!" He knew he sounded petulant, but was too tired to care.

He was saved from further self-pity by the beverage-maker's alarm. "Two cups, Coffee Six," it added, rather ponderously, the admiral thought.

Coffee Six was a high-grade blend, probably All-Jamaica Mountain Combine, made strong and spiked with something Kuwahara couldn't identify. He had reached the point of being ready to tackle lukewarm acid if it had enough caffeine in it, and so was hard-pressed not to gulp.

Baumann had recovered even before the coffee, so she let her's cool, holding her long-fingered hands in a steeple over the cup. The steam trickled up between thumb and forefinger.

"We'll have to divide the job if we're going to do it at all," she said finally. "I'll go beard Mighty Max, or pluck out the beard he's trying to grow. The less you call attention to yourself, the less likely he is to remember you."

"Is there anything I could do with Support and Training?"

"When we're dealing with Max? Surely you have to be joking."

"Sorry, I forgot."

"People have been exiled from the Federation for smaller lapses of memory. Have some more coffee."

More coffee would not help the stress, the main reason for Kuwahara's faulty memory. One reason Maximillian Szaijkowski did not have his Marshal's baton, in spite of his record, was his reluctance to replace the less-than-competent until it was too late. He had a sublime (and not entirely unjustified) confidence that his personal gifts would compensate for the limitations of subordinates.

The other was his outspoken disdain for the Force status of Support and Training. He was the leader of a not-trivial faction within the Army that supported the two combat Forces each having their own support and training facilities directly under their respective commanders-in-chief.

The politest term used among the traditionalists for this faction was "empire-builders." Kuwahara had heard some of the other terms; even in toned-down translations they were remarkably vivid. Some of the terms had come from living Marshals, others from senior War Ministry civilians. The idea would not get far, and nobody who supported it would ever get his baton.

It was still possible to work with Szaijkowski, if you had the rank (as Baumann did) and reasonable tact (which Kuwahara hoped she could improvise). It became impossible if you or some subordinate slapped him in the face by too much dealing with the lesser breeds without the law.

"You run your group, Sho. Run it, and keep it alive. That's your job right now. If there's anything else, I'll let you know after I track down Mighty Max."

Kuwahara sat up and delicately balanced his cup on the arm of his chair. It wouldn't balance and slid off, to thump on the deep brown rug. Fortunately, it was empty.

"What about a few unattributed quotations?"

"What about them? Oh, I see." Baumann picked up her cup, sipped it, then reached into her desk and pulled out a squat bottle shaped like a sitting animal. "I think I need this, if you're about to come up with one of your tactical improvisations."

Kuwahara smiled. "Small-unit tactics only, Admiral. I was thinking of talking to Josephine Atwood."

"The Trans-Rift War rep? Well, she's high enough, God knows. In fact, Media Relations heard a rumor that she was assigned to Charlemagne as a ready replacement for Trans-Rift's Capitol Bureau chief, who is older than the Great Khudr and about as adaptable."

"I didn't know that. I do know that she and Commodore Liddell were friends in college, and somewhat picked up the friendship on Victoria." He shook his head at the senior admiral's interrogative look. "Not lovers, I'm quite sure. But old friends, the kind who will sign on for anything likely to help the other."

"One sees," Baumann said. "So if you tell Atwood that the people after the study group could ruin Commodore Rosie's career . . ."

"Why should I tell her anything else? As far as we know, that is the truth. Or it could be."

Baumann nodded. "I agree. I'll even put my stamp on a full-data scan at Media Relations, on Atwood and anybody else at Trans-Rift who might complicate matters. On one condition. You aren't the source. Not even physically. Find somebody trustworthy but deniable."

"Under the circumstances, that's another word for expendable. I don't have that many people senior enough to be credible but not too good to waste."

"What about Fraziano?"

Kuwahara had the feeling that he had tripped a booby trap and the time fuse was running, with a clock face showing the vanishing seconds. If he didn't speak before the figures zeroed out, he would vanish like the seconds.

"Fraziano is good at staff work and administration. I'm not sure he's the most credible of the senior officers available."

"Who would be?"

"Marcus Langston . . ."

"Let's leave the Army out of it."

"All right. Lena Ropuski is the best all-around. She's also the one I can least afford to lose."

"You also can't afford to send a girl to do a woman's job," Baumann pointed out. This time she set the beverage-maker for voice command.

"Two more Coffee Sixes. No, make that Six-plus."

Kuwahara suspected that meant more of whatever liquor was in the animal-shaped bottle. He decided to end the bargaining before their sobriety departed, as time was critical.

Judicious leaks to the media could add a mob of their people to the military and police strength watching for any sign of the terrorists. The sooner that happened the better, which meant not waiting on the convenience of Admiral Baumann or the ego of General Szaijkowski. It did not mean lightening ship by the weight of one Captain Lena Ropuski.

"I can see one way to avoid trouble," Kuwahara said. "Send me somebody I can slot into Fraziano's place if he folds, and I can send Ropuski. She still won't be expendable, but losing her won't bring the group to a halt or force me to work a hundred-hour week."

The silence lasted long enough for the beverage-maker to break it. This time Baumann got the coffee. Then she stood in front of his chair, looking down from her full meter-eighty with a wry grin.

"What else do you expect superior officers to do when you've bargained them down? Kiss your feet?"

Kuwahara stood and delivered a classic European kiss to Baumann's free hand. She pulled it back and shook it vigorously.

"All right. I admit that Fraziano isn't the ideal man when the Death Commandos land or the toxic-waste line ruptures. I'll reinforce your permanent security and data-retrieval staffs by four people apiece, and start hunting for a backup to Fraziano. But just remember this.

"There are going to be rumors all over the District in days, that the study group is a terrorist target or a career-wrecker. That will weed out a lot of volunteers, and I don't suppose you want me to draft somebody."

"I'd prefer you didn't."

"I'd prefer not to. If we're trying to handle a number of problems discreetly, we don't want everybody noticing that the Navy C-in-C is trying to net a four-striper or two. That kind of gossip could do us as much harm as the terrs, if it gave Mighty Max or the Tomb-Robber an excuse to back out."

Kuwahara nodded and sipped his coffee. "Plus-six" definitely held as much liquor as coffee. He was going to need an hour or two on the couch after he got back to his office. Or even on the couch in the group apartment's living room, if Ropuski was still sleeping off her all-night vigil.

Field modesty was the standard for the study group, now that it was essentially under siege. Under normal circumstances Kuwahara and Ropuski could have shared a bedroom, or even a bed, without implications or comment.

If he did, however, Kuwahara would not have received the sleep he badly needed. Lena Ropuski was a superb officer in most respects, but she snored like a combat ditcher working at top speed in rocky ground.

Fourteen

Victoria:

The shot caught Karl Pocher at a mental disadvantage. Fortunately his combat reflexes hadn't vanished during his years on the farm. He had the direction of the shot, the direction of the nearest cover, and the best route to it estimated before the second shot came.

This one also missed, but not by much. Rock splinters ripped Pocher's skin even through his miteproof coverall. Then Mitch Leary's jumping behind the same boulder triggered a small avalanche from the slope behind the concealing boulder.

Rocks tumbled down, gouging Pocher and making a respectable pile over one foot. He shifted cautiously until he could reach the pile, then pulled the rocks away one by one. The boot was a war-surplus Fed combat model, reinforced all around; the ankle entrusted to it had survived.

"That's not usually the way you get your rocks off," Leary said.

As a joke, it left something to be desired. As a sign that Mitch was a cool head in a crisis, it had something going for it. Pocher raised his eyebrows.

"*Whose* rocks, my friend? *I* didn't try to kick down the cliff!"

"Neither did—" Leary began, then broke off as a rapid-fire burst ripped across the slope above them.

"Are they trying to scare us, hit us, or just keep us down?" Pocher asked, thinking aloud.

"*Trying* to scare us?" Leary said, holding out his hands, then shaking them in a parody of stark terror.

Pocher gently gripped both the hands, held them for a moment, then released one and pointed to the radio on Leary's belt. "If you're not scared speechless, what about calling up some help?"

"Police, or the farm patrollers?"

That was a good question. If the shooter or shooters were out on personal business, they might not know that the farm was a safe house for Victorian Intelligence. They shouldn't learn, either.

If the people were professionals from the opposition (any of several possible ones), they probably already knew too much about the farm. In fact, they might be going after Pocher as part of a campaign against the farm personnel.

Anyway, Leary was covering all angles over the radio, and discreetly, too. The young man was going to do very nicely on Linak'h, if he lived to get there. Pocher's regret at Leary's departure shrank a bit more.

". . . at the foot of a slope, with a striated strip of whiteblood rock toward the top. The other side's got to be in the cover of the boulders on the other side of the depression.

"We don't know if this is serious or scare, but it might be somebody with a score to settle with everybody on the farm. I know that doesn't say much, but anybody who comes for us ought to be ready to face heavy weapons."

That would probably bring out the patrollers; they flew another piece of war surplus, a K/G-96 with plug-in pulser/launcher pods (rockets would have been a bit hard to hide). Add concealed but permanent high-capacity sensors and nav gear, and the patrollers would shift the edge to Pocher and Co.

Somebody replied remarkably fast; Pocher took over the radio and gave coordinates and a few more details about the possible weapons. The acknowledgment and code words for lifting out came within seconds.

Then there was nothing to do but keep an eye to their flanks. Both men carried war-surplus pulser carbines. A frontal attack would be suicidal for either side.

Pocher settled into a niche in the slope where the rocks had fallen out. "Your father's not behind any of this, is he?"

"Dad?" Leary said. "What he thinks, he's already told

you. Mind, I think he also doesn't want to hear what Ginny Osborne would have to say."

"Determined young woman, that."

"Good-looking too, if you don't mind my saying so."

"If I did, I'd have problems keeping friends except my own breed. That's no life for a civilized man."

"Sorry, Karl. Civilized, you certainly are. My type, probably not. Anyway, it's me who's going to have to listen to Ginny, when she learns I'm shipping out for Linak'h. Dad's worrying too soon, the way he usually does these days."

"What the devil for? He's not even sixty yet."

"Don't know. The war put ten years on him, even though we didn't lose much. Then the whole feeling that somebody's still lurking out there . . ."

Pocher followed Leary's pointing hand, out to the gray horizon. It was all rock and sand, with a few patches of vegetation just breaking the monotony of a dozen shades of gray. Come spring, there'd be more vegetation and all of it showing color, but—

A gray blob appeared on the horizon, skimming low over the crests. Pocher shifted so that he could raise binoculars without raising his head into sight of the shooters on the far slope.

It was the patrol lifter, moving low and fast as its high-capacity cells and oversized fans allowed. It was not, however, coming toward them. It was circling rapidly at low altitude over something below. It also seemed to bulge in a few unusual places.

Uneasily, Pocher recalled that there was one of the covert shelters and supply dumps not far from where the lifter was circling. Had something happened to it, possibly at the hands of the comrades of the men pinning him and Mitch into what could still become their grave if the opposition came up with grenades or a launcher?

Pocher picked up the radio, mentally crossed his fingers that issue Victorian scramblers were more sophisticated than the bad guys' portable decrypters, and called up the lifter.

"Patroller Thirteen, this is Amber One. We have you in sight. Do you want us to provide suppressive fire for your approach?"

"Negative on an approach right now," came the voice.

Even scrambled, it sounded like Lucco DiVries. "We have possible hostiles in sight near Security Zone Epsilon. Will ID and discourage before picking you up, if possible."

"I hope we can live with that," Pocher said. "If you're going to be tied up for a while, can we at least have a weapons drop? The position's great, the ammo supply could use improving."

"We'll do our best," DiVries replied. "Good luck, Amber."

The patrol lifter slipped even lower, until it vanished behind crests. Except for their unknown enemies, Pocher and Leary were alone again.

Charlemagne:

When Josephine Atwood received the message, the time and place made her wonder if this was an assignment or an assignation. She had enough of the first, with the Linak'h crisis heating up, and no present interest in the second, although she was always ready to play a situation by ear.

Not ear but eye told her that this was business, when she reached The Nest Egg Grill and saw the woman who'd invited her. She showed more signs of being field-grade military than Atwood could accept as accidental, and that meant some game in Forces politics.

Which didn't exclude either honorable motives or the possibility of a story, of course. Run program back to zero and start again; play this one by ear.

"Good evening," Atwood said. "You're looking for me?"

"You were the one who was obviously hunting," the officer said. "A good cover, around here. This place has back rooms, back exits, discreet staff, and good food. What more could a romance ask?"

"I'm not an authority on romances. It's been a while since one of mine got me even that much."

"I'm sorry. Oh, by the way, Citizen Atwood, I'm Captain Lena Ropuski, Federation Navy. That's not for publication, under most circumstances I anticipate. But you have the right to know."

"I also have the right to stand up and walk right out of here, if I'm not told enough or what you tell me smells wrong."

"I'm here by myself. What did you expect, a Ranger team to silence you if you guessed secrets?"

"Somebody tried to silence Admiral Kuwahara a few days ago. It occurs to me that someone who I think is working with him inviting a media rep to this kind of meeting might have taken security precautions."

Ropuski tapped breast, waist, and ankle. "I have, but strictly personal. What about you?"

"Should I apply for a permit?"

"Why don't you listen and then decide? We'll certainly help you get one if you think it's needed."

"I'm listening,"

Atwood did not have to listen long, in proportion to the amount of information she acquired. She wasn't even tempted to activate her concealed recorder. If her memory couldn't hang on to this much until she got home, she was in the wrong profession.

The attempt on Kuwahara and the attack on Deere and Krazinkow (mentioned briefly in the Violent Crimes 'casts) were probably related. They both arose from somebody planning or allowing terrorism against the Dual-Sovereignty Planet Study Group.

"That's not much new," Atwood said. "Or why would I have known you worked with Kuwahara? No, I won't name my sources, either. Or I could name my own source, but all that would do is force you to ask him to name his, and so on back."

"You don't really need to paint me a picture of how leaky Forces Command security can be," Ropuski said firmly. "Or are you trying to make me feel guilty for adding to the leaks? If you are, don't accuse me of playing games, and give up hope of helping your old friend Rose Liddell."

Atwood had weighted her hand with an empty glass, and was about to jump up in fighting stance before she caught herself.

"That was a dirty trick."

"No trick. Just the truth."

"So Rosie needs help. Out of something you got her into?"

"Out of a situation that the terrorists may be trying to make worse."

Atwood felt manipulated, which meant dirty. The alternative seemed to be abandoning Rosie to take the consequences of whatever was coming down, which would make Atwood feel much worse than dirty.

"Describe the situation."

It didn't take long. Linak'h, it was believed, was a training ground for humans serving the Merishi as mercenaries, spies, terrorists, and assassins. Many or most of these humans came from the Peregrine area, with its baker's dozen (at least) of underdeveloped, marginal, or outlaw colonies.

They were desperate enough to enter Merishi service (and possibly the service of a faction of Merishi in their Space Security who sounded like some human varieties of authoritarian rightist) because they had not been allowed to emigrate from their home planets. The study group had strong suspicions that this illegal restraint had been sanctioned by Federation officials, civil, military, or both.

"That's going against a pretty fundamental law of the Federation and some other civilized polities," Atwood said. "Or are we dealing with some uncivilized ones?"

"We may be, and there could be nothing involved worse than misused resources or badly-set priorities at the Bureau of Emigration."

"But you don't think that, do you?"

"We were open-minded until these incidents, although when the Ministry of War dragged its feet—but I'm getting ahead of my story."

There wasn't much more of it. Ministerial obstructionism, missing intelligence from Victoria (*that* would certainly raise Kuwahara's blood pressure), and now terrorism—it added up to the study group's being on a trail that somebody didn't want followed.

"So what is my publicizing all this supposed to accomplish?" Atwood said. She knew, but wanted to see if Ropuski was expecting miracles or had her head facing the right way. So far she hadn't disappointed, but after twenty years of media work Josephine Atwood took very few people on trust.

Ropuski held up a hand. "One: Scare the people behind this. Not the terrorists, the ones who decided or didn't decide. Two: Make the public aware of the dual-sovereignty problem and the value of free emigration."

"The politicians have been mentioning the second one twice a month since Rosie and I were roommates."

"Politicians can talk the universe into stasis without making the citizen in the street concerned, unless it's something that affects his own life, family, or future. Free emigration qualifies on all three counts, but how to get this across?

"Three, make people aware of the terrorists. That may cause a panic. I trust our citizens a little more than that, however. It should make them keep a better lookout, and also increase pressure on the police to do the same."

Ropuski looked at the two remaining fingers, shook her head, and reached for her glass. "I guess that's about it. I can't promise you'll win any prizes or uncover a conspiracy to overthrow the Federation. You may just help us track down a few basically honest men and women who have each made a mistake or winked at one by somebody else. But enough of those, and you can suspend a mighty weight of trouble from the chain."

"You have a way with words yourself, Captain."

"My mother's a novelist."

"The Ropuski who wrote *Dance of Stars*?"

"Is that your favorite?"

They swapped literary notes and toasted their favorite authors for nearly an hour, until Atwood's head was buzzing softly with much more than the potential story. When she finally stood up, she had to blink to make sure Lena Ropuski hadn't acquired a companion.

"Thanks, Captain. If you ever want to write, put yourself in my hands and I'll see you don't wind up frustrated."

Ropuski frowned eloquently.

"Did I really say that? Anyway, you know what I mean."

"Yes, Citizen Atwood, I do. I wasn't planning on leaving with you, but . . . can you make it home all right?"

"If you do leave with me, it won't look nearly as suspicious. Not from here, anyway."

Then Ropuski's Amazon-grade arm was lifting her, guiding her between the tables and around the robots, and out into the Charlemagne winter night. The wind blew away the mental fuzziness, leaving only exhilaration.

I've owed you something, Rosie, for longer than you know. Now I can pay it back.

Victoria:

Pocher's watch recorded only ninety seconds after the disappearance of the lifter, before he heard its weapons firing. The wind carried the drone of heavy pulsers and the crackle of distant grenade explosions into the valley, and the walls compressed them.

Leary frowned. "What rules of engagement are they using? Can they fire first?"

"Depends on where they find a target," Pocher said. "A Security Zone is free-fire. Otherwise they have to take first fire."

"Let's hope whoever they're shooting at doesn't shoot back."

"That's not sporting, young man."

"I'll be as sporting as you like when my arse isn't on the line!"

"Much better. Being chivalrous beyond a certain point just means the war goes on, and catches innocents. When somebody's declared himself your enemy, put him down or at least out of the fight as fast as you can. I—"

The far side of the valley sprouted heads, flickering weapon muzzles, and a handful of running figures.

Pocher got off a burst that nearly emptied his magazine and put three of the runners down. Then the fire from across the valley seared across the top of the boulder.

"Down that way!" he snapped, pointing. Leary half rolled, half dove down the indicated slope. Rounds flailed the rocks around him, but he was too small and too agile a target to be hit at this range without a great deal of luck.

Pocher followed, and wasn't so lucky. A red-hot staple

seemed to drive into his ankle, and another pricked his temple hard enough to bring tears to his eyes. When he tried to put weight on the ankle, the pain brought more tears.

He swore softly. "Mitch, be ready to break out. I'll cover you. That way seems best."

"Is that an order?"

"No bloody way. Just a suggestion. If you've a burning passion to get killed, be my guest. But I think the gentlemen across the valley are trying to either capture or kill us. If they capture, we're hostages. If they kill, they can go help rescue their friends from our patrollers."

"Um." Leary looked from his friend to the escape route, then across the valley. Nobody was running now, but the suppressive-fire party was still popping off rounds into the general area of the two farmers. Pocher would have placed a large bet that at least one party was not far from their flank.

Leary hadn't learned one basic point of combat: Make up your mind *fast*. Luck saved him from paying the final price for that mistake.

"Amber Party, *Jehosaphat!*"

The voice was Lucco DiVries's, or an impossibly good imitation, but the command . . .

"That's the code to get down and—"

An ear-torturing howl slammed down across the valley, as the walls caught and held the sound of an incoming rocket. No, three rockets. Pocher held his head up just long enough to see three distinct fire pulses and three distinct smoke trails.

Then he and Leary were clasping each other, the rocks, and the odd projecting root as three explosions added to the uproar. When their echoes had died away, silence came to the valley, except for the rattle of falling stones dislodged by the blast—and the occasional scream from the floor and far side of the valley.

Moans didn't carry that far.

"I didn't know you were loading rockets," Leary said, as he crept up the side of the boulder to peer at the scene unveiled as the wind blew away the smoke.

"Neither did I," Pocher said. Evidently DiVries had said bounce the rules, or he had received orders so secret he hadn't informed Pocher. Which had nearly got Pocher and Leary killed by the bandits who must have been mentioned in the orders!

Pocher's nails grated on the boulder. He hadn't had a really good argument with anybody in quite a while. Even-tempered Karl, the perfect gentleman while he courted a young friend, was now going to wrap Lucco DiVries's teeth around his fist—right or left, whichever landed first. . . .

"Captain DiVries must be feeling good," Leary said.

"What?"

"I mean, more of the people who killed his—"

"Damn!" The gap between Pocher and Leary suddenly opened wider than the valley.

"Never say that, don't even think it. Maybe he felt that way at first. I know I did about Mahmoud. But after a while . . . Mitch, come with me."

"Where are we going?"

"Down into the valley. You've seen the casualties after they get to the hospital. I want to show you what they look like on the battlefield."

"Shouldn't we . . . ?"

"Wait? Hades, no. We're supposed to be down there, collecting weapons and documents, snapping pictures of the corpses, and patching up anybody who's still alive."

Leary swallowed. Pocher wanted to reassure him, but was still too aware of the gap between veteran and newlie. Instead he made sure that the radio's IFF was set, then stood up to see if that would draw fire.

Hectares of sand and rocks scarred and blackened to lifelessness were spread before him. Nothing moved except puffs of sand blown by the wind, a wisp or two of smoke, and the sleeve of a body's shirt. No, an arm's shirt-sleeve—the rest of the shirt, like the rest of the body, was fifteen meters from the arm.

Pocher handed the binoculars to Leary and told him where to look. The younger man took one long look, then managed to hand the binoculars back before he dashed behind the boulder to empty his stomach. He was white-faced when he came out, but he had a steady step and a firm grip on his carbine when he followed Pocher down into the valley.

Riftwell:

The incoming call from Frieda Hentsch broke up John Schatz's close-of-day drinks with his chief of staff and flag secretary.

Schatz looked at the calendar—in two more months or at the end of the Linak'h crisis, somebody else would be running Eleventh Fleet from this suite. He looked at the flag secretary—and Commander Fuchida somehow managed to sprint for the door without losing dignity.

He looked at Naomi Xera and winked. That meant, "Listen in, but don't blink loudly; the Pocket Pistol's probably paranoid." (He'd actually said that three times rapidly once after the second stiff drink.)

Xera winked back, patted a microscopic flaw out of her silver-blued hair, and strode out. Schatz took a deep breath, then ordered the call put through to his personal terminal.

Frieda Hentsch's voice came on. The screen remained blank. It was a deep voice for such a small person, and one of her better features. The blank screen, however, meant that she was either in a temper, sunbathing, or both. Schatz hoped it was both. An hour of basking in the sun relaxed her as much as the cats she so much resembled. With the way his luck was running, however, she'd only have just started.

"Hello, John," Hentsch said. "Rumors have come floating by, that you're thinking of reinforcing Linak'h."

"Do you have a telepath on your staff?"

"Not that I know. Do you do your thinking out loud?"

"Like singing—only in the shower."

"Mmm. This opens up a whole new realm of possibilities for Command Group meetings."

"Frieda, that idea was probably first proposed in a Roman legion. If you have to interrupt a staff meeting, could you do it with something original?"

The long silence was broken, to Schatz's relief, with a chuckle. He'd have to guard his tongue, which was growing looser almost by the day as retirement approached. He was still on watch, and part of his job was to keep on good terms with the other senior watchstander, the Pocket Pistol.

"All right. Is it original enough, to suggest that I concur and want the idea put on the agenda for the meeting tomorrow? We might even do some preliminary planning now."

"I have no problem with that."

"One brigade or two?"

"I don't see that we can ship two before the ultimatum runs out and get them field-ready at the other end. Also, I think we'd have to do an in-Zone mobilization, to fill at least one brigade slot and also provide support troops for Linak'h. With two brigades, we're beginning to talk a young corps. And the media will be talking *crisis*.

"One brigade should accomplish our original goal of an orderly evacuation. If Charlemagne wants us to fight a full-scale war, let them tell us."

Schatz's asperity was unfeigned. Forces Command and its civilian overlords seemed to be taking an unconscionable amount of time deciding how to handle the Linak'h crisis. This left the people on the spot with unlimited initiative but only limited resources to exercise it—although even total mobilization of the Federation wouldn't make resources from, say, Fifth Zone (thirteen hundred light-years and a minimum of two months' travel time away) available any time soon.

As with many other dilemmas Schatz had encountered, it only seemed new, when it was probably as old as war. Frieda Hentsch interrupted his vision of some Cro-Magnon warrior complaining that all the new stone axes had been issued to the Deer Clan, and the Wolf Clan was having to make do with clubs.

"All right. I hate to sound lazy, but I suggest we pull one of the three off Riftwell. The roster shows plenty of transport and escort in orbit for one brigade, and this place doesn't have any security problems."

"I was thinking of 233 from I Corps. We have two transports there, one more on the way, and plenty of civilian shipping to charter."

Even on a blank screen, Schatz could tell that Hentsch was both shaking her head and trying not to laugh. The laughter finally escaped.

"John, the quality of your bribes is slipping. I'd like one of my old Hentschmen running a brigade down there, but let's be practical. We want the brigade in, down, and ready to go before the ultimatum expires. That means minimum com lag, ready forces, and no bouncing civilian charters. I don't like those Coordination cruisers."

"The Ptercha'a have limited space-combat experience."

"The Merishi have a hell of a lot. Has anybody gone aboard those cruisers to make sure there isn't a whole tribe of Scaleskin 'advisors' ready and waiting?"

"Colonel Nieg could—"

"If anybody orders Nieg to make a kamikaze of himself, it will be me. I'm more likely to order him to stay off them. There are too many people who think it would make their careers to wring him dry. They're wrong, but we can't do much with a corpse either."

"I take your point."

"Épée or foil?"

"Sabre, actually. It smarts too much."

The three-weapons master on the other end of the circuit laughed again. "Sorry, John."

"No need to be. You pick the brigade, although I note that 218 has the most recent CA qualifications."

"That would be my choice, too. Lev Edelstein knows his business, and I'll see if I can team him up with Uehara."

"That's giving Uehara two bites, John."

"So? Maybe he's got good teeth. In fact, I know he does. Let him try them on the Merishi and the Ptercha'a instead of the Tuskers."

He was not going to admit Uehara's other virtue, which was a stubborn streak that would make him stand forthrightly between Longman and Liddell if he thought it necessary. It probably would be. Given that the SOPS had to be senior to General Tanz, Longman had been about the only choice, but Schatz still felt pangs of guilt at inflicting her on Rose Liddell.

"To quote an admiral of my acquaintance, I have no problem with that. *Auf wiedersehen,* John."

"*Shalom.*"

Schatz was sipping a fresh drink when the rest of the party slipped back into the office. Xera's eyebrows were higher than usual.

"The Pocket Pistol firing practice rounds today?" she

whispered, bending over Schatz on the pretext of refreshing her own glass.

"I have no complaints about her marksmanship," Schatz said. "Get on the circuit to Uehara and ask him what he wants for escorting a brigade, then try to bargain him down to what he really needs."

"Aye-aye, Admiral," Xera said, with a mock salute.

Victoria:

The two police lifters whined away into the grim darkness of a cloudy Victoria winter night. Even with the land frozen hard, a mixture of haze, ice-crystals, and wind-scoured dust and sand could blot out the stars.

Karl Pocher turned as the lifter lights vanished and footsteps sounded on the apron. Lucco DiVries stood there, bearded face just visible under the hood of his coldsuit and hands thrust into its pockets.

"Think he'll be all right?" Pocher asked.

" 'Reesa gave him the best *grappa,* and the police medico had a whole kitbag of soothers and sleepytimes. Add adrenaline depletion, and they may have to roll him off the lifter at his farm."

Mitchell Leary was on his way home to sleep off his first experience of combat, in spite of his pleadings to stay at the farm. When those had been denied, he'd burst into tears and briefly threatened to hide outside the farm perimeter, in spite of darkness, cold, and unknown dangers lurking.

The day's score was nine suspected terrorist bodies, three suspected terrorist prisoners, all badly wounded, and an indeterminate number of unidentified but probably hostile persons escaped, some of them probably wounded. The safe house and storage area in Area Thirteen had not been broached, but DiVries had picked up some sophisticated and hastily shut-down electronic surveillance before he went into action.

This meant a continued terrorist threat, which Mitchell Leary wanted to stay and help meet. Karl Pocher was just as determined to give Mitchell as many more nights as possible at home, before he shipped out for Linak'h.

Teresa DiVries laid on the homebrew (Pocher still couldn't get it down, but Mitchell knocked back two good-sized tumblers), and a police sergeant finally helped Pocher and the farm owners load the reluctant home-goer aboard a police lifter.

"I hope his father doesn't decide to pull him off the expedition," Pocher said. "That would break his heart."

"I thought you'd call that turnabout fair play."

"Luke, that's more than a joke, even from you."

"Sorry. It's the cold. I grew up here, in worse quarters, but the Navy thinned my blood. Let's go inside. I've got something to suggest."

Inside, over cups of tea (with a hint of the *grappa*, but hints Pocher could take; the raw stuff tasted like flarebase), Pocher listened to DiVries's suggestion that he join the Linak'h expedition. Then he shook his head.

"Why not?"

"I'm needed here. I mean, Jo and Charlie already off running *Nosavan*, you up to your ears in patrol and intelligence work, 'Reesa going in old McGuire's place . . ."

"That won't be a problem," Teresa DiVries said, coming into the room with her own cup of tea and a loaf pan full of hot damper. "Kathy McGuire's passed the tests for Master Lift Pilot, which means she can instruct. The Feds are just as grateful to her for the *Mahmoud Sa'id* rescue as they are to her father. Now the only problem is tying old McGuire down long enough to regen his kidney. But that one I'll leave to others."

"No, Karl, it's got to be you. One of the three tops on the farm has to take our squad out. We're the ones cleared for their real job.

"I'm the senior farm owner, so if I can stay, I should. We've gone over why Lucco might not be the best choice."

"I don't see the Feds being that vindictive over his change of allegiance, not after this long," Pocher complained.

"By itself, that wouldn't be a problem," Lucco admitted. "But consider the rest. I've served in the Victorian Defense Forces in ways that involve carrying arms. I've cooperated in the surveillance of Federation intelligence activities on Victoria. I've even participated in combat, as part of a non-combat arm to be sure, but those men

out there are just as dead as if I'd been a power-armored
LI.

"The Feds may not know about most of this. Even if
they do, they're hardly going to send a snatch team of
Rangers to haul me out-system for trial. But if I walk
into Federation jurisdiction on Linak'h, and then get
caught with a pulser in my hand and Fed secrets in my
files—your guess."

"My guess is that I'm going to Linak'h," Pocher said. He
actually felt better, now that it was decided. "But if Jim
Leary thinks I'm going for another chance at Mitchell . . ."

"Tell him that he should be proud to have a son who
can make up his mind," Teresa DiVries said sharply.
"Which is more than his father seems able to do."

She sliced the damper into three generous portions and
slipped each portion, still steaming, onto plastic plates.
"Jam or syrup, anyone?"

Pocher found that he was ravenously hungry. He remembered eating breakfast, but a long day spent mostly
outdoors and partly in combat had followed, and he
couldn't remember another meal. From the way his
stomach greeted the damper, it wasn't likely he was losing his memory—horrible thought, at forty-five.

Too young to lose memory, but not too old for combat, and he was still technically Fed Navy Reserve. Either way, he'd have a chance at more of the people
who'd killed Mahmoud.

*Face it, Karl. The urge isn't as much out of your system
as you were telling Mitch.*

Fifteen

Linak'h:

U-Day minus forty-one.

Candice Shores's command lifter didn't have a calendar, but neither she nor anyone else needed one to keep track of the shrinking time before the Coordination's ultimatum ran out.

The QRF column slipped over the boundary of the Camp Great Bend AD zone. Sensor interrogations registered one by one; one by one IFF's sent back friendly signals. The AD people were good; what they needed (short of no war at all) was an ammo resupply. Tanz, Kharg, and Hogg all both believed in plenty of live-fire exercises. Their battalion CO's agreed, and Longman and Liddell didn't object.

There'd be more supplies coming out with Uehara's convoy and 218 Brigade, straight out of Riftwell. That much was firm. Nearly everything else about the next batch of reinforcements was rumor.

Shores turned the controls over to Warrant Konishi, she to study the formation on the big display in the command suite in the rear. The copilot climbed out of the jump seat and slipped into Shores's place.

On the way aft, Shores stuck her head up into the transparent armorplast bubble that took the place of the turret in this lifter. She didn't like these VIP command models, even if she now rated one as a de facto battalion commander.

When it came down hard, all the firepower on Linak'h arriving in half an hour wasn't as good as just enough on hand right now. The light pods on either side of her new lifter could mark targets or discourage a mob. Suppressing heavy weapons or trained ground-pounders using Linak'h's multiple-canopy forests for cover was beyond them.

Thirty lifters rode in formation, five boxes of six. Twenty-four held troops; five were heavy haulers with mixed loads, including a platoon's worth of LI armor suits. The sixth heavy was an ambulance, on a ferry flight.

Gunships rode on either flank and behind, with a rover now below, making a pass over Little Herd Valley. (Not too low, or the stock farmers would scream, human and Ptercha'a for once in perfect harmony).

Above rode the "tagalong" group, civilian lifters authorized to join the convoy for security, as long as they could stay above the troop level. That left behind a lot of the old clunkers, and since most of those were human-owned, there'd been complaints of "pro-Pussycat prejudice," as one wit (well, maybe that was *half*-right) had put it. The rest had it made, whether attack came from above or below. From above, all they'd have to do was wait until the troops evaded, then dive for the deck. If somebody popped missiles from below, forty sets of jammers, decoys, and weapons lay between the civs and the bad guys. Not to mention as many lucrative targets.

Above the "tagalongs," eight light attackers in four pairs covered all the cardinal points of the compass, weaving occasionally to clear the air for long-distance scans from their "mother." A heavy attacker with a slip-in fuel tank in her weapons bay, the "mother" also provided AEW protection for the whole formation.

Out of sight, but not out of either friendly or (one could hope) unfriendly minds, the heavies and satellites in orbit would be swinging by. Linak'h Command's AO was now under continuous observation, with an orbital QRF of heavy attackers and dedicated buses. It might not wind up supporting Shores's own ground QRF, but the two had worked together, and her people would have first call if they got stuck into something that needed strategic-level firepower.

The whole formation was the classic layering of defenses for a tactical air movement. This movement wasn't strictly tactical, but they were doing it as if the trees below might sprout enemies at any moment. Training arms and legs, eyes and ears, was useless without training the minds that controlled them all, and treating routine air marches as tactical operations was one way to do that.

The Yellow Father had just slipped past the zenith. She'd seen him climb all the way up from the western horizon at dawn, without a single cloud anywhere even for a moment. There'd been thirty days like that, at least inland, and the long-range weather forecasts promised no improvements.

Livestock had stored fodder or browse. Synthetic-calorie plants could be brought on-line if crops failed. Even imported food might come in empty transports or chartered merchanters, to stave off famine.

But Linak'h stood alone against its drying forests.

Already the Rules of Engagement had incorporated weapons restrictions based on the fire hazard. You couldn't use flame compounds or most HE in HIGH or CRITICAL hazard areas. If you were over a stand of mature *zyrik* (nobody had given it a human name), loaded with sap and exhaling it into the air, you just didn't shoot, period.

"Course change coming up, Colonel," a voice said in Shores's helmet phones. "Scheduled change to one-nine-five true. Maintaining speed and altitude."

"Execute," Shores said.

She stayed in the dome, watching the formation change course, until everyone had lumbered and lurched around the turn. Not that she would have done superbly well if she'd been piloting one of the lifters herself; her flying hours made her competent rather than expert, and thirty sets of fan-wash was a pain even for experts.

She was developing a reputation for sleepless vigilance, though—the good kind, that detects both good and bad work and can tell them apart; the kind worth some sweat to maintain—such as watching formation turns as if you knew what you were seeing.

It would be nice, if it were as easy to persuade Ursula Boll that her offer to take the children for a ride was not a bribe!

As the command lifter steadied on its new course, Shores dropped down into the miniature Combat Center. On the edge of the map display was their next turn, Bissozara Hill, which cut the Big Herd Valley nearly in two. Then a straight flight to LZ Campione, where they'd practice approaches and exits to a hot LZ, with the LZ's caretaker party simulating bad guys with flares, low-power lasers, and smoke grenades.

If nobody stepped in it, they'd be home-free to the Zone before dinner. Once a week, you wanted an exercise that stressed everybody to their limits, just to remind them what combat would do. The rest of the time you could pace the troopers—and yourself, as Nieg *would* remind her.

She looked at the fiberplast sheet taped over her command display. It was one of her father's sketches for "The Young Queen," done with her holding a borrowed dress sword—Herman Franke's, she thought. He'd done it at the end of a busy three days for Shores, and Nieg had pointed out that the young queen wasn't supposed to look as if she'd been cleaning out bunkers with demo charges and a carbine!

What was worse, her father had agreed with the colonel. Worst of all, *Ursula* had agreed—and was it paranoid to wonder why the woman had apparently stopped caring if Shores dropped dead or not?

It was, but it might not be useless, either. Shores adjusted the seat for maximum recline and closed her eyes. A brief memory returned, of a nineteen-year-old recruit sure she'd never be able to sleep aboard a lifter, and then Shores's eyes closed and she slipped deeper into her seat.

Even that modest effort was wasted. She'd been asleep for less than fifteen minutes when the pilot woke her.

"LZ Campione's under attack."

"Who?"

"Doing the attacking? Our friendly local terrs, of course. Light weapons only, and they're standing off, so far." Konishi made several traditional gestures of aversion.

The pilot had answered Shores's question more intelligently than she'd asked it. Her usual corollary of easy sleep was slow waking.

Linak'h:

Aromatic smoke floated from Herman Franke's pipe as he looked over Colonel Nieg's shoulder at the display in front of them.

It was a general-officer quality display. Nieg had contacts which allowed him a free hand with equipping his highly unofficial operations room. But only a very modest or junior general would have put his displays or anything else in the manager's office of a disused warehouse in the Zone.

Only a very senior general would have risked running Nieg's informal intelligence operation—a very senior general or an ex-Ranger. Add: an ex-Ranger facing a situation where the main field force on his turf was determined to dominate intelligence with their own assets. Worse, Kharg (with Longman's obvious prodding) had penetrated Linak'h Command's intelligence, so that what 222 Brigade didn't control it could at least neutralize.

Nobody had put up a poster of General Tanz with a target superimposed. Nobody needed to; the objective of keeping Tanz from jumping borders again was too plain to require stating.

Since it was also plain to General Tanz, he suddenly discovered that he had interests in common with Nieg. Nieg was no longer a Trojan Horse for Banfi. He was a potential ally against what appeared to be the actual menace of Longman and Kharg.

Nieg was also deniable and expendable, more so than the other candidate for the job, Colonel Hogg. Nieg suspected she wouldn't have accepted if offered it. Hogg didn't have stars in her ambition, but didn't want to get sucked into a brawl at the back door while real enemies stood at the front.

Hogg could afford that detachment. Nobody was going to shut down her de facto brigade—the Linak'h BEU, the Fourth/222, the Linak'h Reserve Battalion, and Shores's QRF. Nobody but a complete idiot, anyway, and none of the seniors on Linak'h qualified for that rank.

Nieg's operations were different, so he was willing to cut corners to keep them going, and even to recruit miscellaneous talent where he could find it. When the unofficial Command Group of his nonexistent operation met in this covert HQ (not that it ever did), he had himself, Commander Franke (sent dirtside to keep him out of Longman's sight), Lu Morley (for access to the police),

Juan Esteva (not kicking and screaming too loudly at being back in intelligence), and Colonel Davidson.

He would have liked to add a reliable Ptercha'a, a reliable Reservist (the longer on Linak'h the better), and somebody from 222 Brigade. But perfection was for the spirit world or Marshals; in this world, with his present rank, he just had to make do.

Right now, making do meant watching the tactical and message displays as the QRF rode to the rescue of LZ Campione. What they were rescuing it from, Nieg wasn't sure. The amount of reliably reported incoming fire suggested a probe or a small-scale attack by a local guerrilla commander with more initiative than sense.

Either could still have nasty consequences. A probe might be intended to suck the relieving force into an ambush. That seemed to have occurred to Candy, but she might need help to detect and defeat an ambush loaded with AD weaponry.

The ambush was the worst case—and not just because it might get Candy killed. Even the sloppiest attack could also inflict casualties on the troops at LZ Campione— and a well-handled one might give serious trouble to its two rifle platoons and AS&M team. Then there'd be nervous senior commanders, faced with a choice Nieg had to admit would make him nervous too.

Divide Linak'h Command's ground troops to defend the LZ's needed for a decent TacAir system, abandon keeping up such a system, or rely on space-based firepower to save small isolated units under attack?

The first immobilized too many troops. The second conceded defeat on the spot. The third was vulnerable to an opponent's using the elementary tactic of closing in until long-distance fire support was unusable out of risk of hitting friendlies. Whoever the opposition was, Nieg would concede them a mastery of elementary tactics.

But in more than one language, the same word could mean "danger" and "opportunity." Nieg pointed a pair of tightly crossed fingers at the communication board.

"Call 'Formaldahyde.' "

Franke knocked out his pipe and tapped in the code. It wasn't likely anyone was listening, but why take chances? As the com displays gyrated, Nieg put his sec-

ond screen on line and pulled its security hood over his
head and shoulders.

"Hello, Colonel," Tanz's voice said. Both Nieg's ears
and the voice-print program confirmed that it was Tanz—
FORMALDAHYDE. "The Campione attack?"

"Yes. If you don't mind giving the QRF another piece
of the headlines . . ."

"What headlines? Shores has what she needs for the
job, doesn't she?"

"Yes. But if my suspicion is right, and this confirms
the Cu Chi Hypothesis, we may have to push for more
publicity."

"Time to worry about that when we have something
to publicize. How are we doing for biosensors? Loaded,
ready, emplaceable ones?"

Nieg thought an obscenity. "The Navy hasn't been
keeping you informed on their assets?"

"The last report was three days ago."

This time Nieg muttered the obscenity aloud. "We can
do it with low-altitude passes and armored LI on the far
side. But try to squeeze something out of the Navy while
you're alerting the suit people."

"I was thinking of going out at least as far as Campione
myself."

"Sir, with all due respect, I have a feeling our main
problem is Admiral Longman." Also General Kharg,
who was senior to both Tanz's deputy and his chief of
staff, but Nieg choose to err on the side of tact and
brevity. "I suggest a division of labor on the basis of who
is best qualified to deal with which opponent."

That was pushing Tanz as hard as Banfi ever did, and
Nieg had neither the rank, the quasi-legal position with
the Ptercha'a, nor the sheer experience of Linak'h conditions to make the push stick. The only hope was that
Tanz would choose the most intelligent way of regaining
his reputation.

"How much respect is that? Never mind," Tanz added,
with a tone that implied a shrug. "I'll stay where I am.
But keep the QRF air support together, or we will have
to cancel if we don't get those sensors."

"Yes, sir."

Nieg rubbed aching ears after he took off the security
hood. Franke had lit another pipe. The colonel wondered

if it was true, that he didn't dare smoke when he was with Lu Morley. Fortunately for both of them, she was on duty today. If this blew up into an Alert One or even Two she'd be on duty until the QRF operation was finished, one way or another.

Just as well. Morley might not have a real vocation for the military, unlike her brother Gerald, but being forced to resign never went down well with a family like that. Franke was also protective of Lu's career prospects, at least when she allowed him to be, and offending Franke could mean offending the Kishi Institute.

"When are we going to be able to use those allegedly on-planet Rangers?" Franke said, apparently addressing the smoke cloud from his pipe.

"Nothing alleged about Ram Daranji," Nieg said. "Nor a couple of others. I know where to find them, and they know where to find the rest of their people. That satisfies the legal requirement for a Ranger Detachment being 'under command.' "

"It doesn't let us take the heat off Colonel Shores."

"That, I'm afraid, is Tanz's doing. He's afraid that turning the Forces's wildings loose to hunt tunnels will generate another river-crossing incident."

"Then Tanz is—"

"That is a hypothesis I have entertained myself," Nieg interrupted smoothly. "But don't dwell on it, please. We have enough real enemies without imagining more."

Instead of saluting, Franke salaamed, then made *namasti,* and finally clicked his heels and thumbed his nose.

Linak'h:

Candice Shores had all kinds of assets for turning her QRF detachment into a CA-capable force. It took her only thirty seconds after she woke fully to make a mental list.

She had a battalion's worth of air support for her company-sized force. Two companies (C/Fifth/222 and *Shenandoah*) were represented overall, but platoons, squads, and weapons teams were intact. Everybody had a one-plus-three ammo load at least, and the lifters could do some shooting. They had eight combat-loaded suits, which meant less than a work-hour apiece before they could go into action, and six techs for the eight suits. C-cubed assets were sufficient or improvisable . . .

So much for the material. The people weren't perfect, but they were getting better. She didn't have Eppie Timberlake, but she had Lieutenant Kapustev (*check if he's eligible for a field spot to first lieutenant*) and the Juan & Jan Show.

She finished the list and started on the orders. The "tagalongs" were ordered to clear the area, remaining low over the densest forest canopy they could find. The military lifters went into a gypsy circle while four of the light attackers burned sky toward LZ Campione. The heavy climbed to altitude, to start a 360-degree scan, and the map of LZ Campione came up on the displays of the troop lifters.

"Nothing fancy," Shores concluded. "I'll go in with the CA force, but at the rear so I can eyeball the big picture. If there is one," she added.

"Nonlethals for the first load?" somebody who hadn't been listening clearly asked.

Rude remarks on the circuit broke com discipline. Shores took a few square cems of skin off both the poor listener and the undisciplined voices.

"We don't have to take first fire," she concluded. "Hot LZ rules apply. But we may have friendlies and whatever else is around mixed up. Probably will, if it stays at personal-weapons range. We don't want to kill friendlies, and we do want prisoners."

Somebody muttered, "Are we eating Pussy now?" but Shores ignored it. "CA Formation—Standard Four. Counting down—three, two, one, *mark*! Formate."

To the untrained eye the lurching and weaving of thirty lifters trying to form into two columns looked like a badly-done ballet of flying grumblers. By Shores's more sophisticated standards it was a model of precision, if not speed (and personally, she risked those day-ruining midairs only when actually under fire).

Two flights of assault lifters now surged forward, Factual Flight pulling ahead of Temporal, while the heavier lifters held well back. Shores stepped forward to the copilot's chair and motioned him clear. It might be hogging the view, but she wanted *eyes*, not electronics, showing her what lay ahead of her people.

Aboard U.F.S. *Shenandoah*, off Linak'h:

The com display at Rose Liddell's station in the Combat Center was blank, but Admiral Longman's voice came through the scrambling in fine style. By now Liddell could almost read her superior's likely expression from the voice. Right now it was probably skeptical, possibly about to turn hostile.

Liddell crossed her fingers, and would have crossed her toes if she hadn't been wearing the first shoes she grabbed when the action started dirtside. They were almost too stiff for comfortable walking, let alone crossing her toes.

"Was this operation authorized by General Kharg?" Longman said. "It's in his AO."

The question hung in the air. Liddell hoped that it didn't hang in the two hundred kloms of vacuum between the two flagships. Scramble, squirt, tight-beam as you would, there was no such thing as perfect communications security.

There was also nothing more valuable to an enemy, next to learning strategic plans, than learning about a quarrel among senior commanders.

"It was my understanding that this situation developed so quickly that it would have been handled under any circumstances with the forces available, even by General Kharg. As it happened, he appears to have been out of communication during the critical decision window. Also, the most available forces were under Colonel Hogg."

Who does not *insist on being informed before a single platoon of her brigade can be used under somebody else's command.*

Silence on the circuit, except for a little static and a frequency spillover. Scrambled, Liddell could not make out what was spilling over, but it sounded faint, like incoming from the convoy. They must be only a few hours from the transports Jumping to Riftwell and *Somtow Nosavan* heading home to Victoria. One less thing to worry about once they'd Jumped, no Merishi trouble so far, and the escorts able to take care of themselves on the way back to Linak'h.

But that way would be more than three days, and during that time *Shenandoah* was a larger than usual fraction of Linak'h Command's space-based ground support. There was no way a quarrel with Longman could be allowed to restrain her movements.

At this point Liddell noticed that Pavel Bogdanov was frantically trying to get her attention. She nodded, and saw him hand-signaling numbers.

Of course. Longman was a fanatic for being able to quote the proper regulation or at least give its number. (She was also a fanatic for not having subordinates listen in and not having two senior officers in the same CC, but what she didn't learn wouldn't hurt *Shen*.)

"I think this is a case of Field Regulation 123—tactical emergencies, available forces, and junior commanders' initiative."

Longman sounded mollified when she spoke. "That's true up to a point. But who is the real commander in this situation?"

"Have your communications been garbled?" Liddell asked.

That definitely caught Longman on one foot. "Not that I know. Why?"

"Because what we've received aboard *Shenandoah* makes it fairly clear that the OTC is Colonel Shores, acting on orders from Command HQ. For all we know, General Kharg may have been fully informed and simply given an acknowledgment we didn't receive. I sometimes wonder how well we pick up the Army's tactical net, even when they want us to and aren't in a hurry."

"I hope they don't think they can hide a tactical emergency and then ask us to get them out of it when things go sour," Longman said. "Things" wasn't the only bit of sourness in that reply.

"It won't help if we lose Army people waiting for their chiefs to shout for help," Liddell said. *Now to move in for the kill.* "What about some preliminary movements of the Low Squadron?"

"Of course. I'll leave the details to you." Longman valued the image of leaving subordinates some initiative after the shooting started. In fact, she usually managed the reality, not merely the image.

"Thank you, Admiral."

Liddell blinked her vision clear and wiped sweat off her forehead. She wanted a hairbrush to subdue hair that she was sure must have turned into a Medusa's coiffure in the last few minutes, but also wanted the Old Lady's dignity.

"Pavel. Another heavy attacker flight down to support Campione. Also, alert our ready attackers. Launch in five minutes."

"Suggestion, Commodore. We launch the first of the readies immediately, but wait ten or fifteen minutes for the one with the Mark 40's. We have forgotten to tell Admiral Longman that we now have one alert attacker loaded with sensor packages at all times. I think it would be useful if she did not learn that fact until after this engagement is over, at least."

"That won't do any harm. We'll want an eyeball situation estimate from Colonel Shores anyway, and she's at least ten minutes out."

Bogdanov nodded. Liddell switched her com to the Low Squadron tactical frequencies and started tapping in the batch of three-number codes that would send the assigned ships into action. Voice commands would have been faster, but Liddell wanted the extra minute or so, to find answers for questions that might come back.

She also wanted to find answers that didn't reveal Nieg's role in handling this engagement. His being right wouldn't help if Longman or Kharg (or Longman pushing Kharg) made a fuss about his being involved at all!

Linak'h:

Shores got the word on the Navy support twelve minutes out from LZ Campione.

Seven minutes out, with the attackers already over the battle, Shores's command lifter swung out of formation and dropped back to the rear of the first wave. Lieutenant Kapustev was now leading. Shores trusted both his head and the eyes in it more than most people's.

Four minutes out, she learned that the attack was over.

Shores was tempted to order Konishi to dive the command lifter in over the LZ for an improvised personnal reconaissance. However, that nobody was now trying to shoot up LZ Campione didn't mean they had packed up and left entirely. A low-flying command lifter was just the thing to tempt a frustrated rear guard into folly (expensive for them, but too common for safety; expensive for both sides if they had any AD hardware).

Talktalk with the CO at Campione had to be the starting point.

"Huntress to Thermal One. Any hostiles in sight at all?"

"Negative on that. No, wait. Somebody's indicating a visual, bearing zero-two-zero true, on a strip of open ground about one point-five kloms from our perimeter."

"Identified hostile? And what kind?"

"Not identified, not ours. On foot, no race ID—could be Catpeople."

The bearing and position meant that Factual Flight and Shores herself would be passing directly over the mystery people on the way in to the LZ.

"Factual Flight, emergency dogleg turn, two-klom legs, now! Attackers, EW support, now!"

The comparatively neat formation ahead seemed to disintegrate. Either on Kapustev's orders or on their own initiative, the pilots were alternating left and right turns. This would bring them into the LZ a little late and a lot more sloppily, but give hostile AD gunners and sensors a major headache on the way.

Then radio and radar blanked out as the heavy attacker at ten thousand meters and the lights at four thousand all started jamming. The total amount of effort the QRF was putting into countering the unidentified infantrymen was enough to give a battalion headaches.

If there wasn't a battalion, it would give Shores's people good live practice and the morale of the LZ Campione garrison a boost. From their CO's tight voice and fuzzy data, it sounded as if they needed that boost.

"Factual Three to Huntress. We have a firm visual on the LZ's sighting. Ptercha'a, possibly one human, no Merishi. Wearing packs, field footwear, tunics, all civilian-style. No weapons visible."

Shores started, as if the earplug had given her a shock. "Repeat that last, Factual Three. Negative weapons?"

"On ten-power magnification, no weapons visible. We can scan the ground behind them if you want."

"Hold on that, Factual Three."

Doctrine, decency, and common sense converged here. She doubted that the Ptercha'a were civilians who'd wandered through by mistake. The battle had gone on long enough and loudly enough to warn them off, unless they all lacked hearing, speech, and sight.

But if they'd ditched their weapons, they might be trying to surrender, even defect. Their intelligence value joined doctrine, decency, and common sense in shaping Candice Shores's orders.

The temptation was to just lay down a cloud of UC gas, but the troop lifters weren't carrying quite enough, given the wind conditions. Using the heavies' loads meant either exposing them to possible hostile fire or shifting loads, giving the Ptercha'a time to escape if they changed their minds.

Fortunately there was an adequate if more complex solution. A lack of elegant simplicitly never bothered anybody except tactics instructors, and not even them if it worked.

Cut the jamming, so she could *give* the orders. Then smoke bomb ahead, to warn that they'd been sighted. Smoke barriers behind, to cover a force coming up from the rear to seize them. And a psywar drop—a converted sensor package, with a recorded message giving orders, promising good treatment, and containing food, water, and medical supplies, also a couple of unpleasant surprises for unpleasant people (such as those who faked a surrender to lay a trap).

The flight had two of these packages, one human and one Ptercha'a, both racked and ready. That was Nieg's idea, and another of the ones he hadn't bothered to mention to superior officers. One of these days she might mention that habit to him, but not today.

The light attackers laid down the smoke, red in front, blue behind. One reported that the party had stopped. Then the psywar package went down, rocket-boosted for precision, then braked to a final landing by a monofilament chute.

When the Ptercha'a started gathering around the package, Shores issued her final orders:

"Factual Three, take two lifters and execute the capture. I'll bring in the other Factuals. Temporal Flight, circle as planned until you receive either hostile fire or my orders."

The acknowledgments came in. Shores tapped Konishi on the shoulder and pointed at the LZ. The lifter's nose dipped as it started its final approach.

Sixteen

Linak'h:

The QRF HQ was split up for the flight back to the Zone, in case of accidents or enemy action. Juan Esteva found himself in Factual Two, one of the pair of lifters Lieutenant Kapustev was leading to the capture of the mystery Ptercha'a.

Esteva was glad that Kapustev and Colonel Candy usually knew what they were doing. This was more than he did right now, which made him wonder if he'd been so smart in leaving Intelligence. There at least he usually had a piece of the Big Picture.

But remember all the times you complained that you couldn't do anything with the knowledge? His conscience now tended to reproach him in Jan Sklarinsky's voice, even when it was about things that had happened well before they'd met again.

Then the lifter bumped and wiggled to a stop, the ramp slammed down, and the squad leader was shouting "Go, go, go!"

Esteva went at the same run as everybody else. Getting out of the lifter was one moment when a squad couldn't help being a little bunched up. The only hope was fast running, helped if possible by sloppy shooting on the other side.

The squad ran, Esteva keeping on the opposite side of the formation from the squad leader. Kapustev, and the squad leader from his lifter, did the same on the other side of the grounded machines. Esteva had just checked his pulser to make sure that his loaded magazine was nonlethals, when the lifters took off in a blast of fanwash.

The squads had covered most of the way to the smoke

barrier, and the lifters had backed most of the way to the perimeter, before Esteva recognized Jan in the other squad. He waved, she waved back, Esteva's squad leader started to say something but thought better of it, then they were up to the smoke barrier and the point men were taking a deep breath before plunging into it.

"Hold up!" Kapustev called. He pointed left and right, toward the trees that flanked the open ground. The open area was no more than two hundred meters wide, and the forest loomed like a green wall on either side, with spots of blue and yellow and sinister masses of shadow for variety.

"I want the SSW's in the trees just the other side of the smoke barrier before anybody goes through on foot."

"But the colonel . . ." somebody began. Somebody who did not know Candice Shores, and whom Esteva expected to see handed his head on a platter.

Either Kapustev was in a good mood, or he thought that even an empty head was better on its owner's shoulders. He shrugged. "The colonel can come down and take point herself, if she's in that much of a hurry. SSW's to the flanks—*move out!*"

The four troopers of the two SSW teams moved out, at a run.

Linak'h:

Candice Shores saw Kapustev hold up his advance, and spent the next ten seconds composing a royal ass-chewing. Then common sense fought and defeated urgency. She called up the light attackers, who could see beyond the smoke barrier.

"Any Magnet Flight in visual contact with the Ptercha'a? Are they holding position?"

A jumble of pilots' voices as they argued over who was seeing what, then somebody came through with the best proof of all, a visual transmission to the command lifter.

The Ptercha'a had done more than remain in position. They were clustered more tightly than before around the psywar package. Some of them looked as if they had unpacked medical or food packages and were treating one another or grabbing a snack.

They didn't look hostile or in a hurry to get anywhere. They looked like people waiting to be captured. The trees on either side looked like an excellent hiding place for snipers at least, maybe other and more potent enemies, for whom a pair of SSW's was at least a temporary solution.

Kapustev could get on with his job and she could get on with hers, as soon as she could define it. She was almost tempted to take the high watch position herself, to allow some thinking time. But then everybody would suspect her of hesitation, lack of confidence in Kapustev, or both.

Life was easier, Candy, when you were virtually invisible to generals.

Easier, yes—but since she was a private first (officer-trainee selected) she'd done what she'd expected—found a place and a purpose in the Army. More place and purpose than her mother had ever allowed her, more than her father had been allowed to give (or might have been able to, with the best will in the world), more than she had sometimes expected to find at all.

She would just have to write off sweating out generals' opinions of her tactics as part of the payback. At least until she became a general herself—and what was the name the Greeks had for that, which her father had taught her?

Oh yes. *Hubris,* getting so above yourself that the gods noticed and lost their tempers.

Linak'h:

The SSW squads moved fast, considering that they were each carrying a thirty-kilo load, when you added in everything from the SSW itself to the last aromatic in the bottom of the loader's ass pack.

That was ten kilos more than the average LI unarmored load, and meant that SSW teams needed the muscular and aggressive. Esteva was glad he was only the second. Platoon- and company-level crew-served weap-

ons had a long history, which he'd once read up on.
Three things stuck in his memory as holding true, from
the First Terran War up to the last firefight on Victoria.

The weapons were vital assets to their own people.

They were also prime targets for the other side.

Therefore, the weapons crews had a combat life-expec-
tancy measured in minutes if they were lucky, seconds if
they weren't (or if they lacked body armor, or if the
opponent had armor-defeating weapons deployed far
enough forward).

While he waited for the SSW's to get into position,
Esteva asked his squad leader's permission to do a walk-
around, eyeballing this sector of the battlefield. He
wished he'd brought a recorder, so he could take pictures
of any weapon traces, but that was the problem with
being Intelligence in a company HQ. You had to think
like both a trooper and an analyst, and sometimes you
accidentally wound up not thinking like either, or even
not at all.

Esteva roamed back and forth, as the smoke bombs
continued to pop, keeping up the visual barrier between
the Ptercha'a and their prospective captors. By the time
the bombs had stopped and the barrier had begun to
fade, Esteva was satisfied that any attack from this direction had probably been Ptercha'a, with personal weapons
only and not much ammo.

Of course, a lot could already have been trampled out
of shape, but crew-served weapons and the boots of Ptercha'a carrying heavy loads left deep and distinctive impressions. There was expended brass from hunting weapons
pressed into military service (*or maybe used for sniping?
Have to ask Jan about that,*) discarded field-dressing
wrappers and medspray injectors, a few blood traces, and
one definite trail.

Esteva tried to follow the trail, but it petered out after
taking him forty meters toward the forest to the right.
He looked at the trees with new wariness, told himself
that anybody still there would have seen the two squads
and let fly, then decided that was Kapustev's decision.

By the time he reached Kapustev the breeze had risen
and the smoke was almost gone, spread out into a light
haze over most of LZ Campione. Three hundred meters

away, the Ptercha'a sat in a rough circle around their gift from the Federation.

Esteva felt a mild urge to hit the dirt and crawl the rest of the way, but Kapustev was standing so he couldn't. (Of course the lieutenant and Jan, who was beside him, both made hard targets. He was so short and she was so slim, except in a couple of relevant places.)

Mind on job, not on Jan, amigo, his conscience said, for once in a neutral voice.

"Yes, Sergeant?"

"I found a blood trail back there. It only ran about forty meters, but it headed that way," and he pointed.

Kapustev turned around—then spun the rest of the way, throwing his hands up as he lost his balance and toppled.

Sklarinsky was already on her way down when the sniper's round tore through the air where she'd been standing, so it glanced off Esteva's vest. He didn't try to keep his balance, but went down as if he'd been punched through the heart.

Lying still to improve the act, all he could see was a patch of something grass-like, with tiny yellow-white flowers. He could hear clearly, though, as Ptercha'a battle rifles and Federation pulsers and SSW's opened up, distinct at first, then blending into a vicious uproar where any additional weapons just added volume.

Linak'h:

Candice Shores saw the opening of the fight relayed from the high lifter. She saw the rest from the cockpit of her own machine as it climbed back to observation altitude. Afterward she could never remember when the one gave way to the other.

Since there were about five different time estimates for each key event of the fight, the best she could do was average them and extrapolate. Since that wasn't very good, she conceded defeat.

Weapons flickered in the tree line, and Kapustev, Sklarinsky, and Esteva went down. After that Shores stopped taking names.

Rage gave her one idea: Command-detonate the frag charge in the psywar package. The Ptercha'a were faster than Candice Shores's reflexes. They sprinted away from the package, even the visibly wounded keeping up a good pace with help from their comrades.

Some of them ran toward the trees to the left of the open ground. Some of them ran toward the Federation capture party, those who had hands free waving them desperately.

A few ran toward the firing position. They remained untargeted by either side, as far as Shores could see. The tree-line shooters were friendlies, and the Federation was too busy with armed enemies. One did go down, but two friends snatched up the unlucky one and practically dragged him/her out of sight.

That UC gas might not have been such a bad idea, after all, Shores realized. Too light a dose would have lost prisoners, but also spooked them into running off before their comrades could set the ambush that had probably killed Federation soldiers.

Hindsight is always perfect, and usually futile was a very long-memorized maxim. Also, the situation wasn't past repairing. The SSW's were already in action, and the hostile fire was already diminishing just from their efforts.

Then orders crackled on the tactical net, too fast for Shores to keep track of them. She knew they were being recorded anyway, and thought she recognized Esteva's voice.

The high lifter rose higher, its turret swung, and its gun started pumping rounds into the tree line. Smoke puffs said antipersonnel rounds, with small charges producing lots of fragments and hopefully no flash large enough to start fires in the undergrowth.

The other lifter slid sideways to the right, also firing, apparently 22-mm solids and an occasional burst from the podded pulsers. It landed with its rear toward the right-flank SSW team, who didn't have as good a field of fire as their left-flank comrades. They ceased fire, scrambled aboard, and rode across the open ground to join the base of fire on the other side.

Then the low lifter scooted back into the center of the open ground, again landing bow toward the enemy and turret blazing away. (No blazes in the forest, yet, and Shores hoped the lifter crews were being careful with their ammunition selection.) The crew and able-bodied troopers on the ground snatched up the wounded, and the whole party crammed itself into the lifter for the ride to the left flank.

At this point Shores thought of calling down smoke to cover the defecting or at least non-hostile Ptercha'a, but a quick look changed her mind and orders. They were dead or at least immobile, shot down by their comrades with the same ruthlessness shown to human defectors along the Braigh'n.

Somebody on the other side was playing very rough, and when Candice Shores learned who they were, she was going to perform surgery on them with a dull blade. Except that she would probably have to stand in line, if there were any knives left on the planet.

That kind of crude cold-bloodedness paid off only in the short run. But the long run could be too long, for the Federation or at least a lot of her people.

"Well done, rescue party," she said. "Casualties?"

"No KIA yet, four WIA," and this time it definitely was Esteva.

"Kapustev?"

"Concussion at least, maybe a fracture, but his eyes are fair and his vital signs okay. We got a medic down here, but I've been to better parties."

"We'll do something about the party-crashers. Keep their heads down if you can, yours if you can't."

"Can do, Colonel."

That established who was in command for now on the ground. What next, for the one in command of the whole show (at least until somebody with stars decided that a temp light colonel was too junior to hog all the fun)?

She punched up maps and lists of both ready and stored weapons in the QRF formation, then formed a plan. She also briefly thanked the Creator for lift-field vehicles. They'd already prevented a skirmish from turning into a bloody nose for the Federation. A little luck added to her people's skill, and they might turn the skirmish into a Federation victory.

They might even confirm Nieg's Cu Chi Hypothesis. If

they did, she would ask him who or what Cu Chi was or
had been.

Meanwhile . . .

"Factuals Five and Six, take position two kloms in
from the tree line, bearing one-eight-zero relative to the
hostile position. Got a clear sight on it?"

Two "Rogers" came back.

"After that, one lifter take watch, the other find open
ground to land, and alternate at one-hour intervals. We'll
arrange for an aeriel recharge as soon as we get more
heavies in and reload the lights.

"If you find any sort of trail . . . anyone carrying air-
droppable charges?"

"We can influence-fuse grenade bundles, if that'll
help."

"Better than nothing." Her people seemed to take that
attitude in a lot of places—better *something* now than
perfect tomorrow, when you could be dead or the other
side got away. *May this continue.*

"Okay. If you detect any movement, shout. Otherwise
hold position. We'll be putting people on the ground as
soon as we can find both the people and the ground."

The "Rogers" were a little less enthusiastic this time.

The CO of Campione was not at all enthusiastic about
Shores's next orders, which were for the whole Temporal
Flight of the QRF to proceed to the next safe LZ, LZ
Barbarossa, escorting the heavy cargo lifters, and land
there.

"Don't we need more people on the ground here?"
the CO asked. He sounded just as nervous as before,
almost whining.

"No. You drove off the first attack. The second's being
held by my people. If there's a third, we've got air support up the arse. We need to think of bagging those
people in the trees. Intelligence, Captain, intelligence."

Which you had better start displaying . . .

"But—"

"I don't have to explain, Captain."

She also had to leave him in command for now, or at
least not relieve him of command over the air. He was
from the Third/222, and his CO would hear about today,
but unless he completely lost it he would keep his job
for now. Shores didn't have anyone to replace him, since

a 222 platoon would not take kindly to orders from a Linak'h Reserve platoon leader.

Discretion, or someone whispering in his ear, silenced the captain. Shores went back to giving her orders.

The techs at Barbarossa would only have time to bring the eight suits up to a "vanilla" configuration, with minimal weapons and reduced endurance. But "better than nothing," and the heavy attackers were all equipped to handle deep penetrators. The only way to discourage people from building underground bunkers was to be capable at all times of cracking them like eggs. (People who were part-burrower tended to have a burrower's short sight and slow wits, but if you weeded them out of the gene pool at periodic intervals you reduced their potential for doing harm.)

She modified her plan slightly at the suggestion of the Reserve platoon commander. Her people were all raised in the woods, she said. A squad or so coming in on the flank or rear of the people in the trees might give them a major new headache.

"I have no problem with that," Shores said. "Just make sure they swing wide so they aren't spotted going in. I don't want you losing people to ambushes, booby traps, or friendly fire if you get stuck in too close for us to help you out. Want a sniper?"

"Thank you, Colonel, but I have two already. With God's blessing, their work will be good and sufficient."

Shores went off-com, to lean back in her seat and contemplate the displays as they showed Temporal Flight breaking out of its circle and heading west toward LZ Barbarossa. It was tempting to go with them to hustle them along, but they didn't need hustling and the Campione fight might need her again.

Shuttling back and forth among critical areas was a good way for a CO to be out of touch with all of them when she was needed, or at least as out of touch as modern communications technology allowed. Far better to pick one place and stay there.

"Okay, Mr. Konishi. This time we land and stay."

"Mind if I down the port fans for a diagnostic? The signs are a little off."

"No sweat. A little walking will do me some good."

Linak'h:

Juan Esteva had been enjoying his temporary command for just under twenty minutes when Colonel Shores arrived. He'd almost started thinking of it as "Task Force Esteva," since technically he had organic heavy weapons, lift transport (doubling as logistical support), and medics.

However, he was reconciled to the arrival of superior rank as long as it was Colonel Candy, not that cretin from LZ Campione. She brought a lifter-load of ammo and other supplies and sent out the wounded on the same lifter. And Esteva couldn't really blame anyone for wanting to stay away from the captain and be unavailable to the generals who would sooner or later start noticing a fight of this size.

"We've got lifters swanning about over a good quarter of the area between Camp Great Bend and the Zone," Shores said, unwrapping a ration bar. "It would take flag officers dumber than I ever want to have over me not to notice that."

"What about the Pus—the Administration?" somebody asked.

Esteva looked around to see which somebody had nearly used a bad word for the Ptercha'a, but couldn't pick out any guilty looks under the camouflage cream and dirt. The two squads and lifter crews looked trained and ready for a fight. Their eyes would have told any experienced observer that they hadn't really been in one yet.

"We can shoot or even arrest anybody who shoots at us," Shores said. "That's in the agreement, along with not having to get approval for troop movements. I don't expect we'll have to do anything more to accomplish our mission today."

Esteva and Jan Sklarinsky exchanged looks. Esteva knew, and the sniper had guessed, enough about the Cu Chi Hypothesis to suspect that Colonel Candy was lying through her well-polished teeth. Esteva also suspected that, pushed by Nieg, Shores would in turn push both herself and her people to the farthest limit of what was allowed, to catch those Ptercha'a.

Sometimes Esteva had flashes of his old feeling toward

Candice Shores—kid brother looking at an older sister who has involved herself with a brilliant, weird, and even older man. (He wouldn't deny Nieg's claim to brains.) Flashes only, because there hadn't been a lot he could do about it when she was a captain, and there was even less now that she was field-grade.

But it still itched, like a mite that's got into your armor and you don't notice before you go into combat or even into vacuum!

Linak'h:

Shores's lifter crew had just finished unloading the last of the resupply when a sonic boom heralded the arrival of a new heavy attacker. She crouched in the bushes, getting the best view she could without exposing herself of the sleek, glistening cylinder whipping by overhead.

"Vermilion three, calling Huntress. Reporting on station. Azure Six is about ten minutes behind us. They're carrying the Mark 40's."

"Huntress here, Vermilion Three. Your first job is to recharge the two lifters you'll see low over the treetops. Report to me when you've done that. Altitude and course at your discretion, but take their advice."

The silence after the acknowledgment was eloquent. The attacker crew didn't enjoy being ordered to power up a pair of troop lifters, instead of leaping upon the enemy with all weapons blazing, dropping, or whatever else their load did.

That was their problem. Shores was juggling the desirability of capturing prisoners, the usefulness of throwing light on the Cu Chi Hypothesis, and the necessity of not starting any forest fires. Vermilion Three could best help with all of them by obeying her orders—which they did.

"How many penetrators are you carrying, Mark 72 or heavier?" she asked, when Vermilion Three came back on the air.

"Didn't they transmit our load?"

A quick check to the command lifter and the CP of LZ Campione showed no record of Vermilion Three's ordnance load. If it had been transmitted, either it hadn't been received or been lost after receipt.

Hang, draw, and quarter afterwards, Shore told herself. *And then only if harm's been done.*

"We've got four Mark 77's, but one of them's gone down since we left *Shen.*"

Gain nearly an hour on an enemy able to use that time to evade, and gamble that three would be enough? Yes. The Barbarossa people could continue, and be ready as a backup in case there were more targets for the penetrators.

"Be ready to use all four, in two pairs. Sheer kinetic energy might be enough. But can you set the boosters so that *brennschluss* is at five hundred meters?"

Another of those eloquent silences at which Vermilion Three's pilot seemed so expert followed, ending in another voice. "Weapons Warrant Fong here, Colonel. It'll take a little time reprogramming the onboard brains, but if you've got the time we've got the capability."

"Do it," Shores said. She watched Vermilion Three climb supersonically, to vanish behind clouds roiled by the shock wave. Not rain clouds, though, and the stand of forest was rated HIGH for fire-danger under these conditions.

"I'd like to stay and watch the fireworks," Shores said. "But I've got to watch them from someplace with C-cubed. Good luck, people, and don't try to be heroes. There's a shortage of both body bags and medals, the last thing I heard."

As she headed back along the concealed route to the LZ, she thought she heard explosions from the opposite tree line. A quick stop, and she was sure. Explosions that might have been grenades, small-arms fire that sounded like both pulsers and battle rifles, and the rest of the sound effects of a firefight, all muffled by taking place well inside tall timber.

Shores could see that the squad with her, mostly overaged Reservists, were looking nervous. First-combat jitters could make anyone suspicious of anything not in the program, not to mention dangerous to their own people.

"Your CO was putting a squad of your wood-smart

into the trees to hit the Ptercha'a in the flank. They must have made better time than I expected."

The feeling of security that notion gave everybody lasted until they reached the CP. Then the Reserve platoon leader listened to Shores's description of the fight and said, "What squad?"

"It isn't them?"

"Not unless they can be in two places at once." The platoon leader pointed. A squad of heavily laden troopers was slogging toward the tree line, the point about to enter it where they would be invisible from the enemy position.

"You said 'be sneaky,' and I added 'load up on ammo,' and they obeyed both of us."

The platoon leader just missed being old enough to be Candice Shores's mother, and anyway frontier-planet Reservists were a bit weird anyway. (Anybody who'd served on Victoria might be excused for using stronger terms.) Shores didn't object to the brusqueness.

What she objected to was the situation, which was not the platoon leader's fault. *But don't assume chaos until you've checked with everybody; start with the two lifters on hover patrol. . . .*

"Negative on people on the ground," both Five and Six said. "We did see some movement about three, four minutes before the firing, in a thin spot in the trees. Couldn't get a positive ID even to race, though, and they moved too fast for a fire solution."

Shores did not suggest that under the circumstances a running firing solution would have made sense, because a moment's thought ended her anger and told her it didn't. There were too many spots for one lifter's on-board computer to keep solutions on all of them.

This put the situation finally out of her hands. Friendly forces might be in the area; they might get hurt when the penetrators went down. If she kicked the situation upstairs, the delays might let the enemy evade. But if she killed friendlies without checking on their presence, she would be a bad as well as an ex-soldier.

She told the lifters to both get airborne and not fire unless fired upon, then sat at the com console for a call to FORMALDAHYDE.

Linak'h:

Linked to the CP, Juan Esteva listened to the unfolding
confusion without trying hard enough to keep mingled
wonder and dismay off his face. Jan Sklarinsky noticed,
so did the others, then he had to explain.

When he had finished, Jan looked up at the sky and
rolled her eyes. For a moment Esteva thought she'd seen
Vermilion Three launching a penetrator.

Then Jan raised both hands in a mockery of prayer.
"Hey, up there. One question. How many sides are there
here today?" Silence, then:

"Okay. I know it was a stupid question. Sorry I
asked." She looked around. "Bets on how many sides
there are?"

"Counting us, or just Ptercha'a?" somebody asked.

"Oh, throw in everybody," came another suggestion.

The "how many sides" pool got up to eleven bettors
before the idea ran out of steam. Then a couple of troopers started arguing about prepayment, so that if a bettor
got KIA their money would still be in the pool, and
somebody else suggested that if somebody got popped
their next-of-kin ought to get the money back. Various
factions were getting ready for that debate when Colonel
Shores came back on the air.

"We have a negative on friendlies in the area. *Officially* friendly, anyway."

"Firm?"

"Firm, as to official friendlies."

He could tell what she wasn't saying because she
couldn't. "Official friendlies" meant Federation and Administration troops. It left out Confraternity people.

There was no way Shores could have asked about
them, no way to send warning, and probably no way the
Confraternity could keep track of all their people. Esteva
still had a bad feeling about killing people who might be
fighting the people who killed you.

"Okay, people," Shores said, and Esteva could tell
that she was on the all-hands circuit. "The penetrators
will go down on my call. If that suppresses all hostile
fire, we'll move in on the enemy position from both the
open ground and the forest. Only prepositioned squads

will be in the initial wave. Each platoon at LZ Campione should have one squad loaded and ready to lift out as reinforcements, though."

Esteva wondered about the Reservist flankers, but whatever Shores and their leader did about them, it wasn't done on the air. The next thing Esteva knew, the TacAir strike alarm was whining in everybody's ears, and the squads broke up into the dispersed formation used when waiting for friendly air to move in.

Esteva raised his head enough to see the golden flash high up, as the first penetrator fell free and ignited. Each Mark 77 was a two-ton tube of ceramic and steel, very much the same stuff as a starship's sphere-shell, with a base-fused explosive charge. They could penetrate thirty meters of concrete and turn the CP at the bottom into business for Graves Registration.

Esteva had never heard what they could do in virgin forest, with eighty-meter trees in soil. He expected it would be interesting to find out.

The rocket booster blazed until Esteva had to look away as it grew larger and brighter. They must have dropped the beast from nearly maximum altitude for the kind of accuracy they wanted.

Then the rocket died. Esteva barely saw flame turn to smoke before the penetrator vanished into the trees.

A moment later, an enormous padded club seemed to strike the ground from underneath. Esteva felt like a bug on a drumhead, tossed into the air by forces beyond his control.

The earth shook. Across the open ground, more earth rose in a towering column mixed with smoke, shattered branches and whole trees, rocks, and what might have been flying bodies. In the cloud of debris, other trees swayed as if in a gale sent by forces stronger than nature. Some lost the struggle and toppled.

Another flare in the sky, another silver glint riding the flames down to earth, and another eruption of smoke, earth, and shredded forest. This one was to the left of the first strike. Whoever was calling the shots was walking them northeast, away from the Reserve patrol.

As the second explosion's echoes rumbled into silence, Esteva heard everyone around him bracing themselves for a third. He looked up, saw the glint of sunlight on Vermilion Three, estimated her altitude at twelve thousand meters, and waited for the golden flare of the booster.

It didn't come. Instead, Shores cut through static on the circuits with another brisk stream of orders.

"Well done, Vermilion Three. Hold the other two in reserve and take a position above our scanner. You can take high watch while he takes low.

"Ground units, check in. Damage or casualties?"

Esteva was able to report none, and apparently so was the squad in the trees, although Esteva didn't hear their message.

"All right." A lifter rose from the LZ, and the background to Shores's voice was now fan-whine. "Ground squads, advance on the target area. Two and Three, take support positions. Five and Six, remain on-station, but be ready to drop your troops as reinforcements to the first section."

Esteva stood up. There was no firing from the tree line or inside it, as far as his battered ears could make out. In the target area itself, it was hard to imagine anybody being alive, let alone in shape to fight. The smoke and dust were settling or blowing away, revealing hectares of ground heaved up and trees tumbled like a basket of giant toothpicks.

"Rifle teams, move out," Esteva said. "Standard formation."

Standard formation took them right and left, giving the SSW's and the lifters clear fields of fire. Esteva told himself that two penetrators before and five lifters directly supporting the advance of three rifle squads really had to be enough.

He still felt unpleasantly naked out on the open ground, a hundred meters from anything that would stop a bullet. Then they came to their first body.

It was Ptercha'a—they could recognize that much. It was impossible to tell sex, region of origin, or civilian vs. military. A private standing beside Esteva bent over and got rid of her lunch, breakfast, and probably midnight snack.

"Easy does it," Esteva said, resting a hand lightly on her shoulder. "First fight?"

"First . . . ulp . . . first time I ever saw a dead body."

"That one's no way to start, either. Better get up and

moving, though. This *pobrecito* may have live friends getting their wits back."

They moved on, feeling the fan-wash as lifters cut low overhead, stirring up dust, leaves, and strips of bark. Ahead, the target area looked worse with each meter of advance. It was as if someone had run the forest through a coarse-set food blender the size of *Shenandoah*.

A command lifter stopped just inside the tree line, and it was listen-to-the-colonel time again.

"Any activity, hostile or otherwise?"

"None. A couple of what might be spotfires."

"Continue the advance. Use dirt on the spotfires. Save your water. This search may take a while."

"What are we looking for?"

Esteva hadn't really expected an answer now. Instead he heard laughter in the colonel's voice.

"Tunnels."

Linak'h:

Candice Shores laughed to herself at the tone of Esteva's reply. He must have thought she'd gone loco, officially proclaiming the search for the Cu Chi Man Who Might Not Be There.

It was the last laugh she had for a while. After a little longer that description of the mission didn't seem funny.

The penetrators had been the alternative to having a fire bomber standing by, within the range of portable AD weapons. The Fire Guard would not have thanked her for getting one of them shot down.

However, the penetrators had churned up the target area so thoroughly that it was impossible to tell what might have been under it before. Shores remembered some of the battles of the First Global War, where artillery had churned battlefields into gigantic marshes where wounded soldiers drowned in the puddles! She wished she had remembered that historical detail before calling down the penetrators.

They did find one Ptercha'a body in the forest. But it was in civilian clothes from an Administration store, and its (*his*, Shores thought) one remaining boot was Administration Warband issue. The body didn't have any weapons, but remnants of harness suggested it had been armed—and the harness was Ptercha'a style but *Federation*-made.

Shores refused to try adding this up; she recognized an invitation to intellectual vertigo. Instead Esteva recorded the body where it lay, and then it and everything about it were bagged for return to the CP. (This might be the only piece of intelligence they found; she would not have it carried off in a counterattack.)

No counterattack materialized. The Reserves found a couple of trails with recent Ptercha'a prints on them, but they petered out after a few hundred meters. Shores called the troopers back in and settled down to assembling her forces.

Call in the rest of the QRF. LZ Campione isn't under attack; it has secure space for the extra people. Have the eight suits assigned to troopers, but don't have the people suit up yet. Bring in geoprobes as well as the biosensors already on the way—no, they've landed at Barbarossa and the attacker pilot sounded impatient about not being allowed to drop and head upstairs.

"The Mark 40's have built-in geophones," Esteva reminded her. "Not much range, but maybe enough. Also, if we go for more hardware, that means more authorizations from On High." He looked at the sky and bit his thumb at a cloud.

"I forgot. Okay. We'll bring in the Mark 40's, drop the remote-area ones, and have the suit people lay down the rest. Let's look at a map of this stretch of forest."

The display came up; Shores and Esteva bent over it. "If I were a Ptercha'a-sized tunnel, where would I be?" she muttered.

"Colonel!" It was the Reserve squad leader, running and waving his arms. He tripped over a root, which ended the running and arm-waving but not the shouting.

"We've found a tunnel! Back there, when we took a second look at the end of one of the trails! It's hard—well, come and see for yourself."

He levered himself up on his arms, then winced as weight came on his ankle. "See the medic," Shores said, pushing him back down. "Sergeant, you play bodyguard."

"Me and a little help," Esteva said firmly, in a tone that denied even the concept of argument.

Seventeen

Linak'h:

The Ptercha'a "tunnels" were actually more like covered trenches, but they were covered a meter or more deep by the natural debris accumulation of the forest floor. This ran two or three meters deep in most places; add a meter's depth with a trench in the ground, and you had plenty of room for any number of Ptercha'a to move and to move freely.

In the tunnel that Shores's people had found, the cover was held up by woven branches and the sides of the trench by split logs. The floor of the trenches seemed to have drain-holes and was covered with more split logs.

"All the material is local. Nothing to haul in," Shores said, contemplating the shadowy gap in front of her.

Esteva nodded. "Right. No metallic signature, no electrical signature, no thermal signature."

"None?"

"There are always patches of actively decaying stuff in the debris accumulation. They create hot spots, and bio-sensing by purely thermal means is a tricky proposition underground anyway. Only a little confusion might be enough to make a difference."

"What do you mean, 'might'?" Shores asked. "We were all in the dark about this. Except for Nieg and—Sergeant, did you know the whole picture?"

"*Nobody* knew the whole picture. I suppose Colonel Nieg told me more than he did you. I'm expendable."

"There are two opinions on that, Sergeant, and Nieg is going to learn that mine differs from his," Shores said.

Esteva saluted. "Yes, ma'am."

"Oh, shove the robosoldier act. Right now, we're going to booby-trap this tunnel, so it'll warn us if any

Ptercha'a use it. Then we go back to the target area and start digging."

"Digging?"

"I used a common Anglic word, Sergeant. I don't give a Baernoi's bounce about the tunnels right now. What we need is intelligence. Specifically bodies, to find out how many sides there were in this forest.

"Oh, and I'll send out a lifter with more shovels and any power diggers we can have. Also some volunteers, to police up the bodies in the open."

"Yes, ma'am."

Shores smiled. "Sorry to be taking it out on you, Sergeant. It hasn't been a good day, and I'm not optimistic about the night. But we'll just have to muddle through somehow."

Shores returned to the LZ Campione CP to discover that the captain had shown some initiative, for once. He'd chased down all the power diggers and shovels he could spare and loaded them on a lifter. He'd also punched an image of the dead Ptercha'a from the forest through to Command HQ, and they had it on the way to the Administration police files for a computer match.

"The last message I had, the Ptercha'a were promising their highest priority," the captain said. "We may have the word by dinner."

Dinner (two ration bars, hot coffee, and rehydrated fruit) came and went, with no message. The Red Child vanished; the Yellow Father sank low.

Shores was also sinking, onto a cot in her command lifter, when she became aware that Juan Esteva was standing in the doorway, dark with dirt and shadow—and more.

"Word from On High," he said.

"Say it, and let me get to sleep."

"ID on our mystery Ptercha'a. He was one Sogan Ba-Lingazza."

"Sounds like an exotic kind of pasta. Anything else?"

"He owned a couple of hardware stores in Och'zem. He died a long way from home, and they're wondering why. The Ptercha'a—the police, anyway—say he was a VIP in the Administration's Confraternity."

"Right." Her foggy wits slowly assimilated the implications. "Who was he shooting at?"

"They'd like to know too."

"Charming of them." Shores swung her feet off the bunk and remembered not to straighten up until she'd stepped out from under the targeting-laser housing. Otherwise she'd crack her skull, which right now felt as fragile as an eggshell.

"Okay. This means an all-night dig. We rotate so there are always three squads out there. But we bring in the power-suit people as soon as they're ready, which gives us two unarmored squads digging and one resting. Post snipers for extra security, give everybody night-vision gear, and set out IR glowballs. Where's that bloody terminal?"

She thought Esteva held her arm to guide her to the console.

Linak'h:

The gray whiskers on Marshal Banfi's screen twitched. Black lips wrinkled with age drew back from teeth that still shone white.

"You ask too much," the Ptercha'a said.

"Do I not know it?" Marshal Banfi replied, in the True Speech. "But do you doubt my word and those of other humans, that the deaths were an accident?"

The silence seemed long, even though it could only have lasted seconds. The Hunter on the screen was not known for being slow to decide anything.

"When one considers all that is known, I do not doubt. I will even ask others not to doubt."

"Best of all, can you ask others to guide their movements, so you Hunters do not mingle with those serving other masters? Our warriors are wise and skilled, and few hate the Hunters, but I beg you: Do not ask them to be magicians." Nor was "beg" a mere verbal ritual; not tonight.

The silence this time seemed even longer, and Banfi realized it was no illusion. The face on the screen seemed almost ready to begin meditation.

"You realize that this means more communicating

with our Warbands? What if such communications are overheard?"

"We have enough serious business for our communications and intelligence people to keep them out of your ruffs."

"If you can do that, and none complain, well and good. But what about the Administration, or the Coordination?"

Banfi frowned. This might not be the best time to reveal his knowledge of Confraternity strength on Linak'h. But not all Confraternity leaders were clones of old Boronisskahane; some talked more freely. They had given Banfi knowledge that he had intended to conceal until the right time, but perhaps now was the right time.

Make that "probably." A prominent Confraternity leader and some of his Warband, accidentally killed by Federation troops while engaging Coordination or Merishi-sponsored Hunter guerrillas, was bad enough. Having the deaths start rumors that a) the humans had declared war on the Confraternity or b) the Confraternity had been joining the guerrillas, would be worse.

In fact, it could turn both ugly rumors (already spreading on the streets) into bloody truths.

Banfi recited a few unbloody truths about Confraternity strength in the Administration and the Coordination. He added a few names that could only confirm his knowledge. He did not add where he had learned the names, although the face on the screen briefly seemed to be all teeth when Banfi refused that information.

"Would you not agree that you have your own resources, for such communication as will make your Warbands safe?"

"Would you not agree that you are trying not to take sides between the Confraternity and the Administration?"

Answering a question with a question was a subtle breach of manners for Ptercha'a, but the mouth was closed now, even smiling faintly. Banfi returned the smile.

"Our own laws bind me closely enough that even this conversation is questionable," he added. "You must use some of your own resources in your own defense, if you wish us to use ours in the future in defense of all of us."

"That is not the way I would have phrased it," Boronisskahane said. "But perhaps it is a proper choice of words nonetheless. Farewell, Marshal." He used the Anglic word. "What I can do, shall be done."

The screen blanked, leaving Banfi in a study dark except for dimly-lit displays and the skyglow through the northern window. It was also silent, except for the distant sound of cutters as some late-working timberjack cleared away a damaged tree.

Also footsteps on the rug behind Banfi, and then Colonel Davidson's voice.

"You were right about the laws."

"What's it to you, Colonel? Afraid for your commission, or is your sister a secret Imperialist?"

"Bugger my—no, let me put that another way. I'm not worried about either my commission or my sister's opinion. I'm worried about your ability to do any good here."

"So am I. That's why I had to deal with that old *z'dok*. How much of the conversation did you hear?

"Apparently not enough."

"Apparently." Banfi summarized his exchange with the dean of Linak'h's Confraternity. When the Marshal was done, Colonel Davidson looked no unhappier and somewhat less confused.

The timberjack had finished work, but now two low-flying gunships whined overhead, running at low speed on coarse pitch for maneuverability. Sergeant Major Kinski was "patrolling," with Lieutenant Nalyvkina on his wing.

Actually, he was giving her extra training so she could transfer to the TacAir wing with no questions asked, if the shooting started. Also, if Banfi no longer needed her then.

Not much "if" about that, the Marshal realized. If matters worked out one way, he would not need a second pilot. If they worked out the other way he would need no staff at all, even if his quarters might be more capacious than the standard three-by-two-by-one of a grave.

Linak'h:

Nikolai Komarov stood outside his door until the lifter carrying Healer Kunkuhn was out of sight. He stood in plain sight on the doorstep, reckoning that anyone in hiding would still shoot at the lifter first. He could be witness to the incident and still run inside safely, maybe even alert troops in time for them to catch the attackers.

No. It was nice to think that his request would immediately reach someone like Candy (she was still out at the battle site, if the mediacast before they took off was truth), and that they would descend in their wrath and strength to deal out justice. The Federation lacked the strength and skill, and others lacked not only that but perhaps the will, after tonight's news.

"Nikolai, is that you?" Ursula sounded welcoming rather than querulous.

"Who else, *liebchen*?"

"It could be—oh, with what is going on, it could be anybody!"

She sounded frightened, and when she had opened the door Komarov could see that she had been crying.

"Is anything wrong, with anybody?"

"No, I just—well, Peter is frightened. I had to look under his bed, to tell him that a bad Ptercha'a is not there."

"He did call them that?"

"Yes."

"Good. If he starts using any of the other words, *I* will frighten him."

"This is the wrong time to be fussy about such things."

"On the contrary, it is the right time. Especially with both pro- and anti-Confraternity Ptercha'a wondering what the humans will do next."

"What about pro- and anti-Confraternity humans, Niko?"

"What about them? We know where we stand, and I will not have my son talking like some uneducated refugee from a thousand kloms inland!"

Ursula sighed. "I do not wish him to do so either, but some of those refugees are paying for your work and teaching, so why call *them* names?"

He kissed her, glad that she was only willing to quarrel, rather than determined. She returned the kiss.

"How is it in town?"

"No incidents that I have heard of. Businesses that cater to both races were having a slow night, but many of them close early anyway. City Hunters like to be home before dark even in better times. Nobody seemed to be getting drunk, the police were patrolling in mixed squads, and I saw no large gatherings."

"It could be worse."

"It will be, before this is over, I am afraid," Komarov said. He opened the door and started passing in bags and crates. Ursula counted and inventoried as they came in.

"Where is the new cooker?"

"Well, we have not been doing much entertaining lately, and feeding only ourselves and the children. . . ."

"Nikolai," she said, an edge in her voice. "Where is the new cooker?"

"Since we didn't need it," Komarov said hastily, "I bought this instead." He reached into his jacket pocket and pulled out the jeweler's packet.

"What is that?"

"A gift for Candice."

Before he could stop her, she'd ripped open the packet. The bar of silver thumped to the floor. She reached to pick it up, but he was there first.

For a moment they glared at each other from a distance of no more than ten cems. Then Ursula straightened up and kicked the empty packet at him.

"Go ahead. I suppose you'll be wasting time making something out of it, as well as wasting money buying it."

Komarov experienced a momentary fantasy of wrapping the silver around his hand like brass knuckles. It passed quickly. He had survived marriage to three difficult women, and ugly divorces from two, without raising a hand to any of them.

Nor would he begin now. If the Confraternity was about to become a storm center, no man connected with it would help himself with a charge of spouse-abuse. Or his wife, or *any* of his children.

He could not do much about Candy. But if there was something else that was bothering Ursula, from her past or her intelligence work, maybe Colonel Nieg would help. Now, if there was just a way to reach Nieg without having to go through Candy. . . .

If there was, he could find it tomorrow. Nikolai Komarov picked up the packet, rewrapped the silver bar, and closed and locked the outer door.

Linak'h:

In the floodlight glare pouring over Pad Eight, Brigitte
Tachin had no trouble rereading the letter from Brian.
In fact, she had almost memorized it in the three days
since he'd sent it down from *Somtow Nosavan,* a few
hours before the ship left for Victoria.

It would have hurt more if he had been ending their
affiliation, but been easier to understand. This long
frustrated . . . *whine,* she had to call it . . . sounded
like a man who did not know what he wanted. Brian
had admitted to times of being like that in the past.
Brigitte judged that one of those times had cost him
his first marriage.

That divorce had given him scars that he thought had
healed. Otherwise he would not have given himself to
her as he had. She had begun to wonder about the
healing, but hoped that what time had begun she could
finish.

Now this letter, and phrases that smelled of paranoia:

> . . . don't know who could have it in for me enough
> to want me off *Shen* at this time. But it doesn't make
> sense to send a Com OOW like me as part of the
> security party. Com people, the Vics already have.
> What they need is muscle, and you know how much
> good I am at that job.

> Dear God and all saints, won't they just let me
> settle down to do one job that I know how to do? Do
> they have to keep jerking me around, so that I'm
> always afraid of messing up?

"Hullo, Brigitte?"

It was Elayne Zheng, loping cheerily across the pad,
with a shoulder bag swinging. She wore a flight suit and
carried her helmet under one arm.

"Allo, Elayne," Tachin said. "What brings you here?"

"Messenger for some EI." She lowered her voice until
Tachin could barely hear it above the fan whines and jet
shrieks. "We think the Baernoi may have deployed some
more capable satellites."

"A fine time they pick."

"Always at your inconvenience, the Tuskers." She looked at Tachin again. "Man trouble?"

"Well, Brian has gone off on *Somtow Nosavan*. . . ."

"And you're worried about him falling for Charlie Longman. I beg pardon, Chief Engineer Longman." Zheng bowed elaborately.

"You have sex on the brain," Tachin said, trying to hold on to her gloom in the face of Zheng's bubbling spirits.

"I wish I could have it somewhere else," Zheng replied. "You interested?"

"I repeat my previous comment," Tachin said with dignity, then laughed. "But I can offer you a drink in the Navy Ground Party Club. There's one room for the officers."

Floodlights along a quarter-klom stretch of perimeter died, leaving an area lit only by the maneuvering lights of a dozen troop lifters. Then the big lights came back up, at half their previous level. The two officers heard ramps clatter down and saw armed troopers filing down the ramps, to vanish in the shadows beyond the perimeter.

"Trouble here?" Zheng asked. Her voice suddenly wasn't light.

"No, I think that's just the pad-alert force from Third Battalion. They went on pad alert . . . oh, it must have been about the time Candy's little fight got on the media."

"Then Kharg knows."

"Why shouldn't he?"

"Oh, naive Navy child, let one of age and wisdom tell you about the scum-eating General Kharg. . . ."

Tachin heard a good deal, most of it probably rumor, and the price of this monotonous conversation was a hefty bar charge. Although Elayne Zheng had not been working like a quarry slave in the naval section of the Zone Arsenal, she was obviously under her own burden of stress and fatigue.

Tachin thought briefly of offering the other a massage. No more—her own libido was nearly flat, and any sex done out of sympathy she would save for Brian. He was likely to come back in a mood to need it more than Elayne ever would.

Linak'h:

The Tree of Gold was as notorious a Confraternity meeting place as the temporarily closed Renko's. Unlike Renko's, it had never been a safe house, except in the sense that one could safely do almost anything there. Whole roomfuls of Hunters had spent entire evenings bellowing Confraternity songs, and only been stopped when they became audible on the street outside.

So the argument in one of the small rooms five ranks to the rear was unlikely to bother anyone except the participants. They were Emt Desdai, Seenkiranda, Drynz, and a fourth Hunter, a messenger who gave only the Confraternity name of Ebla when she came that afternoon and still hadn't given her true one. (Desdai had begun to think her one of those Confreres who never thinks of herself by any other name.)

"You are quite sure that the order is no more operations until further orders?" Drynz said.

"I am sure," Ebla said. She sounded weary, as well she might. Desdai had lost count of the times this exchange had passed. More often than the glasses had been refilled, by a generous margin, he was sure. It almost seemed as if Drynz thought he could change the order, if he questioned it often enough.

Seenkiranda seemed ready to join him in that question, which annoyed Desdai more than he dared let show. She did not really know enough of the Confraternity to be sure that the order was unwise. Also, he suspected her desire for more combat assignments. Was she a born warrior now finding her true path, or one who hoped to use field experience to command better positions in her old line of work?

That was a question that neither pair-mating nor Legion experience could answer for Desdai. All that would give the answer was time, and he feared that might be short.

Certainly Drynz's temper was. He slammed his glass down on the table so hard that two others jumped off. One of them broke, and the bar-guard raised ears and twitched both whiskers and tail.

"No operations means letting the Slaves and humans

strike us down as we lie belly-up and throat-bare, like clawless babes!" he shouted.

"No such thing," Ebla said. It seemed to reach her at last, that she had to explain as well as merely pass messages. *Now, pray that you can do so.*

"The orders are also to withdraw bands deployed for operations," Ebla went on. "We must be able to protect the secrecy of our messages out of our own resources. We cannot trust the humans, the Administration, even our Confreres across the border for help. Protect our messages, and we protect everything else, so that it will be ready for a better time."

Desdai's muzzle twitched. So, in the back of his mind, did the thought that Ebla was probably of higher rank than a messenger. But then, tonight a great many Hunters had probably gone straight from reprogramming robots or watering fmyl patches to visiting friends and neighbors with urgent messages.

"Drynz, can you see your way to obeying?" Desdai asked. He was technically Drynz's senior in rank, if not senior in line of command. As delegate from Victoria, he would have been high among the seniors of the Linak'h Confraternity, but for two difficulties.

One was his being a leader without a Warband. Victoria had sent him and only him. He could do little without more aid than Seenkiranda could provide, except tell the seniors about Victoria.

That was the other problem. The Confraternity seniors of Linak'h would barely recognize the existence of other planets, let alone the knowledge of delegates from them.

"I hear and will obey, upon my tail's integrity," Drynz said.

Accepting tail-lopping if one broke one's promise was still a fairly potent oath. Also, Drynz's posture and ears showed that he was happier taking the order if it came through Desdai, no matter who originally gave it.

Desdai would like to know. He also wanted the answer to a question of his own.

"What about the sixteens? I trust you know which ones I mean."

Ebla showed that she did, but said nothing. Desdai stifled impatience. It was not a question of his own status. Some of the leaders of the Confraternity sixteens discreetly attached to Administration cohorts feared losing status if the sixteens were disbanded or suspended. Desdai feared more for the good will of those, particularly the eager young, who had hopes of fighting for their own chosen cause for the first time in their lives—or, for all they knew, the whole history of the Hunter race.

(That was not quite true. Those Hunters who died in the Hive Wars and many of the lesser conflicts afterward had served their people well, even if they had also served Humans or Folk. But the memory of youth was short, and its knowledge of history often scant.)

"I have heard nothing said about them one way or the other," Ebla said. Her voice and face both confessed shame at this ignorance, as well as some irritation with the seniors for leaving her in that ignorance. Desdai felt warmer toward her, seeing this.

"May I make a suggestion?" Drynz said. "We are more likely to make the humans notice us by withdrawing the sixteens than by continuing their training. Of course, I suppose we can avoid training in places overrun with hostile humans. . . ." This with a sideways glance at Desdai.

"That will mean transporting weapons, ammunition, training texts, and much else besides the warriors," Seenkiranda put in.

"Only when they must travel for training," Drynz corrected her. "How can we know which sixteens must do that, if they are kept separate?"

"I think I can help a trifle there," Desdai said. He explained how he knew only his own sixteen and the other sixteen-Leaders of his own Legion, but that many in his sixteen had kin with other Legions. It violated the rules of silence, but if the seniors needed this knowledge and did not have it, what else to do?

"We can do it thus," Desdai concluded. "Ebla, ask if the seniors know all this. If not, we shall begin asking on our own."

The amount of communicating the Confreres would be doing now might actually increase, when the seniors wished it decreased. But the seniors did not seem to know how much knowledge needed to be shared when one faced war.

Desdai laughed, amused even though he found his

glass empty. It was an idea to be treasured, this possible ignorance of war among the Confraternity seniors. Set it against the human notion that every Hunter was born with a warrior's skills of mind and body, and one could only laugh even harder.

Until one thought of those who would die of the ignorance, and then one did not wish to either laugh or drink.

Aboard R.M.S. *Somtow Nosavan*, the Linak'h System:

"Attention, all hands, this is the Captain."

Joanna Marder's voice would have carried better on the Bridge without *Nosavan*'s elderly intercom system, or so Brian Mahoney thought. But then, he didn't really want the bad news from Linak'h being passed around the ship. He felt quite irrationally that it would be less true, and Brigitte in less danger, if it wasn't.

"We have received a report from Linak'h, relayed through our Navy escort. An Army post in the Territory was attacked by terrorists this afternoon. Our forces engaged and defeated the terrorists, who appear to have been Ptercha'a.

"In the course of the engagement we discovered a substantial Ptercha'a-built tunnel complex in the area. The search for other such complexes is proceeding, with the cooperation of the Administration authorities.

"Confraternity militia units of indeterminate strength were in the area at the time of the action. There is no evidence that they took any hostile action against Federation or Administration forces."

Marder took a deep breath, let it out slowly, then let the silence drift on another few moments. Mahoney contained his impatience. It was stale news to him, but then he'd been Communications OOW when the message arrived. (Just as well; the Navy officers who handled the relay sounded like a blue-and-golder who might not have talked to a merchanter type.)

"People, I won't pretend this is good news. But we can't wait around for more details. We don't have the receiving power ourselves, and our Navy friends are less than an hour from Jumping. We go with them, or we stay here bare-assed.

"Personally, I think the best thing we can do for Linak'h is to get the Victorian Civil Action Group back here as fast as possible. If there is serious trouble, every warm body with a brain and two hands attached is going to be needed. If there isn't, we can all have a *serious* party.

"Mr. Mahoney."

Mahoney pulled his thoughts back to duty, and even remembered not to start at being addressed as "Mister." In the Navy, that was reserved for warrant officers; aboard merchanters it covered all officers, unless they were addressed strictly by title.

"Record, scramble, and squirt a request for further information back to your Navy friends. Tell them we really want to know, if they have any more intelligence."

"Waste of time, asking those Navy—ah, anyway, I don't suppose they'll answer," Boatswain Butkus said. He currently had the helm, but his low opinion of the Navy seemed to be permanent. Naval officers, Baernoi, most Merishi, and some Ptercha'a seemed to be equivalent lower life forms, in his book.

"Keep your supposition to yourself, Boatswain," Marder said. "Station check, at one hour seventeen-thirty before Jump." She looked at the overhead. "Command Nominal."

The voices went around.

"Communications nominal," Mahoney said.

"Navigation nominal," from behind him.

"Controls nominal," from Butkus.

Then Life Support, Passengers, Cargo, and Engineering, in rapid succession, with Engineering coming through in Charlie Longman's voice. Really recognizable as Charlie's, too, after enough days aboard *Nosavan*.

I thought I had a good berth aboard Shen, *even if Brigitte was dirtside. Now who am I shipmates with? Our old FADS case, who's made department head three years from reporting aboard* Shen!

Not to mention that Charlie looked like he was finally getting enough, and from his captain, of all improbable people. It was enough to make a far-faring, frustrated Killarney man dream of mutiny!

Linak'h:

Nieg stared at the displays in front of them. He had been in this chair, most of the time staring or studying the displays, for eighteen hours with only minor breaks.

Even his combat-trained body was protesting. The supposedly ergonomic chair felt as if it were twining around him like a constrictor serpent, scraping him with its scales. It hadn't started biting, getting a grip to swallow him, but he supposed that was next.

It had to be past dawn, even into full daylight outside. But he didn't want to leave the data now, when it was right on the edge of falling into a pattern that he could incorporate in the report.

The Confraternity. Involved in the incident at LZ Campione—two established facts. Unless Sogan Ba-Lingazza had somehow been out in the woods as a private citizen? Forget that—and Nieg knew that he had been trying to forget such implausible hypotheses for hours, but they kept intruding.

Also intruding from time to time was the thought that he should really go to bed, before serious sleep-deprivation set in. He had been awake now for thirty-one hours, and on duty for nearly all of it.

"I can't order you to go to bed, Colonel, but would a friendly suggestion help?"

Nieg decided to take the voice's suggestion, since his hearing Lu Morley implied that he had started to hallucinate. No, that would be true only if he heard Candy behind him, when he'd heard her on the radio from LZ Campione only ten minutes ago. . . .

"I second that, Colonel."

Now, Herman Franke's presence was logical. And Major Morley's was real, if not logical. Unless the hallucinations were not only audible but visible. And tangible . . . ?

"Ouch."

"Colonel, with all due respect, if you wish intimacy with Major Morley, I suggest that you let her take the initiative."

"Also clear it with Colonel Shores," Morley added, patting Nieg's offending hand. "She outranks me on several counts."

Morley brushed hair back from her brown forehead and frowned at the screen. "What's that?"

"Need to know?" Nieg asked.

Franke nodded.

"A Baernoi TO&E."

"I can see that. But . . . that's light weaponry, isn't it? Is it militia or . . . Ptercha'a?"

Nieg glared impartially at both people behind him. Franke shook his head. "I didn't tell her, Colonel."

"He didn't. But there's a pile of material in the MP files on rumors within the Confraternity. They had all the field-grade MP's not out with the troops checking it over last night. The Baernoi training Ptercha'a has about fourteen references."

Nieg stretched, and felt Morley's hands slipping onto his shoulders and neck. "Try not to put me to sleep, if you want the story."

He laughed. "Our Baernoi Ptercha'a-trainer, Behdan Zeg, would be very unhappy if he learned how little security he has maintained. Orgint, satellites, EI, and now the Confraternity rumor factory."

"Unless Zeg doesn't care if we know," Morley said.

"He'd have to care about the Governor knowing," Nieg said. "That goldtusk is one of our biggest assets. I may mail him a commendation after this affair is over."

"Unless the Governor changed his mind?" Morley asked.

"Hey, Lu, I thought *I* was supposed to be the Intelligence expert of the pair," Franke said plaintively.

"I'm a police officer. We have to do the same thing as an intel type—put ourselves inside the other side's mind. As for the colonel's information—yes, it's been suggested that I switch to Intelligence. Several times. I may yet do it. But not today."

Nieg held up a hand, although it felt as if he were wearing a lead glove on it. He tried to ignore the shaking and the extra fingers.

"Anyway, the TO&E adds up to a light battalion of Ptercha'a, trained by Zeg and a mixed-race cadre, probably to be led in the field by Ptercha'a. Armament is as you said, Baernoi militia-grade equipment, which means easy maintenance. Transport, logistics, medical—all I can say is, neither race has a habit of ignoring them."

"So what are they going to do?"

Nieg pulled away from Morley's hands to stab at the screen. "I was trying to form a hypothesis that I could put in the report to Tanz and Longman. There has to be some reason for the battalion to reach IOC at the same time the Confraternity sticks its neck out."

His look dared the others to even think the word *coincidence* too loudly.

"I'll stand dinner all around if you'll sleep on it," Morley said. "Seriously, Colonel, that report won't be worth doing until you've talked with Colonel Shores, and that may take a while."

"Oh?"

"General Kharg got up this morning with the urge to see LZ Campione himself," Franke said. "He lifted out about ten minutes ago. I couldn't reach you on the secure line, so I came myself."

Nieg looked at the secure line's indicator. It was blinking furiously, indicating that more people than Herman Franke had tried to reach him while he was wrestling with sleep-deprivation.

"One of my instructors described a shaky hypothesis as 'undernourished with data,' " Nieg said. "This begins to look like one."

It might change right back again after he had some sleep, but sleep he would have. If Candy was about to cross blades with General Kharg, there wasn't a thing he could do about it by staying awake, and not much he could do if he was half-dead tonight, when she would need him.

Need him. An egotistical thought, at least now, but absolutely and under all circumstances?

Nieg fell asleep pondering that question.

Linak'h:

Brigadier General Kharg at least had the good sense to keep a low profile in the field. So he didn't start by giving Candice Shores security headaches.

In fact, when he arrived she was down in the tunnel, watching a team of snoop-lifter operators evaluate the tunnel as a suitable environment for one of their robot scooters. Esteva brought the news that an unmarked cargo lifter had just come in, with a gunship escort, and somebody who looked like rank had climbed out.

They were on the way back out of the forest, to be liftered to the LZ, when the new arrival settled down on the edge of the excavation of the penetrator drops. Several meters of the pit's side crumbled, not burying anybody but wrecking several hours' work.

Shores chased the digging crews out of the excavation with a raking glance, succeeded in making her hair dirtier by trying to smooth it with her hand, then planted herself to wait for the visitor.

Kharg's battledress was clean and his bandolier light, but he satisfied regulations for senior officers visiting troops in the field. Question: Would he satisfy her?

Shores decided to salute. "Welcome to the dig, General."

"Good morning, Colonel." Kharg returned the salute, then began a slow walk around the excavation. Shores's eyes kept the work crews at a distance where Kharg would have had to shout to bring them in. He apparently had too much dignity to do that, in spite of his regulation field-ready clothing and gear.

He finally came back to Shores and led her inside the lifter. She was quite sure it was wired for recording, and knew that she had the right to protest, but why assume she had nothing to lose?

"Good work, Colonel."

Shores swayed. She'd had just enough sleep to know she needed more.

"Thank you, sir." That never hurt.

"It would have helped if the . . . Cu Chi Hypothesis? . . . had been communicated through more regular channels. I hope I won't have to remind you and anyone you've been in contact with about this again."

"I can assure you of that." With the Cu Chi Hypothesis proved, Nieg would have a solid base of strength for dealing with Kharg and Longman without getting Tanz involved. Or her, come to think of it.

"I do hope so. With the Confraternity allying itself with the terrorists, we can't waste intelligence assets."

"With the—"

Shores broke off, before she incriminated herself but

not before she saw the look on Kharg's face. The trade he was proposing was almost self-evident: weight the evidence in favor of Confraternity hostility, and he would forget about Nieg's irregularities or anything she might have done to give him reason to move.

Kharg couldn't actually relieve her of command. She was in his AO, but her direct superior was Barbara Hogg. Except that Kharg ranked Hogg, if it came to bringing charges, and might have Longman's support.

It added up to trouble.

Serious trouble, if Kharg had Longman backing him all the way to the point of a confrontation with the Confraternity. Serious trouble for the whole Federation, not just Linak'h Command.

Which in turn required the assumption that Longman was crazy or stupid and would also not be overruled by Riftwell or Charlemagne. Shores was willing to assume that Longman was, if not crazy, wired-up, so that dampening her fuse would be a lot harder than triggering it.

Right. Longman backs Kharg, forcing Tanz aside. That meant most of the time between now and the ultimatum, the Federation and the Confraternity on Lanak'h would be glowering or even shooting at each other. It would take at least that long for those On High to hand down orders, longer still to restore damaged trust (if it could be restored at all).

A further thought chilled Shores more than her tealess, sock-less waking-up in the brisk highland dawn. The Federation had its share of officers—flag rank, many of them—who had no more use for the Confraternity than the Merishi did.

Few of them were serious Imperialists, none of whom she'd heard of actual Furphobes. Many thought that the long-standing human-Merishi friendship made sense, particularly against the Baernoi. This was the wrong time, they said (most of them quietly, to do them justice) to interfere with the Merishi and Ptercha'a working out their own relationship.

These hands-offers, or their ancestors, had supported human recognition of the ban on the Confraternity. They or their descendants would probably have to face a Confraternity ruling the whole Ptercha'a race before they'd change. Cultural inertia was a fascinating subject for historians; the actual victims tended to use other adjectives.

Meanwhile, Shores faced not an abstract anti-Confraternity cabal but a single ambitious brigadier general who was blackmailing her into going along with one of his schemes.

First step, stand to attention, salute, and say "Sir!" in your best reporting-for-duty tone.

That got Kharg's attention. It even seemed to surprise him a bit. Whatever he'd expected from Shores, it wasn't that.

"Have I presented you with a problem, Colonel?" The surprise didn't show in the silky voice; the alertness of a serpent ready to strike showed in the dark eyes.

Next step to be taken very carefully, Candy.

She had to avoid any sign that she'd recognized a threat and refused to yield to it. That could trigger a man like Kharg into a direct order, one which she would have to obey even if it was illegal, *then* protest. For direct disobedience, even a superior officer outside her unit could suspend her from duty, even if he had to go through Hogg to unplug her permanently.

"Frankly, yes," Shores said. "I accept some of the blame for it, authorizing the use of the penetrators. They're fine for wiping out a target without setting the forest on fire. They're not so good for leaving identifiable bodies behind."

"What does that have to do with anything?"

"Just that our case against the Confraternity rests on one identified body. It's the most complete body we've found, too. Otherwise we're getting a lot of pieces. The best we're likely to be able to do is count up the pieces and divide."

Kharg looked as if he had a staffer's stomach when confronted with that kind of gross detail. Shores pressed her advantage.

"As I said, I'll accept any blame that's going around for this situation. But it's one we do have to face. Unless the Ptercha'a have DNA files . . . ?"

"Not in the Administration, at least." Kharg looked as if the admission was as pleasant as passing a kidney stone.

"Very well. Then I'm not sure that the physical evidence

available supports a charge of full-scale Confraternity hostility. There may have been only one Confraternity member, an observer with the terrorists, maybe even unauthorized by the Confraternity seniors."

"I somehow doubt that."

"Sir, I do too. But it's not a question of what you or I believe. It's a question of what the people will believe, after the media get at them. The mediacasts tend to be rather pro-Ptercha'a, under most circumstances."

There. Got him by playing the old card: soldiers together against the dreadful mediacasts. Now find a strong mouthwash.

"I have not spent the bulk of my life on a planet with no exposure to the interstellar media system," Kharg said. "I have to confess that you've made your point."

Damned right. Between which two ribs?

"Thank you for your time, Colonel. I will be happy to enclose your evaluation of the situation in my report. I expect it will receive serious consideration."

It took ten minutes after that understatement for Kharg to finally make up his mind to leave. By the time his lifter was airborne, most of the evacuation team was back at work, without waiting for orders from Shores. She was glaring at them when two dark figures rose from almost under her feet.

She stared. It was Juan Esteva and Jan Sklarinsky, both stripped to their underwear and smeared from head to foot with a mixture of mud and camouflage cream.

"We guessed Kharg wouldn't have thermal sensors in his shoulderboards," Sklarinsky said, sketching a salute.

"Ah, the excavation team . . ."

"Right, but we weren't on it. So your orders to them didn't apply to us."

Shores got her mouth under control. She wasn't entirely sure about her brain. On the whole, she would rather mud-wrestle Baernoi than challenge Kharg again,

"So you were . . . what? Practicing infiltration tactics?"

"You might say that," Esteva replied. "You might say we were going to provide witnesses, too. Just in case there was anything to witness."

"But you didn't leave him an opening," Sklarinsky chimed in. "Good work, ma'am."

Shores tried to glare and ended up stammering and

giggling, which she hadn't done in years. Somehow she managed to say, "D-don't you kn-kn- . . . know . . . that it's ag-g-gainst custom . . . to compliment your s-s-superior officer?"

"Yes, ma'am," they chorused, snapping off parade-ground salutes. Then they dashed off, without waiting to be dismissed.

Shores sat down on a stump and spent the next five minutes getting the giggles out of her system. She was able to stop before any of the diggers came over to ask if she needed help.

Then she called a lifter for a ride back to the LZ. As soon as Kharg left, she or Esteva had to ring up Nieg's HQ and warn him what might be coming down. Kharg had withdrawn one probe of her defenses; she doubted it was the last he'd make.

Eighteen

Charlemagne:

Admiral Kuwahara had never briefed all four C-in-C's and their entourages before. He had always known intellectually that if he reached high enough rank, he would be doing enough Forces Command duty to make that assignment likely.

Now prospect had become fact. He could not help remembering the description of one classmate (who already had a solid third star, so it might be said she knew what she was talking about):

"You feel like the banquet entertainment on Mount Olympus."

Kuwahara had noted early on that the Support and Training C-in-C's were deferential but not obsequious toward the two combat chiefs. As between Baumann and Szaijkowski, it would have required delicate sensors to measure who deferred to whom.

Kuwahara finished his briefing with the TO&E of Linak'h Command as it would be once the reinforcements bound from Riftwell arrived, then sneaked a look at the clock. Four minutes forty-eight. Keeping briefings under five minutes was not a fixed rule, but if you could hope to cover the topic in that time you were expected to give it a visible try.

From the expressions on the dozen faces Kuwahara could see clearly, he had succeeded reasonably well. But a major-general behind Szaijkowski was raising a hand.

"How are the evacuation plans coming?"

Kuwahara ignored a number of laser stares aimed at the general. It appeared that several of his colleagues had either branded him "defeatist" or wanted to give the impression of doing so.

"As I said, the Administration has pledged full cooperation in the evacuation or security of all humans who wish to leave Linak'h, regardless of their reply to the Coordination. The Federation forces expected to be available in the Linak'h Theater at the time of the ultimatum's expiration will be sufficient to implement a non-opposed evacuation."

Nobody, fortunately, needed telling what would happen in the event of an opposed evacuation. Ultimately, it could be the Big Brawl. Immediately, it would be a great many dead Ptercha'a and Merishi, and fewer but still too many dead humans, in uniform and out. The infrastructure of the Coordination made a good hostage to the Federation, so Ptercha'a civilian casualties might be fairly modest, but any Choosers of the Slain would have their pick of heroes from three races and half a dozen forces.

The next question didn't surprise Kuwahara. The source did. Admiral Sloane, the Training C-in-C, looked more like a retired teacher than an officer with three combat awards. Those combat awards probably said more about her than her present position.

"Have we any more data on the Confraternity's position?"

Kuwahara was tempted to reply that Confraternity Ptercha'a probably used the same positions as other Hunters, there being no Confraternity edition of *The Book of the Magic Mat*. However, the image of a dozen senior faces glaring at his joke swiftly removed temptation.

He did not resist the temptation to give an open-ended answer. That was all an open-ended question deserved, even if it fell on you from the height of four stars.

"We really don't expect to learn more about the Confraternity's position on Linak'h before the ultimatum expires. Not unless they tell us, and you can judge how much it's worth wagering on that."

Smiles instead of glares replied, even if they were thin ones. Encouraged, Kuwahara went on.

"In the Coordination, we know that there is a substantial underground Confraternity presence. Probably a tolerated underground, but definitely not legal.

"Linak'h is a fairly important Ptercha'a homeworld, after all. It's not one of those minor settlements out beyond Jumpoff, where the Confraternity could openly take power and it might be five Standard years before the rest of inhabited space learned.

"So the Confraternity presence will be a low-profile one. More than that I can't state, even as a reasonable hypothesis."

"A low-profile presence," Sloane almost murmured. "But . . . too low to be dangerous, if they decided that they could win Coordination approval by fighting against the Federation?"

Kuwahara knew he must be gaping, because Sloane wasn't the only one smiling. However, he also wasn't the only one gaping.

"It seems to me we shouldn't make assumptions ahead of our data," Sloane continued. "We have been assuming that the Coordination is working so tightly with the Merishi that the Confraternity will automatically be against the Coordination. But are the Merishi using the Coordination, or is it the other way around?

"In short, is the Confraternity still the only Ptercha'a group advocating a more independent position for the whole race?"

Sloane, obviously, had not only thought the unthinkable but said the unsayable. The shocked looks could have many causes, and Kuwahara would be curious to know them.

More critical than satisfying his curiosity, however, was getting Sloane's notion to Marcus Langston. The senior Army representative on the study group had been convinced since he'd joined it, that the real issue at Linak'h was future human-Ptercha'a relations. The Merishi were a bunch of—what was the word Marcus had used?—oh, *kibitzers*, adding background noise without really playing a part.

How many Ptercha'a thought the same?

Victoria:

"By the way, Captain Oczuk, what is a Fryer when it is spelled as it is in your ship's name?"

The captain of Payaral Na'an's new charter, *Freiherr*

von Leventzow, stared at the Merishi for a moment. Then he laughed.

"It's not the same thing as the cooking implement. It's a title, in Old Germanic. I think it was one of the lowest grades of nobility."

"Well, I hope your service to Simferos Associates would earn you a higher grade, if we had it in our power to award it."

"Our best service will be yours."

They went through the parting rituals, which Oczuk performed as elegantly as any Consortium chief who remembered old customs and had not yet grown too stiff to honor them. Rather like Na'an's father, when the Councillor had leisure to think of it.

His visitor not only gone but escorted clear of the Trade Mission building, Na'an called up the Ships' Status file. *Somtow Nosavan* was in orbit, undocking her own shuttles and being fitted with a module for docking the shuttles from Victoria. They would be up soon enough, bringing resupplies of consumables in one wave, then the Civil Action Group in two more.

Her escort, heavy cruiser *Anjou* and a scout for which Na'an did not yet have a name, were riding close to the Merishi cruiser *Gyn-Bahr.* The Merishi ship had been in Victoria orbit so long that one almost wondered if she was intended as a depot ship, with any serious fighting to be done by ships not yet in-system or at least not revealed.

Na'an hoped that none of the Folk had plans for spreading the fighting back to Victoria. His own profit and safety and the safety of those who obeyed him would hardly survive such a measure. The Victorians would not readily tell one Merishi from another in such a crisis.

Unless he could get everybody off-planet aboard *Freiherr von Leventzow?* No. That would mean keeping the ship hanging in orbit for so long that everyone who could read a Ship's Status display would know that the Merishi Trade Mission was biting its claws with apprehension. A foolish admission even if true, total madness when false.

Better use for the ship: Send her to Linak'h. Insurance would be a problem, but a deposit in one of the shadow accounts at the Freylinghusen/Victoria bank, to go to the crew's kin if the ship did not return, should ease other matters.

What about a cargo? Not much that would sell on Linak'h available on short notice—short, because *von Leventzow* ought to be able to go out to Linak'h with *Nosavan*, sharing her escort. (Which might solve the insurance problem, too.)

Passengers? Send out a staff and guards for Emt Desdai? Yes, although be discreet about it—Na'an remembered the couriered letter from his father, indicating that rumors of Desdai's affiliations had reached Folk determined to attack the reputation of Simferos Associates. Or was it merely that in the eyes of the rumor-spreaders, all Ptercha'a were guilty of Confraternity affiliations unless they exhibited such slavish servitude as Na'an would not ask of a pet?

Very possibly the latter, Na'an decided, given the particularist influence on the rumor-spreaders. But he would help Desdai. Na'an had a secure list of people known to have worked with Desdai, if not necessarily on Confraternity business. He would ask for volunteers, however. Even the most dedicated warrior might be forgiven for not leaping gladly from the roasting spit into the cookfire.

Other passengers? None of the Civil Action Group; they were already contracted to *Nosavan*. Besides, there would have to be Federation and Victorian security parties aboard *von Leventzow* if she carried Victorians. That was not something Na'an cared to drop on Captain Oczuk at the last moment.

But on the return voyage? A few maintenance technicians aboard the ship on the voyage out, and she would be fit to carry scores, even hundreds of refugees on the way back. Back to Victoria, of course; but if war broke out on Linak'h, the refugees with money might be less demanding about their first destination. *Nosavan* could have carried two or three hundred on her return voyage, if she'd been going somewhere more pleasing to the sensitive and overcivilized than that dustball Victoria.

Who owed him enough, to be asked to supply the techs? Human, by preference, and definitely not Folk.

"Ship-maintenance service operators, all files," Na'an

told his computer, and called for a snack while he waited for the data to emerge.

Charlemagne:

Josephine Atwood caught just the tag end of the Foreign Minister's press conference. Half the questions seemed to be about a communal crisis in Harounabad on Ganges, which as far as she could tell had been caused by somebody's not reading the legal codes.

It had been established some centuries ago that tending the Sacred Herd of a Hindu temple was *not* a Federation-service equivalent. This was based strictly on the religious-impartiality clause of the Federal Constitution, and not on any doubt that tending sacred cows (real ones, that is) was hard work.

But somebody on Ganges had protested, and the Moslems had protested the protest, and there had been at least one riot in addition to a great deal of publicity. No doubt there were enough Moslems and Hindus with long memories and short tempers that Aung Bayjar couldn't ignore the potential for trouble, particularly if the media asked him.

But what about Linak'h? Two dead in Harounabad, more than two hundred on Linak'h, and that was just the counted bodies. How many more in the high forest in silent, secret incidents, or even the fires reported to Charlemagne—two, with forty thousand hectares burned over, which had to mean some of the firefighters at least in the hospital . . . ?

At least Rosie is up in space, out of the path of the fires and assassins. Josephine Atwood vowed to slap her old friend again if she went dirtside and made a target. . . .

"Citizen Lefebvre?"

Atwood knew at least one rule of covert work: Memorize your cover name so it's second nature to answer to it. She looked up.

"You're late."

Chief Yeoman Krazinkow sat down. She wore baggy clothes that hid her remaining dressings and supporters but didn't hide well-maintained contours. In fact she looked rather like a licensed commercial-sex partner, which made sense in this particular bar. The fading visible bruises and the stiff movements would just make people think she'd had an argument with a customer a few weeks back.

Atwood wondered what her own clothes made people think. *Probably buying rather than selling,* she decided. Certainly nobody would suspect Krazinkow of being military, and so many professions included sex-buyers that Atwood would be almost as hard to type.

"Can this be quick?" Krazinkow said. "I think I was followed."

Atwood felt her pulse jump, but managed to hide quickening breath. No point in their both being nervous.

"Anybody you know?"

"No, although I suspect they weren't too professional. I made them several hundred meters back."

"You came on foot?"

"I had to ditch my police tail, remember."

"You might have been safer with the police, if somebody's setting up for another shot at you or Deere."

"It will be me, which is why I want to talk. If you still want to?" Krazinkow was craning her neck toward the door beyond the corner of the bar, looking for either her tail or a robot with a quick drink.

Atwood was not a veteran of anything more than the obligatory Federal Service military-orientation course, but she'd be damned if she'd appear easily scared. Among other points, Krazinkow might talk, and what she said might concern somebody who wanted to intimidate Atwood. (There was a long list of those people, only a few of them with any possible connection to the Linak'h situation. Twenty years of media work accumulated enemies, even if one was nicer than Atwood had ever managed to be.)

"Sure."

"I was warned by the police not to talk to reporters, you know."

"Anybody besides the police? Warning you, that is?"

Krazinkow grinned at Atwood's slip. "Nobody in the Forces, if that's what you mean. But I thought you'd be safer than anybody else. I know that Lena Ropuski's been seeing you."

A couple of men at a nearby table turned at those words. Atwood bit her lip to control laughter. They probably thought they were overhearing the emergence of a three-woman triangle.

"So she has. What do you have to add to what she's been telling me?"

"I suppose you can't tell me what that is?"

"No." That was one slip for Krazinkow. The source who asked leading questions to get something on their bosses was depressingly familiar to Atwood. It was also an accusation she wouldn't level at Krazinkow on the basis of one slip.

"Not really. It's mostly background stuff, and if you handle classified material, I'm sure you know much more about it than I do. What I wanted to know was anything about the attack that you didn't put in the police report."

"What makes you think that there's anything like that?"

"I don't know that there's anything." Atwood held up a hand. "Before you jump me or jump up, any connection with Deere is none of my business. I don't think you would have hidden anything about it that could help the police."

"No. They know that Ken's separated from his wife, and I'm single. They asked me about his wife hiring people, too, but she's on Monticello and not rich."

Atwood decided the evening wouldn't be wasted. This kind of background material would go straight into the files for now, but could be useful later.

A robot that must have picked up a signal Atwood overlooked rolled up with two drinks. Krazinkow shoved one of them across the table to Atwood. "Unless you don't like lemon vodka?"

"It and I get along," Atwood replied. Having a source buy the drinks was a sufficiently novel experience that she intended to enjoy it. Besides, she had the standard immunizations against any of the easily-administered toxins.

"To peace?" Krazinkow said, raising her glass.

They clinked and drank. Atwood felt the subtle bite of really good vodka and fought a brief flare of suspicion. *Chief Yeomen aren't poor. Just because she's willing to spend on good liquor doesn't mean she's taking from someone.*

"All right," Krazinkow said. "There's one thing—just an impression, so I didn't put it in—but maybe it's worth something. I don't mean stellars," she added. "I mean, as part of the picture."

Atwood was familiar with the process of psyching yourself up to make a revelation, of either opinion or body. She'd experienced both from both sides.

"The more details I can choose from, the better," Atwood said mildly. "A story's something like a piece of stone sculpture. You have to start with a block that's a lot bigger than the final piece."

Krazinkow nodded, looked like she wanted to order another drink, then swallowed. "I think one of the . . . people . . . wasn't human."

"One of the attackers?"

"No. There were only two. A third—this one—he or she stood back. Security lookout, maybe."

Or ready to go into action if the humans disobey orders. The analogy to some of the fights on Linak'h was too plain to ignore.

"I thought there might have been a fourth, the one really in command, because the third one kept looking off to the left every so often. Once, I caught a glimpse of his head in silhouette. That was the part that didn't look human."

"Could you give a guess at the race?"

"I didn't see him move."

That said a good deal. Dressed up in cold-weather clothing, with face masks and heavier headgear, both Ptercha'a and Merishi could pass for a human while standing still. It was harder to confuse them when they moved; the Ptercha'a lope was distinctive.

At least that let out Baernoi. There was no recorded case of them succeeding with any disguise less complete than an EVA suit. Even then the different limb proportions could give them away.

So. Possibly Merishi, possibly Ptercha'a, possibly no non-humans operating on Charlemagne—at least in connection with this case.

Emphasize the "possibly" even in your own files, but pass it back to the study group, too. Atwood had an all-over warm glow for a moment, as she thought of the revelation of human bunglers accidentally joining hands with nonhuman spies.

She'd emphasize both the "accidentally" and the "bunglers," too. Ropuski was probably right; what they were seeing was the end of a long chain of minor mistakes.

Except that chains had killed quite a few people, by accident or on purpose. The chain-maker had some responsibility, either way. . . .

A thump brought Atwood's attention back across the table. Krazinkow had slipped down in her chair and caught her battered jaw on the edge of the table. Her eyes were glazed with pain. Then all the intelligence went out of them and she slipped under the table.

Atwood's heart nearly stopped before she could duck under the table and discover almost normal pulse and respiration. She was also checking vital signs with her purse monitor when one of the human staff appeared.

"Should we call an ambulance, Citizen?"

"Just a taxi, thank you. We were celebrating her getting a clean bill of health from the doctor. I guess the painkiller and the liquor didn't get along."

"Happens often enough," the man said. He took Atwood's "Danielle Lafevbre" card without comment and returned with it and a thermos bottle.

"For her stomach," he said. "I've had a few problems like that myself, back when I worked as a bouncer. This stuff helps."

After an analysis, maybe it would. No, she hoped it would. Krazinkow probably didn't have anything wrong with her that a night's sleep couldn't cure, but there would be fourteen kinds of Hades let loose if she did!

Victoria:

The police line looked awfully thin to Charles Longman, but the mob they faced didn't look terribly determined. The problem was, it needed only one hothead taking down a police officer to get the Civil Action Group off on the wrong foot.

Not to mention creating a personal crisis and even danger for one Charles Varin Longman, currently senior *Somtow Nosavan* officer dirtside and therefore stuck on gangway watch aboard the shuttle.

"Team Yellow!" somebody shouted. No, the same shouter as before—a hefty woman who had to be police or military even if she wore civvies. If you crossbred Baernoi and human . . .

"Team Yellow, count off!" a voice replied from the warehouse door. Longman could have sworn it was Karl Pocher. He hadn't been on the last roster Longman saw, but had that been the updated one?

"One. Julius Maszowski."

"Two. Paul Ferakkis."

"Three. Kathy McGuire."

As each person called off name and number, they strode out the warehouse door, along a strip of green carpet, and onto the shuttle's stairs. Media crews on top of the warehouse and on the opposite side of the carpet from the demonstrators busily recorded everything.

Also on the roof of the warehouse, several alert-looking men never moved their hands far from their pockets. On more distant roofs, openly uniformed figures squatted, stood, or lay behind SSW's. A few lifters completed the picture, drifting back and forth apparently aimlessly across the Thorntonsburg Air-Space Center.

"Thirty-nine. Karl Pocher."

It really was Karl, striding with that mix of grace and bull-like pushiness along the carpet.

"Hullo, Karl!" Longman said, saluting.

Pocher stared. "Charlie? What are you doing down here?"

"My duty," Longman said ponderously. "I always do my duty."

"Oh, I thought you only did your captain now. Sorry. It's serious?"

"For her, yes. For me . . . well, I begin to wonder if it's serious for *both* of us."

Pocher stared. "Then the age of miracles isn't passed yet. Your reforming may make a believer of me yet."

"Don't hold your breath," Longman said. He signaled to the cockpit. "Or hold up progress, either. Anybody missing from your group?"

"Two got reassigned to Team Green. They're coming in as soon as the demonstrators get tired."

Longman waited until the shuttle was sealed and they were on the way to the cockpit before he replied.

"Why not just clear them away?"

"Put it down to Gist's decision to make the leave-taking public. He figured that the people who think we're upholding the planet's honor would keep the others quiet. Then he either had too much nerve or too little sense to cancel the public show, when the demonstrators showed up."

"What's got into them anyway?"

"A lot of general xenophobia, reinforced by the war and now by this Confraternity business. What some people will believe about the Ptercha'a reminds me of the old blood libel that—"

"The what?"

"Old fairy tale used in religious warfare, about Christians drinking Jewish babies' blood. No, wait. It was the other way around. The Jews were supposed to need Christian babies' blood for some sort of ritual food."

"Lovely."

"Right. About a quarter of the people think the Civil Action Group is heroic. About a quarter think we're letting ourselves be buggered by aliens. About half would like to get the whole bloody business over with and the foreign ships out of our sky!"

"What about you?"

"I'm a retired hero, fleeing a broken heart."

"Turned you down?"

"Yes, then he volunteered for the Force. Don't try him, though." Longman's face must have given something away. Pocher stared. "You know, I think you *have* settled in with Marder."

"Hope that won't spoil your trip."

"Your ego hasn't shrunk, I see. Or your mouth."

"Somebody has to provide an element of stability in a constantly changing universe."

Pocher made a rude noise and a ruder gesture. "Take care, Charlie. I've got to go back and see that my people are all strapped in."

Charlemagne:

"What's the latest report on Chief Krazinkow?" Kuwahara asked. He tossed his coat toward the closet, hoping that for once it would catch on a hook.

Instead, it slid and slumped to the floor as usual. Kuwahara was conscious of Captain Ropuski's eyes fixed on his back as he hung up the coat, then saw her look away as he turned back.

"Out with it, Lena."

"Krazinkow's fine. But she might not be. Did you know what you were turning loose, when you tapped Atwood to run media-jamming maneuvers for us?"

It would be true to say that Ropuski had not objected, had even found Atwood "fairly sensible for someone who's never served." It would also be an evasion of a commander's responsibility to his people, which Ropuski obviously thought he had already failed to show toward Krazinkow.

"I will personally apologize to her as soon as I have time to stop by." He looked at the clock. "That may be this afternoon, if I can leave without being dragged into any more marginal conversations."

"Yes, Admiral," Ropuski said. She'd need more practice, but she was getting almost as good at a glacial manner as Admiral Baumann. "Oh, there is a courier file in from Linak'h. The Third Watch decoded it."

Since he had not been, and obviously was not going to be, offered a friendly summary of it before Ropuski went off-duty, Kuwahara went into his office. The printed file was on his desk, or at least a destruct-equipped packet about the right size was.

As tired as he was, Kuwahara managed to open the packet without either cremating its contents or scorching his own fingers. After he'd read it, he almost wished he had cremated it.

Everybody on Linak'h was like the legendary wolf that "huffed and puffed and blew the house down." Kuwahara didn't remember whose house the wolf had blown down, but he knew that the study group might be a house of cards falling on his head—and possibly career—if matters got much worse.

Not that the study group hadn't done its best. Nor was this war likely to lead to the Big Brawl. The Merishi still seemed to be almost as divided as the Ptercha'a, and the Baernoi were doing the sensible thing, given their strength on Linak'h—i.e., sitting this one out. (Probably with every sensor in their Territory monitoring everything anybody else did; the best Baernoi Inquirers would go on collecting data while being slowly disemboweled.)

Beyond that, the outcome on Linak'h was becoming the province of guesswork. Kuwahara had no time to inquire about legendary wolves; he had too much data to digest. Much of it was routine, even if it painted a disagreeable picture of the two sides lining up for a confrontation.

Some of it was less so. The Confraternity rumor refused to die. So far, no Confraternity members were known to have done so, but that could change.

The Baernoi were evaluated as having armed a force of Ptercha'a mercenaries, strength less than a battalion, combat effectiveness uncertain, intentions totally unknown. (Kuwahara wondered if the Inquiry mission on Linak'h had given that job to Behdan Zeg to keep him busy while they did the serious work. *Some* explanation was needed, why Zeg and his half-brother Rahbad Sarlin had been able to work in the same mission this long without murder being done.)

Then the forest fires. Three big ones worth noting, one firefighter (Ptercha'a) killed, six (four Ptercha'a, two humans) seriously hurt, more than fifty lightly injured. Kuwahara read through depressing statistics of increasing timber destruction, increasing fire risk, and decreasing stocks of fire-suppressants, and rang for the communications yeoman.

"Sir?"

"Memo to Admiral Baumann. 'Strongly recommend immediate high-priority despatch of shipload best-grade fire-suppressant chemicals to Linak'h.' No, make that 'highest-priority.' "

The yeoman read back the message. "I'll have it ready for your authorization in a minute, sir."

"Thank you. When you're done with that, can you call me up files on some of the other dual-sovereignty planets? There may be something we've overlooked for Li-nak'h that will show up elsewhere."

"Aye-aye, sir."

Even if nothing did, it would be a change from watching three allegedly sapient races lurch toward war.

Aboard R.M.S. *Somtow Nosavan*, the Victoria system:

"Captain, we've got a stowaway."

Joanna Marder woke up from an erotic dream (centered around Charlie, so she had a clear conscience about it) to hear the intercom repeating these words. After the third repetition, she recognized Boatswain Butkus's voice.

"A stowaway," she said slowly. "Human?"

"Yeah, and just a kid."

"I'm going to be seventeen next birthday, and I've got a legal emancip!" a youthful voice put in, high-pitched with indignation. Marder still recognized it. She had no intention of letting anyone know that, however.

Let the little bastard sweat a bit.

"I'll be right down. Where did we find him?"

"Unh . . . it wasn't us found him, Captain. Kathy McGuire of Team Yellow was checking out one of the lifters, said the telltales read funny. She saw the kid— okay, this fine young man—waving from the cockpit."

"Didn't the cargo scans reveal him?"

"We don't know when he got in. Could have been after the lifters were loaded, before the compartment was sealed. Anyway, the scans didn't include biosensors. I mean, we were rushed, and nobody puts bombs in a fruitcake."

"No, but people can have bombs implanted. Run the med-scanner over the stowaway right now!"

"Aye-aye, ma'am."

She had to give some order that would keep people busy for a while. She had nearly had bombs implanted in her, in the underground terrorist base on Victoria where she'd been interrogated. Such a bland word, for describing what had happened to her—and whose memories were now making her shake, sweat, and grip a hand-rail by the cabin door.

She closed her eyes, but at least tears didn't stream out. She also didn't need to vomit or use the head. The flashbacks still came, but not as bad as they used to be. The difference really wasn't just her doctor's wishful thinking anymore.

By the time she'd washed her face, Butkus was back on the circuit.

"He's clean, ma'am."

"Of *course* I'm clean!" the young voice said, now indignant bordering on furious.

"Boatswain," Marder said. "Who was responsible for the decision to omit biosensor scans of the cargo?"

The decision had a complex lineage, rather like a tribal Ptercha'a clan, but a little pressure squeezed out enough of the truth to count. Both Charlie and Butkus had a share in the responsibility, and there were others.

"All right," Marder said. "You, the Chief Engineer, and the other culprits are going to make a physical search of every piece of cargo large enough to hide a stowaway. Then you can start on the working spaces. Meanwhile the Victorians can search the passenger spaces. Start as soon as you've finished escorting the stowaway to my cabin."

"Aye-aye, ma'am."

Five minutes later Butkus more or less pushed the stowaway inside, gave something that was more wave than salute, then vanished. Marder had already announced the stowaway and search over the intercom. Now she folded herself into lotus position on her bunk and stared at the young man.

He looked closer to fifteen than seventeen, and it was hard to believe that he'd ever had a legal emancip declaring him an adult or, for that matter, eaten a decent meal. But he met her look without wriggling, there were muscles under the faded shirt, and the dirty blond hair had been roughly combed.

Just about what she would have expected of BoJo Johnson, orphan at nine, war hero at fourteen, farmhand at the DiVries's at sixteen, and now bound for another war.

"Why, BoJo?"

"I wanted off Victoria. I don't mind the people, most of them, at least at the farm. But I'm not going anywhere from there, and I don't want to stay in the outback all my life."

"So you decided a planet about to go to war was better?"

"Easiest to get to, anyway. I mean, there's bound to be somebody needing help. I can farm, paint, do carpentry, drive groundcars, help mechanics fix a lot of things, maybe fix an organics plant or recycler myself, cook or tend bar."

"You weren't thinking of getting into the fighting?"

"What's the problem with that? A legal emancip means I'm old enough."

"It does not, at least for Federation forces or any that value Federation good will. Also for your information, your much-prized emancipation means that you can be tried as an adult for stowing away. That is a felony with a five-year minimum work-colony term, the last time I looked."

Marder's blast seemed to take another six months off Johnson's age. He no longer looked like even a pretense of an adult. In another moment, Marder suspected, he was going to start to cry. Her seeing him do that would be a blow to his fragile pride that would cause problems for everybody.

She stood up and gave him a maternal hug. "Hey, relax. I'm just reminding you that stowing away is fairly serious business. Did you check to see if those lifters were going to be stored in pressure, for example?"

Indignation restored the lost maturity. "Of course I did. You think I'm a complete twit?"

"No, but you're a problem, and not one with an easy solution. There's no way either we, Simferos Associates, or the Navy are going to send an escorted ship back to Victoria for one stowaway. So you're going to Linak'h.

"But I'm going to sign you on as an apprentice, with articles valid for one voyage. That means you *work* your passage, starting with helping search for other—"

"Ma'am, I didn't see any. I suppose—"

"—that you should also learn some basic manners, like not interrupting your captain."

"Yes—aye-aye, ma'am."

"That's better. As I said, you'll be on the ship's books as an Apprentice Hand. Your immediate superior will be Butkus. Next comes Mr. Longman. If I have to personally give you any more orders, you may spend the voyage in the brig.

"If I have to do that, you'll be turned over to the Federation authorities on Linak'h. They may be too busy to sentence you to a work-camp term. They'll probably just ship you back to Victoria.

"So if you can't stay off my ship, at least stay out of my hair!"

Johnson nearly poked her in the eye with his attempt at a salute, but his "Aye-aye, ma'am!" came out firmly.

Nineteen

Linak'h:

Brokeh su-Irzim counted the Ptercha'a climbing into the lifter and came up with thirteen. Even allowing for the lighter weight of the Furfolk, it was a substantial load. Add Behdan Zeg, Rahbad Sarlin, and the Lidessouf twins . . .

"Are you sure you won't need a second lifter?" su-Irzim asked.

The last Ptercha'a apparently understood some of the People's tongue. He rolled his black-pupiled eyes toward the ruddy twilight sky, then pantomimed walking bent over, eyes on the ground, arms dragging.

"He says you are an old woman, Brokeh," Behdan Zeg said.

"Old women are sometimes the only ones who take thought for dangers the young are facing," su-Irzim replied, in the same tone. "Seriously . . . ?"

"Seriously, this brute is no racer, but it will get us to where we must start walking. Also, have you looked at the badges?"

Su-Irzim had. They were the badges of a healing house. "Are they within the law?"

"As long as we do not shoot from this lifter or cross the border in it, we violate no law. We mean to deceive Federation spies and satellites within our own Territory. Otherwise . . . is it our fault that the one who sold us the lifter did not paint over or burnish off the old badges?"

"It will be your fault if I am crushed to death before even facing a live enemy!" Rahbad Sarlin growled from within the lifter. Grunts echoed him, suggesting that the Lidessouf twins and several of the Ptercha'a shared these sentiments.

"Guard the house with honor," Zeg said, striking the ritual blows at su-Irzim. The Fleet Inquirer was so startled at this gesture from the Khudr of the unmannerly that he nearly forgot to block.

"Its honor is mine," he replied, to Zeg's retreating back. The man vanished into the crowded lifter, the interior lights came on as the ramp came up, and a moment later the fans whined into life.

It seemed to take a long time for the lifter to even rise to treetop height, a longer time for it to vanish in the darkness. By the time it had done so, su-Irzim realized that Zhapso su-Lal, Fygos Dravin the steward, and Lyka ihr Zeyem the communications chief had all come out to join him.

From below, a Ptercha'a threw a keening cry at the stars as they winked to life.

"The farewell to the death-sworn," su-Irzim said.

"You've been studying the—those beings?" su-Lal asked.

"It might be wise for you to do so," su-Irzim replied. "If it succeeds, we may hold it in our power to prevent the war, if it serves the People that we do so."

Su-Lal stared hard at his fellow Inquirer. "I do believe you wish you were aboard that lifter!"

"I had a moment's dream of that," su-Irzim confessed. "But it would never have left the ground. Also, I am comfortable in a chair, not so comfortable in a lifter with my snout in another's ear and another's elbow in my ribs, and hopelessly at a loss in the wilderness."

Ihr Zeyem bowed. "By the Lord Most High, he admits a fault!"

"I have more faults than the Circle of Fire," su-Irzim said. "Fortunately I do not erupt as often."

"No. Here Commander Zeg does that for all of us."

Su-Lal frowned. Su-Irzim let the remark pass. Lyka ihr Zeyem had grown sharper of tongue lately, as the time of war approached. Her work, however, was even better than before, and there was so much more of it that su-Irzim wondered she had any strength left for amusement in bed.

He decided that he would formally propose that she be elevated to command rank. She deserved the honor, and could doubtless learn the leadership skills required.

It might set a barrier between her and the Lidessouf twins, but if she ignored it, so would they. Or the three of them might mutually agree that it was time for all to move on to new partners.

More Ptercha'a keening rose from now three, now five, now what seemed a dozen places around the hill. The house was well-guarded; su-Irzim hoped the Ptercha'a oaths would leave it as well guarded if the patrol bound for the Merishi training camp never returned.

Yet the mission had to go, and to be led as it was. The Inquiry work was valuable, and must go on. It was the Special Projects fighters, however, who would stand between the mission and the judgment that it sat and played the nose flute while a witless war harmed the People.

Merish:

The voting on the Council of Simferos Associates was done in the old-fashioned style. Each Councillor stepped into the silver-plated room that held the small shrine of the Serene, and picked up one of the stone bowls stacked on a table of balgos wood by the door.

Then he crossed to the shrine, prostrated himself before it, and placed the bowl where its color demanded. Black bowls were to the right, white to the left. When all had placed their bowls, the doors were closed, to allow time for the Spirit of the Serene to witness their numbers, positions, and colors.

Once, Zydmunir Na'an knew, this kind of voting was a matter of life and death. White bowls set to the left meant their owners were to be cast out of the tribe, to wander in the desert until death claimed them. Sometimes this was punishment for crime, oath-breaking, nest-fouling, or unlawful killing. Other times, it had been a way of deciding who would die, when there was so little food that if some did not die all would.

It had been a point of honor to vote honestly and not move another's bowl, even if no other living being saw one's vote. There were tales of modern votes in which a recording camera watched the shrine and recorded the votes. In one case where the suspicion was strong, the Association had been ordered dissolved. (Na'an suspected that it had been revived within two years under another name, and with small loss to the Councillors and Associates, but the scandal and shame had been considerable.)

Na'an was not voting. The seventeen Councillors of Simferos Associates currently on Merish, a majority of the total Council, were voting on his fate. It would not, however, be a disgrace to his name if they voted to end his place on the Council. Indeed, quite the contrary.

His place on the Council would be taken by his son Payaral. He would be nearly the youngest Councillor of any of the great associations or consortia, and highly honored by this.

He would also be more than seven hundred light-years from Victoria, his staff, and whatever he was doing there or allowing them to do. The election would honor the house of Na'an; it would also serve as a bribe of star-shaking proportions to Payaral, to end his dubious connections and resume the duties of the kind of Merishi the humans called "merchant princes."

Having studied both the language of the term and its roots in human history, Na'an judged that it was accurate and intended to be complimentary. He wondered if his son had studied as deeply, for all that he spoke better Anglic than his father.

Abler, yes. The lad—a lad old enough to have nest-free children himself, had his first marriage survived— was vastly gifted, fit to turn his hand to anything where his claws could grip. Had this facility led him to try too much, dare too much, bend the laws more than a little?

Melancholy thoughts when your son was about to triumph, but not unreasonable. Returned to Merish (the alternative was flight, leading to unthinkable outlawry), Payaral would find the old and slow-witted dominating the Council. He would have frustrating years of listening to them and persuading them to his views before he wielded as much influence as his father had.

Would he endure the frustrations, when he had been ruler in all but name, even if he was called a servant? If he did not, there would be more than two hands' worth of enemies ready to denounce him for visible crimes and errors committed by the light of the Great Sun, not rumors of things done on a far-distant planet not even ruled by the Folk!

The next Councillor entered the chamber. Na'an heard one click as he picked up his bowl, another as he put it down. He was a real traditionalist, voting barefoot; Na'an heard the scrape of sole-scales on the tile floor.

They were in the presence of the Serene, trusting to its judgment. Zydmunir Na'an turned his back on the door, asking that the Serene enter him and give him some of its essence.

Then he smiled. One thing was certain. Those who expected an easier time after father gave way to son on the Council would be sadly disappointed!

Linak'h:

On the screen a flight of six shuttles swept by *Shenandoah,* dropping toward the night side of Linak'h.

From the battle cruiser's altitude, the planet was almost a complete sphere, and city lights were only twinkles in the darkness. After a while, one's eyes became adjusted to detecting the different tints that told of different races' cities.

Rose Liddell could have played that game if she hadn't been so tired. Providing cover to the landing of 218 Brigade was almost done, and she thought the Low Squadron had done it well. At least 218 Brigade's CG, Lev Edelstein (a charmer, and *mercifully* senior of Kharg; in fact, already selected for two stars) had said so.

Longman hadn't said much at all these past few days. One could interpret that as her having said everything she thought needed saying and then shut up, leaving her subordinates to get on with their jobs. There were disagreeable senior officers like that, who needed to outgas more than normal people, abused their rank to do so, but were more an annoyance than a menace.

Liddell hoped so. What she feared was Longman going the other way—drawing more into silence, more into herself (or at best her staff), as a situation that she didn't feel she could face came closer. Fifteen days now—no, it was past midnight in the Zone, which was the Linak'h Command's standard time. Fourteen days before the ultimatum expired.

Sherry at this hour would only keep her awake, but maybe if she took her shoes off? And if her shoes, why not a few more clothes?

After a while Liddell was in a loose robe, in the lotus position, mixing yoga and a quantity of sherry that would have appalled her old yoga instructor. He would have made a good Merishi, that one; he worshipped serenity so much.

Let the mind run free. Suppose the Administration comes up with a definition of refugee that we can live with? What do we do if the people the Admin wants to go back don't want to go? Force them—the Ptercha'a, anyway? (The Administration wasn't going to be stupid enough to ask the Federation to hand humans back to Merishi justice. She hoped.)

Not a war, that forcing. Even after the third glass of sherry and the fifteenth hour of duty, Liddell could tell the difference between a war and a police action. A police action fought to prevent a war.

Prevent one war, but maybe start others? The security of refugees is one of the things the Federation has fought for, all through centuries and across light-years. What happens if refugees or prospective refugees lose confidence in the ability of the Federation to protect them?

There was already a smell of winking at emigration restrictions, at the root of this crisis. Nieg had told her about that smell years ago, when *Shen* was still in orbit around Victoria. Apparently hard intelligence on the business was missing, but to Nieg the smell was even stronger now. And what was Sho Kuwahara up to, with that study group his letters referred to so cryptically?

Liddell set down her glass and bowed her head until her hair brushed the mat. Then she stretched, neck at full extension and arms over her head. Weariness flooded in, but it was the kind of weariness that allowed sleep.

She knocked over the glass as she stood up, leaving a stain on the mat and another on the hem of her robe.

Leave it to Jensen—a thought which normally would have revolted her. But it was amazing how fifteen-hour days coarsened the conscience.

Merish:

The last Councillor went into the chamber as quickly and intently as if he direly needed to void and nothing had any reality until he had done so. When he came out, he came at a more decorous pace, with a thin smile on his face.

Zydmunir Na'an walked to the far end of the great chamber and sat down on a bench. He thought of prostration or contemplation, but knew that what he really wanted to do was enter Assimilation Mode. That would let him retain in memory most of what he expected to overhear, in the time before the vote was announced and also in the time afterward. That would be useful data, regardless of the outcome of the vote.

Assimilation Mode here and now would be a gross breach of manners, also regardless of the outcome of the vote. Indeed, it would hardly be less offensive for him to copulate publicly with the not yet nest-free child of one of the Councillors. It would be surprising if the penalty for Assimilation Mode was not another vote, which he would certainly lose and his son might not win in any sense.

A murmur of voices broke into Na'an's thoughts. He recognized the ritual call for the drawing of lots, to pick three of the Councillors to go in, count, and proclaim the outcome. Since he could not be one of them, he chose instead to assume the posture of contemplation, with eyes directed at the floor to add an element of humility to the contemplation.

At some point, far enough in the future for an entire rotation of the galaxy (or so it seemed), he heard a silence more audible than speech. He looked up, to see three expressionless faces staring down at him.

This, I shall face standing.

The middle face seemed to grow larger. Dollis Ibrad, the oldest of the Councillors, was stepping forward. In his hands he held a stack of bowls.

"Let it be said by me and understood by all," Ibrad intoned. "The judgment of the bowls has been given, with the blessing of the Serene.

"Eleven favor retaining you as Councillor. Four favor

removing you in favor of your son. One appears to favor having both father and son on the Council."

The wrinkled, brown-spotted face broke in a thin smile. "I think the health of those of your age and mine could hardly survive that last experience, so I do not consider that a valid choice. But only one made it, so no great matter."

"The Serene has blessed this voting with wisdom," the other two judges intoned solemnly. Na'an thought that the one on the right must have been one of the opponents. He certainly had some trouble getting the words out as smoothly as ritual required.

"Praise the Serene and the wisdom of voters," Na'an replied. He tried not to sound too pleased for manners, and in fact this was not hard. "The wisdom of voters" existed more often in prayers than in practical reality, and the larger the voting population, the lower the average of wisdom. Or perhaps it was only that the same amount of wisdom was more thoroughly hidden, in the massed ranks of the unwise.

Na'an's musings on political philosophy were interrupted by the soft chiming of the bell calling for evacuation of the chamber, for the next group needing a ritual vote. He did not remember who it was, but even if it was a dispute between two members of the mason's guild, it was gross discourtesy to delay them.

As fast as he could without holding up his robes, Na'an hurried out of the chamber. He stepped aside as the next group—a merchant and a dissatisfied customer, he judged, with a group of voters mostly women—hurried in, too fast for strict custom.

It was only when the door had folded shut behind the next voters that Na'an saw he was not alone. Apart from the two guards with their ceremonial axe-clubs, Dollis Ibrad had remained behind.

Na'an suddenly felt all his years in his heart and lungs. What was about to be said would decide his future more surely than the vote.

"Do not think that we all love either your son or you," Ibrad whispered. He also turned so that the guards could not read his lips.

When Na'an replied, he hardly even whispered. He knew that Ibran could read lips. "That is no surprise.

Nor do I ask the true reason. I ask only why you waited behind, if that is all you have to say to me?"

Another of those thin smiles. If a pricklefruit could have jested, its smile might have been much like that.

"In ten days, come to my house at sunset. Meanwhile, what you wish to do for your son, feel free, as long as you use only your own funds. He may need more resources.

"Until ten days, Cousin." Ibrad turned and walked away, more swiftly than anyone five years older than Na'an had any right to cover floor!

Na'an never believed in standing gaping, and still less before witnesses. He was in his flyer before he relaxed vigilance and leaned back to search memory.

"Cousin" was not entirely an honorific fiction, between him and Dollis Ibrad. Go back enough generations, and one did come to a pair of brothers who had married sisters, with each couple producing four or five children. Within the traditional definition of kinship (customary if not legal, and in ritual settings perhaps even legal), he and Ibrad were cousins.

This might mean much or little. Na'an thought more of the word Ibrad had used for "resources." It was an archaic form of that word, still in common use but with a different meaning. That meaning was "ships."

More ships for Payaral, as long as only Na'an family funds were used for them? Not illogical. Indeed, a very promising option, one that deserved as thorough an examination as one could make with both haste and discretion. And after the examination, action.

Linak'h:

"Hey, Sarge!" a voice called from up ahead. "Is this the last hill?"

Jan Sklarinsky's voice replied, "Yeah. The next one's a mountain."

That got a laugh. Two kloms farther, Shores was going to clamp down on noise discipline, but right now everybody was too fresh to make it worth keeping them quiet.

Two kloms farther, they'd be five kloms out of camp

on the twenty-klom outward march. That far out, they would need full march discipline and security, besides the lifters on both high and low watch.

Twenty kloms out, set security, run a field problem, allow time for eating a meal and treating blisters, then twenty kloms back and a duty-free day tomorrow. Nothing demanding—*Shenandoah* Company could do it without working up a decent sweat, and C/Fifth/222 was about as good. Even the Reserve rifle company and the Support units were getting up to that standard.

Everybody, however, would get just tired enough for a couple of good night's sleep. Sleep untroubled by nightmares about wars, forest fires, terrorism, riots, or anything else that they'd faced or might face. Sleep so untroubled that once they woke up they might be able to handle all of those things again.

Even the Old Lady might get a good night's sleep.

Shores dropped back, watching the column of march pass in the shadows. It was just past Father-set, but this stretch of road was flanked by massive axeberry orchards. Shores had never seen a fruit-bearing tree that tall, except for a few pecans on Quetzalcoatl, and only Ptercha'a would enjoy the amount of climbing needed to pick berries growing sixty meters above ground.

The trail platoon was Lieutenant Fiske's. At least he'd always been fit in body, if not sharp of mind. He was striding up and down the platoon, trying to look alert and vigilant, covering two meters to his men's one.

"Good evening, Col—ah, ma'am," he said, remembering just in time not to salute.

"Hello, Fiske. Don't sweat yourself dry too soon. I don't have a canteen to spare."

In fact, Shores didn't have a canteen at all. She was deliberately seeing if she still had some of her LI School endurance, by making the whole march out and back without drinking. She'd guzzled before leaving, of course, but forty kloms and twelve hours even at night should be a good test. It was a hot night, too, like the last twenty nights and (so the weather predictions said) probably the next twenty.

Shores fell into step with the platoon and listened to Fiske giving orders, with her critical faculties fine-tuned. His diction was still a little formal, and he tended to repeat himself more often than he should. This probably meant nerves; it would certainly *say* nerves to troops who didn't know him.

But Fiske was improving, and he was giving the right orders. Shores was no longer tempted to put in Fiske's Evaluation & Report the phrase "needs two competent officers to keep him from being more dangerous to his own people than to the enemy." Justice now demanded something like "an officer who began with apparently limited grasp of his duties, but who has improved to an exceptional degree while under my command."

No, that would sound as if she were claiming credit for something that had to be the result of what Fiske had in him to begin with. Phrase it, "to an exceptional degree with experience of duty in command of a rifle platoon."

"Hello," the shadows said.

They spoke in Nieg's voice, so Shores didn't startle anyone by dropping into combat stance. She shortened her stride instead, to join Nieg as he leaped from the top of the orchard wall, across the drainage ditch, to land spring-legged on the road.

"Show-off," she muttered, and punched him lightly in the shoulder. He rode the punch and mock-kicked at her knee.

"I *thought* this was where I'd find you," he said, as they fell in at the rear of the platoon.

"When I couldn't reach you, I wondered if you and Kharg had finally come to blows," she said.

"Not yet. All the brawls today were Ptercha'a on Ptercha'a, with maybe a couple of human refugees thrown in on one side or another. No shooting, though. I think having 218 Brigade working up by patrolling Och'zem is discouraging snipers. They fear getting off on the wrong foot with the brigade by accidentally hitting one of its people while shooting at someone else."

"Let's hope they stay scared."

While he talked, the colonel had been studying her. It was a familiar gaze, one that included a mental undressing but didn't stop there.

"No canteen," he said.

"Is it your business?" she replied.

That made it impossible to keep it her business, of

course. In five minutes he had the story of the deteriorating situation at her father's house out of her.

"Sophie didn't say what this was doing to Peter," Shores concluded. "But she's scared, and she's old enough to understand."

"Have you thought of stepping aside until your father and Ursula thrash this out between them?"

"Several times. Do you have to insult me as well as mind my business?"

"I do not have to show any concern for you at all, Candy. I *want* to, but it is not a matter of duty on either side."

Shut up, Candy, before you've added messing up Nieg to messing up your father's family.

She took a deep breath. "So what form do you want your concern to take?"

"What about my taking the children flying? Frankly, battalion CO's are going to be busier than intelligence officers for the next two days. Also, I will be less of a threat to Ursula than you will. I hardly think she suspects me of trying to undermine her authority over her children."

Shores winced, although the shadows mercifully hid it. She'd admitted that suspicion of Ursula and even of herself to herself, but having Nieg see it so plainly made her feel several degrees beyond naked.

"I hardly mean to insult or bribe you, Candy," Nieg said more gently. "But I know things about large, or at least complex, families that you do not. I can look at your father's household with different eyes."

That was the truth, even if it hurt to have it pushed in her face that he knew it. Fortunately Nieg said nothing more for a while, although he did pull a loaded canteen from his pack and silently hand it to her.

She drank half of it, then slung on her own belt as they hurried to catch up with the rear guard.

Twenty

Linak'h:

One of the Ptercha'a said something that made Behdan Zeg grin. She practically had to shout to be heard over the howl of the wind in the treetops.

Rahbad Sarlin recognized at least one word, *wind*. He wished he'd been allowed to bring along his portable translator, but Zeg said that the People's reputation was too much at stake. So was Sarlin's ability to understand what his battle-comrades were saying well enough not to be killed by accident, but Zeg did not seem to have thought much of that.

"Yes!" Sarlin shouted back. "There is wind!"

The other two exchanged glances, and even what looked like smiles. Sarlin had grown used to the idea of his half-brother being capable of smiling. He had not quite learned the range of Ptercha'a facial expressions.

Zeg said something in True Speech, and the Ptercha'a nodded.

"I said the wind has muscles!" Zeg called. "That's one of their phrases!"

It was also a vivid and accurate one. In the open, not just dead leaves and needles but cones, fair-sized branches, and even rocks were rolling along before the wind. Above, the trees were not merely swaying but whipping back and forth like old-style antennae.

It was a dry wind, too. Although its source in the northwest and their altitude cooled it, Sarlin still felt it sucking the moisture from every scrap of exposed skin. He drew his hood tighter about his face. Never mind cramped and aching ears; the external phones would supply the place of nature. He wanted to keep that wind from his skin and the debris it hurled from his eyes.

Zeg raised both hands and jerked both thumbs toward the open. The Ptercha'a four assigned to the lead tightened their straps and masks and picked up their weapons. Sarlin saw them stagger as they reached the open, then take a firmer stance before they spread out into their tactical formation.

The wind made him stagger, too, when he faced it in the open. What it must be like up on the ridges, after sweeping across fifty marches of open country, he did not care to imagine.

He turned on his receiver and tried to untangle messages from the static. Even a commercial weather forecast would be useful. But the Yellow Father was breaking out in starspots, with the usual effect on radio reception.

Higher up reception might be better, if one did not need all one's strength, limbs, and attention to keep from being blown off the ridges. They would certainly need more time than they could afford, to make such a diversion to satisfy mere curiosity.

In this weather, carrying heavier loads than usual, the Ptercha'a would be slowed, and even the People would need to tread warily. It would take a good half-watch for the final stage to the Merishi training camp. The battle itself should be swift, but the withdrawal might face the same weather and would probably enjoy pursuit.

Was that a rumble of thunder off to the north? Sarlin adjusted the earphone.

"Freeze!"

A Merishi lifter with the markings of a well-known farm-machinery consortium rode overhead, rocking and weaving as it fought the winds. It might have no connection with the camp, but Zeg and su-Lal had between them established that this area was forbidden to normal air traffic.

The lifter also showed none of the required navigation and warning lights. Not a commercial machine off course, then. Sarlin hoped it was the War Lord's will, that the lifter crew was too busy fighting the wind to closely observe the ground below.

The lifter battled its way out of sight. Looking at the treetops where it vanished, Sarlin saw the stars beginning to fade, even follow the lifter into oblivion.

"Clouding up!" he shouted.

Zeg looked up and frowned. Was it the clouds, or his half-brother noticing something before he did? The old jealousy between them was less robust than it had been, but hardly dead.

"Did you hear thunder, just before the lifter came?" Zeg called back.

"I thought I did," Sarlin admitted.

"That makes two of us with the same thought."

Thunder, above a forest dry as straw.

"All the more reason for striking tonight," Sarlin said, more cheerfully than he felt. "They will not be able to hear a thing over the wind save their own thoughts, and those thoughts will all be on the storm."

Zeg thought that remark worth translating to the Ptercha'a, and Sarlin saw ears raised and tails waved at him in reply. *Must give more time to learning the True Speech. Why did I waste so much on Commercial Merishi?*

Because he'd lacked foreknowledge, being an Inquirer, not a prophet. It was the same answer he'd given to a score of different questions, but it grew no more comforting as he grew older.

Aboard U.F.S. *Shenandoah*, off Linak'h:

"Commodore Liddell here."

It was Pavel Bogdanov. "Sorry to bother you, Commodore, but there are thunderstorm formations showing up on the satellites." He sounded tired, but not putting nearly as much effort into hiding this fact as he would have when they first met while commissioning *Shenandoah*.

"Where?"

"Between the Alliance border and the Hyssh'n. The formations extend over a line roughly four hundred kilometers long. Ground stations also report winds gusting up to one hundred kilometers an hour."

When the weather on Linak'h broke, it broke with a vengeance. Before the night was over, Linak'h Command, its friends and foes, would have gone from worrying about forest fires to scrambling clear of flash floods. (Although the dry debris layers, and bush-grown open terrain, would soak up a lot of water before it reached the streams and rivers.)

"Thank you, Pavel."

"Oh, it may not mean much. But there is more than the usual air activity around the suspected training camp. Twelve percent greater than the average."

That hardly seemed significant. "Do we have anybody in the area they might be looking for?"

"I can inquire."

"No, I'll do that, as soon as I'm free."

It would make sense for the Merishi and their hirelings to be either evacuating or reinforcing the camp, with ten days to the ultimatum's expiring. Whether this would lead to war was still anybody's guess, at least partly because communications between the Administration and Linak'h Command had become rare and brief. Most of what there were came through Governor General Rubirosa, who seemed to be enjoying being in the spotlight (or at least useful) after months of being relegated to the sidelines by the bubbling military activity.

Meanwhile, nothing good could come of being rude to Rear Admiral Uehara. Ignoring a senior officer you had invited to dinner was uncouth, impolitic, and unprofessional (take them in any order you wished).

"My apologies, Admiral," she said, turning back to her guest. "I'm sure you've long since learned that we're keeping a close eye on the weather in the fire-hazard areas. This thunderstorm formation is upwind of literally millions of hectares of them."

Uehara looked at his watch. "In that case, it might be wise for me to thank you for an excellent dinner in pleasant surroundings, and return to *Intrepid*. They should have my quarters cleaned by now."

Uehara flew his flag in the light carrier *Intrepid*, a name with a long history, now attached to a big merchanter converted last year to carry two heavy attacker squadrons. The conversion had been thorough and sound on the military side, less so for crew accommodations or storage space. Uehara had spent the voyage out in his watch cabin, while flag quarters served as a storeroom.

"It's been a pleasure having you over." Liddell rose, saluted, and bowed slightly. You couldn't tell, with a

man from Meiji, which side of the Bad Manners Wars
his ancestors had been on, so a bow never did any harm.

Uehara returned both salute and bow. The bow was
precisely matched to Liddell's—he had superior rank, she
was the host. Then for good measure they shook hands.

Uehara's aide entered to collect him, as Liddell alerted
the ready shuttle. Two robots came in as the guests left,
followed by Chief Jensen.

"I had the bakery do up a case of bagels for him," the
steward said.

"Bagels?" Liddell replied.

"Seems he has a passion for them, and *Intrepid*'s
bakers don't know the first thing about them. Although
it might not help if they did. Anyone would think *Intrepid* was converted at Columbia Dockyard."

Liddell smiled and let the steward get on with the
cleanup. The intelligence network among senior officers'
servants would make Alliance Field Intelligence envious,
and the legend of Columbia Dockyard being full of people who couldn't find the right tool for a job was older
than she was.

She went into her study to be out of the way, and saw
that Bogdanov had fed a real-time weather display onto
her screen. Superimposed on it was an announcement
that R.M.S. *Somtow Nosavan* was entering unloading
orbit, with a crew of twenty-eight and three hundred
twenty-three passengers belonging to the Victoria Civil
Action Group.

That was no surprise, although *Freiherr von Leventzow*
had been. Longman had ordered her stopped, boarded,
and searched before letting her into unloading orbit, over
Captain Oczuk's protests. (Rather strong protests; although Liddell didn't know any Turkic, a man who looks
ready to throttle his interrogator is not in charity with
the universe.)

*Keep an ear out for protests from the Merishi over this
kind of handling of one of their charters*, Liddell noted
mentally. Otherwise, *von Leventzow* had come up clean,
and *Nosavan* had chosen a good time to arrive. Her people could be down, briefed, equipped, assigned, and
maybe even at work before the shooting started or the
fires and floods hit. Also, Linak'h Command would have

the ships of the escort force back, and *Shen* would get back the eight crew who'd ridden *Nosavan* to Victoria.

More mental notes. Liddell wanted a copy of the eight's debriefing, and Pavel ought to give them a duty-free day, maybe two. *A dirtside pass, too, if they want it—as Brian Mahoney surely will.*

And now that Uehara was out of embarrassment range, it was time to discreetly check with Colonel Nieg, on who might be doing what near the Merishi camp.

Linak'h:

Rahbad Sarlin and the Lidessouf twins took the lead as the patrol approached the camp. They had been there before, knew the way (important in the darkness), and could tell if the sensors or patrols had been increased.

"Better send a four of Ptercha'a with us," Sarlin added. "They can see better in the dark, and we can use them for more exposed observation posts. Our being seen gives everything away, but what's one Hunter more or less?"

"If the camp's security is careless, not much. But if they are watchful, exposure even of a Hunter could be a death sentence. Or do you not care?" Zeg added.

"If you are going to insult me, mother's son, insult me in a tongue these Hunters do not understand. This is no time for a quarrel between us."

"This is also no time for the Hunters to learn that you are reckless of their lives. They hope for more of the People than they have ever had from the Masters or the Smallteeth."

Sarlin renewed his vows to learn the True Speech. It could be important to learn whether Zeg was telling the truth even about this band of Ptercha'a. If what he said was true of more than a handful of Ptercha'a, much might come of People and Ptercha'a working together, to the advantage of both.

It was also possible that Zeg was so convinced that he had found a way to make himself useful to his own race, that he would be as ruthless with the Ptercha'a as he suspected his half-brother of being. At least that vice would be corrected, sooner rather than later, by the Pter-cha'a themselves. None of the People would need to scrape a fingernail to bring Zeg to justice.

Yet Sarlin realized that in his heart he hoped the Pter-cha'a and Zeg were both telling the truth. Not only because the People would gain from it, either. His mother's son would have at last found those who would follow him, and a cause he could serve.

It was too much to hope that this would make him clean, polite, and gracious in the society of the People. But it would increase Zeg's happiness, which Sarlin now realized was closer to his heart than he had ever been willing to admit.

Nor would he admit it now, unless this mission faced them all with imminent death. The mission first, kin-rites afterward.

"I will stand beside you, mother's son, to see that the Hunters gain what they wish. But can you see if one four will offer themselves, to go forward with us?"

Zeg had his mouth open to reply, when a bolt of lightning tore across the sky. It was so close that dazzling flash and ear-battering thunder came almost in the same breath. Even on the wind, the smell of lightning-gas reached Sarlin, making him fight not to sneeze.

One of the Ptercha'a went down on his belly and crawled forward without orders, seeking a view of where the lightning had struck. He came back almost at once, signaling the absence of danger. A few questions passed between him and Zeg, and the commander turned to Sarlin.

"That one was high on a ridge. He saw no fire, and not much to feed one if there was flame he could not see. Also, high up, the wind may blow out a fire rather than spread it."

"May it be so," Sarlin said. He did not say aloud the thought that even a Hunter might have found it hard to see any great distance. The sky was now starless, although if one looked hard one could see hints of the cloud masses driving before the gale.

"What about that four? Our chances of taking enough prisoners will grow if they come." Sarlin wondered why he had not thought of that argument before. Had the wind and the fear of fire battered his wits?

Zeg nodded. "May you prove wise. But I will expect you to help pay the kin of those who do not return from playing bait."

"Both wisdom and honor demand *that*, mother's son. Am I a fool, not to know that?"

Zeg seemed about to reply, but instead turned away toward the Ptercha'a.

Linak'h:

Candice Shores woke up, trying to recall if she'd been having a real nightmare or just restless sleep. Everything had been shadowy while she slept; now there were more shadows in the bedroom.

She realized that some of those shadows had to mean that there was a light on in the living room. It followed logically that she should also hear voices, particularly since Nieg hadn't been in the bed when she awoke.

Shores pulled on a robe and stuck her head through the doorway. Nieg, in another robe, was sitting at his computer. Commander Franke was just coming out of the kitchen with a tray, while Major Morley sat in an armchair, in full uniform, sipping tea.

"What the Hades . . . ?"

"Hello, Candy," Franke said. "There's an Alert Two and a Security One Yellow. Lu dropped me off and came up for talktalk while her people take their positions covering the area."

"Ukkhh," Shores said. She trusted no one would take that for insight or opinion. Well, maybe opinion.

"Who did what to whom?"

"Thunderstorms up in the high forest," Nieg said. He pointed at the main display. A blue snake writhed across a map, while several orange spots gave the snake the appearance of a bad case of wort-welt.

"No rain, but quite a few lightning strikes, and we have IR indications of some fires."

"That big, that fast?" Shores asked. "Or are those old fires as well as new ones?"

"There is some extrapolation, but not much. It seems to be a major cyclonic pattern generating the thunderstorms. No rain yet, but lots of lightning and winds holding steady at Force Ten."

Shores used a Merishi obscenity. The ideal conditions for the Hades of a big fire had been described in detail several times. (Gruesome detail, when accompanied by pictures of the aftermaths of some of the really big biomass disasters.) Now those conditions had been met.

"That's why the alert?"

"Mostly that, but it could be handy for something else. The Administration is supposed to be planning to hand back the 'criminals' in the next few days. Somebody talked to my liaison in the Admin's Special Branch, so it sounds reasonably official."

The belt of Shores's robe seemed to tighten around her like a constrictor, and she swallowed. "How do they define 'criminal?' "

"Damned if I know," Franke said. "It seems to be all Ptercha'a, but that may be only because they don't have ID's on the humans."

"Or because the Merishi behind this whole situation don't want to admit the humans' existence," Morley put in.

"Could be," Franke agreed. "But I won't bet the definition's anything we can accept, regardless."

An expressive silence replied. Nieg nodded. "Candy, you can go back to bed if you want. I'm not sure you need to be involved in this."

If she'd thought she could sleep, Shores would have gone back to bed, if only to see if it was nightmares or shadows again. Since she was now awake to stay . . .

"What's 'this'?"

"Finding a safe place for the refugees who can't afford to go back," Franke said. "It's possible that the Coordination and the Merishi won't go beyond making a few examples, but none of the Ptercha'a we've talked to are willing to trust them. Even if they were ready to sacrifice themselves to avoid war, they can't sacrifice their families."

"So we've been looking at the idea of a neutral location. One where they won't be under Federation jurisdiction but also can't be hit easily," Morley added.

"Have you thought of the Alliance Territory?" Shores said.

Nieg frowned. "Candy, have you added to your other passions one for being court-martialed?"

"I was joking. What about you?"

Nieg was silent, but his bowed head and slumped shoulders told an eloquent tale of exhaustion. Shores stopped feeling sorry for herself over her insomnia. She'd had a few hours of sleep, and she didn't have lives depending on her staying awake.

Or did she? "I think I'd better get over to my CP."

"Your XO called," Nieg said. "He said he has sounded the recall and lined up field equipment for combat, security, or firefighting. He also says he has your kit packed, so all you need to do is show up if the alert goes to One."

Shores blinked. Her XO might be a slow learner, but it seemed he'd grasped at least the basics.

"All right. I'll stay. Where are we going to put our friends—or let them seek asylum, if we can't offer it to them?"

"Herman suggested *Somtow Nosavan*," Morley said. "She's Victorian-registered, Merishi-provided, with a mixed but largely human crew and room for five, six hundred Ptercha'a for a little while. With resupplies, of course."

"Best of all," Franke said, "she's a *ship*. That means that if the crew won't let Admin types board, there's not much the Administration can do. They have no navy."

"The Coordination does," he added. "But the laws of physics and space apply to them too. Also, any hostile act against *Nosavan* offends a neutral party. It could even be interpreted as starting the war early."

"In which case," Morley said, baring her prominent incisors, "we turn the Coordination's excuse for a navy into the biggest space-debris problem this side of Aphrodite."

"Why am I not ecstatic at that thought?" Nieg said.

There were several good reasons. For one thing, the chain of command would have to be associated with this, and Admiral Longman at least had no love for or faith in *Somtow Nosavan*. Implementing the plan without higher officers' participation might be construed as mutiny; it would certainly resemble a do-it-yourself colostomy too closely for comfort.

Then there was the problem of anti-Federation sentiment on Victoria, as well as the Merishi Trade Mission's chief, Payaral Na'an. Arousing the first or embarrassing the second would be unwise, to say the least.

"What about simply bringing them into the Zone?" Shore said. "It seems to me that we can line up transport for a lot more than five hundred refugees under cover of preparing to move firefighters. We may even be ordered to do it anyway.

"Could we arrange for the refugees to ask Rubirosa and Tanz for asylum, while we're lining up the lift? Then we could take out the fire teams and bring back the refugees. Once they're in the Zone, nothing short of a fuser will get at them."

"Not quite, Candy," Morley said. Her handsome face looked positively demonic when she was grim, and now she looked very grim indeed. "That might do for any humans. But most of the Ptercha'a are supposed to be Confraternity.

"What happens if they're mobbed by humans who've bought into the story of Confraternity hostility? Or if the terrs stage a serious incident hiding behind a mob? The Ptercha'a will think we can't protect them from our own Pussy-haters. They may retaliate, and then—"

Shores held up a hand. She didn't know if she was begging Morley, or her own now very real nightmares, to stop.

Morley stopped. But the sound of the wind outside kept on, the howl of lost souls.

No, not lost souls. Damned souls, seeking to feed on the living with teeth of fire.

Linak'h:

The Merishi had put out more of a sensor net than before, Rahbad Sarlin quickly realized. However, it was thin and of limited capability. They were still relying mostly on concealment and sheer lack of suspicion, and only secondarily on the sensor net.

The net itself seemed to be older or less capable units, the kind used by Merishi private security units or Ptercha'a. That also made sense. The latest Ground Security equipment squatting here in the wilderness would arouse the suspicion of a tribal Ptercha'a feather-hunter. Units one step away from the recycler might be so many things that only a trained Inquirer would bother to consider half of them.

They were coming in on the camp from the west this time. It meant a longer march, and sacrificed familiarity with the terrain. It also saved slogging through particularly deep debris, and kept them away from the area where Virik ihn Petzas had died and the enemy was most likely to be alert.

Rahbad Sarlin felt a touch of unease at not having at least a token body of water between him and the likely direction of any fire, but knew that was less than rational. Lightning was striking all around them. The air would have reeked with lightning-gas if it hadn't been for the wind. The wind was also holding so strongly that Sarlin thought it might be blowing out fires as fast as the lightning started them. Only a sheltered area would allow flames to get a firm grip.

Meanwhile, it was time to put those elderly sensors to good use as bait. Zeg translated Sarlin's instructions. The party would disable a sensor, then the Ptercha'a would go and imitate a repair party. Anyone who came out would be lured into an ambush, executed with stun slugs (gas would be useless in this kind of wind), knives, and hands.

Once they had a reasonable number of prisoners, they would withdraw, keeping them conscious but constrained as far as the pickup point. If the alarm went up before they had enough prisoners, they would drug the prisoners with amnesiacs, leave explosive traps in their wake, and withdraw by one of the alternative routes. Friendly wounded who could not be moved were also to be killed.

Sarlin thought that Zeg said this last with more zest than seemed appropriate. But he had no doubt that his half-brother would face that fate himself with courage, if not necessarily zest.

The Ptercha'a repeated their orders with no more lapses than Sarlin would have expected of shrewd but inexperienced warriors. The extra ammunition was distributed, and the eight-warrior vanguard of the patrol moved out.

Sarlin brought up the rear for the first few hundred

paces. Looking back, he saw the quickgun team busy piling fallen but still fresh branches around their weapon, until even Sarlin had to look twice to see it. Clearly his half-brother had picked Hunters with war-sense, if not necessarily war-seasoning.

As he moved forward to take his customary position in the middle, Sarlin thought he smelled smoke. He wanted to believe it was his imagination, then he saw Kalidessouf lifting his nose to the wind and wrinkling it up.

The twin brought his face around, and his eyes met Sarlin's. Sarlin nodded, then spread his hands. Kalidessouf hesitated, then did the same and turned back to the trail.

They could do nothing about the source of the smoke, which might be near or far, great or small. They could not even be sure that fleeing now would outdistance flames driven before such a wind. They could only continue with their mission.

Linak'h:

"This way, this way!" a hoarse voice shouted. "No, to the right. *Your* right!"

The Victorians surged back and forth in response to the shouts, heads bowed against the wind, clutching their hand baggage.

Karl Pocher, who had his personal kit in a backpack, had both hands free. He cupped them around his mouth and bellowed:

"Listen up, people! We're going to the warehouse. The one marked 'Carzos Brothers,' with the open cargo-platform door. You'll see two people in Territorial Reserve uniforms standing there. Show your cards to them, then sit down and don't get excited. I'm sure there's nothing wrong."

Pocher had a carrying voice, and with the wind in his favor Victorians three Teams behind his own Greens heard him. The aimless surge turned into a disorderly but recognizable movement toward the indicated door.

Pocher waited outside until the last of this flight's Victorians was inside. Kathy McGuire would make a pretty good substitute for him, if the Greens needed any leading while they were sitting in a cozy warehouse waiting for orders and assignments. Too bad the briefing had been postponed until they got dirtside, and there'd better be a damned good reason for this hustling that had everybody's nerves on edge—the Linak'h'ers' too, if Pocher was any judge.

Finally Pocher came up to the Reservist. "What's your count?"

"One-twenty." The woman handed Pocher a rough-print list.

"There should be one hundred twenty-two. We got all three Teams off the shuttles."

They noted the names of the missing. "I'll call for volunteers to join the search."

"You will do no such thing," the Reservist—a warrant officer, Pocher now saw—said firmly. "We know the streets. You do not."

"Our people know us. They don't know you," Pocher replied.

"You sent out paranoids?" the woman said, frowning.

Pocher recognized a mind made up past altering with facts, and threw up his hands in dramatic disgust. The woman stepped aside, muttering something about "offworlders with more enthusiasm than sense," as Pocher stepped into the warehouse.

Inside, the Victorians were forming into two lines to be issued what looked like loaded backpacks and yellow-covered pamphlets. Pocher took one from another Reservist, and had just started to read it when a third Reservist climbed up on a heap of crates and shouted for attention.

He was a while getting it. Once again it took a cupped-hands shout from Pocher to get order. Kathy McGuire added a whistle, two fingers in her mouth, and the Reservist finally had everybody's attention.

"Welcome to Linak'h, people. I'm sorry we couldn't provide a briefing upstairs, but we had to get you down fast or leave you in space. There are some big fires up north, and a lot of lift is being tied up for hauling fire-suppressants and work crews.

"But there are portable showers coming in, and the bathrooms are down that way and ready." He pointed.

"There's a day's food and a canteen you can fill at the faucet in each of those packs, in case any of you didn't bring your own."

"What about the rest of our baggage?" someone shouted.

"That'll come down on the first available shuttle after the people are dirtside," the Reservist said. "Seriously, wouldn't you rather have your baggage up there to be shot at, then yourselves?"

The laughter was at least polite. "Now, I don't want to say we're breaking our promises about assignments," the Reservist went on. "Wherever possible, you Vics will be assigned by Teams. But we'll be happy to take volunteers with special skills for individual assignments.

"I don't know how many of you are qualified lifter crew, or have experience flying in high winds and poor visibility. . . ."

The laughter was the heartiest Pocher had heard in months. He joined in it, watching the Reservist turn several interesting colors.

The man hadn't done worse than show ignorance of Victorian conditions, but he'd done that spectacularly. Outside of the towns, Victorians lived by, often for, and sometimes by their lifters.

When the laughter had died down, McGuire shouted, "Hey, chum! Try flying in a Victorian sandstorm at night, then tell me if *that's* not high winds and poor visibility."

"All right. Anybody with Master or Senior Pilot ratings or any sort of lifter-tech cert, we can use you tonight."

"Shower and eat first?" McGuire asked.

"Of course. It'll take us at least that long to get your transport ready. You can sleep on the way north."

"Who with?" somebody yelled. More laughter, and McGuire made a rude gesture in the general direction of the speaker.

Pocher stepped forward and caught Kathy's arm.

"Hey, I had you picked for my second-in-command, besides keeping an eye on BoJo."

McGuire laughed. "There's no way in God's created universe I could do both. Find somebody else. Like an LI Sergeant Major, preferably male."

Pocher flipped through his manual. "Nothing in there, I'm afraid."

"Keep looking, Karl. And take care." She hurried off toward the bathroom.

Mitch Leary? Pocher shook his head. Good for taking care of BoJo, maybe. Making him second-in-command would look like favoritism. Besides, Mitch was a potential sub-Team leader—and never mind the promises, they had to plan on the Teams being split up.

Pocher decided to sleep on it. In the morning he might have more ideas, or the job might look like something he could do single-handed.

Linak'h:

The wind blew the patrol's foam bomb off-target, so that it landed downwind of the sensor unit. The foam that would have blinded and baffled the units sprayed into the wind and vanished like spittle in a campfire.

Rahbad Sarlin wondered if they should have tried a grenade. He tapped the Ptercha'a with the launcher and signaled for another shot.

They had to delay a hundredth-watch, while two more lifters slid overhead. These were heavy-duty ones, with no pretense at a civilian appearance, and they were outbound.

They were also flying fast for the visibility and altitude, and the smell of smoke seemed just a trifle stronger. Sarlin added the two and came up with another displeasing sum, as unalterable as duty.

The second foam bomb struck its target. The Ptercha'a put down his weapon and joined his three comrades in trotting forward. Each of them had something in one hand that could pass as a tool, and a weapon in a tunic pocket waiting for the other hand.

All four of them could in fact pass for Ptercha'a from the camp, as far as Sarlin remembered. Perhaps not by daylight, but tonight, with true darkness over the land, even Ptercha'a night-sight would leave a relief party confused until it was too late. A little acting ability by the Ptercha'a would help, of course. . . .

Solidessouf slipped into place beside Sarlin. He held a heavy quickgun lightly by the barrel, as if he intended to use it as a club. He probably could do so, and well, if he had to. The Lidessouf twins had taught the "Improvised Weapons" course at the Special Projects Field School, as well as in the Assault Force training camp.

The other twin was off to the left flank, with Zeg, nearly out of sight. No, there they were—or was that a Ptercha'a with them? Trouble in the rear, or had Zeg borrowed an extra to act as messenger? Probably wise, but certainly something he should have asked. . . .

Seven figures appeared in the trees. Here it was a mixture of virgin trees and second growth; settlement or fire had done some clearing. The approaching seven moved rapidly, even though only two of them stuck to the trail. The others divided three right, two left, and moved with the ease of practiced ground-fighters.

Except that they were all Folk. Sarlin barely needed his night sights to make that out. The Scaleskins were hardly bothering to disguise themselves, wearing only form-fitting tunics, baggy trousers tucked into low boots, and helmets with the usual light ground-combat instrumentation. That, and pouches sagging with ammunition for the quickguns in their hands.

The notion that the Folk would not put ground-fighters into the field when they could send Hunters seemed to Sarlin in need of revision.

So did his plans. The capture or death of this many Folk would create an uproar that might lead to a demand for the Mission's closure, regardless of what Inquiry value prisoners might have. The drugs were supposed to be adaptable to all four major sapient biochemistries, but believing that demanded faith.

Something Sarlin did believe, however: He had to act now or his half-brother would, and afterward claim the leadership outright because he had acted.

Zeg or the Ptercha'a four-leader gave the first command. The four Ptercha'a scattered in what seemed like more than four different directions, so swiftly did they move. Lightning striking close by once more helped them; the Merishi wore night-vision goggles and the glare dazzled even their light-resistant eyes.

Then the Ptercha'a were coming in from the flanks,

striking with knives, stun-powder grenades, clubs, and
strangling cords. Sarlin wasted no time on being surprised
at seeing the last; they were an obvious weapon when
silence meant survival. He did finger his own neck, hoping that the Ptercha'a would remember that the cords
were illegal even in the People's Territory.

A Merishi raised his quickgun, seeking targets; Sarlin's
own sleepgun found a target first. The Merishi toppled,
firing a wild burst as he went down, rolled over, and
pressed the firing stud so that his own weapon sent slugs
tearing through his head.

One who won't need any further thought.

From upwind came three explosions close together.
Sarlin recalled the pattern they'd deduced for the sensors; Zeg and his team must have bombed the nearest
unit.

Sarlin's eyes scanned the forest, searching for the next
sensor unit to the east. If three units went out, the camp
commanders would think they faced a massive attack.
They would delay reinforcing the perimeter until they
had gathered strength, or even called in help by lifter.

What Sarlin really wanted was a spell of levitation, but
gaining time was a good second-best.

Hand signals guided Solidessouf to his target, and his
marksmanship with a quickgun took care of the rest.
Smoke billowed up around the third ruined unit, as two
Merishi finally had the sense to retreat. Why they had
not done so before, Sarlin could not think. Braver than
they were wise, or perhaps contemptuous of any attack
by their Hunters?

It seemed to Sarlin that the Merishi should learn to
take their furry mercenaries seriously as enemies. Or
they would be putting a greater temptation in their path
than any race could be asked to resist.

At the moment, the greatest temptation facing the
Ptercha'a was pursuing the fleeing Merishi. Behdan Zeg
slowed the urge with a harsh shout, which made some
of the Merishi still fighting stop and gape.

Were they not used to seeing People at all, or merely
astounded to see them here, commanding Hunters? Regardless of the reason for their mistakes three of them
paid for it in the next moment, Ptercha'a swarmed over
them, leaving them stunned and sprawling.

Solidessouf finished the fight by charging forward. His quickgun chopped the legs out from under one of the fleeing Merishi, for all that he was firing it one-handed. With his other hand he flung a green sack forward, into the middle of the brawl ahead.

The sack contained the drug injectors, and mercifully the Ptercha'a heads contained something besides battle-fury. They snatched out the injectors and applied them with much enthusiasm if little skill.

Meanwhile, Sarlin had brought down the last Merishi with a head shot. The range was long for night work, even with night-vision on both his eyes and his rifle, but his shooting skills had not deserted him.

Then he slammed a grenade into the underbarrel launcher and dropped it on top of Solidessouf's victim. A second landed on top of his own. A third for good measure landed in a patch of bushes, which smouldered but did not quite ignite.

Solidessouf looked a question. "Chew up the bodies," Sarlin said, "and they'll find it hard to learn what killed them. Harder still if the fire comes this way."

The Assault Forcer made several gestures of aversion so strongly and so quickly that Sarlin wanted to smile. He remembered in time that, field-wise as the twins were, they were city-bred. Forest fires were to be feared not only as the menace any sensible Lawbound of any race knew them to be, but to the twins they were also to be feared as the Unknown.

Meanwhile, Zeg and Kalidessouf had returned, and the remaining Ptercha'a had come up. Sarlin had to pass out a few sharp words and more than a few sharp looks to keep everyone from bunching up, an easy target for retaliation. Zeg did not translate; Sarlin wondered if his True Speech was improving.

"We have them all, unless another remained behind as watcher," Zeg said. He pointed a boot toe at the three prostrate Merishi, then a gloved hand at the four bodies.

Then a Ptercha'a to the left of Sarlin gave a long, ululating keen. Sarlin recognized the ancient warning call, which needed no words. By now he also recognized a Hunter pointing. He ran to where the Hunter stood, and turned his gaze where the clawed fingers indicated.

A stretch of open ground reached nearly to the foot

of a small hill. It sloped up to the left, out of sight beyond the trees. But to the right, growing even as Sarlin watched, was a yellow-orange glow.

As he watched, blue joined the glow. A large specimen of the sap-rich tree the People here called "Giant's Torch" had just caught fire. In a moment, Sarlin saw more than a glow. He saw actual flames, mostly blue, rising above the hillcrest.

The smoke smell was also stronger, but it was not that which made Sarlin's breath catch. One of those lightning strokes had found a flammable spot, unleashing wildfire on this stretch of forest.

"We will need about two hundredth-watches," Zeg was saying, as he read the instructions off the stimulant injectors.

"Never mind. Either give it to them now or carry them," Sarlin snapped. He gripped his half-brother so hard the other shook off the grip and nearly entered combat stance.

"It will slow—" Zeg began. Then something a Ptercha'a said must have reached him. He stepped up beside Sarlin and looked the same way.

For the first time in many years, Sarlin saw his mother's son speechless. For one of the few times, when Zeg did speak it was conceding not just leadership but wisdom to Rahbad Sarlin.

"Lord Most High. Can we flee in time?"

Twenty-one

Linak'h:

It had been a while since Nikolai Komarov had packed a field kit, but memory was tenacious. He even remembered the spare socks carried next to his skin, and also to bounce the pack on the living room couch. That compressed the contents a bit. Now he could fit in more first-aid supplies, and another print book.

It also helped that he felt intent and focused, as he seldom did except when he was deep in a work. Intent and focused, at an hour of the night when he was usually sound asleep if he was not making love to Ursula. . . .

"Nikolai, what are you doing up?"

Komarov cursed his impulse to bounce the pack. He suppressed another impulse, to hide it. Suspicion was already in Ursula's voice. Making it worse would be a bad idea, to say the least.

"Packing, *liebchen*. I'm going out with the refugees' fire party."

His wife's mouth opened wide, until he could see most of her teeth. They were in remarkable condition, those teeth, considering how she'd spent her childhood. Malnutrition had been only one of the things that eventually drove her parents into flight.

"Why?"

"There's a general alarm out. Crown fires up north, several of them. Both armies and the Fire Guard are going to be stretched. They asked for volunteers from the camps, and I thought I should be one. It will help, the time I and some of the Ptercha'a have spent in the woods."

"I suppose it will," Ursula said slowly. "Will it help if some terrorist shoots you in the back?"

Komarov shook his head, as if midges were whining in his ears. He felt the focus and intensity slipping. He knew it would not help if he became his normal bumbling self, on the line with a crown fire bearing down on him. But the focus shut Ursula out, sometimes even the children. His wife had often said that plainly, sometimes not politely.

This might be the last time they saw each other. It was certainly about the worst time he could have picked to hurt her. Unless the only way not to hurt her was not to go at all. That he would not contemplate.

"It won't, but we'll have good security. The Federation—"

Ursula's face twisted. Komarov went on. "Reliable Federation Regulars, not the kind of people you suspect. Also, I hear rumors of some measures the refugees are taking themselves."

"Which will get them suspected of being terrorists themselves!"

"Perhaps." He looked at his wife. "Ursula, do I have any choices besides breaking a promise and not going, and leaving with you angry at me?"

"Why are your wits always sharpest at a time like this?"

Komarov's focus let him sense an opportunity to speak more clearly than usual. "Because at a time like this, you are usually trying to take advantage of me, which I do not care for."

Ursula sat down on the couch. She wore a light robe over nothing. After a moment she leaned back and massaged her neck.

"Would it do any good if I told you that I don't hate your daughter?"

"I never thought you did, Ursula. But . . . Candy and I . . . we are groping back toward something that maybe we never had, and one day will admit it. But right now . . . what are you afraid she will do with Sophia and Peter? Drop them out of the flyer when she takes them for that ride?"

He was glad to see Ursula give him a sleepy smile, then chuckle. "Did I seem that . . . paranoid?"

"Only to me, and not always. To Candy . . . I don't know. I did not want to make you more jealous by having a long talk with her. But I think it hurt. Could you stop being paranoid, even if Candy is many things you dislike or distrust? Could you at least wait until she *does* something? She and I cannot help being father and daughter."

Ursula blinked and looked at the ceiling for a moment. "No," she said slowly. "I suppose you can't." She stood up. "Very well, Nikolai. I cannot let you go off to the fires thinking I hate Candy, or hate you because of her." She smiled. "I can even let her take the children flying. Only . . . warn her. Peter wants her to wear her full uniform."

"Her dress uniform?" Komarov said.

"He saw one of the pictures you took of her in it. He said it was pretty."

"His would-be pilot thinks it's a pain to wear," Komarov said. "But I will ask." That might also ruin Nieg's plan of making the flight with the children. As far as Komarov knew, the colonel didn't even own a dress uniform.

He bent over Ursula and pulled her to her feet and into his arms in one motion. Her cheeks were wet, but since she was ignoring that, so did he.

The embrace lasted longer than either of them had planned. Komarov finally kissed his wife on the forehead, and stepped back.

"Don't let the children get too far from the house, but I don't think the fires will get anywhere near here. If you smell smoke, it's more likely to be the cooker finally dying!"

"And who bought an ingot of silver instead of a new cooker?" But she was smiling when she said it.

Linak'h:

It was too much for Rahbad Sarlin to hope that the Ptercha'a had misunderstood his half-brother's words. All he could pray for was that they did not know how badly shaken Zeg was. Sarlin had only heard the man sounding this lost four times in their shared lives.

But then, he was another of the city-bred. Where Sarlin grew up, brush and grass fires came every year. Sarlin prayed that they had taught him something that would be useful tonight.

"We can't outrun a fire moving this fast." He looked along the open ground to the southeast. It quickly narrowed to a rough animal trail. Anyone caught on that trail when the trees to either side blazed up would be ashes in a hundredth-watch.

"We go back," he said. "Remember where there is a stream to the right? Beyond it I saw more open ground; that we could clear. I would rather we had proper fire-starters, but we may be able to do something with grenades."

The Lidessouf twins would lead, the Ptercha'a would form a double column carrying the Merishi (with Sarlin's help), and Zeg would bring up the rear. Sarlin thought Zeg would do better carrying a litter. The People's muscles were a precious asset now, when the alternative to carrying the Merishi was giving them heart failure with too-massive injections or leaving them to burn alive.

"Thank you, mother's son, but a rear guard is needed just in case the Scaleskins do not find the fire totally distracting," Zeg said. "Besides, I always thought you were the one with the muscles and I with the wits."

Sarlin threw a mock punch at his brother's throat, and pulled it just before Zeg went into the counter-move. "Then use the wits you claim to possess, and avoid doing anything foolish."

"I can but do my best."

Sarlin had to be content with that. He looked back at the fire. In the moments since it had appeared, the flames had already grown brighter. Closer, too, or just finding more flammable trees where they were? The smoke smell had been so strong so long that to Sarlin clean air had begun to seem a memory or even a myth. Nor was it his imagination now, that the air was beginning to seethe with the mounting heat of the approaching fire.

At least his eye for ground had not failed him. Through a thin screen of peephole trees—thin, and not likely to send out vast gouts of flame even in this wind—Sarlin saw a stream.

Not just a stream, but a pool, with water in it, even if the marks on the bank showed that the level was nor-

mally half a People's height deeper. Splashing into it,
Sarlin felt its icy bite at his ankles—a spring-fed stream
without a doubt.

They splashed across the stream just above the pond.
On the far side was a stretch of dried mud, free of anything that could burn. While Zeg and the Lidessouf twins
stood guard, Sarlin led the Ptercha'a in digging shallow
trenches. Water oozed into the bottom of the deeper
ones.

Better and better. By this time the glow of flames had
banished darkness; a sinister half-light lay over them.
The wind seemed to be slackening a trifle, but the smoke
was thicker and more pungent and the heat mounting
steadily. Already some of the Ptercha'a had pulled on
their chemical masks and goggles.

None of the Merishi prisoners had that luxury; Sarlin
had to make do with tying wet clothes over their faces
before the Ptercha'a tumbled them into the trenches.
Then he poured canteens full of water over their clothing.

Heat pulsed from the flames now, and wind and fire
made such an uproar that all communication was by sign
language. One by one the Ptercha'a soaked their blankets
in the water. Those who had not pulled on their masks
did so. Then one by one they lay down in the trenches.
Some had wanted to lie in the stream, overcoming their
distaste for dirty water, but Sarlin reminded them that in
the pool or stream, an unconscious warrior could drown.

The People remained upright and moving, even though
the approaching fire now made its own wind, and searing
gusts twice knocked Sarlin down. He still set command-
detonated incendiary grenades at four places along the
edge of the brush-field. Then he drew back, until he was
standing beside his half-brother and the twins.

"Down!" he said, sending the firing command. Smoke
and fire erupted along the brush line. The flames leaped
up, the wind struck them—and the whole brush line went
up as if it had been soaked in blastwater.

Sarlin watched the flames racing away across the field
toward the tree line. Now they would not have to face
blazes on both sides, which might overcome even the
help of the stream.

They might win through, even though the fire now
showed as a near-solid wall beyond the peephole trees.

If the masks held up. If the blankets didn't dry out or melt through from falling cinders and debris. If the flames didn't strip the air of its ability to sustain life.

Too late for *ifs*. The air seemed more smoke than not, and Sarlin knew that both his eyes and nose were streaming mucus. He wiped roughly, with the back of his hand, and drew on goggles and mask.

The first peephole tree was going up now, yellow flames with a tinge of green that was quickly lost in the fire-front. Sarlin's trench was ready, and one of the twins was handing him a soaked blanket.

He lay down, and then the fire was upon them.

Linak'h:

The smell of fuel and fire-suppressant chemicals on the pad was so strong that Candice Shores wondered if they'd be able to smell smoke. The fires were still well to the north, but they were putting out a blanket of smoke that had already ended all satellite and most ground observation in the fire area.

So we'll be flying in blind. At least lift-fields can help you get out again, if they've got you into the wrong place.

Can was the key word here. Fighting forest fires was not as bad as it had been once, when everything had to move at the pace of a ground vehicle, or at most aircraft, with limited loads and less ability to land close to the fire line. But building a fine line still meant down-and-dirty work, close to the fire. Sometimes too close, if the one way back was blocked, or a snag toppled and caught you and your crewmates couldn't pull it off you before the flames came.

Shores put the thought out of her mind. She had her dignity to consider, since right now her job consisted of standing on the pad where the QRF Fire Team could see her. "Command presence," or at least physical presence, was about all she could contribute to keeping their minds off what they would be doing in a few hours.

The Territory was turning out for the fires. The burn was already expected to top a hundred thousand square kilometers, not counting what was going to go up in the

Merishi Territory (three big fires there at last count).
Going up against the fires was every piece of fire fighting
equipment the Territory could muster, and what already
must be at least four thousand people of both races, with
the odd (both in numbers and in temperament) Merishi
thrown in.

Fans wound up to an ear-piercing whine, and a big
sling lifter wobbled off the end of the pad into the windy
twilight. Instead of a cargo container slung under its
belly, it had a massive water tank studded with cylinders
of foam-making chemicals.

The specially-designed water bombers were already
on-line. What was going out now were conversions, regular lifters of a dozen makes and models carrying self-
contained water or chemical units. Rumor had it that
Marshal Banfi had arranged for the manufacture of these
units. Rumor also had it that he'd promised to cover the
contractors' bills.

Shores wondered if the last could be true. Marshals
never retired and their salaries were generous, but Banfi
did not live frugally. Not frugally enough to have two or
three million stellars to spare, for contractors who might
be charitable while the air still reeked of smoke but
would have their hands out the moment they could draw
a deep breath without coughing.

Maybe Nieg could be asked discreetly—and speak of
the devil, there he was. He wasn't disguised, and anyway
the disguise that could really conceal his identity from
Shores hardly existed anymore.

"Hello, Colonel," she said, saluting, if perhaps not as
precisely as she would have a more orthodox officer.

Nieg returned the salute. "I volunteered to distribute
the updated map data, me and my team." He handed
her a data insert and also a folder of printed maps, with
one taped to the cover of the folder.

Together they studied the map. Five major fires in
the Territory, although three were so close together they
would be merging before anything but air-dropped opposition hit them. Four major base camps: two Administration Fire Guard, one human Fire Guard plus Reservists
and militia, one Federation military.

"The Federation camp's also taking parties of volunteers from the Vic Civil Action Group and the refugee camps."

"I hope those Vics know something about forests. If I remember correctly, the tallest tree I saw on Victoria was about your height."

"It wasn't *that* short," Nieg said. "They're tough and willing, anyway. But our camp is taking those two for security reasons. We think they will be the prime targets for any terrorist activity."

Shores knew that her eyebrows were rising to an undignified height. "Terrorists, in the middle of an emergency?"

"Forest fires will cover tracks and dispose of bodies. Even if the terrs themselves don't turn out in force, there may be quite a few personal scores settled, both among the Ptercha'a and among the humans. Or between the two races, which is what we are all afraid of."

No purpose in asking what he meant by "we." "I'll be careful."

"There's one other thing you should know," he added, lowering his voice. Something with jets took off, drowning out anything short of a shout. When a reasonable noise level returned, he went on.

"Keep this strictly to yourself, but we're picking up Merishi radio traffic that suggests their training camp has been burned over."

"I would say good riddance."

"So would I, but quietly. If we say it where the Merishi hear it . . ."

"Oh." *Burning hundreds of thousands of hectares of forest to wipe out the camp? Do they think we're insane?* Or had some of the Federation's tame madmen, the Rangers, actually tried to scare the Merishi out of the camp with one fire that they thought might be lost among many?

Nieg saw the question in her eyes, if he hadn't already heard it in her voice. "No Rangers in the area, as far as I know. But I will find out, without your reminding me that I ought to."

He abandoned dignity enough to brush a hand lightly along her cheek. "Take care, good friend. Don't try to hog all the fun."

"My word on it."

Then her beeper was insisting on its share of her attention, and as she suspected the QRF'ers were about to lift out. She also abandoned dignity by kissing Nieg on the cheek, which they had now worked out how to do without him stretching or her stooping. Then she hurried back to her command lifter, conscious of eyes following her all the way.

Linak'h:

Sarlin had been close to brush fires. He had talked with a veteran of the Assault Forces who had survived being overrun by a grass fire. The veteran said it was no worse than most combat, easier than some.

A high-forest crown fire was another matter. This was the kind of fire that rolled forward like a seismic wave striking a coastline. The temperatures at the fire front were hot enough to melt metal and reduced anything organic to ashes. Sarlin had done his best to see that his people were as far from those temperatures as they could, with earth and water to shelter them further from air and fire run mad.

Lord Most High, let that best be good enough.

He kept his eyes closed, even inside the mask; it was not as smokeproof as the manufacturer's instructions claimed. So he judged the progress of the fire by sound.

Some trees crackled, some hissed, some exploded like long, low-order detonations. It was hard to tell if the crackling was always flames, or if some of the trees were toppling where they stood. The peephole trees were tall enough to reach across the pond and strike down those burrowed into the bank; Sarlin said another prayer.

Heat washed over him like a bath, then began tickling, clawing, and even stabbing at him through gaps in his protection. His tunic, breeches, and boots were supposed to resist fire as well as fragments, but in this kind of heat they also held in sweat. Before long, where the heat was not drying off his skin, Sarlin was awash in his own sweat.

The smoke and heat also fought their battle with the mask. Its filter kept out the worst of the smoke, but enough remained to make Sarlin fight off coughing fits.

He knew if he coughed the mask off, he was doomed to lungs battered by smoke inhalation at best, death from lungs seared by flames at worst.

But no flames reached him. Or at least he could not pick out the bite of a flame from the other pains. His mind was no longer capable of that sort of discrimination. The air was barely able to support life now, and the thunder of the fire wall, added to the din of individual trees burning, hammered coherent thought out of a man's head. Sarlin wanted to spread out like a single-celled organism, until he was so thin that one could see through him and everything except the most basic biological functions stopped.

Somewhere in a time he had lost the power to measure, Sarlin became aware that the heat was decreasing. Both the air that reached his skin and the air that reached his lungs were . . . not cool, precisely, but less than a scorching, searing essence of heat.

Cautiously he slipped the blanket off his head. Dead cinders, ashes, a few half-burned cones, and what looked like the bones of some flying creature pattered down all around him. Still more cautiously, he raised his head.

The others all lay like hibernating root slugs, mutated to gigantic proportions. The ground around them was no longer muddy. Traces of mud remained in the pool, which was completely dry except at the upstream end. There water was slowly trickling in. The spring that gave the stream life—that had given Rahbad Sarlin life—still flowed.

He knew a dreadful moment of fearing that he was the only survivor, before a Ptercha'a cough sounded under one of the blankets. Then the blanket began to writhe, like the slug it resembled coming awake after the spring warmth had touched it. Warmth coming, instead of heat leaving . . .

Sarlin lurched to his feet, as one by one the rest of the party came to life. All except two. One of the peepholes had indeed toppled, crushing the life out of a Hunter. And the vital signs monitors on one of the Merishi showed that between drugs, stress, and heat, his heart had stopped.

Behdan Zeg was the last to reach his feet, and he did so with the help of Kalidessouf on one arm and a Hunter

on the other. Then he shook them off and strode over
to his half-brother.

"Well, mother's son," Sarlin said. "I always knew that
green wood is hard to set alight."

"So is stone, particularly when it is found between the
ears."

"Just because you were right once, do not think you
know everything."

At this moment Sarlin regarded it as a considerable
mental feat to remember his own name. "Our mother has
only one son that boastful. I merely make suggestions,"

"Well and good. What do you suggest? I am thinking
we should run the ridges until we are clear of the burned
land. Higher up, there will be cooler, fresher air. I do
not think we need fear pursuit or patrols."

Sarlin looked in the direction of the camp. Certainly
anyone not at least as well protected as his patrol was
dead, or on their way to a sick-house. But he had heard
no explosions, as of ammunition overtaken by the fire.
No ammunition hinted of either deep underground shelters or an evacuation before the fire.

Either strategy, however, could have left behind warriors who knew this country and were fit to trail the
patrol until they found it, then fought it to the death.
For Sarlin, one narrow escape from death was enough
for this mission.

"It will be harder moving our prisoners, at least until
they can walk on their own," Sarlin said. "Also, on the
cooler ridges, we will have a detectable thermal signature
and no place to hide if detected.

"If we stay low, where the fire has burned, there will
be hot spots everywhere. If anyone does detect us, they
will lose us the moment we stop moving. Also, if they
do close to visual range, we will have cover among the
burned growth, and dark ground to hide us even in the
open. Do you know what color you have turned?"

Zeg denied possession of a mirror, more than a trifle
obscenely. Sarlin grinned. "You are as dark as one of
those Smallteeth whose ancestors came from a region
called . . . Avrigha? Anyway, they are sometimes dark
brown, sometimes even black. Against burned ground,
you or they could come close enough for one to spit on,
before being seen."

"Well, none have ever awarded me prizes for fine looks," Zeg said. "So I suppose I have lost nothing I need for now."

He looked toward the Ptercha'a, now divided into those standing guard, those packing their gear, and those watching over the body. The Lidessouf twins had already rolled the tree clear, and one Ptercha'a was kneeling beside the body brushing its fur to help hide the wounds.

"I was thinking of sliding the bodies into the pool," Sarlin began. "When it fills—oh, forgive me. I forgot."

"As well none of the Hunters heard you do so. Losing a body in water is an abominable death. We can drop our late prisoner there, but our Hunter stays on land."

There was no arguing with Zeg's will or Hunter custom, and indeed no call for it. They would need to give the ground a bit of time to cool off before they moved out. Also, this close to the campsite was about the last place their enemies would be searching for them, if they were fit to search at all.

They buried the Ptercha'a—a middle-aged fighter whose name Sarlin only learned long afterward—in the softest patch of ground they could find. His comrades heaped burned branches over the grave, then keened softly, to perform duty without attracting enemies.

Zeg said the People's Warrior's Departure, then a prayer in True Speech. Sarlin caught only a few words, but judged it was much the same as the prayers most races seemed to have found good when one needed to say farewell to a comrade. The essence of all of them was:

"Thank you for sending us this warrior. He fought well and was a good comrade. Now you have taken him home. We will remember him."

The Hunters were keening softly again as they formed their double line. This time the rear guard was Ptercha'a, and each of the twins had a Merishi slung across his back, while their comrades divided up their equipment.

Twenty-two

Aboard U.F.S. *Shenandoah*, off Linak'h:

In a small display cube, the orbits of the forty-odd ships currently off Linak'h had a certain artistic elegance, particularly if one programmed the colors carefully.

It took more than appropriate colors to induce artistic appreciation of the scene, if you were aboard one of the ships and responsible for the safety of others. Commodore Liddell turned off the display and faced her guest.

Captain Marder had come from *Somtow Nosavan* aboard a Navy shuttle. No one intended that as an insult to the commercial shuttles, but apparently Marder took it that way.

Too bad, Captain. I'm not going to put Shenandoah *in a fixed orbit to let you save face for the merchanter shuttle pilots. As for coming aboard* Nosavan—*I didn't hear that suggestion.*

"What can I offer you, Captain?" Liddell said. "Besides an explanation of why you were requested to come aboard?"

"I would call it the next thing to being kidnapped," Marder said. "I had my crew ready to stun your—it looked like a boarding party—if they tried anything."

Marder might have had a disagreeable surprise if she'd trusted her crew that far. Might have, because Liddell could only hope that Nieg had infiltrated *Somtow Nosavan*'s crew. It was a logical corollary of the plan he had for the Victorian ship. Liddell only hoped that Nieg didn't have so many people aboard that he would be tempted to order them to seize *Nosavan* if Marder didn't cooperate.

"They had strict orders not to use force unless they were attacked. What were your orders to your crew? Or are you going to tell me that's none of my business? I'm somewhat responsible for discipline and good order in Linak'h orbit, you realize. So it *is* my business."

"My orders to my crew were not to use force unless there was an attempt to seize me or the ship. Now that I've told you that and you can stop worrying about an incident, why am I here?"

Liddell had rehearsed her description of—to be realistic, Nieg's plan, even if Longman and Tanz endorsed it—for using *Somtow Nosavan* as "neutral territory" for asylum for the Coordination's wanted list. In fact, she had rehearsed it so often that she went through it faster than she'd expected.

So fast, that she could see Marder's doubts scrolling across the captain's long face halfway through the presentation.

"Did Longman put you up to this?" Marder asked.

"I'm speaking with her authority," Liddell said.

"Then why didn't she have me hauled aboard *Roma* and tell me all this herself?"

Liddell looked at the overhead, not really expecting an answer written there but hoping briefly. She toyed with her sherry glass, minus only two sips since the robot had delivered it.

Marder had drunk her sherry straight off, then switched to hot chocolate. She was on her second cup of that; it looked as if the drinking days were behind her.

"Because if you tell a Commodore to go to the Devil, it's all in a day's work," Liddell said finally. "If you tell a three-star admiral . . ."

"Especially the Golden Vanity."

"I have obligations toward my superior officers," Liddell said primly. "But if you tell a Di Longman to stuff herself up her own waste-water pipe, then it tends to make a larger hull breach."

"You're talking as if I actually have the right to refuse."

"You not only have the right, you have the duty, if you think it in the best interests of the Planetary Republic of Victoria. As it happens, you're the senior Victorian official off Linak'h. There are rumors of somebody from your Defense Force Intelli—"

"Colonel Bissell. He's there. Disguised, but not beyond your friend Nieg's ability to recognize. Unless of course he approaches Nieg on his own."

The Victorians, it began to seem, had taken a prudent share of precautions before they'd committed themselves to involvement on Linak'h. "Are you supposed to be telling me this?"

"I don't know, but Bissell will recognize a fait accompli when someone in authority tells him. Such as you or Nieg."

Liddell took a firm grip on her glass and tried to do the same to the situation. "Does Bissell have a veto on your accepting our offer?"

"Let's say that he'll be happier if he is consulted."

"Fine. Consult him, if you know where he is. Explain the situation, have him meet with Nieg, and come up with an answer."

"Even if it's negative?"

"Even if it's negative. If you move fast, we have alternate plans if you say no. If you say yes, we'll be even better off."

Liddell turned the display back on. "A lot of shuttles will be coming up in the next two days. We're organizing a convoy—the transports that brought 218 Brigade, and any merchant vessels that have no more business here."

"Would I be right in assuming that 'business' is going to be defined rather narrowly?"

"Yes. Basically, unless a ship is loading refugees or documented cargo, we want her out of here. A convoy with only a cruiser escort may not be perfectly safe, but somebody has to be ready to start all-out war to attack it. In orbit, 'accidents' can happen."

"I presume you've thought that possibility through for *Nosavan*," Marder said. Her tone was dry, and the words did not constitute a question.

"Short of a kamikaze run, you'll be safe."

Marder closed her eyes briefly, and Liddell felt immediately apologetic. Marder had lost all her shipmates off Victoria to just such an operation. She might be cautious now, but at least she could be no lover of Merishi or their human pawns. Why Longman doubted her was past all understanding—or at least all of Rose Liddell's. Marder pulled herself back from whatever past she had been wandering in and wrapped long fingers around her cup. "So. Lots of shuttles coming up. A few more or less carrying Ptercha'a refugees won't be noticed. Right?"

"Right. Also consumables."

"We're all right for water, oxygen, and life-support spares. But we're short of food, and what we have is all human."

"That shouldn't matter for a few days."

"What if it's more than a few days? Hungry, maybe sick, children, at least. Besides, an unmixed human-style diet gives Ptercha'a diarrhea. I am not going to host five hundred Catmen with the runs aboard my ship."

"We don't have access to a large supply of Ptercha'a rations," Liddell said. "Not unless we approach the Administration's Warband Leadership. That's sending them a holographic invitation to make trouble."

"Not necessarily," Marder said. She took a sip of her chocolate. "Look. Correct me if I'm wrong, but five or six thousand people of both races are on the move down there. Right?"

The last report from dirtside suggested that the fire-fighting effort might eventually involve that many. "Assuming that's so, what are you suggesting?"

"Can't somebody arrange to lose ten days' food for five hundred Ptercha'a?"

"Probably. It might take time."

"Or Nieg." Marder sounded as if she believed in Nieg's reputation but didn't care for his ethics. "Or the Confraternity."

Liddell's face must have given her away; Marder said an extremely obscene Merishi word. Even *kheblass* was acceptable compared to *uitsk*. "How long is the Federation going to tune out the Confraternity?"

"I wouldn't answer that one even if I was at the policy level."

"Would you answer one about your own personal views on the subject?"

"Why should I?"

"Because there are some things about Alliance views on the subject I don't think the Federation knows. Or at least rumors of people holding views. So—trade opinion for rumor?"

"Fair enough," Liddell conceded. She searched for the right words and finally reached an approximation of her views. "I think we should be pressing the Merishi to agree to joint negotiations over recognizing the Confraternity."

Marder grinned. "That view went out of style years ago."

By the time Marder left, Liddell knew a great deal more about what the Alliance Navy thought of the Confraternity. Or had thought, three years ago. Very little of it was probably a secret anymore, but you could never be sure. And there was always such a thing as confirmation, which she had learned in her Intelligence courses long before she met Colonel Nieg.

At least she had something to trade, for his help in getting Ptercha'a food aboard *Somtow Nosavan*. It was impossible for that to do any harm.

Linak'h:

The patrol could not have "run the ridges" even if Sarlin had thought it a wise move. They were limited by darkness (patches of still-burning debris gave light but confused night-viewers), the Merishi burdening the twins, and fatigue.

As the night crept on toward Father-rise, a few stars winked on, then winked out as more clouds rolled in. The wind dropped, then died, and a fine mist settled over the ruined forest.

This was not to Sarlin's liking, for two reasons. First, it would quench the hot spots he relied on to confuse airborne thermal sensors. Second, it threatened to cover the bare ground with a layer of slimy mud, on which even the sure-footed Ptercha'a would be scrambling for balance. Carrying the prisoners might become impossible.

Sarlin finally decided to find reasonable cover by Father-rise and wait out the whims of the day's weather. So the patrol drifted north, feeling like spirits themselves in a land where life existed only in spirit form.

That was not quite true, of course. Some tall, isolated trees had no worse than scorched bark and charred lower branches. They would survive, at least until the horde of boring insects that every planet with forests always harbors discovered easy prey.

There were also animals, some lying, too badly burned to do anything but die a finger at a time, others still on their feet but lame or blind. Sarlin judiciously ignored the Ptercha'a killing these doomed victims, as long as they used their knives. Time they had—a child could have kept pace with the heavily burdened twins—but their ammunition was half-gone, and conserving the rest might be a life-or-death matter.

Half a watch passed, however, with no signs of hostile presence. Indeed, sapient life might have fled from this wasteland altogether. It would also stay away for a while, except for the borers and quick-growing ground vines and fungi, unless the Merishi launched a massive planting operation.

Sarlin doubted if they had either the resources, the skills, or the inclination, even if other concerns did not intervene. The Scaleskins, when all was said and done, were masters of dry-world ecology. Forests were alien to them. Not used, not abused, but if burned, also not something to be immediately restored.

Another half-watch, and Father-rise began to glimmer through the layers of cloud, mist, and smoke. The twins were now walking in the rear, while two Ptercha'a apiece carried the prisoners.

A stand of peephole trees stood nearly intact, some two hundred paces ahead and a hundred to the right. It seemed so intact that Sarlin wondered if it had been saved by sapient firefighters, who might still be there.

Zeg and a Ptercha'a scouted ahead and reported no signs of life. By the time they returned, Sarlin himself had guessed the reason for the trees' survival. Set in a ravine running down from the ridge, they had been protected to either side and to the rear by bare ground. Their front and the grass itself had been largely protected by another pooled stream, now dry and not refilling. But it had done its work before it evaporated, and now the trees had strength to spare for a patrol that had nearly exhausted its own.

Sarlin thought he would be unable to sleep. But in fact he was barely able to give orders for regular checks on the prisoners, security (including two lookouts on the ridge), and checking the water supply, before his legs gave out.

He remembered his half-brother and the Ptercha'a
scout pulling off his boots, and his halfhearted and less
than half-coherent protests. He remembered a yellow
glow that for a moment made him think, "Fire!", so
that his heart nearly stopped before he remembered the
Yellow Father.

Then he remembered nothing else for nearly a watch.

Linak'h:

Candice Shores rode out to Fire Camp Three in the
weapons seat of a gunship, three thousand meters higher
and a hundred km/h faster than her people. She saw
Nieg's hand in the arrangement, and mentally promised
him the removal of skin and toenails if this was being
protective.

If he wanted her on the spot in case of trouble, on the
other hand, she would wait until she learned how much
he knew about the trouble that he hadn't told her. *Then*
she might start altering his anatomy.

In the end, Nieg had paved the road, if not to Hades,
then to Camp Three, with good intentions. Fire Camp
Three lay in the lee of a stretch of ridges, one of the
natural barriers where fire lines were going in. The updrafts from both the fire and the wind carried much of
the smoke over the ridges, leaving the camp's approaches
in clear air.

So Shores's people went almost straight in. By the time
Shores had finished making a visual reconnaissance of
the area, the smoke at her altitude had the gunship pilot
on instruments and caution. They couldn't just cut lift
power and let gravity, fans, and aerodynamic controls
bring them lower, either. With poor visibility and flukey
winds, they wouldn't be maneuverable enough for heavy
traffic—and every time two lifters below landed, three
more took off.

The smoke also seemed to be creeping lower, almost
matching the gunship's controlled rate of descent. They
finally broke out of the murk at less than a thousand
meters above the camp pad. The pilot cracked the canopy, and Shores promptly started sneezing so that her

helmet nearly fell off. She was blowing her nose when they landed.

The QRF Fire Team, fifty troopers from each company plus a proportionate slice of the support units, was already unloading. Some of the people were already coughing, and a few were putting on their masks.

Shores was just about to pass the word to leave off the masks until the smoke got worse, when that rare thing, a tall and stout Ptercha'a, came storming up. She had a somewhat random selection of what looked like bodyguards, recruited from who knew where and armed with far too much.

"Hoa!" she called. "No masks until you hit the fire lines. The rules."

"What rules?" somebody said, and another said, "Who is this big vidjis?" For once somebody using True Speech didn't help; the epithet meant "someone who steals the milk meant for another's young."

Shores managed to get between her people and the Ptercha'a without actually breaking into a run. "I am Lieutenant Colonel Shores, commanding the Quick Reaction Force here," she said in True Speech. "So I am as big a vidjis here as you. Why are you giving orders to my people?"

It was the longest piece she'd ever delivered in True Speech. The impact of her doing it instead of using Commercial Merishi or a translation computer stopped all the Ptercha'a where they stood.

"I am Warden First-Class of the Fire Guard Isha Maiyotz," the Ptercha'a said. "I have authority to enforce any regulation, anywhere in the Fire Camps."

"Very good," Shores said. She took a deep breath and managed not to cough at the smoke jabbing her throat from the inside. "So what is the regulation?"

"No masks except on the fire line," the Ptercha'a woman repeated. She lowered her voice. "Weaklings always go masked from the first. Then their filters are clogged by the time they face the flames close, and they must go to the rear to be changed."

Shores was glad that the woman had lowered her voice before she switched to Anglic. "I do not think we will agree about my people being weaklings. Is there a shortage of filters?"

"Also masks, water bottles, much else," the woman said. "This is all the fires of a single year in one, to say nothing of what the Merishi face. We have offered them supplies . . ."

Shores muttered obscenities in three languages.

". . . but they have refused to let us fly to their fire camps. They insist that all must go through their Warband in its lifters, of which they have so far sent none."

If it wasn't for the potential biomass destruction and environmental chaos, Shores wouldn't have minded letting the Merishi roast on the pyre of their own forests. However, it might come to that anyway, if the Merishi were ready to sacrifice their forests to guard their secrets.

At least neither Shores nor the Warden believed in doing that. This might give them enough in common to work together.

"Thank you for the warning," Shores said, switching back to the True Speech. "I will see that my people conduct themselves properly."

The Warden saluted in the Ptercha'a style and led her bodyguard off at a trot. Shores looked up at the sky. It should have been full daylight by now, instead of this sullen grayness that seemed apart from all times of day or night.

"Sergeant Esteva," Shores said, picking a familiar face out of the crowd. "My compliments to Lieutenant Fiske, and he should go to Camp HQ and find out what our orders are. Sergeant Sklarinsky, start clearing out the command lifter. We'll have a Command Group meeting as soon as Fiske gets back. Also, my compliments to the Team XO, and I'd like to see him as soon as possible."

Salutes flew, and the two sergeants sprinted off along the line of grounded lifters. Shores pulled out her canteen, drank half of it, refrained from emptying the other half over herself, and locked the cap.

A cargo lifter slid out of the north, veiled in the haze until it broke into the clear less than eight hundred meters up. *Ceiling dropping,* Shores thought—*and that lifter has been to the wars.* The whole belly was blackened, and one of the self-contained tank units had ruptured into a mass of twisted metal. It was a miracle that the machine was still flying.

Shores memorized the appearance of the lifter before

it dropped out of sight toward the far end of the field. A few words about it might remind people that a fire like this was nothing to play around with, even in the air.

Linak'h:

Rahbad Sarlin awoke to the sound of lifter fans and a muttered conversation between his half-brother, the twins, and several of the Ptercha'a. His thoughts still sleep-dimmed, he put the first of them into words.

"Go to sleep, mother's son!"

He hadn't realized that he nearly shouted, until a Ptercha'a hand clamped over his mouth. He chopped flat-handed in the general direction of the hand-holder's torso, but struck only air.

He decided that his reflexes were hardly more awake than his wits. Since neither could go back to sleep, he sat up slowly and whispered, "Zeg? What is wrong?"

Zeg came over to him, then knelt. Sarlin was relieved to see that his half-brother also showed signs of being only just awake.

"Pardon for the abrupt silencing," Zeg said. "We have Merishi not as far off as I could wish."

"Visual range?"

Zeg nodded. "The twins are watching."

Close Merishi (or close anybody, except for the marvel of their ride back to the People's Territory) required little noise and less movement. Sarlin had no trouble resisting the urge to move his sleep-slowed limbs and join the twins.

Finally he heard the fans of a lifter climbing. Then a launcher rattled off a burst, the grenades exploded—and what could only be screams tore at his ears. Thin, distant, despairing, but screams and nothing else.

Sarlin shook off Ptercha'a hands, nearly broke Ptercha'a arms, and crawled to join the twins. By the time he reached them, the lifter was nearly out of sight. Through his own viewer, Sarlin recognized it as a standard Merishi military design.

He also recognized the source of the screams. Four or

five bodies—so badly burned it was hard to tell, apart from the smoke still curling up from them—lay in the middle of a deep pile of ashes. Here forest debris twice the height of a Hunter had burned—but long before the bodies now smoldering in the middle of it.

Sarlin increased his viewer's magnification to the limit and set it to record. He could not make out the race of the victims even at extreme magnification, but computer enhancement of the recording might do better.

Then he saw his half-brother and his favorite Ptercha'a partner stripping themselves of all clothing and equipment except loinguards and smearing themselves with ashes.

"They are dead, mother's son," Sarlin said quietly.

"Perhaps some only beg for death, which we will give them," Sarlin said. The Ptercha'a made several signs of affirmation. "Also, we cannot wait for su-Lal's computers to analyze the recording, to learn the race of those the Merishi murdered. They pushed them out of the lifter into the ashes, where they could not run swiftly, then firebombed them from a hundred paces up. If that is not murder, then what is?"

Sarlin suspected he wore a bemused look, less at the discovery of his half-brother's having principles than of his being willing to apply them to those who might not be People or Hunters. An evil gnawing in his belly told Sarlin what those charred bodies probably were.

Zeg returned to confirm that they were human, at the same time as one of the lookouts on the ridge descended to report more Merishi lifters. According to her, two lifters had landed to pick up a party on foot. She believed that the lifters wore sick-house markings, and that the party was Masters (she wrinkled her nose at that word) and Slaves. No humans, no People.

"How sure are you?" Sarlin said.

This time the lookout bared her teeth and said something whose meaning was irrelevant. Zeg hastily calmed her. Sarlin understood that he was telling her his half-brother seldom asked such questions merely to insult, more often because he thought the answer held life or death.

"She says, as sure as she can be without studying their teeth, as I did with the bodies," Zeg said.

"So," Sarlin mused. "They pick up Hunters and Folk, and murder humans. Why?"

"If that is so, then— Does the phrase 'covering one's tracks' mean anything to you, mother's son with leaves between your tusks?"

It meant a good deal to Sarlin. Also death for any stray humans in this wasteland, and an opportunity for the People (and Hunters) to take advantage of the trouble this would surely raise, between Smallteeth and Scaleskins. Conceivably the patrol might add to that trouble, if it found occasion to rescue any Smallteeth and listen to what they said in their relief and gratitude.

Best not go out of their way to seek stray Smallteeth, however. Better to make their way out of this wasteland, with their prisoners or at least their prisoners' information. The behavior of the Merishi lifters hinted at a way. Now, if the prisoners could confirm it . . .

"We remain here for the time of Father-light," Sarlin said. Everyone stared at him as if a stone image had suddenly begun to recite mathematical formulae. He ignored the stares and went on.

"Keep up the security, and anyone in the open freezes when they hear a lifter. Before dark, we should all blacken our exposed skin like Zeg and Tskad.

"For now, we wake up the prisoners. There are a few questions they may be able to answer."

"And if they refuse?" Zeg asked.

Sarlin looked at his half-brother, annoyed that the man needed to play this game of testing another's hardness now, of all times.

"We have two prisoners," Sarlin said. "You know what that means."

With two prisoners, there was always the final and most ruthless method of getting an answer. Kill one, in the way the prisoners' race and culture feared most, and let the sights and sounds of the death work on the other's mind until his tongue had loosened.

This time, if they did kill one prisoner, the other was safe. But they were not going to tell the Master—the word now came easily to Sarlin's mind, at least—that little truth.

Linak'h:

"Is everyone out of the forest?" Colonel Davidson said, to Olga Nalyvkina's reflection.

"I didn't come to answer that question," the lieutenant said.

"Well, I need an answer to it, whether you came or not."

"I didn't notice," she said. "I was checking out the gunships. Kinski's a better armorer than I am, so I didn't find anything wrong."

Davidson stepped to the bathroom window and peered down at the pad. The two gunships squatted at opposite corners, flanking the Marshal's personal lifter. Each gunship now dripped pods—rockets, pulsers, grenade-launchers, and ECM were the ones he could recognize. They had also sprouted booster units in the rear, to get them off the pad at a high gross weight without a rolling takeoff.

"We still need the people out of the forest *now*, and on the evac lifter as soon as possible. If we get a fire in the scrub, anyone who hasn't pulled out may find himself surrounded by fire, booby traps, and fused mines."

The silence behind Davidson was eloquent. The brisk click of the heels of small boots on the tile floor broke it, then gave way to the softer sound of those boots on the bedroom rug. He turned, to see Nalyvkina sitting down on the bed, contemplating the half-packed foot-locker.

"Trust a Scotsman to take more care of his kilts than what's under them," she said.

Davidson wiped the last of the beard cream off his face and used a hot towel. "I have also packed my underwear," he said, with dignity.

"I thought Scotsmen didn't wear any."

"Decadence overtakes us all," Davidson said. "Now, are you here to seduce secret information out of me?"

She started as if he'd slapped her, and her smile was a little forced. "I thought I would ask first. You're not getting the workers out of here because of the fire risk. The fires aren't going to spread this far, and the thunderstorms are breaking up.

"Is it terrorists? Or is it something to do with the work

gang that's been moving the Ptercha'a rations out of the storage bunker?"

Davidson used a couple of rude words in Scots Gaelic.

"That, I assume, means that you can't tell me because if I go into combat and get captured, I might be tortured to tell?"

This time Davidson used English. "The Devil fly away with mind-readers!"

"Yes?"

"Yes. Marshal Banfi's orders. So if you want them changed, try seducing—"

This time the slap was real, and hit Davidson. Or would have hit him, if the lieutenant hadn't pulled it at the last moment. Instead she brushed his cheek lightly with the tips of her fingers. Then she stood on tiptoe and did the same with her lips. He found it natural to put his arms around her—not tightly, but she returned the embrace with comfortable strength.

They stood that way for a moment. "This isn't the time, Olga," Davidson said. "Kinski might come. . . ."

She laughed. "You think he's been playing chaperone? Actually, I think he's been waiting for a chance to tuck us into bed!"

"I think we can manage that ourselves, at the right time. Which is *not* now."

Reluctantly, she stepped out of his arms, then smiled. "I might almost agree. I have too much . . . call it lust . . . stored up for a quick tumble." The smile broadened. "But since you don't have to be ashamed over being seduced, now can you tell me what's going on with the Ptercha'a food?"

Davidson decided that a real breach of security would require that Nalyvkina be assigned to a combat unit, fly combat, be shot down, survive to be captured, and then talk under interrogation. A very long chain of events, every link needed, and unlikely to be forged quickly if at all.

"All right. It will be stale news by the time it reaches anybody through you." Timing himself by the clock on the wall, Davidson explained in less than one minute the delivery of the Ptercha'a rations in Banfi's custody to the Navy for shipment to *Somtow Nosavan*.

"Having custody of that food at all . . ." Nalyvkina

mused. "Then turning it over to the Navy. So it has to have a deniable source." She looked at a blank space on the far wall. "Confraternity?"

Davidson nodded. He was neither surprised nor shocked to learn that Banfi's Confraternity sympathies were no secret to the lieutenant. Whether Banfi would be so equable was another matter.

"I won't ask how the Marshal deals with the Confraternity," Nalyvkina said. "But tell him that if he needs another gunship pilot to help him, he doesn't have to load everything on Kinski."

Words like *career* would have sounded obscene to Nalyvkina. Anyway, she was out the door before Davidson could have said them.

Twenty-three

Linak'h:

Flames towered in the darkness to the north, in half a dozen places Candice Shores could see with her own eyes. A dozen more registered on instruments or were recorded on the command lifter's displays from data squawked in over the radio.

"Ten kloms to the west, then we can turn," Isha Maiyotz said.

"Can do," Shores said. She didn't know the etiquette of dealing with senior Fire Guard Wardens, but had the feeling that Maiyotz wouldn't have stood on it if there was any.

Shores had not expected to end up as the pilot of a flying command post for the de jure CO of Camp Three and all its line crews. But then, she had not expected that all the Federation units would have organized themselves for security. There was no reason they shouldn't have; it made excellent sense. No need for her to worry about its being a slap at the QRF by General Kharg.

However, it left her hundred and fifty people with much less to do than they'd expected. One platoon was assigned for security to the Victorian volunteers, two to the refugee volunteers. Both had orders to turn a blind eye to any "security arrangements" the two supposedly unarmed groups made for themselves, unless these involved active combat.

Esteva also went with the Vics, with a strongly-worded request (not quite an order) from Nieg via Shores, to find Colonel Bissell. Once he had found the colonel, Esteva was to suggest that an explanation of his presence on Linak'h would be appreciated.

"If his presence isn't explained, should I arrange his absence?" Esteva had asked. Shores nearly had a heart attack before the sergeant grinned.

"Not unless you want *both* me and Nieg on your trail," Shores said, and sent Esteva off into the smoky twilight.

Shores herself was somewhat at loose ends when Isha Maiyotz came by and asked if a Federation lifter and pilot were available. Shores recognized in the older Ptercha'a the same urge to get to grips with the fires and the same frustration at having to remain in the rear. If they pooled their resources . . .

Now the Yellow Father was long set, the smoke rose into clouds that totally shut out the Red Child, and only the flames or the floodlamps gave light.

Off in the darkness, at the limits of unaided vision, red sparks glowed, a line of them swelling as Shores watched. Backfires going in, to stretch the line farther along the crest of the Begwinamy Hills. The wind had died now, and there were rumors of rain farther north. None here, so far, although the humidity was rising, but with no wind the fire crews could use backfires when they had to work fast.

A commercial-model treetopper slipped by overhead, half its lights out and belly and cutter hatch blackened. But someone in the cabin door spotted Shores and gave a hands-over-head greeting. Shores couldn't tell if it was Ptercha'a or human.

"Mayday, Mayday," crackled on the radio. "This is Crew 16/Three, in the ravine above the 882139 fire. The retardant drop went in, but dropped too far downhill. They hit the rear of the fire, but the rest has blown up. We estimate ten minutes to our position."

The voice sounded as if it was announcing the weather—bad weather, to be sure, but not life or death for the announcer. Shores called up a display of fire and vehicle positions.

"Can we get another drop there in time?" she asked.

Warden Maiyotz tugged at a whisker so hard that Shores expected it to come out any moment. Then she grinned. "We'll order one up, but we'll also order them up to the crest and take them off."

"Who's going to take them off?"

"Look at the map, Cohort Leader."

Shores looked at the display, and understood why Maiyotz was grinning. She was now a grandmother, but she had begun her firefighting career on the Administration's equivalent of a hotshot crew. She had seen people to either side of her trapped by falling trees or burned alive, survived being overrun by a crown fire, spent half a year in the hospital getting her lungs flushed, her skin regenerated, and her hair regrown. Generally she had long ago learned in a harsh school everything the people on the line tonight needed to know.

Now she could put some of it to use within actual reach of the flames, for the first time in too many years. Shores thought she might feel the same, if she ever wore stars, and fed power to the fans.

"This is Warden Lead Green, calling the 882139 crew. Can you take an overhead drop?" If worse came to worst, a fire bomber could unload a tankful directly on an endangered crew. They would be soaked and smelly, but in the middle of an area that wouldn't burn before they could walk or be lifted out.

"Negative on that," the voice came again. "This is a Vic team. There was a mixup at the camp, and we went out without masks."

The Warden said things Shores dearly wished she understood, but which obviously expressed sentiments the Federation officer shared. Nothing to do about it now, or even say over unscrambled links, but when they returned to the camp, a few people were going to be answering questions. The supply officer who'd left the Victorians maskless, the pilot who'd left a blowup intact and ready to burn those same Victorians, and maybe others.

They slipped over the ridge less than five hundred meters up, filing their altered flight plan and calling up a second firebomber as they went. The ridge dropped off steeply on the north side, so that the last stretch of slope at the head of the ravine was nearly vertical. Add the heat to the natural updraft, and the Vics would be trying to climb up a chimney with a fire burning in the fireplace below.

Shores slapped controls. Displays showed almost what she wanted to see, with one exception. One of the exter-

nal grab bars hadn't deployed. She jerked a thumb at
the crew chief.

"We may have to climb out with people hanging on
to the bars. Can you go out and try popping number
three?"

The crew chief's face registered mixed emotions. Justi-
fying her existence in a command lifter without much
commanding to do was one thing. Doing so by climbing
out on the fan aprons with hundreds of meters of empty
air between her and a forest fire was a different matter.

She made quite a business of rummaging the safety
harness out of the locker, but finally disappeared out the
left rear hatch. Shores cut back the fans and let the lifter
drift, until finally the display light turned from red to
green.

She whipped up the fans again as the crew chief
climbed back inside, then turned the controls over to
Konishi. The warrant officer was a better rough-air, low-
altitude pilot than she was, and anyway Shores had a
little commanding to do. Specifically, she was going to
command reinforcements, in the form of the QRF pad-
alert troops.

One omission where the Vics were concerned could be
an accident. Two, forming a potentially lethal combination, smelled strongly of a plan to turn the Vics into an
"incident."

Linak'h:

The two Merishi prisoners were as uninformative awake
as they had been asleep. Nothing about their clothes or
equipment gave a clue to their identity, either personal
or organizational. They were both male, both middle-
aged, both in good but not the best physical condition,
and both definitely frightened.

This said very little, Rahbad Sarlin knew. It tended
to reduce the possibility of their being combat-experi-
enced ground-fighters, but that left several dozen categories into which they could fall. His personal guess
would have been Space Security, assigned to this secret
Inquiry project because of their political background

and personal ruthlessness. Such were often bullies, who when the odds were turned against them lacked much of the courage they thought they had when they were in superior force.

This had to remain speculation, as there was a limit in the interrogation that could not be exceeded. Noise was a factor, and also leaving the two prisoners in condition to walk. Not just walk, but keep up with People and Hunters hurrying across rough ground, and then act as decoys when a Merishi lifter came in sight.

Eventually the interrogation was finished, and by the time the Merishi were secured again it was nearly Fatherset. It was possible now to tell twilight from smoke, and both from clouds. Some of the clouds to the north even looked fat with rain.

Sarlin wished that the rain, having held off too long already, would play the laggard for a few more watches. A heavy rain on this bare ground would do worse than turn it to a soup of mud and ashes. The runoff would swell streams into torrents, and the torrents would dump mud and ashes by the shipload into rivers that might have escaped having their banks burned over in the crown fires.

The whole fire area would have its own local ecology for the rest of a People's lifetime. It would be as much as anyone could expect, with any Lords' favor, if it did not ruin lands far beyond its borders.

They moved out on Sarlin's command, the Merishi stumbling along, not visibly bound (they could not be allowed to "accidentally" fall and slow the march), the rest of the patrol in a deliberately ragged formation. Everybody had their orders, however, whether a Merishi lifter landed or not.

It would have been well for the reputation of Special Projects if there had been equally sure methods of dealing with either a landing or an attack from the air. It would have been even better for Sarlin's hope of drawing a pension and the Ptercha'a kin's not needing death gifts.

However, Special Projects had no special wisdom to conjure heavy weapons out of a wasteland of ash. If the next Merishi lifter simply came in shooting and the heavy quickguns were not enough to meet it, the patrol would have to scatter.

The Ptercha'a were a trifle reluctant to amble along strung out, as one said in the People's tongue, "like children too young to play at Warband!" But some of them understood, they persuaded the rest, and Zeg's tongue filled in the gaps.

They fooled two lifters, which passed overhead without circling, slowing, or trying to communicate. (If they had done the last, a pantomime of lost or faulty radios had been worked out and practiced.) The third lifter circled briefly, and it must have communicated with somebody on a frequency the patrol's radios did not cover.

It was barely a hundredth-watch later that they heard two more lifters coming out of the night. This time, they also heard fans slowing to hover speed, then saw the shadows of lifters settling down on either side.

Linak'h:

Warrant Officer Konishi didn't know much about fighting forest fires. But he knew the standard tactics for dispersing or spreading smoke with a lifter's fans.

As they came over the ridge, Konishi swung the lifter's nose toward the fire sweeping up the ravine, then lowered it. The forward fans on full reverse blasted wind at the fire, while the Victorians scrambled desperately up the boulder-strewn, brush-choked floor of the ravine. The last few came into sight with their clothes black and smoking; at least they'd had *some* protection.

One tall man with a singed beard was holding back, as if he were the leader who had to be sure everyone under him was clear. A smaller, slimmer man seemed to be doing the same.

Shores yelped like a dog with a stepped-on paw when she recognized the smaller man as Juan Esteva. At least that saved the problem of identifying the taller man. Now that she thought about it, that beard did look familiar, even though it was both dyed and dirty.

There were sixteen Vics in all, counting Esteva. All of

them had dumped their tools. As they saw the lifter ahead, some of them began dumping helmets and outer clothing. Nobody risked stopping to undo, let alone kick off, boots.

A few of the more agile ones climbed up past the lifter, clinging to bushes and even strands of grass. Shores kept one eye on them, another on the people scrambling up on the fan aprons. She prayed that the eager climbers weren't overestimating their strength. There'd be no time to take them aboard if they slid back, and the lifter might not be able to take them anyway, without dumping equipment. There might not be time for that, either.

Six agile climbers made it up the ravine on their own, with only one backslider. Two of his comrades gabbed him and pulled him the rest of the way. Shores thought one of the grabbers was BoJo Johnson, but that had to be a hallucination. It was barely a rumor that he was even on Linak'h!

Esteva was definitely one of the six. Shores thought rude things about such a display of machismo, then decided to drop a word in Jan Sklarinsky's ear. She would say even ruder ones.

The bearded man—*let's not call him by his name in public*—scrambled in. By now the flames were working around the flanks of the fans' artificial wind, the thermometer registered fifty degrees, and Konishi was trying so hard not to look nervous that he was making Shores want to bite her nails.

Instead she jerked her thumb toward the overhead.

"Up!"

The fans' whine changed pitch as they switched to full lift on all four. Shores even imagined the lift generator making noise, which she hoped was imagination. If it wasn't, the generator or power supply was about to fail, and the fat would be in the fire—all the fat of everybody on board, and their bones, muscles, nerves, memories. . . .

The flames surged forward, pushing a wall of hot air ahead of them. Following the laws of physics, the hot air rose, and the lifter rose on the cushion of hot air.

It rose more like a drunken soldier climbing a rope ladder than in any tactically approved manner. Shores didn't care. All she knew was that the temperature began to drop. Then she could look down on the ravine-climbers, who a moment ago had been looking down at her.

Finally there was time to grab a drink from her canteen, remove a strange elbow from the small of her back and a knee in singed coveralls from the region of her crotch, and look across the packed cabin at the bearded man.

His eyes met hers. She pulled her micropad from her jacket pocket, wrote on it:

COLONEL BISSELL, I PRESUME?

—and tossed it to the man.

He held it for a moment, smiled, then wrote a reply and tossed it back.

YOU DO, AND VERY GREATLY, BUT YOU'RE RIGHT. NIEG SAYS WE NEED TO TALK, AND NEITHER OF US IS UP TO ARGUING WITH HIM.

Shores smiled back and wrote her reply:

SPEAK FOR YOURSELF, COLONEL.

Linak'h:

Special Projects assault operations were normally carried out by picked teams, rehearsed on dummy targets over several days at the least. A dozen contingencies would be discussed, each with its own variations, and responses to each of them devised, discussed, studied, and rehearsed (sometimes at random).

Rahbad Sarlin had never imagined himself carrying out a vehicle-assault with a mixed People/Hunter team, after only a hundredth-watch of briefing and two rehearsals not much longer. The same team also had to guard two

Merishi hostages, keep from tripping over charred stumps and falling into burrower holes, and avoid hitting one another in the darkness—the usual mix of unique and normal complications.

Having now leaped over the stage of imagination to the stage of execution, there was nothing to do but thank whoever was responsible for the quality of the team. Every Lawbound on it, of both races, would do their best.

The lifters were coming in bows to the east, one on either side of the patrol. One had a turreted gun in the normal position behind the controller; the other had a large hatch with docking gear in the same place.

It was not until the turret-less lifter flared to land, that Sarlin noticed the sick-house markings under the layer of soot. He jerked head and thumb; his half-brother nodded, and turned toward the other lifter. Zeg's hand signals also turned the rest of the patrol, except two Ptercha'a who faded into the shadows to act as sentries and snipers.

Tskad the scout stepped toward the armed lifter's controller hatch. He was the smallest of the males, probably the fastest (which meant Sarlin's eyes could barely follow him in combat), and at the same time the best at acting innocent.

"Good Folk," he whined. "Please let us in. We escaped the flames, but the two Folk we found are both hurt. I think they cannot go much farther."

The turret groaned but didn't turn. Mutterings in what sounded like High Merishi floated out through a cracked controller's window. Then the hatch slid open.

"We can only take Folk now," the Merishi said, in Trader. "But give us the Folk and your names, and we will be back and—" He broke off. Sarlin took a deep breath. The Merishi frowned.

"You said *two* Folk? I see four."

That was all the suspicion Tskad needed. He whirled in midair, a pinwheel with claws as he flew through the hatch. The Merishi was bloody in a heartbeat, and had time for only one scream before he had no throat to scream with.

Tskad rolled to one side, clearing the hatch and tempting another Merishi to leap toward it. This time Sarlin was ready. His quickgun chopped into the Merishi's throat and chest, nearly ripping his head from his shoulders.

Then the greatest danger to the mission became too many patrol fighters getting stuck in the hatch. Sarlin finally broke the crush and lunged inside by sheer brute strength. He crashed into the other side of the cabin, whirled, holding his quickgun high to deliver headshots or at least fire over the heads of his own people.

Five Hunters swarmed into the cabin, while Tskad struggled with one of the Folk to keep him from reaching the turret. Sarlin scrambled into the turret himself, while the others tried for a clear shot or at least a clear handhold on Tskad's opponent.

At last the two opponents rolled into the midst of the other Ptercha'a. Knives flashed, feet and hands came down with claws out, and a bloody Merishi corpse rolled on the deck. Tskad raised a hand in thanks, coughed until blood trickled from his mouth, and died.

Tskad's blood still flowed when a Merishi quickgun gave its angry ripping from outside. Sarlin frantically sought the turret controls, found them, and swung the turret in time to see Kalidessouf lying on the ground. The other lifter's fans had never entirely stopped, and now they were blurring as they wound up to high speed.

Stopping the escaping lifter had to be done. Stopping it peacefully was no longer necessary. Sarlin's memory of a year's courses in non-Khudrigate weapons guided his fingers from turret to gun controls. No doubt the weapon had controls forward as well; Sarlin only hoped none of the Ptercha'a would touch them!

Channgggg! A burst from Sarlin's gun shattered the controller windows of the sick-house lifter, just as it cleared ground. Blood and screams told the controllers' fate, and the lifter's abrupt descent told of more damage.

Then three Ptercha'a, Zeg, and Solidessouf were opening the nearest hatch and vanishing inside. Sarlin commended those inside to the mercy of whatever they believed, out of all the odd faiths of the Scaleskins. They would pay full price for their violation of the laws of war.

Sarlin waited a decent interval, concluded from the absence of screams that the work was being done silently, and slipped out of the turret. With a muttered "Don't touch any controls" to the Ptercha'a standing guard over Tskad's body, he climbed out and crossed to the other lifter.

He found Zeg and two of the Ptercha'a studying vital-signs monitors on five patients in the back of the lifter. All were best semi-conscious. Two were Merishi, three Ptercha'a.

That explained the absence of screams. Not silent killing, but no killing at all. Except the two controllers, who were bloody ruins in their shattered seats. A medical attendant seemed to be dead, but Sarlin saw his—no, her—chest moving. Only stunned—but what to do about all these witnesses, who could hardly be killed outright but would tell *most* interesting tales if they were not?

"How is your brother?" he asked Solidessouf. Much would depend on that answer.

"He may miss this war," the fighter growled. "But he will not miss the next one, or many parties, kegs of beer, or women. It takes a heavier quickgun than a Scaleskin carries to put down one of us."

Kalidessouf looked ghastly, with blood and torn flesh, but a closer look confirmed his twin's diagnosis. He had taken most of a burst, but none of the rounds had struck vital spots.

"Very well," Sarlin said. "If one of the Ptercha'a will go and get the medical kit out of my pack . . ."

"Ah. The 42/22 pelsh capsules?"

"I trust no one has used them?" Sarlin said in a level voice. For the first time since the training of the Ptercha'a had begun, he felt the old urge to sink his thumbs into his half-brother's neck.

"I do not accept drug users among my recruits," Zeg replied stiffly.

"Not knowingly, I am sure," Sarlin said. "Now, before we quarrel—the capsules."

"Of course." More Ptercha'a left than were needed to bring all the equipment of the patrol. The only one remaining was cleaning, spraying, and covering Kalidessouf's wounds.

"Now, before we lose the whole mission by quarreling—the next time you search my gear, please tell me. Or did you really fear the pelsh meant my dreadful softness was on the march again?"

"If I had, they would not be there, and these"—he pointed at the attendant and patients—"would be dead. That I wish to know more about you than you tell me, mother's son, is not a crime. Or is it?"

Sarlin laughed. "It is not. But what we need to know now is what to do about these unfortunates."

"Simple. See if the patients need anything, then leave them. Give the attendant a capsule, as she has seen us with waking eyes. Then we strip out the power packs from this lifter and add them to ours. We will need normal range and speed, with a heavier than normal load."

"That will leave these wretches alone to die in the dark."

"Not if lifters come by as often as they have. I think we need fear being caught before we leave more than these need fear dying alone. But if your conscience weeps and murmurs . . ."

"Save your breath for words of sense, mother's son."

"I ask pardon." He sounded sincere again. "We have a radio in the lifter. So we can donate our emergency beacon. Set the time to a tenth-watch, and it will start howling a distress signal that they will hear in orbit! By then, we shall be well on our way home."

Ptercha'a muscles were not entirely adequate for wrestling power packs, so they had to leave more behind than Sarlin thought wise. But they could certainly reach the border with what they had, and no power supply would save them if they were intercepted.

Heavy air and a hint of thunder in the north warned of the coming rain, when Zeg took the overloaded lifter off the ground and headed south.

Linak'h:

Warrant Officer Konishi abandoned subtlety and skill and used brute force to get the lifter to the safety of the ridge summit. It was too overloaded for agility, too overcrowded for comfort, and too short on power to haul its load far. So the warrant officer set down in the first open space on the lee side of the ridge.

As he did, he narrowly escaped a fan-mangling midair with a lifter carrying Federation markings. It turned out to be the QRF's reinforcements, under Lieutenant Fiske.

He was not the officer Shores would have chosen, and she was ready to blast both him and the lifter pilot when he led the other aside. From scraps of sentence that floated back on the hot wind, he was administering a perfectly adequate blast himself, not even raising his voice.

Shores decided to limit her own remarks to a "What the Hades . . . ?" at some appropriate time, and turned to Colonel Bissell. They didn't have much to say to each other that could be said with ten Federation LI troopers and a dozen Victorian Civil Action Groupers in earshot, but maybe the colonel thought he deserved an explanation for having Esteva on his trail.

No "maybe" about it. If only because, if Esteva had got crisped in that ravine over there, the Vics would have been off on the wrong foot with a lot of Feds, including me.

"Sorry about our informal method of contacting you," Shores said. "But we assumed you were keeping a low profile for a reason."

She had to repeat that, because a heavy fire bomber droned over the ridge at that moment, so low its fans nearly drowned out the fire. Smoke swirled around it in the fan-wash, and its empty dump hatch was a blacker darkness in the soot-darkened belly.

"As I was saying . . ." Shores began again.

Bissell held up a hand. "I suppose certain people are entitled to an explanation. Even you, and definitely your superior. Otherwise we may have Confucians worse confounded."

Shores closed her eyes briefly. "My superior is not of Sinic descent, as far as I know." *And if you came all the way from Victoria to make rotten puns . . .*

Lieutenant Fiske provided a welcome interruption, slouching up and not even trying to salute. "Evening. Sorry about the trouble, but I had the impression you needed some security in a hurry. It was really my fault as much as the pilot's."

"I'm not going to be blaming anybody, as long as we all get off this ridge in one, preferably uncharred, piece," Shores said. "Anybody else coming in?"

"The rest of my platoon," he said, then turned to Bissell. "Excuse me, are you the Team Leader?"

"Boss of this crew, anyway," Bissell said. He leaned back against a tree, then yelped as spiky bark gouged his singed hide, and jumped upright.

As Bissell straightened, Lieutenant Fiske's head exploded. Someone had fired a high-velocity solid round straight into the base of his skull, at an angle that brought it out through the bridge of his nose. A battle-axe could hardly have been messier.

These details, Shores learned later. Before Fiske hit the ground, there was a general stampede of some twenty-five people in nearly as many directions, some chosen, some random. She was carried away, swept into the command lifter in front of a wave of Victorians, and expected to be swept out the pilot's hatch.

But Konishi had that shut, and was winding up the fans ready for takeoff. The mob slammed Shores against the back of the copilot's seat, and she felt her ribs and one arm creaking. How it might have ended, she never knew, except that suddenly there were angry yells and the pressure eased.

Then she saw BoJo Johnson and Isha Maiyotz rise up from the press of bodies. BoJo was using his fists, with an occasional knee in a vital spot when he lacked room or his opponent was of the right sex. Maiyotz was using her claws on both sexes, but only thrusting almost gently instead of in the raking slashes that made even an elderly Ptercha'a deadly to an unarmored human.

"We can leave, if you want . . ." BoJo began.

"BoJo, shove it," somebody said. A slightly older man, still barely in his twenties, shouldered his way through the pack.

"Ah, ma'am, if you wouldn't mind landing again—there's three, four of us could be helpful, now that it's come to shooting."

Shores knew that he meant some of the Victorians were carrying concealed weapons. However, anything they could conceal was unlikely to be much good in a sniper hunt, which usually turned into a combination of long-range shooting and short-range crawling through the bushes.

"In principle, I'm willing," she said. The young man—his name badge read M. LEARY—and BoJo at least looked as if they'd be not only willing but useful. "But this is above a light colonel's decision level."

It turned out to be above quite a few people's decision levels. The final word came from General Tanz, and it was a strict order against involving any of the Victorians in ground combat.

"Or yourself, either, Colonel Shores," Tanz added. "I don't quarrel with your habit of leading platoon-sized actions, if that's what's on hand when the shooting starts. But tonight my order to a particular pitcher is: Get away from that well, *now*!"

Shores's parody of heel-click was only mildly obscene, partly because she didn't really have room for her long legs under the displays. She asked permission to stay until the other two squads arrived, learned from Esteva (who had probably been listening in) that they were already on the ground and moving out, under his orders, and decided to call it a night.

She still stayed on the pad at Camp Three until the lifter with Fiske's body aboard landed. She was following the litter toward the ambulance, mentally composing her letter to Fiske's family, when a Ptercha'a shape materialized from the darkness.

"Was he a good soldier?" Maiyotz asked, looking toward the litter. The ambulance's lights came up, the siren whooped, and it rolled off toward the hospital. Graves Registration would have Fiske before Father-rise, but right now there was an autopsy, with a forensics expert from Intelligence sitting in on the whole stomach-turning process.

"Not really," Shores said. Her father had always taught her that ghosts are angrier about lies than they are about unflattering truths. Fiske's ghost must be very close now—unless her mother was right, and there was no such thing as a ghost. . . .

"But he was learning," she added. "There are quite a few officers like him. Go in as recruits, leave six years later as first lieutenants, serve out their Reserve time, and do more good than harm without ever making a great name for themselves."

"You are not one of those, from what one hears," Maiyotz said.

Shores grimaced. "I have better things to do than listen to gossip about myself."

"Perhaps. Can you listen to me?"

Shores automatically checked her flanks and rear. It would take a sensitive pickup, visual or acoustic, to eavesdrop on them over the noise of lifters. As for snipers, there was no cover for three hundred meters in two directions, and plenty of armed troopers in the other two.

"Certainly."

"Some of the Victorians—they do not know how much Anglic I speak. So they talk freely. They some of them think the bomber that passed just before the shooting was the same one that dropped in the wrong place. Not by accident, some of them think."

"So?"

"So such a bomber would make a good spotter for a sniper, sent into the woods to deal with anyone who came free over the ridge from the fire."

Not anyone. The prime targets would have been her or Bissell. Probably Bissell, and Fiske got it because Bissell jumped at the wrong moment. A chest shot on Bissell would have been a head shot on Fiske.

Shores slammed one fist into the open palm of the other hand. "It makes sense. But what . . . ?"

"I have rank in the Fire Guard. In the Fire Guard, also, we make recordings of messages sent from our flyers. *All* messages. I can see if anything suspicious was sent from the fire-flyer."

"Or if there are any suspicious holes in the recordings," Shores said.

"That also," Maiyotz said. "Do you wish it?"

"What I wish is not so important as what . . . those superiors I spoke of with Mr. Bissell wish." *Particularly if the lady is Confraternity, and favors to her are favors to them.* "But I can take your proposal to those superiors, with my opinion that your offer is sincere and you are honest. I carry some weight, even though I am not quite a Cohort leader."

Cohort Leader in the Ptercha'a table of ranks was roughly equivalent to senior full colonel, rather than acting lieutenant colonel. "Roughly," because Cohorts had a good deal more autonomy than any human unit normally commanded by a colonel, except for TacAir Wings and the Alliance Independent Regiments.

"Whatever you are, it is something *I* trust. That opinion, too, I will pass on to my seniors."

"Thanks." They shook hands, and Shores watched Maiyotz fade into the shadows at a speed she hoped she could manage when *she* was nearly eighty.

What the Hades! Intelligence ran on barter, if half of what Nieg hinted, or a quarter of what he said outright, was true. And a three-cornered swap—Victoria, Federation, Administration—was nothing unusual, even if it turned out the Administration was really Confraternity!

She adjusted her sidearm for a quick draw and headed for the communications center, to track down progress reports on the fires and the sniper hunt.

Linak'h:

What happened in the hazy light of Father-rise remained with Brokeh su-Irzim forever afterward.

He would as soon have expected the Reincarnation of the Great Khudr as what actually happened. Actually, it reminded him more of the Return of the Generous Wayfarer, when the captured Merishi lifter landed and began unloading.

Live and dead Ptercha'a, live but senseless Merishi, live People (one wounded, three exhausted), and equipment all spilled out of the lifter. Zhapso su-Lal took one look, then had the wits to run for the guards and the camouflage nets. Both came quickly, and everything that could not be moved into the house was covered from satellite or even living eyes before Rahbad Sarlin began his tale of the patrol's mission.

Su-Irzim listened, devoting more effort to commanding his features than he usually did with Fleet Commanders. At last both Sarlin and Zeg seemed to have said all they had to say, yet he still could not make sense of what he had heard.

So he phrased his reply to conceal this. He spoke of how the fires were going out, except for one in Federation territory and another on the Alliance border. The second would be rained out within the day, even if no sapient being came within marches of it.

Zeg frowned and held up a grimy hand to interrupt su-Irzim.

"You doubt our word?"

"No. I merely have difficulty assimilating so much data so quickly."

"And he calls himself an Inquirer," Zeg said, with a look at his half-brother that might almost have been described as affectionate. This seemed even more improbable than the narrative of events; su-Irzim hoped that no one would ask him his views on it.

"Well, we shall sleep," Sarlin put in. "While we sleep, you increase your powers of assimilation. Then we will tell you again."

"And if you do not assimilate then, we will cut your throat," Zeg added, with a touch of his old tone. "We, or these our battle-comrades." They led the Ptercha'a off around the house, leaving su-Irzim standing. At least his mouth was not gaping; Behdan Zeg had not returned altered out of all recognition.

Still, he was not the only one of the mission who might have novelties to assimilate before the last flames died. Intercepted messages suggested that the Merishi were trying to build a case for human agents as the cause of the fire. This was as plausible as the rumors in the Federation Territory that the Confraternity was turning against the humans.

It was also as likely to be believed, and the power of a tale to cause trouble depends on the number of those who believe it, not on how true it may be.

Aboard U.F.S. *Shenandoah*, off Linak'h:

The meal was breakfast, because the time was right, and also because Commodore Liddell, the host and senior officer present, said it was breakfast. This gave Commander Franke and Colonel Nieg a chance at a pair of Chief Jensen's super-omelets, so Liddell heard no complaints about this case of RHIP.

In fact, both men looked too tired to complain about anything. Also too relieved—the fires were going out all over the high forest as rain moved in, casualties among the seven thousand people who'd served on the fire lines had been light, and the sniper who killed Lieutenant Fiske had met the same fate.

Almost the best yet, the sniper was human, and the possibility that he'd received targeting data from a Ptercha'a-crewed lifter could be kept blacked down for the moment. The two days of fighting fires had done much to uphold interracial goodwill; an interracial sniping would not be undoing that work.

The list of refugees to be evacuated to *Somtow Nosavan* was complete, and the shuttles assigned to that job had been judiciously sprinkled in among the regular shuttle flights to the ships heading out tomorrow in the convoy. The only remaining problem was getting the Ptercha'a supplies aboard the Victorian ship.

"Incidentally, I assume that Marshal Banfi's contribution is either from Confraternity sources or was intended for them but is being released with their consent," Liddell said. "Can anyone confirm or deny?"

Nieg and Frank looked at each other. "Come on," Liddell said. She sounded peevish even to her own ears. "I know my role. I'm the Navy's deniable flag officer. If all this canoodling with the Confraternity falls apart,

Longman can repudiate me. If it works, we can all keep quiet—after you answer my question."

"If it's the question I think it is, yes," Nieg said.

"Thank you," Liddell replied. "In return, I'll give you a piece of advice. Unless you're planning to make Colonel Shores another deniable link to the Confraternity, I think you should pull her out of intelligence work."

Franke laughed.

"What do you find amusing about that, Commander?"

"*Somebody* has to," he said. "Both you and Nieg look as if you're attending a family funeral. Shores talking to the senior Confraternity leader in the Fire Guard is no longer a secret. So it's too late for security. I don't know who leaked or how, but three people mentioned it to me in the two hours before I came up."

Liddell thought this news did not improve Nieg's mood. She knew it didn't help hers. Franke appeared oblivious to glowering seniors as he continued.

"Besides, the only way you can completely break Shores from the Confraternity is forbidding her to have contact with her father. If you even *think* that too loudly, Colonel, there won't be enough of you left to interest Graves Registration. Some Hunter gardener will use your remains for—"

"I suppose this is based on a long and intimate association with Colonel Shores?" Nieg said. For a mad moment Liddell suspected sexual jealousy. Then she saw that he was smiling.

Franke grinned. "A long and intimate association, yes, but with Major Morley. She's virtually Candy's sister, though, when it comes to insisting on her share of the fun."

"I suppose that is one possible word for the consequences of illegal contacts with the Confraternity," Nieg said. "Shall we let it stand and return to the original topic of discussion?"

"We'd better," Liddell said. "Captain Marder is being kind, courteous, and cooperative, so far. She has also made it clear that if her ship hasn't got at least five thousand Ptercha'a-days of appropriate supplies aboard, the refugees don't leave the shuttle. Any Federation party who comes aboard to argue the toss will leave, probably by way of the airlock but not necessarily in suits."

The problem had been and still was secrecy for the supply runs. If Coordination intelligence was able to trace Ptercha'a supplies from the ground up to *Somtow Nosavan,* the refugees might as well have been leaving a thread behind them, like Ariadne helping Theseus find the Minotaur. Unfortunately, in this case it would be the Minotaur using the thread to trail Theseus.

"Actually, I think I have an idea. I picked it up from Elayne Zheng."

"Is that all you picked up?" Nieg said.

"Commander Zheng keeps her personal and professional lives a little more separate than she was doing on Victoria," Franke said with dignity.

"Good. I would not think of interfering with your private life, but I could not rely on further work from an affiliate who had insulted Major Morley. Your own phrase about 'remains and Graves Registration' seems applicable. Go on."

Franke had to finish choking on a bite of omelet before he could obey. Then he delivered his usual over-worded but entirely sound presentation.

It made sense to Liddell, even if it added to the operational hours on her already hard-worked attackers. Marshal Banfi's establishment was a likely enemy target, so why not run an air-support exercise over it? Why not have six or seven attackers, all using ECM, flares, and anything else to baffle sensors, organic or otherwise?

Baffle a sufficient number of sensors, and nobody would notice a shuttle taking off from Banfi's and joining up. Since several of the attackers would be returning to orbit after the exercise, nobody would pay much attention to a shuttle taking advantage of their free escort. By then, any link between supply depots and the shuttle's docking with *Nosavan* would be incredibly tenuous.

Liddell respected Coordination intelligence, with or without Merishi help. She also respected Elayne Zheng's expertise at electronic warfare. It would be useful to have a second or even third opinion, but there might not be time, and for an improvised operation Zheng's input would be enough.

They drank their toasts to Elayne Zheng in coffee and returned to their various duties.

Twenty-four

Merish:

Zydmunir Na'an's first meeting with Dollis Ibran was largely ceremonial. They did agree that four ships would not be too few to be useful off Victoria, nor too many for Na'an to charter out of his private resources.

Now, in the wake of the fires on Linak'h, they had to meet again with more haste and less ceremony. Rumors of massive support for the Coordination were running about the streets of the major cities, like afksi in a feeding frenzy. From even the seventh-level eating balcony of Ibran's house, Na'an could hear the distant chanting of a crowd (bought for the purpose, no doubt, by Space Security or those who procured the funds for the eager young bloods in its ranks).

"We need more ships on the scene," Ibran declared.

"What is the scene now?" Na'an asked. "Linak'h or Victoria?"

"For the next flight of ships, it should be Linak'h. I intend for them to stop at Rhaym. After they do that, they will be more useful, or at least less suspicious, at Linak'h."

"What if the caretakers at Rhaym will not release the material?" Na'an asked.

"That would tell us much about what Space Security intends, and how far they are willing to go to carry out their plans," Ibran said. "Would you care to reveal such a secret at a time like this?"

If Space Security intended to alter the traditional role of the great merchant fleets as a reserve in case of war—yes, it was a large secret and one better kept. If they intended to alter this role by taking control of the merchant houses' private supply depots—this was revolution hardly less than recognizing the Confraternity would be.

Na'an thought rites of aversion, then found a less pleasant idea coming to the fore.

"What if they insist on putting security parties aboard the ships?"

"There would be no reason for that, if we sent them out fully crewed," Ibran said. Both his voice and face were as bland as nestlings' gruel.

Na'an could not help feeling that it was as well someone above him had the notion of being prepared for the first private war among the Folk in some centuries. It might not save him, but it had a fair chance of saving his son. Payaral might have no Simferos Associates left, of course, after the smoke blew away, but his wits were keen, and what his claws grasped, they held.

Charlemagne:

Marcus Langston sipped his Rebel Yell bourbon, frowned, then added another ice cube.

"It just occurred to me, Sho. There's one good thing to be said for these rumors about the Confraternity. They'll get people talking about the Ptercha'a."

"That's pretty damned cold-blooded," Kuwahara said. They were in one of the secure private rooms of the Flag Officers' Club, so he didn't even feel like lowering his voice.

"It may have people doing more than talking," the admiral added. "The Coordination may have deferred going to war because of the fire disrupting their mobilization. They may have also done it because they think anti-Confraternity sentiment will make so much trouble in our Territory that the Administration won't want our support!"

"You may be right," Langston said. "I'll tell you one thing, though. If we buy off the Coordination by helping the Administration's thugs suppress their Confraternity, I'm resigning my commission."

Kuwahara's mind leaped quickly through shock, to the stage of contemplation, and finally came up with an idea.

"Marcus, how would you like to resign your commission now?"

"That eager to get me off the study group? I warn you, they may not send a replacement who can charm Lena Ropuski as well as I do. An uncharmed Captain Ropuski . . ."

". . . is my problem, not yours," Kuwahara finished. "Unless you've decided to affiliate on very short acquaintance?"

"Is that really your business, Sho?"

"It is if there's anything between you and Lena that will make her angry at me for damaging your career."

"She's a professional, so am I, and so are you. Now, as one professional to another, what reasons are you offering for my resigning?"

"Very simple. We need somebody who isn't bound by Federation Confraternity policy on Linak'h. Marshal Banfi isn't that somebody."

"No, he's just a Marshal," Langston said, taking a hefty gulp from his drink. "Marshals have a way of objecting to stray observers from outside commands wandering around, trying to sneak looks at their pet schemes. Banfi has that vice in spades, when it comes to him and the Ptercha'a. I presume you know how many times he nearly kissed that baton good-bye?"

"Probably better than you do," Kuwahara said shortly. Verbal games wasted time, which he and Langston did not have in unlimited quantities. Not when Linak'h was a minimum of twelve days away, even for a passenger traveling in starsleep.

"All right. Then you know you're sending me into a lion's den, with only one stone for my sling. And no damned innuendos, thank you."

"I wouldn't dream of them," Kuwahara said. "If I want to put them across, I'll say them out loud." Langston started to glare, then ended by smiling—thinly, but it was a smile.

"They haven't called for a personnel freeze yet," Langston mused. "And generals do get first-class treatment when it comes to processing outs. The only question is, is this supposed to be a secret mission? Major generals aren't so common, even on Charlemagne, that one resigning wouldn't make the media."

"There's an alternative," Kuwahara pointed out. "Resign ourselves to the publicity, and get extra range out of it. Pick a reason that will grab media attention, and use it. Not Confraternity sympathies, I suggest, but anything else that comes to mind."

"Haven't you forgotten that I won't have high-speed Forces transport available if I resign?"

"Forces transport, no. High-speed, yes. I happen to know that the media are arranging for a starsleep run for an eight-body media pool to Linak'h."

Langston threw up his hands in disgust, although he remembered to put his drink down fist. "Is there no hope for me, facing a man who cultivates mediacrats?"

"Spare me the flattery, Marcus. I wouldn't mind you going out on active duty with a regular assignment, except for our needing Szaijkowski's approval for it. We might not be able to have it at all. We certainly wouldn't be able to have it without the Empress using up a good deal of her credit balance with Mighty Max."

"Try to imagine how little I care about Chilly Willi's credit balance, Sho."

"Somewhat less than about our relations with the Ptercha'a, I suppose."

"Precisely." Langston looked at his empty glass, then shook his head. "All right. I'll do it. I wasn't thinking of staying around for a third star, Confraternity or no Confraternity. Besides, this will be Marshal Banfi's first experience of dealing with a loose cannon, instead of being one. It should be entertaining."

To Langston, maybe. But it would be eight hundred light-years from Kuwahara. Both the comedy of service rivalries and the pain of friends dying in battle diminished when they had eight hundred light-years to travel.

Deep in the earth something stirred, and strove to wake. The weight of earth and stone lay heavy upon it, and time gnawed at its blood and bones. A darkness came and went, too swiftly to disturb its slumber, but now at last the chains of sleep began to fall away as day by day it drifted closer to waking. It dreamed foul dreams and the world went mad. Soon its long sleep would end, and the world would tremble when the sleeper spoke its name.

Look for the ROC leader
DOWN AMONG THE DEAD MEN
by Simon R. Green
coming December 1993

If you and/or a friend would like to receive the *ROC Advance*, a bimonthly newsletter featuring all the newest and hottest ROC books and authors, on a complimentary basis, please fill out this form and return it to:

ROC Books/Penguin USA
375 Hudson Street
New York, NY 10014

Your Address

Name _____

Street _____ Apt. # _____

City _____ State _____ Zip _____

Friend's Address

Name _____

Street _____ Apt. # _____

City _____ State _____ Zip _____